Mourn
The
Innocents

Cover design by Brandi Doane-McCann

Formatting and Layout by Billington Media

Print edition ISBN 978-0-9973024-9-3
e-Book edition ISBN 978-0-9973024-8-6

Mourn The
Innocents

A Novel By
Huston Michaels

Gold Miner Books

"Maybe you are searching among the branches,
For what only appears in the roots."
Rumi 1207-1273

For those who hold The Thin Blue Line

CHAPTER 1

The two women were waiting in the LAPD West Bureau interview room when Detective Ben Kaye walked into the adjoining observation room. He glanced again at the Patrol Division incident report from the previous evening swing shift, which his boss, Captain Thompson, had handed to him when he assigned Kaye the case, then turned his attention back to the occupants.

JoAnn and Valerie Weber. Mother and seventeen-year-old daughter.

Mrs. Weber was tastefully dressed and obviously impatient. She sat stiffly upright in the hard-backed chair, her legs crossed and folded hands twisting in her lap, glancing back and forth between the room's door and the mirrored observation window.

It was Valerie, though, who drew Kaye's attention.

She slumped in her chair, legs stretched out and knees visible through the holes in her jeans. A too-big UCLA sweatshirt made her look like a coat hanger, and she had pulled her long, strawberry blonde hair over her right shoulder, twirling it on her fingers as she studiously ignored her mother.

Valerie's left eye was discolored and swollen shut. A jagged line of bristling black sutures occupied the space where her left eyebrow should have been. More sutures, looking like a costume moustache gone bad, crossed her lips about halfway between her left nostril and the left corner of her mouth. Red-turning-to-black bruises extended from her broken nose to her left ear, which was also swollen. Scratches and deep red welts tending to black covered her throat and wrapped around the sides of her neck, leaving the faint outline of a thumb and fingers.

It was obvious to Kaye that somebody had pinned her down with their left hand and pummeled her with their right. The big question was who would do that to a seventeen-year-old?

Let's go find out, he told himself as he turned away from the window. On the way he dropped the incident report on his desk.

"Good morning. Sorry to keep you waiting," he said as he stepped into the interview room. "I'm Detective Kaye. I'd ask how I can help you, but I think I already know."

1

The girl glanced at him sullenly. "You don't look like a cop to me."

"I get that a lot," Kaye said. He didn't look like a cop. At about six one, with long arms and legs, he carried nearly three hundred pounds of solid muscle. He also dressed like a biker, because he was one. It drove Captain Thompson crazy. But Kaye solved cases, so the Captain usually turned a blind eye to his appearance.

"JoAnn Weber," the woman introduced herself. "This is my daughter, Valerie."

"You're not my mother," Valerie mumbled without looking up.

Kaye sat down, put a yellow legal pad and pen on the table, looked at Valerie and said, "Looks like it hurt."

"I've had worse."

"Right," Kaye said. "So, tell me what happened."

"Nothing happened," Valerie mumbled, her tone defiant. "I fell down. Big fucking deal."

"Valerie," JoAnn snapped, "we talked about this. If nothing happened, why do you have stitches all over your face?" She looked at Kaye. "She had the same attitude with the officers that came to the house last night. That's why we're here."

"I saw the report," Kaye said. "This happened at school?"

Valerie didn't answer.

"That's what she told me," JoAnn said, looking at Kaye with total frustration.

"Valerie, is that right? This happened at school?"

"Uh-huh," Valerie muttered without looking up. "Yesterday, after."

Which Kaye instantly knew was a lie. He also knew from the incident report that Valerie attended Westside Alternative off La Cienega and Olympic. But if the time was a lie, odds were the location was, too.

"Did you go to the office?" he asked. "Tell someone?"

"No," Valerie said, still not looking up.

"Why not?"

The girl just shrugged.

"Valerie," JoAnn said, "at least have the common courtesy to answer the Detective's questions."

"Nothing happened. Just let it go, okay?"

"I will not just let it go," JoAnn said angrily. "Because you hid this from me instead of letting me take you to the doctor, you'll now have scars on your face for the rest of your life. Think about what that does to your future prospects."

"My *prospects*?" Valerie said incredulously. "Are you fucking —"

"Valerie Rose Weber!" JoAnn cut her off angrily. "Do not use that language with your mother."

"You're not my mother," Valerie mumbled again.

"I —" JoAnn started to push back.

"Whoa!" Kaye said loudly. "Time out. Both of you. Stop."

The room went silent. Valerie looked down at her hands again while JoAnn glared at her.

"Mrs. Weber, would you mind if I spoke to Valerie alone?"

"She's a minor," JoAnn replied. "I have the right to be present."

"That you do," Kaye acknowledged. "But you're not required to be. If it makes you more comfortable having a woman in the room, I can make that happen."

JoAnn thought about it for a moment.

Valerie never looked up.

"Okay," JoAnn said. "But I would like a woman present. No offense."

"None taken. I understand," Kaye said, sliding his chair back and standing up. "Be right back."

He went to his desk and punched an internal extension number into the phone.

"This is Patty."

Patty Phillips was a Bureau Police Assistant with whom Kaye had worked closely on many cases. She had great investigative instincts and Kaye trusted her completely. He had long tried to convince her to become a sworn officer.

"Patty, it's Kaye."

"What can I do for you, Detective?"

Kaye explained the situation and less than two minutes later they met outside the interview room.

"Mrs. Weber," Kaye said when they entered, "this is Ms. Phillips. We work together."

JoAnn just stared at Patty, who said, "Pleased to meet you, ma'am. Sorry it has to be under these circumstances."

"And this," Kaye said, "is Valerie."

"Hi Valerie. I'm Patty."

Valerie looked up and mumbled, "Hi."

"Mrs. Weber, if you'll come with me, I'll show you to our break room," Kaye said. He turned to Valerie. "You want a soda or something?"

"No thanks."

"I like your hair," Kaye heard Patty say as he closed the interview room door.

"How long has she been at Westside?" he asked JoAnn Weber.

"She just started this year."

"Where was she before that?"

"Grove Charter."

"What happened?" Kaye asked as they entered the break room, curious how Valerie had gone from one of the most prestigious schools around to the alternative high school.

JoAnn paused before she answered. "I blame myself, really. I had complications when Valerie's older brother was born that left me unable to have more children, so my husband and I decided to adopt a daughter. We got Valerie when she was an infant. When she turned sixteen we told her. Big mistake. She had no memories of her biological parents, but she became obsessed with finding them, especially her mother. To put it bluntly, things went to shit in a giant hurry. She's not the same girl she was before. She doesn't even call me Mom anymore. I'm just JoAnn to her now."

"Sorry to hear that," Kaye said. "Has she had other problems at Westside since she started there?"

"No," JoAnn said. "We thought she was doing well. That's why this really bothers us. It happened out of nowhere."

"I'll find out who did this to her," Kaye said. "It shouldn't be too hard. Have a seat and feel free to help yourself to coffee. I shouldn't be too long."

"Thank you, Detective."

He headed back to the interview room. Patty and Valerie were talking in low tones when he pushed the door open. Valerie went quiet as soon as she saw him.

"Okay," Kaye led off after sitting down. "Valerie, the first thing I want to tell you is that you are not in trouble here and –"

"That's what you think," Valerie interrupted, her voice sullen.

Kaye studied the girl for a moment.

"Look," he continued, "you're not in trouble with me. From where I sit you're the victim of a serious beating. I'm not judging you, and I'm not angry with you. My only interest here is finding who did this to you. That's all. To do that, I need your help."

"He's being straight with you," Patty said. "And he's really, really good at his job. Let him do it, please."

"Valerie, tell me what happened," Kaye said.

4

"I already told you."

"But you didn't tell me the truth," Kaye said.

"I –" Valerie started to protest, but Kaye held up his hand in a 'stop' gesture.

"No, you didn't," he said firmly. "I've seen a lot of people who've been beaten up, and worse. Injuries and bruises talk, and yours tell me this didn't happen yesterday after school. Day before yesterday maybe, but probably the day before that."

Valerie stayed quiet.

"Right?" Kaye prodded gently.

Valerie looked up at him and nodded as a tear rolled down her swollen cheek.

"Monday after school," she said.

"But you didn't go to the office?"

"No."

"Did you go to class on Tuesday?"

"No. Yesterday, either."

"When did you go to the doctor?" Kaye asked.

"JoAnn took me yesterday afternoon."

"Why the delay?"

"I didn't want JoAnn to see," Valerie replied. "She's gone a lot, so I got up and left early so she would think I was at school, then came home late and stayed in my room."

"That's why your mom didn't call us until yesterday evening?"

"Yeah. I asked her not to call, but…" She shrugged. "And she's not my mother. I'm adopted."

"She told me," Kaye said. "So she thinks you've been in school all week?"

"I guess so."

"Valerie, who did this to you?" Kaye asked.

"I don't know," Valerie said, dropping her eyes to her lap again. "They jumped me from behind. Some girls, I think. I didn't even see them."

Kaye leaned back and studied Valerie again. Out of the corner of his eye he saw Patty tilt her chin up to get his attention. When he looked, she shook her head ever so slightly.

"Lying to me doesn't help your cause," he said.

"I'm not lying. I didn't see them."

"If they were behind you, how did they punch you in the mouth, and your eye? And it takes a hell of a punch to cut somebody deep enough that they need stitches. Any of the girls at school professional boxers, maybe MMA fighters? Is that who I need to talk to first?"

"No," Valerie mumbled.

"So, who did this to you?"

"I can't tell you," she barely whispered.

"Valerie," Patty spoke up, "did whoever beat you do anything else to you?"

The girl's eyes opened wide. "You mean, like rape me or something?"

"Yes," Patty replied. "That's exactly what I mean."

"No!" Valerie almost shouted. "It's not like that!"

"Are you sure?" Patty asked. "If you like, Detective Kaye will leave the room again and we can continue our talk, woman to woman."

"Nothing happened," Valerie said, and Kaye heard the near-panic in her voice. "He –" She stopped and clamped her mouth shut.

"He?" Kaye asked "Valerie, who is *he*?"

"I can't tell you," she whispered again. "I won't tell you. You can put me in jail if you want. I'm never going to tell you. I want JoAnn now. You have to bring JoAnn back in."

She was right.

"Okay, if that's what you want," Kaye said. He looked at Patty. "I'll be back."

He went to the break room and found JoAnn Weber. On the way back to the interview room he shared what little he'd learned and told JoAnn not to get mad or lean on Valerie to tell her who had beaten her.

"Are you taking her to school from here?" Kaye asked.

"No," JoAnn answered. "I thought I'd let her stay home today."

Ten minutes later he had JoAnn's cell number and had shown the Webers out the front door of the station.

"Did she tell you anything she didn't tell me?" Kaye asked Patty.

"Not really. She also had some bruising on her ribs she was too shy to show you. Left side, just like all the blows to the head. I took a photo. I asked if she had a boyfriend. She got really defensive, but I couldn't confirm it or get a name out of her."

"Must be the 'he' she mentioned. First thing is to find him, whoever he is. Thanks, Patty."

"Any time."

CHAPTER 2

Audie Murphy Elementary School opened in 1951. Classic California architecture: One floor, flat roofed, and finished in stucco painted light yellow. There were no hallways. All the bright green classroom doors, two for each room to satisfy the fire code, opened directly to the outside and inside the classrooms the walls opposite the doors were wide banks of windows. After all, if you live in Shangri-L.A., you may as well take advantage of it.

Over the years the school adapted to the changing times. The original parking lot was expanded to handle bus drop-offs and pick-ups, and another lot was added for teacher parking. An eight-foot chain link fence was put up around the perimeter; not to keep the kids in, to keep the street people out. A security gate was added to the teachers' parking lot.

In the early 1980s the school was closed and abandoned because of the high costs of lead paint removal and asbestos remediation. But the District held on to the property, leaving the buildings standing because it was cheaper than tearing them down.

Twenty years later, when the need for an alternative high school could no longer be ignored, the powers-that-be decided Audie Murphy was the perfect, cost-effective location. After all, high schoolers are smart enough not to peel paint off door frames and windowsills and eat it, and new regulations recognized that asbestos wasn't dangerous unless you inhaled it. The asbestos-containing floor tile was simply covered with glued-down, industrial carpet.

The only physical modification made was the changing of bathroom fixtures to 'big kid' compatible heights.

Because it seemed somehow disrespectful that a school for perceived miscreants would bear the name of America's most-decorated WWII veteran and much-admired Hollywood star, Westside Alternative High School was born.

The teachers' lot still had a security gate. The bus lot was now student parking. Decorative wrought iron bars, which didn't fool anyone, had been installed over the windows and the chain link fence had been topped with another eighteen inches of mesh, tipped inward at forty-five degrees. There was no disguising that it was now to keep the kids in.

Looks more like a prison than a school, Kaye thought as he circled the area looking for a place to park the Road King. He finally gave up, used the slope where the teacher parking entrance crossed the sidewalk and met the street, and rolled down the sidewalk the short distance to the main entrance gate.

An armed security guard instantly exited the main building's double doors and half-sprinted toward Kaye.

"Sir," the guard called from halfway, "you cannot park there."

Kaye waited patiently. When the guard got close he pulled back the right side of his riding jacket to reveal his shield and the holstered Kimber .45 on his hip.

"Detective Kaye, LAPD," he said to the guard. "I'm here on police business. I've been around the block twice and couldn't find a place to park."

The guard eyed him skeptically for a few seconds before saying, "I guess it'll be okay."

"I shouldn't be too long," Kaye said. "Can you point me to the office?"

"Follow me."

Kaye followed the guard to the double doors, which required a key to open, and then inside.

"Right over there," the guard said, indicating a counter on Kaye's left.

"Thanks."

The counter was topped with a thick glass barrier, penetrated only by a slotted, brushed aluminum vent placed more to help facilitate conversation than improve air flow. It reminded Kaye of the visitor check-in counter at the County jail.

A woman at a desk behind the barrier saw Kaye and came to meet him.

"Can I help you?" she asked, leaning forward and standing on tiptoes to get closer to the vent.

"Detective Kaye, LAPD," he said, displaying his badge. "I'd like to see the Principal, please."

"About?"

"I'm investigating a crime that may have occurred on campus." It was the truth, but it didn't really tell her anything.

"Oh, okay," she said. "Let me see if Dr. Fraley is available."

"Thank you," Kaye said, smiling.

She crossed the outer office and disappeared through a door on the far wall. A moment later she returned, trailed by a tall, lanky man, who looked to Kaye to be about forty, dressed in gray cargo pants and a light green polo shirt. The woman returned to her desk and the man opened a door to the lobby on Kaye's right.

"Detective Kaye? I'm Barry Fraley. Come on in."

Kaye walked into the front office. "Thanks for taking the time to see me," he said as he shook Fraley's hand, then followed him back through the door the Principal had come out of.

"Not a problem," Fraley said. "Always happy to cooperate with the police. Have a seat. What can I do for you?"

Kaye sat down. "You have a student named Valerie Weber?"

"Yes," Fraley said immediately. "Smart young lady." He paused, then asked, "Did something happen to her?"

Kaye found it interesting that Fraley immediately thought of Valerie Weber as a potential victim and not a possible perpetrator.

"She was beaten up pretty badly a few days ago," he said. "She claims it happened here, on campus."

"Really?" Fraley said, sitting up straight, a quizzical look on his face. "Here? During the day? I've heard nothing about anything like that. When?"

"Monday, after school."

"This is all news to me, Detective. Did she come to the office?"

"No, she didn't."

"Did she say why not?" Fraley asked.

"No," Kaye said. "She wasn't very forthcoming, to tell you the truth. That's mainly why I'm here."

"Oh?"

"Does Valerie have a boyfriend that you know of?"

"Nobody comes to mind right away," Fraley said. "Valerie's been kind of a loner since she came to Westside. She's a smart girl, good student. Does very well in her English and Literature classes. In fact, she's the assistant editor of our school paper. But she's always been quiet, not real social. No clubs, no teams, nothing like that. I thought she might have an after-school job."

"Can you think of anyone who might have something against her? Maybe somebody she wrote something unflattering about in the paper?"

Fraley shook his head. "Sorry."

"You don't by chance have video cameras, do you?"

"Sadly, yes, we do," Fraley said. "I know this place looks like a prison from the street. I'm trying to change that. But to tell you the truth, Detective, our security measures are more to protect the students than anything else. These days, you just never know. We even have weekly active shooter drills."

"Do you archive video footage?"

"Yes, we do. I still have Monday's, if that's where you're heading. I'd be happy to let you review it."

"I'd appreciate it," Kaye said.

Two minutes later Kaye sat with Fraley in front of the video monitoring console while the Principal brought up Monday's footage.

"We have a closed campus," Fraley said. "Once school starts, students aren't permitted to leave until school lets out. Something else I'm trying to change."

"Why?" Kaye asked, curious.

"These kids aren't, and shouldn't be thought of as, prisoners. Most of them are here because of behavioral problems at their former schools. Truth be told, if you look at our students, you'll find that their behavioral problems often stem from boredom or mistreatment. They were in the wrong place, disinterested, not challenged, not encouraged. Our society tries to cram everybody inside the same bell curve, as close to the ordinate as possible. Like it or not, some just don't fit there, and with young people who don't realize that yet and worry about fitting in, well, that conflict becomes the source of many of their problems."

"Whoever beat Valerie Weber to a bloody pulp wasn't bored or disinterested, Mr. Fraley."

"I know. That's why I'm as anxious as you are to find out who's responsible."

"I noticed you have a student parking lot," Kaye said. "Do all the kids drive to school?"

"Not even close," Fraley said. "There aren't even enough spaces for all the seniors, and permits are granted based on academic and personal achievement. Even then, we have to hold a lottery every semester."

"What about underclassmen?"

"Students with cars but without permits can drive, but they have to put their car information on our list and park on the street. A lot get rides from friends and parents. We also have students who get here by bus."

"Public transit or school bus?"

"Both," Fraley said, then smiled. "I'm not making this easy for you, am I, Detective?"

"Not really," Kaye replied. "Do you know how Valerie gets back and forth?"

"She doesn't have a parking permit, so..." Fraley replied, shrugging. "Should I have Myrna check the list?"

"No, that's okay," Kaye replied, assuming Myrna was the woman in the office.

There were cameras covering the front entrance and a decent portion of the street, both parking lots, and the internal open spaces between classroom buildings. All in all, Kaye thought the coverage was pretty good.

They started with Monday morning. About fifteen minutes before the first bell a silver Range Rover SUV pulled to the curb not far from the front gate.

"That's Valerie." Fraley pointed at the monitor as a girl got out of the front passenger seat, turned to say something to the not-visible driver, then slammed the door and headed into school. "She look angry to you?" Fraley asked.

"Hard to tell," Kaye said, although he'd gotten the same impression.

They watched the front gate camera until the security guard locked it.

"Are there any other places she could get off campus?" Kaye asked.

"Not unless she left through the student parking lot before the gate was closed."

They checked the video feed for that camera and didn't see Valerie. Fraley picked up the phone and pushed the intercom button.

"Yes?" a woman's voice answered.

"Myrna, would you check for me and see if Valerie Weber missed any classes on Monday?"

"Hold on."

A moment later, Myrna came back on and said, "She was here all day on Monday, Dr. Fraley. She's been absent since then."

"Thank you."

Fraley fast-forwarded until the time stamp on the front camera monitor showed the time of the last bell.

Valerie Weber wasn't the first student to get to the front gate, but she wasn't the last, either. The difference was that she stepped out of the way and let others pass instead of going out to the sidewalk, and kept watching the street in the direction of the parking lots.

It was also apparent that she had not been beaten up.

Two minutes later two yellow school buses pulled up. Students streamed aboard and in less than another two minutes the buses were gone. Valerie was still there.

Fraley paused the video and looked at Kaye. "She's waiting for somebody."

"Agreed," Kaye said. "Keep going, please."

Valerie waited another five minutes before Kaye saw her straighten up, her attention drawn down the street, then shift her backpack to her other shoulder before heading quickly for the gate.

Just as she got there, a white SUV passed through the camera's field. It looked like it was decelerating and Kaye could tell the brake lights were on, but it went out of view before stopping. Valerie passed through the gate, turned and hurried in the same direction before being lost to view.

"Do you recognize that vehicle?" Kaye asked Fraley.

"Not specifically," the Principal replied. "But I can tell you it's an almost-new Toyota Highlander."

"How could you tell? They all look the same to me."

"I drive one. But mine's dark gray." Fraley looked at Kaye. "And I know that none of our student parking permits are issued to one."

Kaye pondered his next move for a moment, then asked, "Think I could talk to a couple of Valerie's friends while I'm here?"

"Sure," Fraley said, reaching for the intercom again. "Myrna, would you have Allie Ortega and Neisha Burns come to the office, please. And make sure they know they're not in trouble. I need their help."

"Right away," Myrna replied.

While they waited, Kaye got some background on Westside. Fraley told him there were just over four hundred students and that he tried to tailor the curriculum to each one.

"How do you do that?" Kaye asked.

"Well, they have to take the basics so they can pass the tests and graduate," Fraley said. "But otherwise they can load up their schedules with classes that actually interest them. Valerie's a good example. She wants to be a writer, and there's talent there, so she goes heavy on the English and Literature classes and works on the school paper. Unlike what's happening at most schools that are moving to an almost exclusively STEM curriculum, we still think the arts and humanities have value."

When Fraley made the comment about Valerie Weber wanting to be a writer, he immediately thought about his deceased wife, Amy. An English teacher when they'd first met, she, too, had wanted to be a writer. It took her a few years, but then one of her books hit it big and there was no looking back.

Kaye liked to think he'd moved on, but also knew he would never truly leave Amy behind.

"Sounds like a solid plan," he told Fraley. "You know every student's friends?"

Fraley laughed. "Hardly. I just know that Valerie and Allie are writing a play together that the drama class will perform in the spring, and Neisha is the editor of the paper."

"Allie and Neisha are here, Dr. Barry," Myrna's voice came over the intercom.

"Send Allie in, please."

A moment later there was a soft knock on the door before it opened slightly. Kaye could see a wide-eyed young lady peering in tentatively.

"Come on in, Allie," Fraley said.

Allie Ortega came in and took the chair next to Kaye, glancing furtively at him while Fraley spoke.

"Allie, this is Detective Kaye. First thing is, you are not in trouble. We need your help. Please answer his questions as honestly as you can."

"Okay," Allie said, looking sideways at Kaye again.

"Allie," Kaye began, "do you know Valerie Weber?"

"Yeah, we're friends. We have a couple classes together and we're working on a play. She's been absent since –" Allie stopped abruptly and sucked in a deep breath. "Oh, my god, is this about Val? Is she okay? Did something happen to her?"

"She had a little run-in with somebody," Kaye said, "but she'll be okay. I guess my real question for you is if you can tell me who her boyfriend is."

Allie got a perplexed look in her face before answering. "I didn't know she had a boyfriend. If she does, he doesn't go here."

"She never talks about anybody?"

Allie shook her head. "No, at least not to me, and we're pretty tight."

"Do you know if she has a friend that picks her up after school? Maybe drives a white SUV?" Kaye asked.

Allie thought about it for a moment before saying, "Not that I remember. Sorry."

"Allie, no reason to be sorry," Fraley spoke up. "If you don't know, you don't know."

"One last question," Kaye said. "Is there anybody here at Westside that Valerie's had any trouble with? Anyone at all?"

"Gosh, no," Allie said. "She's pretty private, but she gets along okay

13

with everybody."

"Thanks," Kaye said. "That's all I've got."

"Thank you, Allie," Fraley said. "When you go out, send Neisha in, please."

Allie nodded, got up and went out the door at twice the speed she'd come in with.

Almost immediately there was a strong knock on the door and Neisha Burns strode into the room.

"Reporting as ordered, Dr. Fraley," she said, grinning broadly and saluting.

"As you were, Neisha," Fraley said, also smiling. "Have a seat. This is Detective Kaye. He has some questions for you about something he's working on."

She studied Kaye closely for a moment, her eyes narrowing, and asked, "How can I help you?"

"I'm investigating the assault of a Westside student, and —"

"Valerie Weber, right? Gotta be her. She's been absent three days in a row. She's never absent."

Kaye just stared at her.

"Hey, I'm a journalist. I pay attention to what's going on."

"I'm impressed," Kaye said sincerely. "I guess my questions for you are if you know why somebody would beat Valerie up, and who that might be."

"Sorry," Neisha said. "I have no idea. She's a little slow to make friends, but she gets along with everybody. She's my assistant editor, you know, and she'll be editor next year. She doesn't really have a nose for news, if you know what I'm saying, but, man oh man, that girl knows how to paint pictures with her words. She's teaching me."

"Does she have a boyfriend?" Kaye asked.

"Not that goes here, but I see a guy pick her up after school sometimes."

"Is there a pattern?" Kaye asked.

"Nah, not really. Sometimes it's two, three times a week, sometimes he doesn't show at all for a week."

"Did you happen to see him last Monday?"

Neisha thought for a moment, then said, "We had a school paper staff meeting Monday after last class, so I wasn't out front. Sorry."

"Valerie didn't attend the meeting?" Kaye asked.

"No," Neisha replied. "She told me at lunch something had come up and she wouldn't be able to make it."

"What can you tell me about the guy who picked her up?"

"Nothing, really. All I know is he drives a white SUV and I think he's a college type."

"What makes you think that?"

"His ride has a USC license plate holder and a decal in the back window that says Trojans."

"Can you describe him?"

"Sorry," Neisha said, "but I can't give you much there. I've never seen him outside his ride, and it's got tinted windows. White dude, dark hair. Not bad looking, I guess, if you're into white dudes." She grinned again. "The other thing I noticed is that he always parks down the street from the gate even if he could park right in front and save Val a walk. Almost like he knows there's cameras and doesn't want his picture taken. Weird, huh?"

"Thanks, Neisha," Kaye said. "That's very helpful."

"I told you. I pay attention," she said.

"Thank you, Neisha," Fraley said. "Back to class."

"Yes, sir," she said, standing up. She looked down at Kaye. "When you find that dude, come back and talk to me. I want to do a story about this." She turned and walked out, leaving the door open.

Kaye thanked Fraley for his help, left a business card and returned to the Road King, where he sat for a minute planning his next move.

A guy in a Toyota Highlander didn't necessarily mean boyfriend. It could be a Westside student that parks on the street and isn't in the parking permit database, just doing a favor and taking a friend home. It could even be Valerie Weber's father.

Just to double-check, he cruised the neighborhood around Westside until he got far enough away to start finding available parking spots on the street. He hadn't seen a white Highlander with USC fan displays parked anywhere nearby.

He headed back to the station.

CHAPTER 3

When Kaye got to the squad room he immediately picked up the phone.

"Mrs. Weber, this is Ben Kaye," he said when she answered. "Hope I'm not disturbing you."

"Certainly not," JoAnn Weber said. "Are you calling to tell me you found out who beat up Valerie?"

"Not yet. But I'm making headway, and I have a couple questions for you."

"Go ahead," JoAnn said.

"Does anyone in the family drive a white Toyota Highlander? And do you have a connection to USC? Alumni? Fans, maybe?"

"My husband drives a BMW and I drive a silver Range Rover, Valerie has a yellow Mini Cooper with black stripes and her older brother, Miles, drives a Jeep," she replied. "Neither one of us went to USC, and we're not real big sports fans. Why do you ask?"

"I just finished talking to some of Valerie's friends at school. One of them told me that Valerie sometimes gets picked up after school by a male in a white Toyota Highlander with USC stuff on it."

"I have no idea who that could be. I don't even know what a Highlander is."

"It's an SUV," Kaye told her. "You said Valerie drives a Mini. But not to school, right?"

"Right," JoAnn confirmed. "Only seniors can get parking passes, and her father doesn't want the car parked on the street all day."

"Did Valerie have a boyfriend when she was at Grove Charter?"

"Well, yes, for a while," JoAnn replied. "Nothing serious, really. And I know he did not drive a Toyota SUV."

"How long ago was that?" Kaye asked. People change cars a lot in Los Angeles.

"Let's see, that would've been almost a year ago."

"Do you remember his name?"

"Of course. Kenny Vaughan. You don't think…?"

"I have no reason to believe he has anything to do with the attack on Valerie," Kaye said. "I just need to check him off the list."

"I understand."

"Would you mind if I asked Valerie?"

"Not at all," JoAnn said. "I'll go get her."

Weber put the phone down and Kaye could hear the clicking sound of heels on a hard floor grow fainter as she walked away.

A couple of minutes went by before JoAnn picked up the phone again.

"Detective?"

"I'm still here."

"I'm sorry. I thought Valerie was in her room, but apparently she's not here. Her car is gone."

"Would you mind giving me her cell number so I can call her?"

"I… I think I'd rather not," JoAnn said. "I'll ask her about who's been picking her up when she gets home and give you a call, if that's all right."

"I guess that'll have to work," Kaye said, trying to hide his irritation. "Call me either way, please."

"Of course."

Kaye leaned back in his chair and silently fumed. Having a lead to chase and not being able to do it frustrated him. But, even though she was a victim, Valerie Weber was still a minor and if her mother said he couldn't call her, he was stuck.

The sound of the squad room doors opening caused Kaye to look around. He saw Captain Thompson, his boss.

Thompson was a large, ponderous Black man with nearly thirty years' experience at the Department. The Captain saw Kaye, detoured slightly, and asked Kaye, "Got a minute?"

"Sure," Kaye said and got up to follow his boss.

When the two were seated in the office, Thompson leaned forward, elbows on his desk and hands clasped.

"I just got some news," he said.

"Good or bad?" Kaye asked.

"A little bit of both, I guess," Thompson answered. "The bad news is that I got passed over for promotion again."

"I don't get that at all," Kaye said, shaking his head. "You're the best Captain in the department, at least in my opinion. They're making a big mistake."

"The good news is I've been offered a great opportunity outside the department, and I've decided to call it quits. Take my pension and do something else."

Kaye was stunned. He and Thompson had their differences, but the Captain had always had his back when it counted. Losing him as Boss was almost beyond comprehension.

"What are you going to do?" Kaye asked.

"Remember those two guys that were here a while back?"

Kaye did remember. Suits. At the time he'd thought they were feds, but Thompson had later told him they were recruiters trying to woo him away.

"I do."

"They've offered me a position at Pepperdine."

"Really? Wow, that's great. Doing what?"

"I'll be teaching jointly between the grad schools of criminal justice and public policy. They feel my combination of education and experience is perfect for the job. I guess finishing my doctorate put me on their radar."

Kaye was again stunned. He'd had no idea his boss had anywhere near the academic credentials needed to teach at the university level.

"Your doctorate?" he asked.

Thompson laughed. "I kind of kept it quiet, to tell you the truth, in case I flunked out. Took me almost four years."

"And the department is letting you go? I just… I don't know what to say."

"When they called me in to tell me I wasn't getting bumped up; again; they pointed out that I seemed to have," he made air quotes, "lost focus, which they took as losing interest in being a team player. I tried to point out that writing a dissertation eats up a lot of time."

"I really hate to see you go. When's your last day?"

"The Chief asked for a month, so I gave it to him. I start next semester." He smiled. "Between my pension and what they're offering, I still can't afford your neighborhood, but that also gives us time to house hunt a little closer to campus."

"Any idea who they're bringing in?" Kaye asked. "I hate the thought of having to train another Captain."

Thompson laughed out loud. "That's what I like most about you, Kaye. Your humility."

"I was joking."

"Sure you were. Now, back to business. What's the deal with the young lady that was in here this morning? The one who got the shit kicked out of her."

"Inconsistent story," Kaye said. "She lied about the where and when, but I've got a lead. I just need her mother to let me follow it."

"Is the mom being a problem?"

"Not a problem, really. Over-protective, maybe. The victim's a juvie, so…"

"Got it," Thompson said, nodding. "One more piece of housekeeping."

"Sir."

"Lister has decided she's not coming back."

Detective Melody 'Mel' Lister had recently been wounded in the line of duty while she and Kaye were attempting to arrest a murder suspect, who ended up dead.

"You're kidding? She say why?"

"I guess having a bullet take off her ear lobe was a little too close for comfort," Thompson replied, shrugging.

"Did she say what she was going to do?"

"Just that she'd had enough of police work. Said there were too many assholes with guns out there."

"I hear that," Kaye said. "What are you going to do about the manpower situation?"

"You know a Detective Jim Jefferies?"

"J.J.?" Kaye said. "Yeah, I've run into him. Seems competent."

"He's transferring here, and we're also getting a newly minted detective," Thompson said, then looked at a note on his desk. "Amari Burke. Jefferies doesn't have your experience, but I think he'll do okay as her partner. Plus, if I've got to have somebody running solo, you're it."

"Thanks, Captain," Kaye said sincerely. "And I'm sorry to hear Lister's not coming back."

"Me, too. I was thinking we should get her a going away present."

"Like, maybe, some earrings?" Kaye asked, deadpan.

Thompson laughed out loud before saying, "That's just cruel, Detective. Go back to work."

Kaye headed back to his desk. In the background he heard Thompson mutter, "earrings," and laugh again.

Kaye spent a goodly amount of time documenting his interview with JoAnn and Valerie Weber and his visit to Westside Alternative, then worked on a plan of action for moving forward with the case. He'd been honest with JoAnn Weber; he didn't think finding whoever had beaten Valerie would be that difficult.

He was reluctant to leave his desk in case JoAnn tried to call him with information about the white Highlander, but as the afternoon wore on he finally gave up. He wanted to check one thing, and on the way home had to ride practically right past the place he needed to go.

It was almost 4:30 p.m. when he rolled into the parking lot at Grove Charter. School was out, but as Kaye parked the bike he hoped he could get what he needed in the office.

The contrast between Grove Charter and Westside Alternative couldn't have been sharper. Grove was almost-new construction, looked more like an Ivy League university than a prison, and had lots of extra goodies around the buildings that the students at Westside could only dream about.

It took Kaye a few minutes to find the offices. No armed security guard and no bulletproof glass over the counter.

"Sir, is there something I can do for you?" A woman standing in the space behind the counter asked suspiciously when he walked in.

"Detective Kaye, LAPD," he identified himself, showing his badge. "You have a student named Kenny Vaughan?"

Kaye thought the woman almost laughed.

"The police looking for Kenny? There must be some kind of mistake."

"I think I'm in the right place."

"We do have a student by that name," she said as she stepped to the counter. "Class has been out for almost an hour. I doubt he's still here," she hesitated, then held up a finger, "but he might be..."

"Can you find out?"

"Sure, one second," she said. Walking to a nearby desk, she picked up a desktop telephone handset, pushed a button, waited, and asked, "Mr. Patel, is Kenny still in the lab?" There was a slight pause before she said, "Send him to the office, please."

After hanging up she turned to Kaye, who said, "I heard. Thank you."

The woman went back to what she'd been doing. About three minutes elapsed before a boy walked into the office. He was not very tall, had a mop of unruly brown hair, wore black, horn-rimmed glasses, and looked like he was made out of pipe cleaners. Based on the kid's build alone, Kaye immediately dismissed him as a suspect.

The woman saw the boy come in, made eye contact with him, and nodded her head toward Kaye. When he turned and saw Kaye, his eyes went wide.

"Are you looking for me?" the kid asked.

"Are you Kenny Vaughan?" Kaye countered.

The kid nodded.

"Then the answer would be yes. I'm Detective Kaye. Do you mind if we talk for a minute?"

"About?"

"Valerie Weber."

The kid got a flustered look on his face and said, "Sure, I guess."

There were chairs lined up on one wall of the office's public space. Kenny gravitated to the one in the corner and Kaye left an empty between them.

"You know Valerie?" Kaye led off.

"Uh-huh. I did, anyway."

"When was the last time you saw her?"

"She doesn't go to school here anymore. I haven't seen her since before last summer."

"Not at all?" Kaye asked.

"Uh-uh."

"But you dated her when she did go to school here, right?"

"We, uh... Yeah, we, uh, went, you know, to the movies a few times," Kenny said self-consciously. "But her dad didn't really like me, and I didn't have my own car, so, you know." He shrugged his bony shoulders. "We stayed friends."

"Do you have a car now?" Kaye asked.

"Yeah, I saved up enough to get one. It's a gray two-thousand nine Ford Fusion."

"Does your dad or mom drive a Toyota Highlander? White?"

"I live with my mom. She drives a red minivan. I don't know where my dad is."

Kaye studied the kid closely. There was no chance he could hit Valerie Weber, or anyone else, hard enough to inflict the damage Valerie had suffered. But he had to have friends.

"Kenny, why haven't you asked me why I'm here about Valerie?"

Kenny shrugged again. "I don't know. I guess I thought that she was in some kind of trouble, and if you wanted me to know, you'd tell me, right?"

"Fair enough," Kaye said. "Hold your hands out, palms down."

Kenny did. No scraped or torn knuckles, but Kaye hadn't expected any.

"When Valerie went to school here, did she have enemies? Anyone who just didn't like her, or might have wanted to get back at her for something?"

The kid thought about it for a moment before saying, "Not that I can think of. Valerie's real smart. She'll be a famous writer someday. She did really well here until she found out she was adopted. I told her it didn't matter, that her mom, Mrs. Weber, was her mom because she'd raised her and taken care of her, not because she gave birth to her. But she just sort of went downhill. It was sad." He hesitated before asking, "Did she do something wrong?"

"No, but she got beat up pretty badly. I'm trying to find out who did it."

"Will she be okay?" Kenny's voice was anxious.

"I think so," Kaye said.

"Can I go see her?"

"I don't see why not," Kaye said. "Give her a call." When he said it, he instantly followed up with, "You've got her number, right?"

"I used to."

"Try it," Kaye said. "I'm sure she'd appreciate hearing from you."

"As soon as I get home, I will."

"Not now?"

Kenny blushed deeply. "I don't have a cell phone. We... I can't afford one."

"Sorry, I didn't mean to embarrass you. Believe me, there are a lot of days I wish I didn't have to carry a cell phone." Kaye stood up. "Thank you, Kenny. I appreciate you coming to talk to me, and sorry for dragging you away from what you were doing. Would you do me a favor and keep this conversation just between us for now?"

"No problem," Kenny said as he, too, stood up. "And if you see Valerie before I get a chance to talk to her, please tell her I'm sorry about what happened and I hope she's okay."

"I'll do that," Kaye assured the kid.

"Thank you," Kaye said loudly to the woman behind the counter as he headed out. She didn't look up, just waved.

Back in the visitor's parking Kaye sat on the bike and went over his conversation with Kenny. There weren't any gaps, and, honestly, Kenny Vaughan just hadn't set off his radar. There was no doubt whatsoever in Kaye's mind that the kid had nothing to do with Valerie Weber's beating.

Until he heard back from JoAnn Weber about who was picking Valerie up after school, he was dead-ended. He started the bike and rolled to the exit. Stopping, he checked traffic. It was relatively heavy in both directions. He wanted to make a left, so he constantly swiveled his head, checking both directions and looking for an opening. There were traffic lights less than a hundred yards away in both directions, so he knew there would eventually be a break. As he looked to his right, the light controlling the street he wanted to cross turned red. Before he could look back to his left, though, he saw a white SUV turn out from a cross street and begin to move away. As it straightened from its turn, Kaye, who couldn't tell a Highlander from the Lock Ness monster at that distance, sucked in a surprised breath and stared.

On the rear window of the SUV was a decal just big enough for him to make out.

Trojans.

"Shit," he muttered, quickly looking left. The light in that direction was also red, and oncoming traffic was thinning fast. "C'mon, c'mon," he said impatiently, now wanting to turn right and catch the white SUV. Looking back to his right, though, he could no longer see it, and traffic in that direction was stacking up fast at the light. *Not going to happen*, he realized.

Still, when the opportunity presented itself, he turned right. He wanted to see where the cross street went. He was surprised when he got to the light. The street bordered that side of campus, and about a hundred feet from the intersection was the entrance to the Grove Charter School parking lot.

He turned right, rode down to take a look at the now almost-empty lot, made a quick U-turn, and headed home.

CHAPTER 4

Kaye idled the Road King down the gentle slope of the dead-end street, gassed it when he hit the upslope of his driveway and pulled around the house to the garage.

To the southeast the west-facing curve of the South Bay cities, their lights just beginning to twinkle in the dusk, stretched from Santa Monica to the Palos Verdes Peninsula. From there, the darkening, slate blue Pacific carved a horizon around to the west and Malibu. The sun had set, but low clouds way out still clung to the last silver rays of the sun.

Kaye stopped and stared. There are those who claim that a mortgage lasts a lot longer than a spectacular view takes to become too familiar and unseen, but even after living in the house for years, and without a mortgage to worry about, the enormous beauty of the setting still captivated him.

It certainly wasn't the typical LAPD detective residence. Indeed, it reeked of Hollywood money and, in truth, there was really only one degree of separation.

Then tragedy struck.

On an evening ride along Pacific Coast Highway, heading home from a visit to Amy's parents' house, a drunk driver had drifted across the center line, barely missing Kaye.

But he hadn't missed Amy.

She died before they got her to the hospital.

And the drunk kept right on going.

Against orders, Kaye hunted down the man and arrested him, earning a suspension for disobeying orders. Kaye had no regrets about it at all. The driver was an ex-con and had been sent back to prison.

There was a memorial marker, part of the State campaign to combat DUI, for Amy Kaye on the side of the road at the accident scene. None who passed by knew it was also where Shaeffer Kaye, story teller beloved around the world, had died.

Amy had loved the house. Kaye had been sold on the over-sized garage, a rarity on an ocean-view lot. They'd reconfigured the garage to improve the view and added a second floor, which became Amy's retreat when she was totally absorbed in a story and trying to make a deadline.

Kaye opened the center two-car-sized door and rolled the Harley into the double-deep space. It was his motorcycle shop. In addition to his daily rider, Kaye owned a Flight Red 1941 FL Knucklehead and a Hi-Fi Blue and White 1961 Shovelhead Duo Glide, both of which he'd restored himself. The single space to his left held his pickup truck. The single space to his right had long held Amy's beloved 1967 427 Corvette Stingray. The Corvette was gone, the space now taken up by his current restoration project: A 1951 FL Panhead. The frame had been bolted to a lift and Kaye was slowly working his way through the boxes of parts and pieces, mocking up the bike to see exactly what was there and what wasn't. He'd known it would be a challenge when he bought it, and had promptly dubbed it the Pan-in-a-Box.

He went inside and spent an hour working through his hybrid yoga and strength training routine. Most people took one look at him and pegged him as a powerlifting gym rat. They were wrong. His size and preternatural strength came naturally. What didn't come naturally was flexibility, and while rehabbing from an injury suffered during his Marine Corps days, he'd discovered yoga. From there he'd dabbled in Eastern philosophy and eventually settled, much to the dismay of his evangelical Christian mother, on Buddhism as the approach to the world that best suited him.

After exercising he meditated for a half-hour.

Then he cleaned up and ate, and was just finishing the dishes when his cell phone buzzed.

"Detective Kaye, this is JoAnn Weber. I hope I'm not calling too late."

"Not at all. Did you get a chance to ask Valerie about who's been picking her up?"

"Actually, no. That's really why I'm calling. Valerie hasn't come home. She doesn't answer when I try to call, and she's not responding to my voicemails. It's not like her."

"Have you tried her friends?" Kaye asked.

"I only know a couple of them, and they don't know where she is either."

"Has she done this before?"

"Well, yes, a couple of times, but with her getting beat up, I'm really worried."

"Okay," Kaye said, "here's what I can do. I'll call in a missing juvenile report and have the bulletin sent to every night shift patrol briefing in the city. They'll keep an eye open for her."

"Thank you," JoAnn said.

"One question: Is the Mini registered in your name, or to a business?"

"To us, at our address."

"Do you happen to know the plate number?"

She recited it to Kaye.

"I'll call it in right now," Kaye said. "And please let me know right away if Valerie comes home, no matter what time it is, so I can cancel the bulletin."

"I will. And thank you again."

"Try and get some sleep, Mrs. Weber. She'll show up."

Kaye called the Watch Commander at West Bureau, filled him in, gave him the pertinent details on Valerie Weber and the car, and asked that the information be shared at night shift briefings across the Department.

"If anybody comes across her or the car," he said in closing, "wake me up no matter what time it is."

***

It was 3:45 a.m. when his phone woke him.

"Yeah," Kaye answered sleepily.

"Detective Kaye?" a female voice inquired.

"That's me."

"This is Officer Nystrom at North Hollywood. We found your yellow and black Mini Cooper."

"Where?" Kaye asked, immediately awake.

"A Staples parking lot in the Silver Triangle. Unlocked, keys were in the front cup holder and a cell phone was in the center console."

"Any sign of Valerie Weber?"

"No," Nystrom replied. "The lot technically belongs to Staples, but it butts up against a twenty-four-hour diner. We checked. She wasn't there and nobody remembered seeing her."

"Anything off about the car?"

"Nothing that suggested foul play. Some fast food wrappers and some school books. If I had to guess, I'd say she met somebody, left the keys because she wasn't planning on coming back and is in the wind. You want us to impound it?"

Kaye thought about it for a moment before answering.

"Yeah, probably should, just in case, and have it processed," Kaye said. "Do you mind doing the paperwork?"

"I can do that," Nystrom said. "And there are cameras on the front of the Staples building. Whether they work, or cover the entire lot, I don't know. But probably worth checking."

"I'll do that," Kaye said. "Make sure the bulletin for Valerie stays active, will you? You found the car. We still need to find her."

CHAPTER 5

It was an odd site arrangement. The front of the Staples store didn't face busy Ventura Boulevard. Instead, the store faced Valleyheart Drive one block north. Parking was accessible from Ventura Boulevard, but the main driveways were on Valleyheart. Across Valleyheart to the north was the Los Angeles River, or, as the locals called it, the Big Ditch.

Nystrom hadn't told him exactly where the Mini had been parked, so when Kaye rolled in he stopped to survey the lot and its surroundings. There was landscaping around the perimeter and two driveways that provided access to Valleyheart. Good-sized trees spread over both driveways and sun-starved shrubs tried to fill the rest of the buffer.

The diner Nystrom had mentioned occupied the end space of a strip mall just east of the Staples parking. It didn't share the parking lot, but its side wall bore a sign and it was an easy walk between the shrubs bordering the parking to the diner's front door. It worked out well for the diner, which otherwise had all of about six parking spaces in the strip mall lot. Even as mid-morning approached it was obvious the diner still had more customers than Staples.

He headed for the store, checking the cameras and their placement as he crossed the parking lot and concluded it was going to be iffy.

The manager's name was Evelyn. After introducing himself and explaining what he needed she readily agreed to help him review the previous evening's video.

"Pull up that chair," Evelyn said as she settled into the one facing a console with two monitors mounted above the desk. "Not the best system, but we should be able to get something."

Kaye told her he wanted to start at 7:00 p.m. and she entered commands into the system.

While the system worked, she pointed to the monitor on the right. "This field of view should be the one we're interested in."

An image time-stamped with yesterday's date at exactly 7:00 p.m. came up. The light was still good and it was obvious the Mini was not in the parking lot.

"Fast forward from here," Kaye said, "but not too fast."

"You bet." Evelyn typed in a command and the image clicked forward one minute, held for three seconds of real time, then clicked forward another one minute.

At 7:38 p.m. the Mini was not in the lot. Evelyn clicked forward two minutes, and it was parked in the space next to the east driveway, the one closest to the diner..

"Back it up, please," Kaye said. "Then let it run normal speed."

At 7:38:20 p.m. the Mini swung into the parking space and went dark. It had gotten darker out and the diminishing light had changed the image from decent color to shades of gray.

"Let it run, please," Kaye said, wanting to see if anyone got out.

The recording was typically bumpy, reflecting the fact that it was a timed series of still images rather than actual video, but the interval was short and the resolution, even in the growing darkness, was decent.

No one got out. About two minutes after the Mini had parked Kaye thought he detected a faint glow inside the car. Evelyn saw it, too, and froze the image.

"Looks like she just lit a cigarette, or she's on her phone," Evelyn said, glancing at Kaye.

"Agreed. You can fast-forward if you want, but not too fast."

"You got it."

The image became jerkier and the time stamp advanced at the rate of three recorded seconds per second of real time.

It was 8:23 p.m. when the dim light again came on inside the car.

Another phone call, Kaye thought.

Five minutes later the driver's door of the Mini opened and the dome light came on. Evelyn instantly backed up a bit, then went to real-time playback.

Kaye couldn't have sworn in court it was Valerie Weber that got out, but given the overall circumstances, he was certain enough. She was carrying a small tote bag.

She closed the door and stood next to the car for about ten seconds before heading toward the street. Just as she started to move, the glare of approaching headlights, coming west on Valleyheart Drive, appeared in the frame.

Valerie increased her pace and was almost immediately lost to view under the tree in the planter between the parking lot and sidewalk.

The oncoming vehicle, its presence betrayed only by headlight beams on the pavement, appeared to stop on Valleyheart directly across from the Mini. Five seconds later it drove away, continuing westbound.

"Somebody picked her up," Evelyn said, confirming Kaye's impression.

As the vehicle drove away it was momentarily visible as it crossed the gap in the vegetation where the parking lot driveway connected to Valleyheart. There was a streetlight, and as the vehicle passed under it, it partially illuminated the vehicle's interior.

"Freeze it," Kaye snapped.

Evelyn clicked, stopping the image, then backed it up slightly to get the best view.

Kaye couldn't determine the make, but it was clearly a light-colored SUV.

"Can you zoom in?" he asked.

"I can enlarge the image, but because this is recorded I can't improve the resolution. The bigger we go, the less detail you'll get."

"Try it."

Evelyn clicked the mouse and the image enlarged slightly, as predicted losing some detail.

"One more," Kaye said.

The image enlarged again, the vehicle now nearly twice the size of the original capture. The pixilation was more noticeable, but not extreme.

Kaye leaned forward and studied the fuzzy image closely. The driver looked to be an adult white male wearing a dark-colored, short-sleeved t-shirt and a baseball cap. The window was down, the driver's left elbow was resting on the bottom of the window opening and his left hand was on the steering wheel. Kaye looked more closely at the vehicle itself, but couldn't pick out anything that told him it was, or wasn't, a Toyota. Nor did the camera ever capture an image from an angle that might have shown a license plate.

"Can you create a separate file that covers the time from when she drove in until we get a look at the SUV driving away and email it to me?" he asked.

"I can do that," Evelyn said.

Ten minutes later, Kaye sat on the bike.

Why would she leave her cell phone? He kept asking himself. She made calls while she was sitting there.

He grabbed his phone and made a call.

"Good morning, Mrs. Weber. Detective Kaye."

"Good morning, detective. If you're calling to see if I've seen or heard from Valerie, I have not. I've tried to call her, but she doesn't answer."

"We found her car," Kaye told her.

There was a short silence before JoAnn asked, "Just the car?"

"Yes, ma'am. Valerie parked in a Staples parking lot in the Valley last night before eight o'clock, left the keys and her phone in it, and left with somebody in a light-colored SUV. One of our officers found the car about four this morning."

"How do you know she left with somebody?"

"The parking lot had cameras."

There was another pause, longer this time.

"Why would she...?" JoAnn finally asked, her voice quavering. "I don't understand."

"The officers that found the car said they saw no signs of foul play," Kaye said to calm her down. "And she wasn't under duress when she left. I think she left the keys with the car because she isn't planning on coming back. Mrs. Weber, did she have two phones?"

"Not that I know of," JoAnn replied. "Was the car that picked her up the same one that's been picking her up at school?"

"I couldn't tell for sure from what I saw, but I've got a copy of the video file and I'll have our tech people see what they can come up with," Kaye said, "but it could be the same vehicle." He didn't mention the possible match he'd seen leaving Grove Charter, not wanting to get her hopes up.

"Wonderful," JoAnn muttered, and the edge was back in her voice. "Now, on top of everything else, she's a runaway. Does that mean you won't keep looking for her?"

"Not at all, especially under the circumstances. We need to find her."

"Well, I know the first place I'd look, if I were you."

"And where might that be?"

"Try her birth parents," JoAnn said, and Kaye heard the bitterness in her voice.

"Do you know where I can find them?"

"I have no idea. If Valerie really found them, she didn't share anything with me."

"I'll see what I can find out," Kaye said. "There is one thing that would really help, Mrs. Weber. I need her cell phone number."

"Detective, I told you, I'd prefer –"

"Listen to me," Kaye interrupted brusquely. "I am not the bad guy here. Valerie could be in real trouble, and the longer she's missing the deeper that trouble can get."

Another hesitation.

"Okay," JoAnn said at last. "I guess that makes sense." She gave Kaye the number and carrier information. "Please call me when you find her. I'll come pick her up."

"I'll be sure to do that," Kaye said. Before ending the call he told her the Mini had been impounded for processing, what that entailed and that he would keep her informed.

From the parking lot, Kaye turned west on Valleyheart to follow the path of the SUV that had picked up Valerie. He'd only gone a short distance when he saw that Valleyheart dead-ended where the river channel made a bend. An adjacent parking lot provided access to Ventura Blvd.

Whoever picked her up either had to turn around or cut through there to get back out. He shook his head. That would widen the search area.

***

It took Kaye forty-five minutes to make it over the hill to the Station. He immediately called the law enforcement contact number for Valerie Weber's cell phone carrier.

"Tech services, this is Reggie," a male voice answered.

"Reggie, this is Detective Kaye, LAPD." He provided his badge number and verification call-back number. "I need you to ping a phone for me."

"Do you have a warrant number for me, Detective?"

"I do not. The phone doesn't belong to a suspect in a crime. It belongs to a juvenile female who was badly beaten this week and is now missing. We located her car abandoned in a parking lot about four this morning, and there's evidence she left with someone else."

"What's the number?"

Kaye gave Reggie the number and added, "The name on the account should be Weber." He gave them the Weber's address.

"Hold on, please."

While he waited, Kaye reflected on the strained relationship between JoAnn and Valerie Weber. Given the circumstances, he doubted that the gulf between them was a one-sided development. Telling your teen-aged daughter you weren't her biological mother was tough enough, but having to watch the child you'd raised from an infant then withdraw and focus on finding the people who'd given her away must be heart-breaking. Kaye had grown up with a sister in a stable, two-parent home and couldn't even imagine how to cope with a scenario like the Webers'.

"Detective?" Reggie came back on the line.

"Here."

"Okay, I checked your credentials, and I can tell you that the number you gave me doesn't show any activity since late yesterday afternoon, which tells me it's probably been turned off."

Well, crap. She must've had a burner. That's why she left the other phone, Kaye thought. "Can you flag that number and have someone call me as soon as possible if there's any activity on it?"

"We can do that."

"Thanks, Reggie. Appreciate the help."

Kaye leaned back in his chair and considered his options. He wanted to go to Grove Charter and check the parking lot for the white SUV with the Trojans decal. To him, it was likely the key to what was going on. But he also needed to locate Valerie Weber's birth parents. If he found them, he might also find Valerie.

"Hey, are you tied up on anything right now?" The sound of Captain Thompson's voice broke his concentration.

He spun around to see his boss, a bundle of papers in his hand.

"Sorry, Cap, what was the question?"

Thompson half-smiled and shook his head. "I was wondering if you're too busy to take on an inter-agency assist request that just came in."

"Just working on that battery case I took yesterday morning. The girl, Valerie Weber, is now missing. Trying to decide which lead to chase first."

"Well, while you decide, can you handle this for me?" He handed Kaye the papers. "Meet Neil Gaeta."

Kaye studied the photo on the top of the first page. Gaeta was maybe thirty, tall and thin, wore multiple sets of ear clips, had a nose stud and a piercing outside his right eyebrow.

"Who might Neil Gaeta be, and who's looking for him?"

"To us, a pain in the ass," Thompson said. "To Oakland PD, a valuable witness in a homicide and they're asking for our help."

"Help? I assume that means they want us to find him for them."

"Not exactly. Two Oakland detectives are already in town with a bench warrant. Gaeta failed to appear after being subpoenaed to testify in the trial. They have a tip on where he is and they've asked for local assistance just to keep things on the up and up."

"Why me?" Kaye asked. "Sounds like a job for a uniform."

Thompson's jaw clenched and he said, "Aside from the fact that I'm your Captain and am assigning this to you, check the last known vehicle section."

Kaye scanned the pages, then looked up at Thompson. "I'm in."

Neil Gaeta's last known mode of transport was a 2011 Harley Wide Glide.

"Probably even a good idea for you to wear your colors on this one," Thompson said, referring to the Big Boar MC riding jacket with patches Kaye habitually wore.

Thirty minutes later Kaye rolled into the parking lot of a convenience store on Crenshaw north of the Santa Monica Freeway. The Oakland PD plain wrap white Tahoe was easy to pick out and Kaye pulled into the open spot next to the passenger side. The front window buzzed as it went down.

"Go park someplace else," the woman inside said, holding up a badge. "We're waiting for somebody."

"That would be me," Kaye said as he swung off the bike and pulled his jacket back to show his badge. "Ben Kaye, LAPD."

The woman shook her head, smirked, opened the door and slid out as the driver, a man, got out and walked around the unit. Both were casually dressed in slacks and polo shirts, and wore belt badges and sidearms.

"Tina Magnuson, Oakland PD," the woman introduced herself. "And this," she gestured in the direction of the man coming around the end of the Tahoe, "is my partner, Tom Horton."

Handshakes were exchanged all around.

"Never heard of the Big Boar MC," Horton said.

"There were only a few of us," Kaye said. "I'm the only one left. I wear it to honor the ones who are gone."

"Nice," Magnuson said, nodding.

"My boss says you're here to snag one Neil Gaeta for fail to appear," Kaye said. "What's the plan?"

Horton laid it out. Even though Gaeta was a witness and not a suspect, had no priors and was not considered a threat, their informant had told them there were children in the house and he thought it would be better if they could draw him out.

"Whose house is it?" Kaye asked.

"His grad school roommate," Horton replied.

"Seriously?" Gaeta's picture flashed through Kaye's mind.

"Oh, yeah," Magnuson said. "He looks like a freakazoid in the bulletin photo, but he's a post-doctoral researcher at Cal. Something to do with the psychology of artificial intelligence. Got wrapped up in this totally by accident. Wrong place, wrong time."

"Why'd he run?"

"He's scared," Horton said. "We need him to testify against some pretty nasty people."

"Witness protection?" Kaye asked.

"Turned it down," Magnuson said. "Said he has too much of himself invested in his research to abandon it because somebody else is an asshole. His words exactly."

"I get that," Kaye said. "So if we're not kicking the door, how do we get him to come out?"

"Well, I thought I had a plan, but you've actually given me a new idea," Horton said, smiling.

Twenty minutes later they were set up near the house their informant had pointed them to. It was well-kept and there was a blue, late-model Kia SUV parked in the driveway. No sign of a Wide Glide.

Kaye was on his cell, in communication with Magnuson.

"Tom's making the call now," she told Kaye.

"Think Gaeta will buy it?" Kaye asked.

"Yeah, I do. Our informant is close to him. When she calls and tells Gaeta we know where he is and are on the way to snag him up, he'll bolt. Then he's all yours."

"Why is your informant giving him up? Is she reliable?"

"She's in love with him," Magnuson replied, "which makes her about as reliable as you can get. She wants to protect Gaeta and understands he's better off with us than flying solo." She paused for a second before adding, "Okay, our lady just called back. She got hold of Gaeta and he's freaked out. Look sharp."

Kaye watched and waited. He'd stashed his belt badge in his jacket pocket and moved the holstered Kimber far enough around behind his back to conceal it.

Five minutes later the garage door went up. A tall, thin man Kaye assumed was Gaeta took a few steps into the driveway, looked up and down the street, then turned and went back inside.

"He just stepped outside," Kaye relayed to Magnuson.

"We saw him. If he leaves on the bike, he's all yours. If he takes the vehicle we'll give him a few blocks and make the stop."

"Got it," Kaye said and stashed his phone.

Another two minutes passed before Kaye saw Gaeta roll a Wide Glide out of the garage, stop, get off and close the garage door. A small black duffel was tied to the bike's sissy bar. Kaye was far enough away that he barely heard the rumble of the exhaust when the bike started.

He started the Road King.

Gaeta turned out of the driveway and accelerated away from Kaye's position. Kaye started after him and rolled on enough throttle to narrow the gap.

They got lucky. Gaeta pulled into a gas station and convenience store on Crenshaw near I-10.

Kaye hung back far enough to see if Gaeta was going to the gas pumps or inside the store. When Gaeta pulled up to a pump island, Kaye pulled in and rolled to a stop at the island next to him, their bikes only about ten feet apart. He noted the Cal-Berkeley license plate holder and made a mental note of the number.

Gaeta had his back turned while he put in a credit card to activate the pump. Kaye did the same, keeping his back turned so Gaeta couldn't help but see the Big Boar colors when he turned around.

When Kaye turned around Gaeta was just starting to pump gas. At the same time, Horton and Magnuson pulled into the parking lot and backed into a space in front of the store.

"Nice bike," Kaye said. He noticed that Gaeta was minus the jewelry he'd had on in the photo.

"Thanks," Gaeta responded politely.

"Wish they'd bring it back. One of their best ever."

"Agreed. I like yours, too. Is it new?"

"Almost."

"Must be nice."

Gaeta took his eyes off Kaye to check the gas level in the tank and Kaye took the opportunity to step closer.

"Custom paint, right?" Kaye asked.

"Yeah, I got tired of the whole flames thing." Gaeta made a face.

"Not a real fan, either," Kaye said. "Looks like you're taking a road trip. Where you headed?"

"Not sure," Gaeta said slowly, and Kaye saw a faint hint of suspicion in Gaeta's eyes as he put the cap back on the tank. "I guess wherever the road takes me."

As Gaeta turned to hang up the pump nozzle, Kaye stepped toward the front of his bike to get a better angle. If Gaeta ran, he'd have to run straight at Horton and Magnuson to try and avoid Kaye.

"Lucky you," he said. "I'm always too busy at work to just take off."

"That's too bad. Where do you work?"

Kaye looked him directly in the eye and said, "I'm a detective with the Los Angeles Police Department, and I'm sorry Mr. Gaeta, but I have to cancel your trip."

Gaeta's eyes opened wide in surprise, then looked quickly for an avenue of escape. Kaye's size must have made Gaeta believe Kaye was slow, because he slid quickly between the pumps on his side and took off running.

It took Kaye about fifteen feet to catch Gaeta and grab him by the arm. Gaeta tried to pull away, but instantly realized he was out-matched. He stopped struggling and, shoulders slumped, stood quietly.

"You're faster than you look," Gaeta mumbled.

"Maybe you're not as fast as you think you are," Kaye said, smiling.

Horton and Magnuson must have read the surrender in Gaeta's posture too, because they quickly headed in Kaye's direction.

Gaeta saw them coming.

"You guys just don't give up, do you?" he said, resignation in his voice.

"We can't, Neil," Magnuson said. "The judge issued a warrant. We have to take you back."

Gaeta sighed deeply and looked at Kaye. "What about my bike?"

"I can impound it," Kaye said. "Or, if you trust me, I'll keep it secure at the station until you can come get it. No impound charges."

"I don't know how long it will be."

"Neil," Magnuson spoke up, "you'll only be held until you testify. Probably Monday or Tuesday, latest."

"And then what?" Gaeta asked. "Jail time for not showing up?"

"Let's work on that when the time comes," Magnuson said. "But believe me, you're safer with us than you are on your own."

"I wish I believed that," Gaeta said, then turned to Kaye. "I'll take you up on your offer. Thank you."

"Shall we go?" Horton said. "It's a long drive."

"Do I have to wear handcuffs?" Gaeta asked. "And can I get my bag?"

"Not if you give me your word you won't run," Magnuson answered as she took the bag off the Wide Glide sissy bar, took a quick look inside and handed it to Gaeta.

"I promise. At this point I just want to get this over with."

Kaye handed him a business card. "Give me a call when you want to come get it."

"Thank you," Gaeta said before the two Oakland cops escorted him to their unit and put him in the back seat. Magnuson waved in thanks as they pulled out.

It took Kaye almost an hour to arrange transport for Gaeta's Wide Glide and get it back to the station. He had it dropped in the secure lot, locked it up, and told himself he'd bring a cover for it on Monday.

He pushed through the squad room doors and almost ran into Captain Thompson.

"Did you get him?" Thompson asked.

"We did," Kaye said, nodding.

"Problems?"

"None. They're on the road back to Oakland as we speak."

"Thank you, Detective."

"You headed out?"

"Yeah, going to look at a house. You heading up to see Auggie this weekend?"

"That's the plan."

Kaye had met Augustina 'Auggie' McMaster, a Santa Barbara County restaurateur and winemaker, during the course of a recent homicide investigation. The two had hit if off immediately, but her connection to Kaye had sucked her into the case and put her in mortal danger.

"How's she doing?" Thompson asked.

"Okay, I guess," Kaye replied. "I really haven't talked to her much over the last few weeks."

"Really? I thought you two had really hit it off."

Kaye shrugged. "I'm busy. She's busy. Two-hour trip each way. I'm going to ride up and drop in. I guess we'll see."

"I hope it turns out the way you want it to," the Captain said sincerely.

"Me, too," Kaye said, smiling. "Once I figure out what that is."

"I'll keep my fingers crossed."

Kaye went to his desk and checked the time. It was too late to try and make it to Grove Charter and hunt for the Highlander. Monday would have to do.

He checked his email to make sure the video file from Evelyn at Staples had come through, then picked up the phone and called the Technical Forensics lab downtown.

"Digital Forensics, this is Scott," a man answered.

Kaye introduced himself and filled Scott in on what he had and what he needed.

"Sure, we can do that," Scott said. "I can't guarantee results without seeing the file, but with the original I can do a lot better than you did enlarging it on the screen. Just make sure you book the file in, then email the numbers to me with the file." Scott gave Kaye his email address.

"How long you think it'll take?" Kaye asked.

"We're pretty busy, and a little short-handed. I'll get to it as soon as I can."

"I guess that'll have to do," Kaye said.

After sending the file he grabbed the phone and called the District Attorney's office.

"Ms. Okafor, please," he said when the call was answered. "This is Ben Kaye, LAPD."

Kaye and Assistant District Attorney Kayla Okafor had developed a strong working relationship over the years, most recently when she'd debunked a false stalking complaint against Kaye. She also knew Kaye had two years of law school.

"Detective Kaye," Okafor said jovially when she picked up. "How are you?"

"Doing well, Counselor. You?"

"Hey, it's Friday afternoon. What can I do for you?"

Kaye gave her a quick summary of Valerie Weber's week, the overall family situation, and that he needed to find Valerie's birth parents in case that's where she'd gone.

"And I need a quick primer on how to go about that," he said in closing.

"Interesting," Okafor said, and Kaye could almost hear the wheels turning. "Valerie Weber is still a minor, correct?"

"She is. Seventeen."

"And JoAnn Weber believes Valerie found her real parents?"

"She thinks so, but she's not certain."

"Interesting," Okafor said again, this time mumbling more to herself than to Kaye, then paused for a moment. "Okay, I doubt Valerie located her biological parents. Minors cannot petition the court, and even if the adoptive parents were the petitioners, adoption records are sealed by law until the adopted child turns eighteen."

"That I knew. Can I, as a law enforcement officer, find out who they were? Even if it's just the mother?"

"I honestly don't know," Okafor admitted. "This is outside my area of expertise. My gut tells me no, but let me make some calls and find out."

"Works for me," Kaye said.

"It'll be Monday at the earliest."
"I'm good with that."
"I'll be in touch."
"Thanks, Counselor."

CHAPTER 6

Kaye rolled through Santa Ynez and into the Auggie's Wine'N'Diner parking lot just after 5:00 p.m. As usual for a Saturday evening the lot looked like downtown Sturgis during the annual bike rally.

Auggie McMaster had created a real niche for herself. In addition to being open to the general public, she had homed in on motorcycle club chapters, allocating group reservations on a rotating basis to keep everybody happy. She served great food and backed it up with some of the world's finest boutique wines from local wineries, including her own. She also ran a subscription wine club and sold to exclusive restaurants in southern California.

Like she'd told Kaye the first time they'd met, "These guys dress up and play Marlon Brando on the weekends, but during the week they all wear expensive suits." She was right, and business was good. The fact that she was a rider didn't hurt the cause.

He pushed through the door and was instantly swallowed by the din of a lot of people having a really good time. The inside was a complete throwback to a 1950s diner. Black and white checkerboard tile floor, chromed steel chairs, barstools and booths upholstered in red leather with white accents and tables topped with throwback mottled Formica encircled by ribbed, chromed steel.

A young woman he'd never seen before stood behind the check-in podium. Her badge read 'Britney.'

"Hi, welcome to Auggie's," she half-shouted, leaning forward to be heard. "Do you have a reservation?"

"I'm here to see Auggie," he replied loudly.

"I'm sorry. Auggie's not here. Did you have an appointment?"

"I didn't think I'd need one."

Britney smiled widely and said, "Let me get the manager," before turning and walking away.

Manager? What the hell? Kaye thought as he watched Britney disappear into the throng.

She reappeared almost immediately, trailed by a familiar face.

"Hi, Ben!" Cheri, whom Kaye knew as the former hostess, greeted him. "How are you? Long time, no see."

"Been a little longer than usual," Kaye admitted. "You're the manager?"

"Yeah, there've, uh, been some changes. But we still have your stool at the end of the bar if you'd like to sit down. I'll buy you a glass of wine."

"Is Auggie here?"

"No," Cheri said, checking her watch. "But she should be here in, oh, maybe thirty minutes."

"I'll wait. I can find my way."

Kaye slowly made his way through the crowd toward the bar. It was as busy as he'd ever seen it, the tables and booths all jammed with patrons clad in biker garb, then navigated through the three-deep crowd along the length of the bar.

He finally made it to the single, empty bar stool pulled around the end of the bar and tucked into a corner.

"Hey, Ben," the bartender greeted him. "How's it going? Haven't seen you in a while."

"Doing okay, Billy. You?"

"Can't complain," Billy said. "Here to see Auggie?"

Kaye nodded. "Cheri said she'd be here in a while."

Billy turned to look at the clock behind the bar, spun back and said, "Yeah, usually before six on Saturdays now. You want something to drink in the meantime, or you want to wait?"

"I think I'll wait."

"Let me know," Billy said before turning his attention back to the other customers.

Kaye whiled away the time by surveying Auggie McMaster's domain. He'd suggested to her not long ago that she should consider franchising the concept and still remembered the exact words she'd used when she dismissed the idea.

"Ben, I want to crush grapes, not the competition."

The clock rolled past quarter after six. Kaye was about to give up and head out when he saw Auggie walk in. She was dressed in jeans and a sleeveless, light green t-shirt emblazoned with her vineyard logo on the front. Her left arm was inked from shoulder to elbow, and her long black hair was piled atop her head. A black daypack hung from her right shoulder.

She stopped at the podium to talk to Britney, whom Kaye saw turn and look in his direction. Auggie looked, too, saw Kaye and headed his way. It took her some time. It seemed that every table she passed wanted her to stop and chat, and she obliged.

"Hi," she said tentatively when she finally made it to where Kaye sat. "This is a nice surprise. When did you get here?"

"About an hour ago."

"Have you eaten?"

"No."

"Okay, sit down and I'll get you some dinner and a nice glass of pinot noir."

"Yours?"

"Of course," she chided gently. "Only the best for you."

The last of the stragglers were out the door by a little after 10:30 p.m.

Auggie, glass of water in hand, came and plopped onto the bar stool around the corner from Kaye.

"Tired?" he asked.

"A little," she admitted.

"Looked really busy tonight," he said. "And I noticed some changes."

"Changes?" She stared at Kaye for a second, then added, "Oh, yeah. I forgot I hadn't told you. I reorganized."

"You made Cheri the manager."

"I did. I've made some other changes, too."

"Want to tell me about them?"

Auggie took a deep breath, looked Kaye in the eye and said, "Since, well, you know, I've really been thinking about my life, what I'm doing and where I'm going, if that makes sense."

"Makes sense to me," Kaye told her, knowing the trauma she'd barely survived.

"Anyway, I decided to allocate more of my time to growing my wine business and less to running this place." She hesitated, looked away again, and added, "And as soon as I made up my mind, the perfect opportunity just sort of fell out of the sky into my lap."

Kaye looked at her but didn't say a word.

"One of the first things I did was buy that sixty acres I told you about," Auggie said. "Then, out of the blue, the owner of one of the large, established wineries here on the central coast calls and offers me a job. Well, not a job. A partnership. They want me to make wine from their grapes for their label, but I also get to keep being my own *vigneron* and use their equipment to bottle under my label."

"Sounds like a sweet deal."

"It is. I almost couldn't believe it when they called," she said, stopped to take a deep breath, then said, "But there's a slight catch."

"Oh?"

"Yeah. I'll have to divide my time between here and their other facility in Napa." She looked at Kaye and said, "I'm sorry."

"Why would you be sorry?"

Oh, God, Ben," she said softly, "there's no easy way to –"

"Auggie, stop," Kaye said gently. "To be honest, I've been having the same struggle."

"You have?" Her eyes widened.

"I have. Look, we got thrown into a crisis situation together. It's perfectly natural for us to have bonded, almost like a patient and a therapist. But we have very different lives, very different commitments and priorities. It would be tough enough if we were next door neighbors. Which we definitely are not."

"You got that right."

"Don't get me wrong. You're a beautiful, smart, ambitious, talented woman. Under different circumstances things might be different," Kaye said. "I also have to admit I don't think I'm ready for a serious relationship."

"Your wife?"

"Yes," Kaye said.

"I could tell."

"But you do ride a motorcycle, which is a plus," Kaye said, smiling.

"Yeah, about that," Auggie said, making a face. "I sold the Glide to help pay for the new pickup for the winery. Hated to do it, but…"

"Uh-oh," Kaye said teasingly. "That's a deal breaker."

They both laughed.

"Thank you for making this easy. Well, easier," Auggie said, leaning over and kissing Kaye on the cheek. "Thank you for coming into my life, Ben Kaye. Thank you for saving my life. Twice."

"I'm not throwing your number away," Kaye said. "Is that okay?"

Auggie laughed. "I was just about to tell you the same thing."

***

Kaye couldn't face the long ride home in the dark. When he got to Santa Barbara he got off the 101 and stayed in the nicest hotel he could find, hoping it would take the sting off the evening's outcome.

It didn't, at least not completely.

He took a long, circuitous route home the next morning, rolling up the driveway not long before the sun disappeared into the Pacific. When he walked into the house, the first thing he noticed was the blinking light on the answering machine.

"Kaye, Tom Gannett from Robbery-Homicide. Sorry to call you at home. Hey, first thing tomorrow...Monday...check your email and call me."

Puzzled, Kaye wondered if he should try to track Gannett down now, but decided against it. Gannett hadn't said it was an emergency, and his tone hadn't conveyed that, either.

He spent an hour exercising. After a light, late dinner he turned in.

CHAPTER 7

Kaye pushed through the squad room doors at 7:15 a.m.

Gannett's message had piqued his curiosity. Combined with doubts about his conversation with Auggie, sleep had been difficult. At least getting in early meant he missed most of the worst of the traffic.

He immediately opened his department email and found the message from Gannett at the top of the Inbox queue. There was a .jpg file attached.

The email text was short and sweet.

Is this Valerie Weber, your missing juvenile?

With a feeling of dread in the pit of his stomach, Kaye clicked on the .jpg to open it.

It was a facial close-up of Valerie Weber and there was no doubt she was deceased.

Kaye studied the photo. The stitches were still present, but there were no untreated cuts. The bruises he'd seen had faded somewhat, but were still present. But that meant little to him now because of the significant lividity on the right side of her face.

He tried Gannett's number. No answer. He didn't leave a message, instead heading for the break room to make himself a cup of tea. Captain Thompson, also in early, was getting himself some coffee.

"Morning, Detective. How was your weekend? How's Auggie?"

"She's better," was all Kaye said, wanting to avoid the question. "Getting stronger all the time."

"Good, good."

"How 'bout you?"

Thompson sighed. "I'm becoming resigned to the fact that I'm looking at a hellacious daily commute."

"No luck on a house?"

"Oh, we've seen some great houses," Thompson said as they headed back to the squad. "We just don't want to try and afford any of them. I thought this teaching thing would take the edge off retirement, but now it looks like I'll need it just to cover the bills unless I want to spend three hours a day in the car."

"That's too bad," Kaye said. "Tell you what. I know some people. I'll try and pass the word and see if they can come up with something."

They got to Kaye's desk and stopped.

"Thanks," Thompson said. "So, you got anything going this morning?"

"Trying to get hold of Gannett in Robbery-Homicide about a body."

"Somebody we know?"

Kaye turned and pulled up the photo of Valerie Weber.

Thompson looked at it, then at Kaye. "Hey, isn't that...?"

"Valerie Weber," Kaye confirmed.

"Son of a bitch," Thompson muttered. "What happened?"

Kaye gave his boss the quick and dirty on Weber up until the time she got into the white SUV behind Staples and finished by saying, "I won't know more until I talk to Gannett."

"Keep me informed." Thompson turned and headed for his office. He stopped when he saw a tall, red-haired man with freckled complexion come through the squad room doors.

Kaye turned to look and recognized the man as Detective Jim Jefferies. He stepped forward and the two shook hands.

"Welcome to the squad," Kaye said.

"Thanks," Jefferies said, then turned to Thompson. "Captain, Jim Jefferies. Just call me J.J."

"Welcome, J.J.," Thompson said effusively. "Glad to have you on board."

"Glad to be here, sir."

"Where's your rookie?"

"I saw her looking for a parking place out back right before I came in," Jefferies said.

Just then the squad room doors opened and a harried-looking young woman, a document case clasped under one arm while she tried to straighten her hair, rushed in.

"Glad you could make it, Detective Burke," Thompson said, then turned his head and winked at Kaye. "Have trouble finding the place?"

"No, sir," Burke replied, still trying to compose herself as her gaze shifted rapidly between the three men standing in front of her. "Just haven't had time to gauge the traffic and it was worse than I thought it would be."

"And how do you fix that?" Thompson asked.

"Get my ass out of bed earlier," Burke said. "Sir."

Thompson grinned, stepped forward and shook Burke's hand.

47

"Welcome to the squad, Detective. And don't worry about the traffic. It's L.A. It bites us all in the butt on occasion. Besides, you'll soon find this isn't an eight-to-five job."

"Thank you, sir," Burke said, relaxing noticeably.

Thompson introduced Burke to Kaye and Jefferies, then told the two newest members of the squad to follow him into his office for a get acquainted session.

Kaye spent a few minutes reviewing his reports and notes on Valerie Weber, then tried Tom Gannett again.

The Robbery-Homicide detective must've recognized Kaye's number.

"Kaye, thanks for calling," he said without preamble. "Did you get my email?"

"I did," Kaye replied. "Your DB is Valerie Weber, seventeen. I've been working the assault and battery that gave her all the stitches."

"Okay, good," Gannett said, then quickly added, "I mean, not good she got beat up and murdered. Just glad you recognized her. Until now she's been a Jane Doe."

"What can you tell me?"

"Not much," Gannett said. "A hiker walking his dog found her naked body yesterday morning in the water at the south end of the Hollywood Reservoir. She'd obviously been dumped."

"Did you get tire tracks, footprints, anything?"

"I got nothing."

"Any idea yet on cause and time of death?"

"Still unofficial, but there were no signs of fresh trauma. From the petechiae in her eyes, though, my best guess is she was smothered. Looked to me like she'd been dead thirty-six, maybe forty-eight hours, and lividity didn't match the body position, so she'd been dead for a while before she was dumped."

"Who was the M.E.?"

"Martinek," Gannett said.

"How'd you connect Valerie Weber to me so fast?" Kaye asked.

"It was the stitches and bruises. One of the patrol officers on scene remembered your bulletin from last week and said I should call you."

"Glad you did," Kaye said. "How can I help?"

"I'm not looking for your help," Gannett said bluntly. "I just needed to confirm it was your missing juvie."

"You're sure?"

"I'm sure. It's a homicide now, Kaye, and it's my case. If I need help,

I'll call you. For starters, can you tell me what was going on with the girl?"

Kaye ran it down, leaving nothing out and giving Gannett the names of everyone he'd already talked to and what they'd had to say.

"So, all you've really got is a possible vehicle," Gannett said when Kaye finished.

"That's about it, I guess," Kaye said, irritated with Gannett's attitude. "And I don't even know for sure that the light colored SUV that picked her up behind Staples is the same one that's picked her up at school."

"Good place to start, though," Gannett said. "I'll make sure Newton and Southwest patrol, and the USC campus cops, get the description. Who knows? We might get lucky. You've talked to the parents?"

"The mom, yeah. Multiple times."

"Would you be willing to go with me to make notifications?"

"Sure," Kaye replied reluctantly. He gave Gannett the address.

"Okay," the RHD detective said. "Meet you there in about an hour?"

"I'll be there."

"Oh, and hey," Gannett said before Kaye hung up. "I talked to the crime scene techs. They took prints from Weber's Mini, but I'm betting they'll all be hers since you saw her dump the car. But I'll check."

"I think you're probably right."

"Good," Gannet said. "Thanks, Kaye. See you in an hour."

Kaye hung up, leaned back and shook his head. Gannett's attitude irked him more than a little, but that was the way it worked. He headed for Thompson's office to tell him Valerie Weber was no longer his case.

"I don't want a turf war over this," Thompson said after Kaye filled him in. "Share what you've got with Gannett and if RHD wants to run the homicide, let them. But don't just hand it over and walk away. Follow what you've got, and if you bump up against the RHD guys, smile and buy them a cup of coffee. If they ask what you're doing, officially you're under my orders to work on who beat her up. I'd still like an arrest on the battery, even if it's only to give the District Attorney leverage if RHD finds the killer. That okay with you?"

"That works."

"Good. Use Burke and Jefferies if you need help."

***

Kaye loathed making death notifications. It was, without doubt, the part of his job he'd never gotten comfortable with. As Tom Gannett rang the

Weber's doorbell Kaye still didn't know exactly what he was going to say.

JoAnn Weber answered the door and went ghostly white when she saw Kaye and Gannett standing on the porch.

"What happened?" she asked in a whisper. "Did something happen?"

Gannett introduced himself and asked, "May we come in?"

"Of course, of course," JoAnn said, flustered.

She led them to the living room, offered them seats and sat down on the couch so close to Kaye their knees almost touched. She grabbed a throw pillow and clutched it in her lap, her knuckles white.

"Please tell me she's all right," JoAnn whispered.

Kaye reached out and put one hand over JoAnn's.

"Mrs. Weber," Gannett said, "I'm sorry to have to tell you that Valerie is deceased. She —"

JoAnn Weber broke into long, wracking wails, bending over and burying her face against Kaye's hand.

Kaye could only wait, feeling the heat of her tears.

A young man ran into the room, shouting, "Mom! Mom!", saw Kaye and Gannett and pulled up short. "What the hell!" he shouted and advanced toward Kaye, fists clenched. "What did you do to my Mom? Get out of our house!"

His shouts broke through JoAnn's grief and she raised her head.

"It's Valerie," she barely whispered. "She's dead." She began to sob.

With a confused look on his face, the young man sank into a chair. "What? Valerie's dead? That can't be right. She was…"

"Are you Miles?" Kaye asked.

He nodded. "Are you the cop that's been looking for her?"

"Yes. I'm Detective Kaye. This," he pointed, "is Detective Gannett. We're very sorry about your sister."

"Mom told me about you. She said everything would be okay, that you'd find her."

"I did my best," was all Kaye could think of to say.

"It's okay," JoAnn said, her voice hoarse from crying. "It's not his fault, it's mine. I should have —"

"It's not your fault, JoAnn," Kaye said softly.

"If I had just told you —"

"No," Kaye said more firmly. "There's no way to know that. This is not your fault. It's the fault of whoever did this to her, and we will find them."

JoAnn had gathered herself enough to ask, "Do you know what

happened?"

"Not exactly," Gannett said. "At least not yet. She was found at the Hollywood Reservoir. I wasn't able to identify her until I spoke with Detective Kaye this morning."

"When did you find her?" JoAnn whispered.

"Yesterday morning."

JoAnn broke into sobs again and squeezed her eyes shut tight, as if to try and make it all go away.

"Is your dad home?" Kaye asked Miles.

"No, he left for the office early."

"Can you call him and tell him he needs to come home right away? Are you okay to do that, or do you want me to call?"

"I can do it," Miles said, standing up. "I'll call him from the kitchen. But if he's in court, he, uh, can't answer his phone."

"Give it a try," Kaye said. "We'll wait."

Kaye and Gannett stayed with JoAnn and Miles for almost a half hour before the front door flew open and a tall, dark-haired man in a blue business suit burst into the living room.

"Dad!" Miles yelled, launching himself from the chair.

"JoAnn!" the man shouted as he rushed across the room and knelt down beside his wife. "Are you okay?" he asked as he stroked her hair and looked at Kaye. "I'm Gunther Weber. You are?"

"Detective Kaye, Mr. Weber, and that's Detective Gannett. We can't begin to tell you how sorry we are."

JoAnn Weber looked up and took a big gulp of air. "I'm okay, Gun. I'll be okay." She collapsed into her husband's chest and began to sob again as he wrapped his arms around her.

"What happened?" Gunther asked.

"I'm just getting started," Gannett said. "We still don't know a whole lot."

"Are you absolutely certain it's Valerie?" Gunther asked and Kaye saw faint hope flicker in the man's eyes.

"Yes, sir," Kaye said softly. "There's no doubt."

The hope died, replaced by bottomless despair as tears rolled down Gunther's cheeks.

"Okay," Gunther said after a moment, "what do we -- I -- need to do now?"

"You'll need to officially identify her," Gannett said. "She's at the Medical Examiner's office. I'll need to go with you, but I'd like to ask you some questions first."

"I'll go," JoAnn said, her voice barely audible.

"No you won't," Gunther said softly, leaning down and kissing the top of JoAnn's head. "It's my job. I'll do it."

Gannett looked at Kaye and gave him a nod, telling Kaye he could clear, and that he'd take it from here.

"We'll find whoever did this to your daughter," Kaye said, then turned to Miles. "You stay with your Mom while your Dad is gone. You do *not* go with him. Understand?"

Miles looked at his Dad, who nodded slightly, then at Kaye. "Yes, sir."

Kaye gently slid far enough from JoAnn Weber to stand up. Miles immediately sat down next to his mother and put his arm around her shoulders.

"Call me any time," Kaye said. "Day or night. We'll keep you informed of our progress."

"Thank you," Gunther said. "Please catch whoever killed our daughter."

"We'll do our best," Kaye said, "I'll show myself out. Again, I'm very sorry about Valerie."

Kaye called the Medical Examiner's office from the pickup and asked for Dr. Archuleta, a Deputy M.E. with whom he'd worked before. He told Arch they'd made notification to the Webers, that Gannett was bringing Gunther Weber in as soon as he was up to it, and asked him to pass the info along to Dr. Martinek.

"I'm glad you called," Arch said. "I talked to Martinek. Valerie Weber was smothered to death and an estimate on the time of death would be last Thursday night, late, or early Friday morning. I can also tell you that there was pre-existing lividity and zero rigor, so I don't think she was dumped until late Saturday night or early Sunday morning."

"So whoever killed her kept her body for two days?" Kaye asked.

"That's what it looks like," Arch replied.

"Any sign of postmortem trauma or abuse?"

"Martinek said she didn't find anything obvious, thank God," Arch said, relief clear in his voice.

"Sounds like whoever killed her didn't want her to be found right away, or maybe just didn't have a plan," Kaye said. "Which means the death could have been a spontaneous act, or accidental."

"Gaspers," Arch said. "Sometimes they get carried away."

"Was Valerie sexually active before she died?"

"That I don't know. Martinek and I had a conversation in the hall.

52

I'm assuming she took tissue samples, so we'll know in a couple days. I'll have her send you the final report."

"Send it to Tom Gannett in RHD. He's the lead. But I'd appreciate a copy. And, hey, the victim's dad is a lawyer. If he starts asking questions, spare him some of the details, okay?"

"Think he might have had something to do with this?" Arch asked.

Kaye thought about the Weber family's reactions to the news of Valerie's death. "No, I don't think so. They're just a little tender right now, so go easy."

"Got it," Arch said. "And I'll let Martinek know they're coming in. Talk at you later."

***

It was just after 2:00 p.m. when Kaye rolled into the visitor's parking lot at Grove Charter. The same woman who'd been in the front office when he'd come to talk to Kenny Vaughan was again working. Today Kaye noticed an engraved plastic name plate in a gold aluminum holder sitting on the counter near the wall.

Mrs. Kowalczyk.

"You're back," she said when she saw Kaye. "Who's the criminal du jour now?"

"Don't have one," Kaye said. "Just need some help."

"Do I need to get Ms. Holderby, our Principal?"

"I don't think so, but you decide after I tell you what I need."

She nodded, then stared expectantly at Kaye.

"I'm looking for a particular vehicle," Kaye went on. "I was wondering if your students need parking permits and if you have a database you can check for me."

"Yes on the permits, and yes on the database," Kowalczyk replied. "But don't you need a warrant or something?"

"Not really."

"Are you sure?"

"I'm sure, although you can certainly refuse to search. In that case, yeah, we're going to need Ms. Holderby."

She stared at Kaye again, then asked, "Is this still about Valerie Weber?"

"It is."

"How is she? I couldn't help but overhear your conversation with Kenny the other day."

It was Kaye's turn to stare and make a decision.

"She's been better," Kaye said, not wanting to disclose that Weber had been murdered and start the inevitable rumor mill through the school. "That's why I really want to find whoever beat her up. Will you check your database for me?"

"Yes, of course."

"I'm looking for a late model, white Toyota Highlander, and failing that, any white, mid-sized SUV."

Kowalczyk turned and went to the nearest computer terminal. It took her about three minutes before Kaye heard a printer whir to life and almost immediately disgorge one page into the top tray. She retrieved the printout.

"One white Highlander and three other white SUVs," she said as she handed the sheet to Kaye. "I have no idea what's mid-sized and what's not, but that's all the white ones."

Kaye scanned the sheet. Each entry listed the vehicle make, model, color and plate number, plus the associated student's name and what looked like two random numbers.

"What are the numbers?" Kaye asked, pointing.

"The first one is their permit number and the second one is their assigned space."

"That makes it easy. Is the lot secured?"

"No."

"Do you have students that drive to school that don't have permits to park in the lot? Maybe they park on the streets around campus?"

"They're not supposed to," she said, shrugging. "But we can't enforce parking on public streets."

"Got it," Kaye said. "Thank you, Mrs. Kowalczyk. I appreciate your help. If anybody calls about a suspicious guy prowling your parking lot, that would be me."

That got a half-smile out of her.

"I'll check with you before I leave," Kaye added.

Kaye went out the front door and around the building to the parking lot he'd seen on Friday. It was exponentially larger than the Westside Alternative student lot, and it was full. Each space had its number stenciled in white paint and Kaye was thankful they were visible and not under the car in the space.

Once he figured out the numbering sequence, which to him seemed counter-intuitive, it didn't take him long to work through the list.

There were two Highlanders in the lot. The white one was associated with a male student and lacked the USC regalia. The other was a very light beige and was not on the list. It had no decal, either, but Kaye still made a note of the plate so he could talk to the owners if the need arose. Then he checked the other three vehicles listed. None were Toyotas, none displayed USC references and all three had female students listed as their drivers. He still took notes. Girls often had brothers.

He headed back toward the office. His search had taken him to the far reaches of the lot, so he cut through. As he progressed, he noticed a raised sidewalk that looked to divide off a smaller section of parking.

Sure enough, there was a separate, distinct lot beyond the larger one, and none of the spaces were numbered. Kaye glanced back and forth and saw an entrance at the end of the sidewalk to his right. There was no gate, but he could see the blank back side of a sign planted next to the entrance and went to look.

Faculty Parking Only. All Others Will Be Towed.

Makes sense, he thought. He stood and scanned the lot and saw two white SUVs, but from where he stood he couldn't discern make or model.

The first one was a GMC with no USC regalia.

As Kaye headed for the second one he recognized the Toyota logo in the middle of the front grill, but couldn't tell if it was a Highlander, RAV4 or 4Runner. Still a half-dozen spaces away, he cut through the row of parked cars so he could approach from the back.

It was a Highlander.

Across the back window, about two feet wide and centered just above the wiper, was a cardinal and gold decal. TROJANS. The license plate frame read 'USC' across the top and 'Trojans' across the bottom.

"I'll be damned," Kaye muttered.

He took photos before walking around and looking in the windows. The back door and rear window glass were heavily tinted and he couldn't see much. He saw nothing in the front seat that looked out of place or piqued his interest.

He went back to the sidewalk and called Patty.

"Hey, it's Kaye," he said when she answered. "I need you to run a plate for me."

"What's the number?"

Kaye read it off and she read it back to confirm.

"Hold on," she said.

It didn't take long.

"Detective?"

"Here."

"That plate should be on a two-thousand-twenty-one Toyota Highlander, white, and it's registered to a Dylan Glithero," she spelled it out for him, "at an address I think is in the Hancock Park area."

"Is that the only name on the registration? A wife, maybe?"

"No, just Dylan."

"When you have time, could you see what you can come with on this guy? Driver's license, criminal history, the usual. Put whatever you find in my box."

"I'll put it on your desk."

"Thanks, Patty."

Kaye studied the Highlander again. There was nothing remarkable about it other than the decal and license plate frame. It had a sunroof, and behind that was a satin-finish roof rack that extended almost to the back of the vehicle. Kaye knew little about Highlanders and figured probably half of them, at least, had sunroofs and roof racks. Still…

He wasn't about to go back into the school office and inquire about Glithero. Even without disclosing Weber's murder to Mrs. Kowalczyk, that would start all kinds of rumors, and if Glithero turned out not to have anything to do with the beating or murder, Kaye and the department could be caught between a rock and a lawsuit.

He walked back to the office to let Mrs. Kowalczyk know he was finished looking around.

"Did you find what you were looking for?" she asked.

"Don't know yet," Kaye answered. "I found all the vehicles on the list. Now comes the detecting part."

She laughed. "Do you have any questions about any of the students on the list? I hope you don't mind, but I took the liberty of doing a little checking. None of them are problems, if you know what I mean."

"You have problem kids here?"

She laughed again. "Detective, they're teenagers. Smart, but still teenagers."

"Yeah, you're probably right. I don't have kids, and right now I don't have any questions."

"I'm here if you do," Kowalczyk said, then busied herself with a stack of folders on her desk.

Kaye returned to the bike. He still had over an hour to kill before he could lay eyes on Dylan Glithero. Not that it would do him much good. The image from the Staples video was much too grainy to support an identification. But Neisha Burns' description of a 'college-type white dude' meant that should Glithero turn out to be old, short, heavy and bald, or African American, Kaye could cross him off the list despite the Trojans decal.

On the off chance that a rogue student might actually disobey the rules, he used up some time checking the surrounding neighborhood for white Highlanders parked on the street. He found nothing and went back to a spot that gave him a view of the faculty lot.

He'd decided not to brace Glithero on school grounds. That, too, could prove problematic insofar as the rumor mill. If and when the time came to pour grist into that particular mill, Kaye would do it in a way that would give him the advantage. But it wasn't time yet. He wanted to know more about Dylan Glithero before he started asking the man questions.

An old piece of advice from his first partner after his promotion to Detective bubbled up from his memory.

"Find out everything you can about suspects before you question them for the first time, and then only ask questions you already know the answers to. Quickest way to find out if they're on the up and up or a lying shitbag, and lies give you something to twist them with later."

Kaye would wait.

Twenty minutes later movement across the street caught his eye. He looked and saw a man in slacks and a sport coat, a book bag hanging from one shoulder, walking in his general direction on the sidewalk between student and faculty parking.

The final bell of the day had not yet sounded, so the man's presence raised Kaye's interest.

As the man got closer, Kaye was able to discern some details. White, with dark hair, and based on the cars he walked by, probably a little under six feet. Lean, he walked briskly, held a cell phone up in front of chest with his right hand and was obviously engaged in conversation.

When the man came to an empty spot on the faculty side, he stepped off the sidewalk and cut diagonally across the lot. Kaye sat up straight. The man was heading toward the white Highlander.

Sure enough, about fifteen feet from the Highlander the man ended his phone conversation, pocketed his cell phone and shrugged the book bag off his shoulder into his left hand. He walked to the driver's door, which Kaye could not see from his vantage point, and almost immediately the Highlander's parking lights flashed to signal the doors unlocking.

Dylan Glithero.

Kaye watched Glithero exit the parking lot and turn toward the street that fronted the school.

Running surveillance on a motorcycle is difficult. Generally, there's only one in a driver's rear-view mirrors at any given time, so they tend to get noticed.

Kaye decided to give it a try. He started the Harley, got lucky when another passing car got between him and Glithero, and pulled out to follow.

It didn't take long for Kaye to determine that Glithero was heading to the Hancock Park enclave, which meant that the address on the Highlander's registration was likely current. When Glithero made a turn into the neighborhood itself, Kaye broke off and headed for the station.

When he got to his desk, Kaye found a sheaf of papers on his desk. Affixed to the top sheet was a yellow sticky-note with the name Dylan Glithero printed on it, below which was the initial 'P'.

He also had a message from ADA Okafor, asking for a call in return. He called Okafor first.

"Thanks for calling me back," she said when they'd been connected.

"I always return calls from my favorite ADA."

Okafor laughed. "Yeah, sometimes even in the same week."

"That hurts, Counselor," Kaye said with mock seriousness. "What have you got for me? News on finding Valerie Weber's biological parents?"

"Sort of. I talked to my contacts and they said we could petition the court to gain access to the record, but it's dependent on the terms and conditions of the adoption and the judge's evaluation of the reasons for the request whether access is granted, or not. It's almost a search warrant, but not a search warrant, if that makes sense."

"Would it help if I told you that Valerie Weber is no longer missing?"

"Probably not. In fact, that'll probably instantly nullify any request. Where is she?"

"The morgue."

Okafor went silent for a moment before she asked, "What happened?"

"A dog walker found her body in the Hollywood Reservoir over the weekend. Gannett in Robbery-Homicide got the call. He said it looked like she'd been smothered, then dumped later, but I don't have a final report yet."

"Do you still need to find her biological parents?" Okafor asked. "I mean, under the circumstances it might be better to leave that alone."

"I'd still like to find them," Kaye said. "We can't account for Valerie's whereabouts for almost seventy-two hours before her body was found. If we can narrow that gap it might help us connect where she was to whoever killed her."

"Right answer, Detective. That'll be the crux of my argument to the court. I'll try and get the papers filed today, first thing tomorrow at the latest. Based on the fact it's now a homicide I'll ask the request to be expedited, but it might still take a couple of days."

"Thanks. Let me know."

Kaye immediately dove into the information on Dylan Glithero that Patty had gathered for him.

The top sheet was a blow-up of Glithero's driver's license. His date of birth made him forty-two years old, but he looked younger. It listed him as 5' 11" tall and 180 pounds, black hair and blue eyes. He was an organ donor. The address matched the one on the Highlander's registration. The photo and description matched the man Kaye had seen leaving Grove Charter in the Highlander. Regular features, hair neatly cut with a tinge of gray just creeping in around the temples. Even in the photo the eyes were intense. No facial hair, but Glithero had the kind of beard that gives a guy a five o'clock shadow by lunchtime and makes him shave twice on date nights.

Kaye burned Glithero's face into his memory until he knew he'd recognize the man from any distance less than a block away.

The next page was a printout result of a criminal history search. It had one entry, and it made Kaye sit up in his chair.

Almost twenty years before, Dylan Glithero had been arrested in Orange County, California, for Sexual Battery of a Minor.

But the sheet showed nothing about a conviction or prison sentence, or a requirement to register as a sex offender, leading Kaye to believe that the charges had either been dropped or Glithero was acquitted at trial. Otherwise, the man was practically a choir boy, without even a misdemeanor traffic ticket.

The third page was a note from Patty.

Detective,

I can't find hardly anything about this guy on social media, and for a good-looking, single (?) guy his age I think that's weird. I'll keep digging and let you know if I come up with anything else.

And I know you didn't ask for my opinion, but...

How much does a high school teacher make these

days, anyway? I mean, the guy lives in Hancock Park.
 Just saying…
 Patty

Kaye had wondered the same thing when Patty had mentioned Hancock Park while giving him the vehicle registration return.

Something else to look into.

CHAPTER 8

Kaye dressed like he was going to court; slacks, sport coat, shirt and tie; and he drove the truck.

Sometimes an official image was important.

Just after 9:00 a.m. he pulled into the Grove Charter visitors' parking lot.

Mrs. Kowalczyk looked up when he entered the office.

"How may I —" She stopped mid-sentence and smiled. "Why, Detective Kaye. I almost didn't recognize you."

"It's me," Kaye said, smiling back. "I need to speak to Ms. Holderby."

"About Valerie Weber?"

Kaye nodded.

"Let me see if she's available," Kowalczyk said. She rose and disappeared through a door in the wall opposite the counter. A moment later she emerged, trailed by a woman Kaye guessed at fifty, dressed in a crisp blue business suit.

"I'm Eilene Holderby," the woman said as she approached the counter. "You wanted to speak to me?"

"Detective Kaye, Los Angeles Police Department. I was hoping to get a few minutes of your time."

"Of course. Come through there," Holderby said, pointing to a door to Kaye's right as she reached under the counter to buzz him through. "Let's go to my office."

Holderby closed her office door behind Kaye.

"Have a seat, please," she said as she walked around her desk and sat down. "I assume this is about Valerie Weber?"

"Correct," Kaye said. "May I ask how you heard about what happened?"

Holderby smiled and said, "Mrs. Kowalczyk reports to me, Detective. Officially and quite literally. Now, how can I help you?"

"I'm trying to get some background information on Valerie. Classes she took, activities, friends, things like that."

"I'm sure you're aware that privacy laws prohibit me from disclosing student information."

"I am," Kaye acknowledged. "I don't think anything I'm trying to find out will violate the guidelines, especially given the student health and safety exception."

Holderby stared intensely at him for a few seconds. "I fail to see how —"

"Enough," Kaye said sharply. "I didn't come here to debate privacy laws. You can either answer my questions now or I'll come back with a search warrant, go through every folder in this office if I have to, and take whatever I want."

"It seems to me, Detective," Holderby said, with emphasis on the word detective, "that you're going to a lot of trouble because a delinquent was beaten up."

"That delinquent, as you call her, was murdered over the weekend."

Holderby went pale. "Oh, my Lord," she barely whispered. "What happened?"

"I'm sorry, but I can't discuss an active investigation."

"Point taken," Holderby said, then visibly gathered herself. "Ask away."

"First, just tell me about Valerie Weber."

Holderby told Kaye what she remembered. Valerie had started at Grove Charter as a Freshman, was a good student, quiet but well-liked, and got along well with the other students.

"Until about the middle of last year," the Principal said.

"What happened?"

"I don't know for sure," Holderby said pensively. "She just seemed to give up academically. She seemed angry all the time, became aggressive and spent quite a lot of time in the chair you're sitting in right now. I finally had to send her to Westside. It was such a shame."

"Did you know that Valerie found out she was adopted?"

"She never mentioned it, at least not to me. You can talk to some of her teachers if you'd like."

"Did she have any enemies, questionable friends, anyone that seemed to be bothering her?"

"No. Like I said, she got along with everyone until… something changed. She went from having a group of friends to being a loner."

"Mr. Fraley at Westside mentioned that Valerie was a very talented writer. She worked on the school paper."

"Unfortunately, we have to limit our school paper staff to upper classmen, but I do recall that Valerie excelled in her English and

Literature classes. She even participated in our invitation-only, after-school writing group led by one of our literature teachers. She was the only freshman ever invited into the group."

"Really?" Kaye asked. "Nice to hear teachers will still make that kind of time investment in students."

"Well, Mr. Glithero is one of our best. We were lucky to get him."

One of your best what? Kaye wondered. He now had a link.

"How so?" he asked evenly.

"He came to us from Mountbatten Prep in Hancock Park. Rarely do teachers choose to leave a school like that to come to a public school, even if it is a charter school."

"I imagine not," Kaye said, although he'd never heard of Mountbatten Prep. "Did he say why he left?"

"I don't really know," Holderby said, eyeing Kaye closely. "Are we still talking about Valerie Weber? Because I certainly cannot discuss Mr. Glithero's personnel file."

"I'm sorry, I guess I got a little off track. Did Valerie take classes from Mr. Glithero? Is that how she got into the group?"

"Yes," Holderby said, nodding. "She took freshman English composition from Mr. Glithero. It was his first year with us and he saw her potential right away. I believe she also took sophomore classes from him, but I'd have to check."

"That's pretty exclusive, isn't it? Being the only Freshman? Might that have made other students, even their parents, angry?"

"It wasn't like that. Admission to the group wasn't competitive, and it wasn't capped. Promising students were recommended by their teachers and could choose to participate or not. Although I will say that the group is fairly small."

"So students weren't selected just by Mr. Glithero?"

"No, but he made the final decisions on who was invited into the group."

"Is the group still active?"

"Oh, yes."

"When do they meet?"

"It's flexible," Holderby said. "It isn't a practice I agree with, but Mr. Glithero insists it's a way for him to test the students' commitment to what he calls 'the craft'."

"Is there anything else you can think of that might help me find Valerie's killer?" Kaye asked. "I know it's hard to imagine that her death might be connected to Grove Charter, but I have to check all the boxes to keep my boss happy."

And I just checked off a big one, he thought.

"Nothing comes to mind right now, Detective."

"If anything does, please call me," Kaye said as he stood up. He handed her a business card.

On the way out, he thanked Mrs. Kowalczyk.

"You're welcome, Detective," she said. "And for the record, I like your motorcycle jacket better."

CHAPTER 9

The civic core of Santa Ana, The County Seat of Orange County, occupies several city blocks packed with city, county and federal office buildings, courthouses and jails. Kaye had been there before and parked in the parking garage between the Santa Ana PD headquarters and the County Courthouse.

The line to get through courthouse security was a long string of what Kaye figured were workers returning from lunch and the afternoon's first round of litigants and their lawyers, so he stepped aside to wait. That drew the attention of a uniformed security guard, who came from behind the barricade and approached, stopping just outside arm's length. Kaye could see the man's nameplate. Cox.

"Sir, can I help you find something?" Cox asked as he eyed Kaye carefully.

"Detective Ben Kaye, LAPD," Kaye said and held up his open badge wallet. "I'm here to check some old case records. I am armed and figured I'd wait for the line to shorten up a bit to avoid delaying people."

"May I?" Cox said as he reached out for Kaye's identification.

"You bet," Kaye said, handing it to him.

The man studied it closely, comparing the photo on the ID to the man standing in front of him before handing it back.

"Sorry, Detective," Cox said, "but you can't take your sidearm into the courthouse. I'll secure it for you and return it when you leave."

"No apology necessary," Kaye said. "Same rules where I work."

"Habit," Cox said, smiling. "I've been around long enough to remember when public buildings actually belonged to the public. But I can save you from the line. Follow me." He led Kaye back through the exit he'd used toward a bank of metal lockers against the far wall.

"How long you been doing this?" Kaye asked as they walked.

"Almost five years now."

"Where'd you retire from?" Kaye asked as they got to the lockers. Most were open and had two orange-tipped keys hanging from their locks, a few were closed and had no keys.

Cox looked sideways at Kaye.

"What can I say," Kaye said, smiling. "It shows."

"I'll take that as a compliment."

"I meant it as one."

Cox nodded and said, "I was OCSD for twenty-six years."

"Why are you doing this instead of going fishing every day?"

"Keeps me involved," Cox said, then paused for a moment before adding. "I'm also old enough to remember when it didn't cost five hundred bucks to walk into a doctor's office. We need the extra insurance."

"I hear that."

Cox shrugged and said, "Pick a locker and put your pistol inside, please."

Kaye followed the instructions, dropping the magazine from the Kimber .45 before locking it and the pistol inside.

"You keep that key," Cox said as he twisted the second lock closed and took the key. "See me when you come back down. You'll want the third floor."

"Thank you," Kaye said as he turned and headed for the stairs.

"Elevator's faster," Cox called after him.

Kaye turned and looked as he opened the stairwell door. "I need the exercise."

Cox laughed and shook his head.

The Court Administrator and Records Office was bustling when Kaye stepped through the door. The office was using the tried-and-true 'take a number' customer service model and Kaye was dismayed when he saw the 'now-serving' number and compared it to the paper ticket hanging from the dispenser. It wasn't until he stopped and looked around that he noticed another window, separate from the four counter stations serving walk-ins, with a sign above it. Law Enforcement Only.

The window was unattended, but there was a button on the counter with a handwritten 'push for service' note taped next to it.

He pushed the button and waited. It wasn't long before a smiling young woman appeared.

"Hi," she said. "How can I help you?"

"I'd like to see the records for an arrest and trial that happened quite some time ago. I'm looking for background on a case I'm working now."

"Can I see your identification, please?"

Kaye laid his badge wallet on the counter and she wrote his particulars onto a log sheet. Then she looked up and asked, "Okay, who are we looking for?"

"The arrestee's name is Dylan Glithero," Kaye said, then reached into his pocket, pulled out the record sheet Patty had given him and slid it across to her. "That's all I have."

She picked it up and immediately frowned. "Wow, that's a long time ago." She glanced up at Kaye, back down at the sheet and back up at Kaye. "This is way before our seven-year look-back window, and that's all I have access to. I'm not even sure this will be in our digital records database."

"Can you find out for me, please?"

"Sure. Hold on."

She disappeared into a back office, returning about two minutes later.

"Okay," she said, "I asked my supervisor. He searched the name and came up empty, which he said means it's not scanned into the system yet."

"How do I get my hands on the paper record? It's possibly related to an active homicide investigation."

"Let me find out."

She disappeared into the same back office again and this time returned almost immediately, trailed by a balding man wearing glasses and dressed in slacks, shirt and tie, his tie loosened and his sleeves rolled up almost to his elbows.

"Detective Kaye?" the man asked. "Marvin Sunderland, Court Administrator. You're looking for information on Dylan Glithero?"

"I am."

"Unfortunately, those records haven't been digitized and are in our paper storage warehouse. You can fill out a request form and we'll get them for you, but it might take us a week or two."

"I understand. It was a long time ago."

"That it was," Sunderland said. "I'd only been here about a year. The name didn't click with me right away, but as I recall it was quite the spectacle. That's the only reason I remember it."

"Spectacle?" Kaye asked. "How so?"

"The citizens were really up in arms. If they'd had their way, they would have lynched those two guys."

"Two guys?" Kaye asked.

"Oh, yeah," Sunderland confirmed. "Glithero and… I'm sorry, I can't remember the other guy's name, but he was a teacher, too."

"Glithero was charged with sexual battery of a minor," Kaye said. "Are you saying that he was a teacher and the victim was a student of his?"

Sunderland didn't answer immediately, and Kaye could tell the man was dredging his memory.

"That's what I recall," the administrator said finally, "but it's been so long you'd need to check the record to be sure."

"I can't find a record of a prison sentence or sex offender registration. Were the charges dropped? Was he acquitted?"

Sunderland nodded. "He was. That's what started all the brouhaha. Again, my recollection could be off, because there were two very similar cases tried at the same time. I seem to remember that Glithero testified on his own behalf, but don't remember the defense strategy. Whatever it was, it worked, because the jury found him not guilty."

"You said there were two teachers involved."

"Yes," Sunderland said. "The other guy was older. I wish I could remember his name. He was charged with multiple counts of rape."

"Did he walk, too?" Kaye asked.

"Oh, no," Sunderland said, shaking his head. "But as I recall, the prosecutor cut a deal when Glithero was acquitted and agreed to lesser charges and a lighter sentence."

"They had separate trials?"

"I'm not sure they were actually co-defendants. There was a lot of buzz about the other teacher. The rumors were flying when the prosecutor retired right after the case wrapped up."

"I bet," Kaye said. "If nothing else, terrible optics. Do you remember the Prosecutor's name?"

"I think his last name was Chilton, or Clifton, or something like that, but I don't remember his first name. Don't even know if he's still alive."

"So Chilton, or Clifton, was the prosecutor in the second guy's trial, not Glithero's?"

"I think so," Sunderland said. "I don't remember who prosecuted Glithero. Sorry."

"That's okay."

"The kicker was that the Judge accepted the pleas, but ignored the sentencing recommendation and put the guy in prison," Sunderland said. "The guy went berserk in the courtroom. Injured two bailiffs."

"Who was the Judge?" Kaye asked.

"DeVilbiss. He passed in twenty twelve."

"But you can't remember the other defendant?"

"No, sorry," Sunderland said. "I'm really surprised I remember what I do. I was a first-year traffic court clerk back then." He stopped for a second, then said, "I just remembered the name of the school, if that would help."

"Can't hurt."

"Moulton High School, down in south County."

Something about the name tickled Kaye's memory.

"I'll check it out," Kaye said. "I would like to make a formal request for the records."

"Certainly," Sunderland said. "I'll see what I can do to speed up the process. And I have another suggestion for you."

"What's that?"

"Try the Sheriff's Department. With all the advances in forensic technology they never throw anything away, and their storage is more readily accessible."

"Thank you, Mr. Sunderland. I appreciate your help."

"You're welcome, Detective. May I ask you a question?"

"Sure."

"Is Dylan Glithero a suspect in the homicide you're investigating?"

"Honestly, I don't know," Kaye said. "His name is one of several that's come up and I have to chase them all down."

"I understand," Sunderland said. "We'll get those records to you as soon as possible." He tapped the counter twice with his knuckles before turning around and heading for the back office.

The young lady working the window helped Kaye with the records request paperwork, and fifteen minutes later he had retrieved his Kimber and was headed around the block to the Sheriff's Department headquarters.

Kaye had to wait in line while the desk deputy patiently explained, multiple times, to a woman that she was in the Department headquarters building, not the county jail, and that she needed to go to the jail if she wanted to post bond for her son. She finally gave up and complained all the way out the door.

"Sorry about that," the exasperated deputy said when Kaye stepped up to the desk. "What can I do for you?"

Kaye held up his ID. "I'd like to talk to one of your senior investigative staff, if anyone is available."

"About?"

"I'm trying to find information on an old case. I went to court records and they're going to search their warehouse, but it could take a couple weeks. The Admin, name of Sunderland, suggested I check to see if you still had the reports and any evidence on hand."

"You should probably talk to our records Lieutenant. Hang loose a sec and I'll see if she's available." He reached for the desk phone.

Kaye stepped away to avoid the appearance of eavesdropping and scanned the portraits of past Orange County Sheriffs that hung on the walls. They were in chronological order and Kaye noted that it hadn't been all that long ago that they'd all posed for their official photo wearing a uniform and white cowboy hat. Then, abruptly, business suits had taken over. Kaye thought it probably marked the transition of the post from lawman to politician.

"She'll be right out," the Deputy called to Kaye as another group of customers pushed through the front door.

"Thanks," Kaye said in return.

It wasn't thirty seconds before a woman in uniform, a single silver bar on each side of her collar, came through a door into the lobby. She homed right in on Kaye.

"Trish Adamson," she introduced herself as she approached.

"Ben Kaye. Thanks for taking the time to see me, Lieutenant."

"No problem," Adamson said. "You're looking for old case files?"

"One in particular, yes," Kaye replied, then gave her a quick background and time frame.

"Wow," Adamson said, "that was a long time ago. Come on back with me and we'll see what we can come up with."

Kaye followed her into the secure area and around a corner into an office. Adamson sat down at the desk, put on the glasses that were atop it, and spun toward a computer monitor while Kaye sat down opposite her. He reached into his pocket that pulled out the small spiral notebook, which he called his paper brains, he habitually carried with him.

"What did you say the guy's name was?" Adamson asked.

"Glithero," Kaye replied, then spelled it out. "First name Dylan, as in Bob." He slid the arrest record he'd brought with him across the desk.

Adamson grabbed it and laid it next to the keyboard, tipped her head slightly to get the right focal length, typed in the name and hit enter.

Almost immediately the screen refreshed and Kaye could see a photo. He leaned sideways to get a better angle, and it wasn't hard to deduce it was the same, just much younger, Dylan Glithero he'd seen at Grove Charter.

"Got him," Adamson said, turning to look at Kaye before she looked back at the screen. "Yep, sexual battery on a minor. Date matches. And we got the case number."

"Can you read that to me, please?" Kaye asked, grabbing his pen.

"How 'bout I just print this for you?"

"That'll work." He put the little notebook away.

Adamson scrolled through several screens of data that Kaye, from his angle and distance, couldn't see well enough to read. She grunted several times, scrolled back to the top of the data, clicked the mouse, spun toward Kaye and dropped her glasses back onto the desk just as Kaye heard a printer he couldn't see come to life. When it went silent, Adamson reached under the side of her desk, came up with the printout, and handed it to Kaye.

"That's your copy of the booking report face sheet," she said. "And there's good news and bad news."

"Bad news first."

"Apparently, because Glithero was acquitted the investigative reports were," she paused two beats, then added, "not maintained."

"You mean they were destroyed?"

"It's not something we do as policy," Adamson replied. "There has to be a court order on a motion from defense counsel. Probably something to do with exoneration and Glithero avoiding future fallout from the charge."

"What about physical evidence?"

"According to the computer, no evidence was booked. Must've been strictly a 'he said, she said' situation."

Well, crap, Kaye thought as he scanned the printout.

"What about the detective on the case?" he asked, finding the page. "G. Sebaly. Where can I find him?"

"I don't know," Adamson said, shrugging one shoulder. "I've been here almost nine years and that's not a familiar name to me. Sorry I'm not being much help here."

"That's okay," Kaye said, rising to leave. "Been a long time."

"Wait," Adamson exclaimed, holding up an index finger. "I just had an idea."

Kaye sat back down as she grabbed her glasses again and spun toward the monitor. Her fingers flew over the keyboard for a minute before she turned to Kaye and said, "I hope she's on-line."

Kaye waited while Adamson nervously tapped her desktop. A moment later her computer made a sound and she leaned toward the monitor. Seconds later she slumped back into her chair.

"Damn," she muttered, turning to Kaye. "I just checked with Finance. They don't have anybody named Sebaly in the pension system as a payee, which tells me he didn't retire from here."

"Or he did, and he died," Kaye pointed out.

Adamson made a face and said, "Yeah, could be. I didn't think of that."

"Good idea, though. Thanks for trying."

The two exchanged business cards and Kaye headed for the parking garage.

As he passed the courthouse he had a sudden idea and turned to go inside.

The line for security was now almost non-existent and the same guards manned the station. Kaye stepped aside and caught the eye of Cox, the guard he'd talked to earlier. Cox came out to meet him.

"You're back," Cox said.

"I am," Kaye acknowledged. "Not having much luck finding what I'm looking for and thought you might be able to help me out."

"Me? How's that?"

"You said a while ago that you worked for the Sheriff's Department, right?"

"I did. Twenty-six years."

"When did you retire?"

"Little over five years ago."

"Do you remember a guy, a detective, named Sebaly?"

"Greg Sebaly?" Cox asked. "Yeah, I remember him. Why?"

"He was the lead, at least his name is on the reports, on the case I'm trying to track down," Kaye said. "I'd like to talk to him."

"That was a long time ago," Cox said.

"That's what everybody keeps telling me," Kaye said, half-smiling. "I found out he either didn't retire from here, or he died, because the County doesn't send him a check every month."

"Sebaly didn't retire from here," Cox said. "Left to work someplace else."

"Law enforcement?" Kaye asked.

Cox nodded.

"Do you know where?"

Cox thought for a moment before saying, "I'm pretty sure he went up north, one of those counties on the coast, but I don't remember which one."

"Do you know why he quit?"

Cox studied Kaye closely before saying, "You must be looking into an old child molestation case or something like that."

"Something like that."

"Well," Cox said, "that's why he quit. He worked sex crimes for too many years. Burned him out, I guess. I heard he was telling people he was tired and wanted to go back to writing speeding tickets on quiet country roads instead of always dealing with molesters and rapists."

"Have you kept in touch?"

"Me? No. We weren't buddies or anything like that. I worked patrol and was a TacTeam sergeant, and he was a suit." Cox stopped abruptly before quickly adding, "No offense, Detective."

"None taken," Kaye said easily.

"In fact, I probably wouldn't even remember Sebaly if it wasn't for all the shit in the papers when he quit."

"Really?" Kaye said. "What happened?"

"People thought he took money to throw a case," Cox said. "A lot of people."

"Did he?"

Cox shrugged. "All I can tell you is that there was a full investigation because of the public outcry. He was cleared, but I don't think people outside the Department bought it. They thought it was a cover-up."

"Why?"

"Because a prosecutor also quit right before Sebaly," Cox replied. "It was a real mess. I spent a lot of days in full gear guarding the courthouse during the trials. There were a lot of protesters."

Kaye picked up that Cox had said 'trials', plural, and realized Cox was talking about the Dylan Glithero case. And his possible co-defendant. He needed to find and talk to Greg Sebaly.

"Do you know anybody who still works for the Department that might have kept in touch with Sebaly?"

Cox thought again before answering. "Not that comes to mind. That was --"

"A long time ago." Kaye finished the sentence. "I know. Thank you, Sergeant Cox."

"I'm not a sergeant anymore," Cox said.

"Once a sergeant, always a sergeant," Kaye said. "At least in my book."

Back in the parking garage, Kaye slid into the pickup and opened the search engine app on his phone. He typed in Moulton High School and tapped the search icon.

At the top of the search results was a system message: Did you mean Moulton Junior High School?

The first return showed a school building next to the caption identifying it as Moulton Junior High School in Orange County, California. It also gave a street address, next to which was a map. Kaye clicked on the map and instantly knew why the word Moulton had triggered his memory.

When he and Amy had first started dating, Moulton Parkway had been on his route to her apartment. He enlarged the map and fixed the school's location in his mind.

He followed a couple of links until he found an historical summary for the school. It had been Moulton High School when it first opened, then converted to a Junior High about ten years ago when two adjoining school districts decided to merge. There was no mention of the teacher sex scandal that had rocked the school years before that.

He cleared the search field and had just started typing 'Greg…' when the phone rang.

"Detective, Kayla Okafor."

"Hey, Counselor, what's up?" Kaye asked.

"I just got back from Judge Franklin's chambers," she replied. "He showed me some of Valerie Weber's adoption information."

"Already?"

"Yes. When I told him she'd been murdered he cut through the red tape. I wasn't allowed to see the entire file or make copies, but I've got some information and an old address for you."

Kaye grabbed his pen and paper brains from his pocket.

"Go ahead," he said.

"Valerie's birth mother's name is Rachel Lowden." She spelled it out. "And get this. She was barely seventeen when she had Valerie."

"That might explain why she gave up her baby," Kaye said.

"Probably so," Okafor said.

"You get any information on Rachel's whereabouts? Or who the father was?"

"Not from the Judge," Okafor said. "But what he showed me listed an address in Northridge." She gave Kaye the street number. "Since she was only seventeen, odds are it was her parents' address, so I called the County and asked them to check tax records. The house is still owned by Leon and Monica Lowden. Doesn't mean they still live there. It could be a rental now. It's been a long time."

"I've been hearing that a lot today," Kaye said. "If it's a rental, the tenant has to send rent someplace. I'll find them."

"Where are you now?"

"Santa Ana. Looking into an old case tied to a possible person of interest in Weber's beating and murder."

"You've got a suspect already?" Okafor said. "Wow, Kaye, even for you that's spectacular detective work."

"Don't pop the champagne yet, Counselor. I'm nowhere near calling this guy a suspect, much less making an arrest."

She laughed. "How about I just keep it on ice?"

"You do that," Kaye said. "Thanks for the info on Rachel Lowden. Appreciate it."

"Sure. Hope you find her."

Now that he had a connection between Valerie Weber and Dylan Glithero, finding Rachel Lowden's birth parents slid down his priority list. He momentarily thought about just turning the information over to Gannett, but rejected the notion almost immediately. He'd chase it. He owed JoAnn Weber at least that much.

Kaye put his phone away and started the truck. It wasn't until the dashboard display lit up that he noticed the time. Trying to get back to the station now would probably become an exercise in traffic futility.

He sat for a moment, thinking, then muttered, "What the hell. Why not?" and headed for the garage exit.

When Kaye got to I-5 he passed the northbound ramp entrance, went under the freeway and caught the green arrow for the southbound ramp. It didn't take him long to realize that southbound traffic was probably as tough as northbound, so when he got to the Hwy. 133 exit, he took it and headed toward Laguna Beach, got off at Lake Forest and cut over to Moulton Parkway.

Much had changed, and it took him a while, and a few wrong turns, to finally find the apartment complex. His first thought was that the buildings looked shabbier than they had back when he'd rolled in on his first Harley to pick up Amy for their first date. Then he realized it wasn't the apartments that had changed. His frame of reference had matured.

He drove through the complex twice before he gave up, chagrined that he couldn't tell for certain which building Amy's apartment had been in. The trees and landscaping had grown and changed the entire look and feel of the place. Still, he parked and just sat, remembering.

From the apartments, Kaye headed south on Moulton. If he remembered right, at some point it changed names and became one of the famous Dana Point 'Lantern' streets that would take him directly to Pacific Coast Highway and the yacht harbor.

Again, it took him some time, but he wasn't in a hurry. He crested the last rise while the sun was still above the horizon. The headlands of

Dana Point rose on Kaye's right and the glittering Pacific stretched to the horizon.

Kaye turned south on U.S. 1. It wasn't long before he crossed the bridge over San Juan Creek. After a bit of disorientation because of highway construction and realignments, he found the turn for Camino Capistrano and headed inland.

The creek was the only real break in the coastal bluffs for miles in both directions, and the street had been traveled for centuries, first by the natives, then by Fr. Junipero Serra, founder of California's glittering string of Missions. For nearly two hundred years it had been the unofficial 'Main Street' of the small, unincorporated village known informally as Capistrano Beach.

The highway realignment had changed that, even since Kaye's days at Harley Charlie's bike shop. As the sun set, he made two passes up and down the now unfamiliar street, searching. Finally, he pulled into a big box home improvement store parking lot, parked, and tried to get his bearings.

"Son of a bitch," he finally whispered, clenching his jaw.

The building that had housed Harley Charlie's and two others housing adjacent local businesses were gone, replaced by a national franchise tire and auto shop. Its lights glared in the twilight as the employees scurried around trying to take care of the customers before closing time.

Dispirited, Kaye drove back to Pacific Coast Highway and turned north. He pulled into the familiar Dick's Arco station across from Doheny State Beach, filled up the truck and continued north.

In Laguna Beach he slowed as he passed the spot where Amy had died.

The memories still haunted him. The realization that the oncoming car was drifting over the center line. The instinctive lean and swerve to avoid being hit. The sickening sound of impact as the car hit Amy, just behind him to his right. The gruesome injuries, the blood, the sirens, the flashing lights.

But mostly the look on her face, in her eyes, as she drifted away forever, her last words, "I love you Ben."

Then the absolute rage when he realized the driver had just kept going.

The memorial sign bearing Amy's name, part of the State's campaign to curb drunk driving, still stood as a reminder of what Kaye considered the worst moments of his life.

He stayed on PCH all the way to Newport Beach, picked up Hwy. 55, and headed home.

As he passed LAX and its ever-present string of landing lights in the eastern sky, his phone rang yet again. He pushed the hands-free button on the dash.

"Kaye."

"Is this Detective Kaye?" asked an unfamiliar voice.

"It is," he replied. "Who am I speaking to?"

"This is Neil Gaeta. We, uh, met last week when you arrested me."

"I remember," Kaye said. "How'd it go? Did you testify?"

"I did," Gaeta said. "Yesterday. The judge made me spend the night in jail for not showing up the first time, but I got out this afternoon."

"I'm assuming you'd like to come pick up your bike."

"That's why I'm calling," he said. "You still have it, right?"

"Of course. It's parked in the secure lot at the police station, as promised."

"Okay, great," Gaeta said and Kaye heard the relief in the man's voice. "I'm booked on an early flight to Burbank in the morning and was wondering if I could come get it."

"What time does your flight get in?"

"Eight fifteen."

"I'll be at the station when you get there," Kaye said. He gave Gaeta the address. "Just ask for me at the front desk."

"Thank you, Detective. I'll see you tomorrow morning."

It was late when Kaye pulled around to the back of the house and put the truck in the garage. In the dim light cast by the garage door opener he looked across at the partially mocked-up 1951 Panhead bolted to the lift. He hadn't been spending a lot of time on it lately.

Should have plenty of time now, he thought, his feelings ambivalent as he remembered his last conversation with Auggie McMaster.

He locked up the garage and headed inside. On the drive home he'd planned to meditate, but the long day and late hour now conspired to dissuade him. His practice had gone to pot over the last couple of months or so, he knew it, and he knew he needed to visit Kyokoku-Dera and sit *zazen* with Roshi, his mentor, to try and get back on track.

Once inside, Kaye left the lights off, grabbed a bottle of water from the refrigerator and went back outside. He sat on a patio chaise and stretched out his legs. It was late enough that the wind chased the sound of the coyotes singing in the canyons above down toward the beach and kept the sound of the surf at bay. The moon had not yet risen and the ocean was a vast smear of inky blackness. Just where he thought the horizon must be, Kaye could make out the running lights and the hazy aura of bridge lights on a large vessel, its cargo probably oil or containers of goods destined for Big Box stores, slowly crawling a heading that would round Point Vicente and take it to port in San Pedro.

To the southeast the lights of the South Bay carved a glittering arc from Santa Monica to Redondo Beach, and with no moon Kaye could easily spot the aircraft departing from LAX, climbing out of the airport traffic pattern before finding the shortest heading to their destinations.

He sipped the water and watched the world, oblivious, he was sure, to him and his woes, and reflected on his day. Harley Charlie's shop had died with Charlie, but knowing the building had been demolished had gotten to him. After not being able to pinpoint Amy's apartment it seemed as if there was a conspiracy afoot, not just to fade his memories, but to obliterate them completely.

He rose with a sigh, headed inside, dropped the empty bottle into the trash and went to bed.

CHAPTER 10

Back on two wheels, Kaye made it to the squad room by 7:30 a.m. He wanted to talk to Tom Gannett before Neil Gaeta showed up to fetch his Wide Glide.

He went to the break room and brewed himself a cup of tea. His phone was ringing when he got back to his desk.

"Kaye."

"You're early."

Kaye recognized Gannett's voice and said, "I could say the same thing about you."

"No shit," Gannet said. "I've got court in an hour and I wanted to talk to you first."

"About?"

"I happened to call a Ms. Holderby at Grove Charter High yesterday afternoon to set up a time to meet, and guess what? She told me she's already talked to you about Valerie Weber."

"I sat down with her yesterday morning," Kaye said. "For future reference, if you need to know what's going on at Grove Charter, talk to Mrs. Kowalczyk, the office lady. Holderby might be the company commander, but Kowalczyk is the senior NCO."

"I'll remember that. Are you planning on sharing what you found out?"

"That's why I'm here early," Kaye replied, trying not to let his irritation creep into his voice. "I was about to call you."

"Okay, so?"

"Well," Kaye began, "I think I found out who was picking Valerie up after school over at Westside." He went on to fill Gannett in on finding the Toyota in the Grove Charter faculty lot, connecting it to Dylan Glithero, the man's sexual battery of a minor arrest when he was younger, and the subsequent acquittal.

"Good catch," Gannett said, "but we still can't connect that Highlander to the SUV that picked Weber up behind Staples."

Kaye took Gannett through his conversation with Holderby about Weber's time at Grove Charter and how she and Glithero had intersected.

"Holy shit," Gannett said softly. "Sounds like he homed in on her from the get-go and started grooming her. And I don't mean to be a writer."

"That occurred to me, too."

"Did Holderby pick up that you were fishing on this Glithero guy?"

"I'm not sure. I tried to make my questions about Valerie, but when I asked about Glithero more directly she pointedly refused to answer. She kept bringing up confidentiality rules."

Gannett laughed. "There are no confidentiality rules in a homicide investigation, especially when the victim's a kid."

"I pointed that out to her," Kaye said. "I'm not sure she was convinced."

"Too bad for her. So Glithero has a prior, but a long time ago. Where's he been in the meantime?"

"I don't know yet," Kaye said. "And don't forget, he was acquitted."

"But they had enough to charge him."

"I'm still looking into that. Might take a while."

"And you haven't talked to him at all yet, right?" Gannett asked.

"No," Kaye replied. "I figure the more I know about the guy and the more he relaxes because he thinks we're not looking at him, the better off we'll be when it comes time to talk to him."

"Can you send me some notes about what we just talked about?"

"Sure. I'll get them to you this morning."

Gannett was quiet for a moment, then said, "This court thing could drag on into tomorrow. Stay away from Glithero for now, but I'll get a search warrant for the Highlander as soon as I can and attach your notes to the affidavit." Gannett paused, then asked, "You don't mind being cited as a brother officer, do you?"

"Of course not."

"Good," Gannett said. "I'll call you as soon as I have the warrant. We'll set up a forensic team, serve it on Glithero at his house and see if we can hold his feet to the fire about killing little girls."

As soon as the call ended Kaye went to work putting together the notes Gannett had asked for. Because he also had to update the chronology in the case file, he was pretty much able to cut and paste.

He was just about done when his phone rang again.

"Kaye."

"Detective, this is Navarrez at the front desk. There's a guy here to see you about a motorcycle. A Doctor Neil Gaeta?"

"Ask him to wait, and tell him I'll be just a minute."

Kaye quickly wrapped up his notes and sent them to Gannett. He grabbed the Wide Glide's keys from his desk drawer and headed downstairs.

Neil Gaeta was dressed in riding gear and his overall appearance was even more conservative than it had been last week. A pair of riding gloves stuck out of the helmet dangling from one hand, and in the other he held a small day pack.

"Doctor Gaeta?" Kaye said as he entered the lobby.

Gaeta turned to the sound of his voice and smiled. "Detective Kaye, good to see you again. I can't even begin to thank you."

"Not a problem," Kaye said. "Us bikers need to stick together. Follow me."

Kaye led Gaeta though the station and out back to the secure parking lot. He spotted the bike immediately and increased his pace, making it to the bike several steps ahead of Kaye.

"What do I owe you?" he asked when Kaye caught up.

"Nothing," Kaye said as he handed over the keys. "Glad I could help out."

"Are you sure?"

"Positive. Just be safe on the ride home."

"Thank you so much." Gaeta said sincerely. "I should be home by dark. If you're ever in Berkeley, look me up at the computer lab at Cal. I'd love to buy you and your significant other dinner."

"I'll do that," Kaye said, smiling. "Go ahead and start it up, and I'll open the gate when you're ready."

He headed for the exit gate's keypad. From there he watched Gaeta bungee cord the day pack to the Wide Glide's sissy bar, don the gloves and helmet, and cinch the chin strap tight before he swung over and pulled the bike up. Seconds later it rumbled to life. After a short idle period, Kaye heard the transmission go into first gear and the bike slowly rolled his way.

He punched in the code and the gate opened.

"Thanks again," Gaeta said loudly as he rolled by.

Kaye watched Gaeta stop, check traffic, then accelerate up the street until he disappeared. He closed the gate, stepped out onto the sidewalk, made sure the gate closed all the way, then headed for the deli around the corner to pick up an early lunch.

Back at his desk, Kaye slowly worked on his sandwich while he tried to track down former Orange County Deputy Greg Sebaly.

His search returns mostly referred to old newspaper articles from the Dylan Glithero case days. Kaye scanned through them and noticed the tone of the coverage change from praising Sebaly's work on the case to a print assassination of the man's character for being a crooked cop. It reminded him that right or wrong, the internet never forgives or forgets. Near the bottom of the screen he found a result that read 'Officer critically injured in shooting' and the name Greg Sebaly was listed in the summary. He clicked and was directed to the site of the Ukiah Daily Journal.

The story, dated several years ago, detailed how Deputy Greg Sebaly of the Mendocino County Sheriff's Office had unknowingly walked into the middle of an armed robbery at a convenience store in one of the county's small towns. Sebaly had killed one of the robbers, but another had shot him several times, including once in the head. The article gave no specifics on Sebaly's condition or subsequent outcomes of the investigation.

Well, at least I know where to start looking, Kaye thought. *Hope he made it.*

Kaye immediately looked up and called the number for the Mendocino County Sheriff's office.

A Deputy Vann answered.

Kaye went through the standard introduction and told Vann he was looking for a Greg Sebaly he thought used to work there.

"I found an old article in your local paper about a Deputy Sebaly being shot during an armed robbery," Kaye said. "It's a pretty unique name, and I'd like to talk to him about an old case."

"I'm sorry," Vann said. "I'm not authorized to release that kind of information over the phone. I'm sure you understand."

"I do," Kaye admitted. "Our policy is the same as yours. How do I need to do this?"

"If your commanding officer verifies who you are, you should probably talk directly to the Sheriff. He'll probably tell you what you need to know."

"Is the Sheriff in now?"

"He is not," Vann said. "What did you say your name was?"

"Detective Ben Kaye. I work out of the LAPD West Bureau and my Captain's last name is Thompson. The station number is in the book. If you could have the Sheriff call our desk number and ask for the Captain, he'll be able to verify who I am."

"I'll give him the message," Vann said.

"Can you at least tell me if Sebaly's still alive?"

Kaye heard the click as the line went dead.

The call hadn't been a total waste of time. When Kaye had mentioned Sebaly, Vann hadn't said 'never heard of the guy', which to Kaye meant he was probably looking in the right place.

Now he just had to wait.

Kaye checked the time. If he hustled he could make it out to Northridge before afternoon traffic and check the address Okafor had given him for Leon and Monica Lowden.

He gathered his gear and was headed for the door when he heard Thompson calling his name.

He turned to see the Captain hurrying in his direction.

"What's up?" Kaye asked. "Did the Mendocino County Sheriff call already?"

Thompson gave him a look that told Kaye the Sheriff hadn't called, then said, "Just had a call from Jefferies. He needs you on Wilshire, just east of Westwood Boulevard, a.s.a.p."

"Did he say why?"

"A drive-by."

Kaye started to ask his boss another question, but the look on Thompson's face stopped him.

"On the way," he said instead as he headed for the door.

Kaye pushed the Harley, using every traffic-beating technique from his motor officer days, plus some not-exactly-legal passing maneuvers, to make it to Westwood Village in near-record time.

Wilshire was closed in both directions between Glendon and Westwood Boulevard. The uniformed officer directing traffic at Glendon recognized Kaye and waved him through.

Ahead, Kaye could see multiple cars and trucks parked in the street, then a knot of marked units, their overheads flashing, blocking the street beyond them. An unmarked unit he assumed belonged to J.J. and Burke was pulled up close to the marked patrol cars. A fire truck was also on-scene.

Most of the uniforms were busy directing traffic, working perimeter security and crowd control. Kaye slowly threaded the bike through the parked cars, pulled up behind the unmarked unit and shut down. He hung his helmet on the handlebars and, keeping an eye on the surrounding crowd, walked through the maze of marked units.

He spotted J.J., notebook in hand, on the north sidewalk talking to a man and woman.

Burke spotted him at the same time he saw her, disengaged from the officer she'd been talking to and headed toward Kaye.

"What've you got?" Kaye asked when they met. He kept going.

"Looks like a drive-by," Burke replied, spinning around and catching up. "Vehicle-to-vehicle, though."

"On this stretch of Wilshire?" Kaye finished the question just as he rounded the last patrol unit between him and the scene. He pulled up short and stared.

Lying in the right lane, bent and broken from the dump and subsequent slide, was a custom painted Harley Wide-Glide. Kaye immediately focused on the Cal-Berkeley license plate frame.

"Is he alive?" he asked Burke, his voice low.

"He was when they loaded him into the ambulance, but it wasn't good."

"Injuries?"

"Looks like he took multiple rounds," Burke said. "One to the head that looked like it penetrated his helmet." She paused for a beat before adding, "The EMS guys left the helmet on, just in case."

"How'd J.J. know to call me?"

"The first-on-scene said the vic asked for you by name just before he lost consciousness. Do you know the guy?"

"In a way," Kaye said. "His name is Neil Gaeta. I arrested him last week and he came and picked up his bike this morning."

"What did you pop him for?"

"He had a warrant out of Oakland," Kaye replied.

"A fugitive?" Burke asked.

"No, fail to appear. He was a witness to a homicide," Kaye said. "He was afraid to testify, even though the Oakland PD offered him protection."

"Did he testify after you hooked him?"

"He did."

Burke went silent for a moment, then said, "So, this could have been a hit."

Kaye looked sideways at her and said, "You know, you might make a good detective one day."

She laughed. "Thank you. Coming from a legend, that means a lot."

"Don't believe everything you hear."

She laughed again. "Detective, if I only believed half the stories I've heard, well, let's just leave it at that."

It was Kaye's turn to laugh. "As long as the half you believe isn't the half that comes out of Internal Affairs, we should get along just fine."

"Sure a lot of laughing and slapping going on over here," J.J. said as he walked up. "Does that mean you two have already broken the case?"

"Kaye knows the victim," Burke said.

"Really?" J.J. asked, looking askance at Kaye. "A friend of yours? Is that why he asked for you?"

Kaye told J.J. what he'd already told Burke about Neil Gaeta.

"Oh, a biker thing," J.J. said knowingly. "I get it. You want to take lead on this?"

"You were assigned," Kaye said. "You take lead and I'll help as much as I can."

"That'll work," J.J. said. He turned and looked at Burke. "You okay with that?"

She nodded.

"So," J.J. asked her, "what do you think happened here?"

"We…" Burke stammered. "Uh, I think it could have been a hit because he testified."

"Do you know who he testified against?" J.J. asked Kaye.

"No," Kaye replied. "The Oakland PD cops that came down to get him called them really nasty people, but didn't give me specifics. You can call them and find out."

"I agree on the hit theory," J.J. said. "Fits with what the witnesses told me."

"What did you find out?" Kaye asked.

Jefferies related that the couple he'd been talking to had been in the car behind the motorcycle, westbound on Wilshire, stopping at the same lights, keeping pace with traffic and such, with no sign of the suspect vehicle. Just as they passed through the light at Selby, the man, who was driving, saw a silver SUV coming up fast behind him. Traffic was heavy, but the SUV was trying really hard to get ahead and moved into the inside lane just as it came up on him, making the car there brake hard to avoid a collision. The SUV then slowed down and went with the flow of traffic.

"Probably pacing Gaeta, looking for the shot," Burke said.

"Probably so," J.J. agrees. "Anyway, the red light at Westwood is causing everybody to slow down. The light goes green, the SUV pulls up alongside the bike, an arm comes out the passenger side window, and boom, boom, boom. Three quick shots. He goes down and the SUV gasses it westbound."

"Did they see the driver?" Kaye asked.

"They did not," J.J. replied. "Said the windows were too tinted. But the woman in the passenger seat saw the shooter's arm. She said he was white and she could see a tattoo, but not enough to be definitive."

"Not much to go on," Burke said.

"Ah, but wait," J.J. said, smiling. "Turns out the guy is in the car business. He gave me make, model, year, everything right down to the brand of the oversized custom wheels. He called it a 'banger wagon' – his words, not mine -- and said the wheels are so expensive they're only sold by special order."

"Don't suppose he got a plate?" Kaye asked.

"He did," J.J. said. "You get one guess."

"Stolen," Burke says instantly.

J.J. smiled. "Not stolen, but the plate doesn't match the vehicle and it's not current in the system."

"So, where do we start?" Burke asked.

"I think with car dealers here and in the East Bay area," J.J. replied. "The suspect vehicle is a current model year. They had to buy it somewhere. Same with the wheels."

"If you want to start chasing that," Kaye said, "I'll go check on Gaeta. I'm assuming they took him around the corner to Reagan."

"They did," Burke said.

"Oh, and J.J.?" Kaye said.

"Yeah?"

"Talk to media relations. Spin it however you want, but keep Gaeta's name and condition out of the news."

"Got it," J.J. said. "No information released until next of kin located and notified."

Kaye returned to his Harley, carefully rode through the remaining vehicles, turned north on Westwood Boulevard and headed for Ronald Reagan UCLA Medical Center.

A few minutes later he parked near the emergency entrance and went inside. He headed straight for the E.R. registration desk.

"Can I help you?" a man in scrubs behind the counter asked.

"Detective Kaye, LAPD," he said, holding up his badge. "A shooting victim, a young man, was just brought in. What can you tell me about his condition?"

"Stand by, Detective. I'll get somebody to help you." He left the counter and headed down a hallway.

Kaye waited almost ten minutes before a figure in full scrubs approached, raised the goggles she wore onto the top of her head and pulled down her face mask.

"I'm Doctor Prakesh," she said, eyeing Kaye closely. "You're here about the young man who was shot?"

"I am," Kaye replied, holding up his badge. "Detective Kaye. The victim is Neil Gaeta."

"At least now I know his name."

"He didn't have any ID on him?"

"Detective, I didn't have time to check."

"What's his condition?"

"Critical," Prakesh replied. "They just took him into surgery."

"Injuries?"

"He sustained three gunshot wounds. One was a through-and-through of the upper left arm that then struck his torso but did not penetrate the thoracic cavity. Another entered below his left axilla, expended most of its energy breaking a rib, fragmented, and punctured a lung. He also sustained leg injuries from the crash itself, but none of those should require surgery. He was pretty lucky, actually, all things considered."

"You said three gunshot wounds."

Prakesh's expression darkened. "The third bullet penetrated his helmet. I was able to remove the helmet and assess the injury. The bullet penetrated the scalp layers but did not obviously fracture his skull."

"That sounds like good news."

"Yes, and no. The helmet absorbs some of the energy," she hesitated, "but some is also transferred to the skull and subsequently to the brain. It can be as bad as being hit in the head with a big hammer without having a helmet on."

"Best case scenario?" Kaye asked after a moment.

"A concussion and a few days of nasty headaches," Prakesh replied, her expression telling Kaye she didn't think that was the likely outcome.

"Worst?"

"A severe traumatic brain injury that leaves him in a persistent vegetative state."

"For how long?" Kaye mentally crossed his fingers.

"Possibly for the rest of his life," Prakesh said softly.

"He was able to talk to one of the officers at the scene," Kaye said, hoping it was a good sign.

"That's potentially good news," Prakesh said. "But not predictive. We won't know until we get full imaging and a thorough evaluation by a neurologist."

"I'm going to need whatever bullets or bullet fragments the surgeons take out of him."

"We have chain of custody protocols for that, Detective. They can be retrieved from our security department after twenty-four hours."

"Excuse me, Doctor," a nurse said as she walked up. "We need you in seven."

"I'll be right there," Prakesh said, then turned to Kaye. "I'm sorry I can't be more definite. There are just too many variables at this point. Now, if you'll excuse me."

"Certainly," Kaye said. "Thank you, Doctor."

It was too late to try and make it to Northridge.

Kaye decided to call it a day and head home. Instead of catching Sunset over to Pacific Coast Highway he decided to take Wilshire through Santa Monica and catch PCH there.

CHAPTER 11

Kaye was dog tired and more than a little wet when he walked into the squad room. It had been mostly cloudy, but dry, when he left home, but on the way in he'd been caught in a brief, heavy shower. His helmet and jacket kept his upper body dry, but his pants, his thighs in particular, had taken the brunt of the rain.

His first stop was the locker room and the dry pair of jeans he kept in reserve. Then he headed for the break room and brewed himself a cup of tea. On the way to his desk he grabbed the fresh batch of Dailies off the board and went through them while the tea seeped into his bones.

He thought about calling the hospital for an update on Gaeta's condition, but knew there was likely zero chance of getting even an acknowledgement that Gaeta was a patient.

He'd just hung the Dailies back on the board and headed for his desk when his phone rang.

"Kaye."

"Ben, Tom Gannett. Happy National Crime Day."

"There's a National Crime Day?"

"Three hundred and sixty-five of them every year," Gannett deadpanned. "One extra in leap years."

"Got it. What's up?"

"I thought I'd let you know that I served the search warrant for Dylan Glithero's Highlander –"

"You were supposed to call me," Kaye interrupted.

"I know, I know," Gannett said. "But the whole thing got fucked up. You didn't miss anything."

"Do tell."

"Hey, I know you're pissed," Gannett said. "I would be, too. But get this. Glithero no longer owns the Highlander."

"What?"

"He made a deal for a new one last Saturday afternoon."

"The white Highlander with the Trojans decal was parked at Grove Charter this week," Kaye said. "I saw him get in it and drive it home."

"Hey, I believe you," Gannett said defensively. "I saw your photos, remember? When I asked him about it he told me he wanted the dealer to change the wheels and tint the windows on the new one. He claims their shop was backed up and he couldn't pick it up until yesterday. I hate to admit it, but it fits. I was sitting there with a forensics team, waiting for him, when he drove up in a new, red Highlander hybrid. He showed me the paperwork."

"Did you check the garage?" Kaye asked.

"I did. No white Highlander," Gannett replied. "When I asked why he traded in an almost new car for basically the same thing he got all excited about the saving the planet hybrid thing."

Kaye went quiet, his mind churning as he considered options.

"Did you call the dealer?" he asked after a moment. "Ask about getting the black box?"

"Just hung up from talking to them," Gannett said, defeat in his voice. "They verified the delivery delay and already had Glithero's old Highlander in the detail shop getting the once over. Including wiping the box."

"Damn it," Kaye muttered. "Did Glithero ask why you had a warrant to search his car?"

"He did. As soon as I mentioned Valerie Weber he asked for his lawyer and that was the end of that. He's our guy, Ben. I could feel it. Now we just have to figure out how to prove it."

Kaye had a flash of irritation at Gannett's use of 'we' after, at least in Kaye's mind, mucking up the whole thing.

Instead, he asked, "Traffic cams?"

"I put in the requests for the cameras around Staples and the approaches to where Weber's body was found right after you gave me the Highlander information. Might take a while to go through it all, but if it's there I will find it. If it's not there, I'll start looking at private security cameras in the same areas."

"Can I help?"

"Thanks, but the Boss has already assigned some extra eyes."

"Anything else I can do in the short term?" Kaye asked.

"Keep chasing Glithero's background," Gannett said. "Eventually we're going to need all the leverage we can get on the guy."

"I'll see what else I can come up with. What about you?"

"I'm going to Grove Charter and pry the names of the other female students in Glithero's writing group out of Holderby and start nosing around there."

"Good luck with Holderby."

Gannett laughed. "Hey, I already told you that, in my book, anyway, there are no confidentiality rules in a homicide. If Holderby gives me a hard time I'll arrest her for obstruction and we'll fight about it later."

"Keep me posted," Kaye said.

"You do the same."

Kaye ended the call, pulled up his case notes and spent fifteen minutes updating them. He was still angry that Gannett hadn't called him about the warrant service. He'd really wanted a chance to get up close and personal with Glithero and get a read on the guy. That chance was now gone.

But it was what it was. Nothing he could do about it now. He'd just have to keep digging into Glithero's past and hope he could come up with a skeleton big enough to flush the teacher out from behind his lawyer.

***

Kaye got lightly rained on again going over Sepulveda Pass to the Valley. He chastised himself for not paying closer attention to the weather, then beat himself up even more for letting a little rain bother him. It never had before.

His inescapable conclusion was advancing age.

The house in Northridge still owned by Leon and Monica Lowden was on a quiet street less than a block from an elementary school built in the same Shangri-La style Kaye had seen at Westside Alternative. Unlike Audie Murphy Elementary, though, Tribune Elementary had benefitted from the demographic shifts of the 1950s and since, and the square-block school grounds now hosted multiple portable-turned-permanent classroom buildings.

The neighborhood had also fared well over the years. Palm trees now towered over everything and many of the ranch style tract houses had been updated and added on to. In Kaye's mind that raised the odds the Lowden's might still live in the house.

Using the school as a landmark, Kaye had no trouble finding the address. The house was well-kept and a silver Ford SUV bearing a handicapped plate occupied the driveway. A ramp led from the entry walkway up to the level of the front porch and a wide, gentle wedge smoothed the bump between the porch and front door threshold.

Badge in hand, Kaye rang the camera-equipped doorbell, stepped back, and waited.

A moment later a woman's voice spoke through the doorbell speaker.

"Hello. How can I help you?"

"Ma'am, my name is Ben Kaye." He held up his open badge wallet. "I'm a detective with the Los Angeles Police Department. I'm trying to locate Leon and Monica Lowden and I found this address in the tax records. Do you know the Lowdens?"

There was a brief silence before the woman answered.

"I'm Monica Lowden. May I ask what this is about?"

"Mrs. Lowden, I'm trying to locate your daughter, Rachel."

Another silence, longer this time, before the door opened. A woman Kaye guessed as mid- to late-50s deftly blocked the doorway with her wheelchair as she held onto the doorknob.

"May I ask why you're interested in my daughter after all these years?" she asked, eyeing Kaye suspiciously.

"I'm sorry?" Kaye said, detecting a note of hostility in the question.

Lowden studied Kaye for a moment, then said, "Oh, my goodness. You don't know, do you?"

Kaye didn't know what to say, but Lowden rescued him.

"My daughter took her own life many years ago."

"I had no idea, Mrs. Lowden. I'm truly sorry. Had I known, I wouldn't —"

"No need to apologize," Lowden interrupted. "It was a long time ago."

"I'm very sorry to have bothered you, ma'am," Kaye said. "That actually tells me what I came to ask about. I'll let you get back to your day." He turned to leave.

"Excuse me," Lowden said quickly. "I'd still like to know why you're looking for my daughter."

Kaye turned back around.

"I'm working on a case and your daughter's name came up."

"Really? Must be one of those, oh…what do you call them? Cold cases?"

"No, ma'am, it's a current case," Kaye said, then figured the best approach would be the direct one. "Mrs. Lowden, did Rachel give up a baby girl for adoption when she was younger?"

Monica Lowden's eyes hardened and her jaw clenched. "Yes, Rachel gave up a baby for adoption. Although I fail to see how that's the business of the police."

"I'm not here to judge, Mrs. Lowden. Some information came to light on the case I'm working that the baby your daughter gave up might have tried to locate her birth parents. Obviously, she couldn't have found your daughter."

"Obviously not."

"There is one thing I'd like to ask about, though. It's a sensitive question and you don't have to answer if you'd rather not."

"I'd like to hear the question first," Lowden said.

"Did Rachel know who the father was?"

She hesitated for a moment, then answered, her voice now bitter. "Do you mean 'was my daughter a slut'?"

"No ma'am, that's not at all what I meant," Kaye replied. "It's just that my information concerns both birth parents. I'd like to find the father, if possible."

Lowden hesitated again, then said, "Yes, of course she knew. His name was Trevor. His last name was... Oh, my goodness, t's been so long I can't remember. I think it started with R-O-W, or something like that. He was a horrible boy, all kinds of trouble. After we found out Rachel was pregnant, my husband... we... forbade her from seeing him and he just abandoned her. When the time came my husband wouldn't allow Rachel to list him on Crystal's birth certificate to keep him from possibly causing trouble in the future."

"The baby's given name was Crystal?"

Lowden nodded.

"How did Rachel know Trevor?"

"They went to the same school." She paused and Kaye could tell she was dredging up old memories. "Rachel said she loved him, but they were so young, too young to have any idea what it takes to raise a child, especially an... illegitimate one."

The anger and bitterness in Monica Lowden's voice surprised Kaye.

"It was a very tough time in our lives," Lowden went on. "I'd been diagnosed with multiple sclerosis a short time before that. At first the episodes were infrequent and I had long periods of remission. That changed quickly. Then, when Rachel... died... the doctors told me my condition had worsened to the point where another pregnancy would have been dangerous." She sighed and stared into nothingness. "Had I known how things would turn out, well, let's just say we might have done things differently instead of giving up the only granddaughter I'd ever have."

"I'm sorry for your loss, Mrs. Lowden. Might you know where Trevor is now?"

She shook her head. "He moved away before Rachel had the baby."

"Do you know if his family still lives in the area?"

"I have no idea," she replied. "Nor do I care."

"I understand," Kaye said. "I'm sorry for bringing back bad memories, Mrs. Lowden. I appreciate you taking the time to talk to me." He handed her a business card and left a grieving Monica Lowden to her memories.

"Detective?" she said as he turned away.

"Yes, ma'am?"

"If you find Trevor, what's-his-name, please don't tell him you talked to me. Those who say the Lord only gives us burdens we can bear are liars, and I'd just as soon not add him to my list."

"I'll do my best, Mrs. Lowden."

Back at the bike he grabbed his paper brains and wrote down the name Trevor R-O-W. Neither JoAnn nor Valerie Weber had made a specific reference as to which parent Valerie was trying to locate.

You never know, he told himself as he put the little notebook back in his pocket. It might be interesting to find this Trevor kid and see if he grew up to drive a white SUV.

CHAPTER 12

Kaye walked into the squad room and almost bumped into Captain Thompson, briefcase in hand, as he headed out.

"Oh, hey," Thompson said. "Perfect timing."

"Good or bad?" Kaye asked.

"Good. I just left a note on your desk. The Mendocino County Sheriff called a little while ago to verify I have a Detective Kaye working here. He said you're looking for somebody up there?"

"I am. One of his former deputies. It's connected to the Weber case."

"Well, he left his number. Said you could call him direct."

"Thanks, Captain," Kaye said. "I'll give him a call. You headed out?"

"Yes," Thompson said. "Downtown to meet with the brass."

"Uh-oh."

"I don't think so." The Captain smiled. "I think they're going to ask me to stay on for a while."

"Really? Would you do that?"

Thompson shrugged. "Never make a decision until you're sure you have the other guy's final offer."

"Excellent point. Good luck."

"Thanks, Detective," Thompson said as he went out the door.

Kaye went to his desk and found the note. The name Earl Merritt was written down, along with a phone number. Kaye checked his call history and saw it was different from the number he'd tried already.

He made the call.

"Sheriff Merritt," a gruff voice answered.

"Sheriff, this is Detective Ben Kaye from the LAPD. You spoke to my boss, Captain Thompson, a while ago and gave him this number."

"I did. You called looking for Greg Sebaly, right?"

"That was me," Kaye confirmed. "I found an old story on-line about him being shot. Is he still working for you?"

Merritt ignored the question, instead asking, "What do you want with him? Is it something I might be able to help you with?"

Kaye explained to Merritt that he was digging into one of Sebaly's

95

old Orange County cases as part of a current homicide investigation.

There was a brief silence before Merritt, his tone measured, asked, "Is this about a guy named Glithero?"

"It is. Do you know the case?"

"Not the details. But I heard about the scandal at the time, and when Greg applied here I looked hard into his background and hooked him up to a polygraph before I hired him. You want my professional opinion?"

"Sure."

"If there was anything rotten about that case," Merritt said, "it wasn't Greg Sebaly. If you could straighten it out, I'd sure appreciate it. And I know Greg would, too."

"So he's still alive?" Kaye asked.

"Yes," Merritt replied, "but he suffered a brain injury and is confined to a wheelchair. The docs called it transient aphasia. His ability to listen and comprehend mostly came back, but he pretty much lost his ability to speak. He communicates through a computer."

"Sounds like I'd need to come talk to him in person."

"That would be best, Detective Kaye. Mentally, Greg's still sharp as a tack. In fact, he now does all my department's digital forensics. He just has difficulty communicating verbally."

"I'm still waiting on some things down here," Kaye said. "When I get them I'll decide if I need to make a trip up there to talk to him. Thanks for your time, Sheriff."

Kaye leaned back in his chair and ruminated on how unkind fate had been to Greg Sebaly. So much for writing tickets on quiet country roads.

The thought steered Kaye's mind to Roshi, his mentor at Kyokoku-Dera monastery. He hadn't been to visit Roshi since the old monk had helped him unravel some mysterious Kanji notes that led Kaye to a brutal murderer. He needed to go by.

J.J. and Burke pushed through the squad doors, saw Kaye, and headed his way.

"Glad we caught you here," Burke said.

"What's up?" Kaye inquired.

J.J. answered. "We've got a call set up with the Oakland PD in," he glanced at his watch, "ten minutes. We'd like you to sit in, if you have the time."

"I've got time," Kaye said, grabbing his pen and a legal pad.

Burke led the way to an interview room set up with a conference phone and they took chairs around the table.

At the appointed time, J.J. dialed the number. It rang for nearly twenty seconds and J.J., a disgusted look in his face, was reaching to disconnect when a male voice finally answered.

"Hello?"

"Hello," J.J. said, looking askance at Kaye. "This is Detective Jefferies, Los Angeles Police Department. Who am I speaking to?"

"Sergeant Osmond, Oakland Police Department."

"Sergeant, I'm here with Detectives Burke and Kaye. We were supposed to have a call with your Detectives Magnuson and Horton about a shooting here in Los Angeles that might be tied to a case there."

"Oh, yeah," Osmond said. "I heard them talking about something like that. And, uh, sorry about how I answered the phone. It's at an unoccupied desk and I figured it for a wrong number. Hang on."

There was a loud crackle and hold music started.

"What the hell?" J.J. blurted angrily.

"I guess we wait," Kaye said.

"Is being a detective always this exciting?" Burke asked without looking up from the pad she was doodling on.

Minutes passed before the hold music suddenly stopped and another voice, this one female, came on the line.

"This is Lieutenant Chen. How may I help you?"

J.J. shook his head in bewilderment, then went through the reason for the call again.

"And what did you say your victim's name is?" Chen asked.

"Neil Gaeta," J.J. replied. "He was a witness –"

"Never heard of him," Chen interrupted.

Kaye leaned forward. "Lieutenant Chen, this is Detective Kaye. I arrested Gaeta last week on a failure to appear warrant issued by an Alameda County judge. I was accompanied by your detectives Magnuson and Horton, who took custody of Gaeta at the scene.

"Yesterday, Gaeta returned to Los Angeles to retrieve his motorcycle, which I had impounded. He told me he had testified in a murder trial and did an overnight in jail on the warrant. On the way out of town, Gaeta was shot off his motorcycle. It wasn't an accident, and it wasn't random. It was a hit." Kaye paused briefly before asking, "Ring any bells now?"

"I already told you," Chen said flatly. "I've never heard of... what's his name. Sorry I can't be of assistance. Have a –"

"One more question," Kaye interrupted brusquely.

"Our weather's very nice today, thank you for asking," Chen said

97

sarcastically.

The call went dead.

"What the hell was that all about?" Burke asked.

J.J. shrugged and said, "That's a first for me."

Kaye sat quietly for a moment. When Burke gathered her pad and stood up to leave, he said, "Hang on a minute," took out his cell phone, spent a minute searching the web, scrolled through his call history until he found what he wanted, tapped the screen and held the phone to his ear.

Burke and J.J. exchanged looks and Burke sat back down.

"Tina," Kaye said seconds later, "this is Ben down in L.A. Got a minute? And can I put you on speaker?"

Kaye immediately took the phone away from his ear and again tapped the screen before putting the phone on the table.

"Okay," he continued, "you're on speaker. I'm here with Amari Burke and Jim Jefferies. They work with me. We just had an interesting conversation with a Lieutenant Chen."

Tina Magnuson laughed. "Kaye, you're lying. Nobody, and I mean nobody, has ever had a conversation with Chen that could be called interesting."

"Then I'll get to the point," Kaye said. "Can I ask you a question, strictly off the record?"

"You can ask. I can't promise I can answer."

"Why the stonewall job… on our mutual friend?" Kaye was careful not to mention Neil Gaeta by name.

Magnuson was silent for a moment before answering. "I can't tell you anything material to the case, but I guess I can tell you why I can't tell you. There's a gag order until the trial is over."

"The trial's still in progress?" Kaye asked.

"Yep," Magnuson said. "Probably another week, at least."

"Let me guess. The court's afraid of a mistrial if word of what happened down here gets out."

"I think that's an excellent deduction, and I think the concern is legit."

"Agreed, but know we've got a tight lid on this," Kaye said. "And who's Chen? She's not even on the Oakland PD org chart."

"She runs a gang task force," Magnuson replied. "Very *sub rosa* and lots of interagency stuff."

"That's kind of what I thought," Kaye said as Burke and J.J. exchanged a quick glance.

"Can I ask you a question?" Magnuson said.

"Sure."

"How's our friend doing?"

"Too soon to tell," Kaye replied. "Could be okay, could be catastrophic."

"Shit," Magnuson muttered. "You know, sometimes life just sucks."

"Amen to that," Burke murmured softly, drawing a scowl from J.J.

"Have you talked to his girlfriend?" Kaye asked. "Does she know?"

"I was told not to."

"Okay, we'll make the notification if it comes down to it," Kaye said. "Thanks, Tina. I'll keep you in the loop."

"Thanks, Ben."

Kaye ended the call.

J.J. leaned back in his chair, tossed his pen onto the table and said, "What a bunch of bullshit."

"Look on the bright side," Kaye said.

"There's a bright side?" Burke asked.

Kaye nodded. "Neil Gaeta was shot in Los Angeles. We work for the LAPD, not Oakland PD or Chen's task force. Their orders don't apply to us."

"Right," Burke said, visibly brightening. "They can't tell us to stand down and keep our mouths shut."

"I think keeping our mouths shut is advisable in this case," Kaye said. "But we're not folding up our tent and going away."

"Without information from Oakland PD we've got nothing to go on," J.J. protested.

"Not true," Kaye said. "When I arrested Gaeta he was hiding out at an old college roommate's house. Go talk to the roommate. Maybe Gaeta told him, or her, what's going on."

"I can do that," Burke volunteered.

"And," Kaye went on, "see if you can figure out how to contact Gaeta's girlfriend up north, just in case."

"His girlfriend?" J.J. asked. "Why?"

"She's the one who burned him to the Oakland cops," Kaye replied. "She'll tell you whatever she knows if she thinks it'll keep him safe."

"She'll have questions," J.J. pointed out. "Want me to hold back some of the details?"

"Be circumspect, but don't lie. If she presses, just explain the situation, ask her to lay low, and tell her we'll be in touch. In the meantime, keep up the total press blackout on this."

Burke and J.J. looked at each other, then J.J. said, "I haven't told Media Relations anything."

"Good," Kaye said. "Let's keep it that way for now. Any and all questions are answered 'no comment'. Got it?"

"Got it," the other two answered simultaneously.

"You've got the roommate's address, right?" Burke asked.

"I do," Kaye replied. "Come with me."

They left the interview room and Burke followed Kaye to his desk. It only took him a moment to pull up the outside agency assist report on Gaeta's arrest and give Burke the roommate's address.

***

Kaye idled the Harley through the gates of Kyokoku-Dera monastery, then came to a stop on the crest of the gravel driveway before it sloped gently down to the monastery grounds and took in the view. The small ponds, the fountains and beautiful landscaping imparted a sense of calm to him after a busy day. The building itself, less than a hundred years old, looked as though it had occupied its piece of the earth for a millennia and always took his breath away.

Kaye sat and looked for a minute, then idled the bike down the hill to a spot near the monastery's main stairway. The flat stone Roshi had long ago placed there to support the weight of Kaye's motorcycles fulfilled its task.

Kaye removed his helmet and gloves, stuffed the gloves into the helmet and hung it on the handlebars. Then he turned to look, expecting, as usual, Roshi waiting for him atop the stairs.

The old monk had once told him, "Your motorcycles betray your presence, Benkei."

Roshi wasn't there.

A sudden sense of foreboding washed over him as Kaye retrieved the fresh cantaloupe – his traditional gift of respect – from the saddlebag.

When he straightened up and looked again a monk he recognized, but whose name he didn't know, stood at the top of the stairs looking down at him.

Kaye mounted the steps and formally greeted the monk, extending the cantaloupe in both hands.

The monk accepted the offering, then said, "Benkei, you honor us with your presence."

"I am honored to be welcomed into your house," Kaye replied, his anxiety mounting.

"You have, of course, come to see Roshi Munan."

It was the first time Kaye had ever heard what he assumed was Roshi's dharma name.

"Yes," he said, nodding.

"Sit, please," the monk said, gesturing toward the top step.

Kaye sat down and the monk joined him.

"Benkei, I have sad news."

Kaye's throat closed and he lost his words. He knew Roshi was deep into his nineties.

"Did he die?" Kaye was finally able to whisper.

"Not yet," the monk said softly, "but he is very ill." He paused, then added, "The doctors say that his body is simply tired, winding down. It is only a matter of time."

A tear dropped from Kaye's eye and spotted the ancient stair tread between his boots.

"How long?" he managed to ask.

"Not long. Days, perhaps a week or two."

"Where is he?"

"He is here, in his quarters."

"I'd like to see him."

"He would like that," the monk said as he stood up. "Please, come with me."

"Thank you," Kaye said, standing up. He stopped, embarrassed, then looked at the monk and said, "I don't even know your name."

"Seicho."

"Thank you, Seicho."

Kaye took off his boots and followed Seicho deep into parts of the monastery he'd never seen before. He and Roshi had often sat *zazen* together in Roshi's beautiful private garden, but they had always entered through an outside gate.

To say the quarters were austere would have been an understatement. A small bathroom and a bedchamber perhaps twelve feet square, furnished with a single bed, a small desk and chair, a dresser, and an ancient altar stand, beautifully painted with scenes depicting the life of Gautama Buddha. Atop the altar stand a wooden Buddha, intricately carved in the singular Japanese style and backed by a golden Mandorla, sat in the Lotus position atop a bed of lotus blossoms. A door beneath a decorative moon gate allowed access to the outside, and through it Kaye could see the familiar garden.

A sleeping Roshi-sama, covered by a blanket, looked very small on the bed.

"I will leave you two alone," Seicho said softly, then turned and left the room.

Kaye grabbed the chair away from the desk and sat down next to the bed. He gently took Roshi's hand, expecting him to awaken. But the monk stayed still. Kaye looked at the old man's face and could only imagine all those eyes had seen.

"Roshi-sama," he whispered, "if it is time for you to go, then leave knowing that my love for you is as strong as that of a son for his loving father. I will grieve your passing, but I will celebrate your arrival in Nirvana, for if there was ever a spirit deserving of the title Buddha, it is you."

He sat with Roshi for nearly a half-hour, remembering their first meeting at an open invitation seminar on Buddhism and the unlikely friendship that sprang from that chance encounter. Roshi became his rock, someone to whom he could turn in times of doubt or trouble, always offering sage advice, usually in the form of a question that guided Kaye through.

"I must go now, Roshi Munan," he finally whispered. It was the first time he had ever uttered Roshi's Buddhist name and it tore at his heart. "But I will return. And know this. If I am, as you believe, the warrior-monk Benkei, you have been my Yoshitune, my guiding light. I will always honor you, and when the stars align we will meet again and sit *zazen*. I promise."

He gently squeezed his mentor's hand. He would never know if it was just wishful thinking, but for a brief second he thought he felt Roshi's hand gently squeeze his in return.

The tears flowed freely as he left the quarters. Seicho waited for him in the hallway and grasped his shoulder to comfort him.

"Remember, Benkei," the monk said, "death is not the end. It is a new beginning."

***

Back outside, Kaye said his goodbyes to Seicho, then sat on the bike for a long time pondering life in general and death specifically. Everyone dies, but Kaye thought some were luckier than others. He just wished there was some universal linkage between the value of one's life's work and the longevity of the life. Were that the case, he knew Roshi would live for another hundred years.

He took some comfort in knowing that Roshi's life's work surely must have brought the old monk closer to Satori and a place in Nirvana.

Makes you think, he thought, then sighed deeply and started gearing up.

***

Forty-five minutes later Kaye walked into Reagan Medical Center, went to the information desk, held up his badge and asked what room Neil Gaeta was in.

When he got to the floor he asked at the nurse's station for Dr. Prakesh and found out she wasn't in the hospital.

"Dr. Skaggs is Mr. Gaeta's attending," the nurse told him. "Let me find him. If you'd like to go see Mr. Gaeta, he's down the hall," she pointed, "second room on the right."

"He's conscious?" Kaye asked.

The nurse grinned. "Doctor Skaggs will fill you in."

Wires and tubes sprouted from Gaeta like snakes from the head of Medusa, connecting to IV stands and a bank of monitors and displays that rivaled a television production control booth.

Gaeta's right leg was outside the covers and slightly elevated, a cast covering it from his toes to the knee.

Kaye was encouraged by the fact that Gaeta wasn't intubated. As he walked to the man's bedside, Gaeta's eyes fluttered open. He stared vacantly for a few seconds before finding and focusing on Kaye.

"Hi," he managed to croak, then made a sour face.

It was clear to Kaye it hurt Gaeta to talk.

"Hello," Kaye echoed. "I came by to see how you were doing."

Gaeta managed a small smile. "Been better," he whispered.

"I bet," Kaye said. Before he could continue, he heard a man behind him say, "Hello", and he turned around.

"I'm Doctor Skaggs," the man said as he held back one side of the curtain. "You're Detective Kaye?"

"I am," Kaye replied. "How's he doing?"

"He's doing great," Skaggs replied as he stepped to the opposite side of Gaeta's bed and quickly scanned the monitors. "Mr. Gaeta is a lucky young man."

Gaeta tried to laugh, and instead coughed.

"Medically, I mean," Skaggs qualified, smiling. "He might have some headaches for a while, but there are no signs of permanent injury to his brain and his other injuries are healing nicely. His biggest inconvenience, really, will be getting used to the crutches he'll be using for a couple of months."

"I'm right here, you know," Gaeta managed to croak.

Skaggs laughed, patted Gaeta on the shoulder, then turned to Kaye and turned serious.

"Any leads on who did this?"

"Some," Kaye replied, "but nothing solid yet."

"If you want to ask him some questions, feel free," Skaggs said. "He's up to it." He looked down at Gaeta. "I'll be back to check on you later."

"When can I go home?" Gaeta asked.

"We'll talk about that," Skaggs said, then said to Kaye, "Nice meeting you, Detective."

"Thank you, Doctor," Kaye said.

Skaggs lifted a hand in response, then swept the curtain aside and left the room.

"Neil, is it okay if I ask you some questions?" Kaye asked.

Gaeta nodded. "As long as I can whisper. It really hurts to talk."

"Probably from the ventilator. It'll go away." He grabbed a chair, pulled it to a spot where he could see Gaeta's face, and sat down.

"Can I go first?" Gaeta asked.

"Sure."

"My bike. How bad is it?"

"It's probably a total," Kaye replied, grimacing.

"Fuck," Gaeta whispered. "I loved that bike."

Kaye let the man grieve for a moment before asking, "Can you tell me what happened?"

Gaeta looked at him and shook his head.

"I don't remember a damn thing."

"That's okay," Kaye said. "We've got a few leads to chase down."

"Do you think this is about me testifying?"

"I do."

"Have you called --" He coughed roughly, "Tina Magnuson?"

"I did," Kaye replied. "The Oakland PD won't tell us anything."

Gaeta's eyes widened and he whispered, "Why?"

Kaye explained that the trial was ongoing, the concerns that a mistrial would be declared if word of Gaeta's shooting got out, and about the gag order.

"I was hoping," he said in closing, "that you could fill me in."

Gaeta looked away for a moment, as if deciding, then looked back at Kaye.

"I went for an early morning run down by the Bay," he whispered. "I saw two guys shoot another guy and dump his body into the water."

"And they saw you?"

Gaeta nodded.

"Did you get a good look at them?"

"One of them, yeah," Gaeta replied. "He stepped right into his car headlights when he saw me."

"How'd you get away?"

"I went off the breakwater and swam for it. They shot at me, but it was still pretty dark and I can hold my breath pretty good."

"Any idea how they found out who you were?" Kaye asked.

"I run a loop, so I rode my Glide down and parked it. They must've seen the bike, figured it out, and found me through the license number. Or…"

"Or what?" Kaye asked.

Gaeta hesitated for a second, then said, "Somebody in the police department told them who I was."

"You think that's a possibility?"

"Detective Magnuson seemed to think so."

"And that's why you turned down police protection."

Gaeta nodded and said, "The man I saw kill the guy and testified against was named Peter Li."

"That name doesn't mean anything to me," Kaye said.

"He's the head of a street gang called Tiger Boys. At least that's what I was told."

To Kaye, that explained why Lieutenant Chen had taken their call, but not told them anything.

"I've never heard of the Tiger Boys," Kaye said, "but we'll look into them. Has Skaggs given you any idea how long you'll be in here?"

"Not yet, but I'm hoping next week."

"Have you called anybody up north about what happened?"

"I tried. She didn't answer."

"Your girlfriend?"

Gaeta nodded.

"Does she know what's been going on?" Kaye asked.

"Oh, yeah, right from the get-go," Gaeta said. As soon as the words left his lips, the color drained from his face and he muttered, "Oh, shit."

"Give me her name and number, please," Kaye said.

"Alina Crenovitch," Gaeta said, then gave Kaye a phone number. "It's her cell. We don't have a landline."

"Is she also at the University?"

"Yes, she's an associate professor of art and architecture."

"We'll call her," Kaye said. "You concentrate on getting better, and hopefully by the time you're discharged it'll be safe for you out there."

Gaeta gave Kaye a look and said, "Yeah, right."

"Okay," Kaye said. "Safer. How's that?"

Gaeta smiled.

Kaye found Skaggs at the nurses' station, poring over papers.

"Excuse me, Doctor."

Skaggs turned around. "Oh, hey, Detective. Are you done with my patient?"

"For now. He said he'd probably be released next week. Is that about right?"

"That might be a bit optimistic," Skaggs said slowly. "But we'll see how he does. Why?"

"Just need to keep tabs on him, for his own safety," Kaye explained. "We're trying to keep this out of the media for the same reason."

"Understood," Skaggs said. "Doctor-patient confidentiality keeps my mouth shut, and the hospital's confidentiality rules should take care of the rest."

"That's what I thought. Thanks, Doc."

From the patient floor Kaye found his way to the Security office and retrieved the bullet parts and pieces the surgeons had taken out of Gaeta. He was pleased to see that one bullet was pretty nearly intact and should be good for ballistics.

As soon as Kaye left the building he called J.J.

"Jefferies."

"J.J., it's Ben. Hey, tell Burke she doesn't need to spend time running down the old roommate."

"Really? Why?"

"Yes, really," Kaye said. "Gaeta is awake and alert. He doesn't remember the shooting, but he filled me in on the background stuff. You ever hear of a gang called Tiger Boys?"

"Nope."

Kaye relayed what Gaeta had told him about the murder in Oakland, the Tiger Boys, and Peter Li.

"So it is gang related."

"It is," Kaye confirmed. "He also told me he thinks someone inside the Oakland PD may have burned him with the Tiger Boys."

"That's not good," J.J. said. "You still want me to find and call the girlfriend?"

"Yeah." Kaye passed along the contact information for Alina Crenovitch. "Give her a call and tell her what's going on, but ask her not to try and contact Gaeta because of our blackout. In fact, you might suggest that she go visit her family or a friend for a few days if she can."

"You think the Tiger Boys would go after her to get to Gaeta?"

"We can't ignore the possibility."

"Gaeta's already testified," J.J. said, "so it's about revenge now. What better way? And I'll call our gang guys and see if the Tiger Boys are on their radar. They might have a chapter here in L.A."

"Or friends," Kaye said. "Gaeta wasn't on the ground here long enough yesterday to drive from there to here, much less find him and track him. To me, that says the shooter was a local. And it also supports what Gaeta said about them being fed inside information."

"They knew he was coming?"

"Had to," Kaye said. "I'm betting they picked him up at the airport and followed him all day, waiting for the right spot to make the hit."

"Shit," J.J. muttered. "Pretty sophisticated."

"Call the gang unit and see what you get. And have Burke sit in on the call to Crenovitch."

"Will do," J.J. said.

Kaye ended the call. He hadn't even put his phone away when it rang again.

"What'd I forget?" he asked, assuming it was J.J. calling him back.

Silence.

"Hello?" Kaye said.

"I'm sorry. I think I dialed the wrong number."

Kaye recognized the voice as JoAnn Weber's.

"Mrs. Weber, this is Detective Kaye," he said quickly. "My apologies. I thought it was somebody else. What can I do for you?"

"I was wondering how the investigation is going. Is there any new information?"

Kaye was a little taken aback by the question.

"Have you spoken with Detective Gannett?" he asked.

"I haven't heard from anybody at the LAPD since you and Detective Gannett came to my house." JoAnn didn't try to hide her irritation.

"I'm so sorry, Mrs. Weber. Valerie's case is officially assigned to Detective Gannett. I assumed he was keeping you informed."

"Well, he's not. Can you fill me in?"

Why not? Kaye thought, not caring if Gannett's toes got stepped on.

He briefed her on the little progress they'd made. They had a possible ID on who'd been picking Valerie up after school, the similarity between that person's vehicle and the one seen picking Valerie up the night she disappeared, but no concrete connection between the two. Yet.

He didn't tell her he thought it was because Tom Gannett had fucked up.

"Can you tell me who was picking her up at school?" JoAnn asked.

"Not yet," Kaye told her, "but when I'm sure, you'll know."

"Did you find Valerie's birth parents? Did they have anything to do with this?"

Kaye thought about how to answer the question, then replied, "I've found absolutely nothing to suggest they are involved in, or even remotely connected to, Valerie's death."

"How can you be so sure?" JoAnn asked pointedly.

Just tell her, he thought. *She deserves some peace of mind.*

"JoAnn, Valerie's birth mother died when Valerie was still a baby. I'm looking for the father, but I've got very little to go on. But there's just no way Valerie could have found either one of them, or they could have found her. The records are still sealed."

JoAnn went quiet for a moment.

"So, you're still investigating?" she asked finally.

"I'm still investigating," Kaye echoed.

"Good," JoAnn said. "I have this horrible feeling, a premonition, really, that if *you* don't find whoever killed Valerie, no one ever will. Please keep me informed."

"Will do," Kaye said. "You have my word."

She ended the call without saying anything else.

Kaye's first reaction was a flash of anger aimed at Gannett. The RHD detective was, Kaye knew, good at his job. In the Department hierarchy, you didn't get to Robbery-Homicide by being a so-so investigator or slacker. Gannett not calling JoAnn Weber wasn't typical and Kaye couldn't help but wonder if something was going on with the RHD detective he didn't know about.

He wasn't about to brace Gannett, though, for the lack of communication. Kaye knew there was no standard playbook for being a good detective. There were standard procedures and the basics everyone followed and knew, but above and beyond that, things became more esoteric and intuitive, requiring skills and qualities not everyone possessed or even applied in the same fashion.

Kaye's conflicts with Captain Thompson stood as evidence of that.

Before he started the Harley, Kaye decided he'd take a more active role in the Valerie Weber homicide investigation and see if anyone told him to back off. If he did run afoul of RHD, he'd simply point out he wore the same badge they did. If that was a problem, tough shit.

CHAPTER 13

Kaye got to the squad early and was surprised to see Captain Thompson already in his office.

Curious, he knocked on the boss's door.

Thompson looked up, saw Kaye, and said, "Come on in."

Kaye took his customary chair.

"What do you need, Detective?" Thompson asked, studying Kaye.

"I talked to the Mendocino County sheriff. I won't be going to Ukiah, at least not right away."

"Why not?"

Kaye laid it out, recapping his conversation with Merritt.

"That's too bad," Thompson said. "And I don't mean just because you lost a source."

"I can probably get most of what Sebaly would have told me by reading the trial transcripts, if I ever get my hands on them."

"Do you know when that might be?"

"No," Kaye said, shaking his head. "They said it could take a while."

"Well, stay on it," Thompson said, then, expecting Kaye to leave, turned his attention to the papers on his desk.

Kaye didn't get up.

Thompson studied him again, then asked, "Is there something else, Detective Kaye?"

"How'd it go down at The Office?" Kaye asked.

The Captain shrugged and said, "Okay, I guess. I was asked to stay on for a month, maybe two."

"That's good, right?"

"Depends," Thompson said with a slight shrug.

"What's the down side?" Kaye asked.

"It would create a huge conflict in my time line."

"So, what are you going to do?"

"I told them I'd give them my decision by the end of next week. But I did my due diligence by listening to The Man's final offer."

"You trust him?"

"What kind of question is that?" Thompson asked sharply.

"A valid one, I think," Kaye replied. "Did he put anything in writing? Give you a copy?"

"Jesus, Kaye, you're one cynical s.o.b."

Kaye smiled. "Hey, somebody has to be the Plan B guy."

"That's true," Thompson said. "I'll figure it out. Now, go do some detecting, will you? I've got things to do."

Back at his desk, Kaye bent to the task of trying to locate 'Trevor'.

Fifteen frustrating minutes later, he gave up, picked up his desk phone and punched in an extension number.

"Hi, Detective Kaye," Patty Phillips answered. "What can I do for you?"

"I need your help tracking somebody down whose last known whereabouts go back almost twenty years. Can you do that?"

"I can try. What've you got?"

Kaye filled her in on Trevor, last name possibility starting with R-O-W, that he could be Valerie Weber's biological father, his approximate age, the area where he went to high school and what little else he knew.

"I know it's not much to go on," he said in closing, "but it's all I've got."

"I'll see what I can find."

"Thanks, Patty."

"And, hey, Detective? How's the case going, overall?"

"It went to Robbery-Homicide."

"Really? I hadn't heard that," Patty said, sounding disappointed. "Can I pass along something I dug up on Dylan Glithero?"

"I didn't know you were digging."

"Well…" Patty stammered. "I hope you don't mind. I just keep seeing Valerie's face beaten to a pulp and remembering she was killed almost right after I met her."

"Don't let it get too personal, Patty. It'll drive you crazy. But I don't mind at all that you're digging into it."

"Thank you. Remember how I said Glithero had almost no social media footprint?"

"I remember."

"So, anyway, I did some checking around," Patty said. "I found out he has an ex-wife and the divorce was pretty recent."

"Really?" Kaye asked, intrigued. "Do you know who initiated the divorce?"

"His ex-wife, Roslyn, was the Petitioner," Patty replied and Kaye heard the satisfaction in her voice. "You'll never guess what the grounds

111

were."

"Adultery," Kaye said instantly.

"Yes," Patty confirmed excitedly. "Fits, right?"

"That it does. Do you know if the ex, Roslyn, kept the last name Glithero?"

"She did not. She is now Roslyn Reingold, with a residence address in the Wilshire Center area." Patty read off the address. "Unlike her ex-husband, Roslyn is all over social media. She was easy to find."

"Did you happen to notice where she works?"

"I did," Patty said. "She's some kind of investment person." She gave Kaye the same street address again. "Her name's even on the building."

"That would explain the house in Hancock Park," Kaye said. "Thanks, Patty, I'll pass it along."

"I'll let you know what I come up with on the Trevor guy."

Kaye leaned back in his chair and pondered his morning thus far.

Getting some details on the Glithero case from Sebaly might have filled in some blanks. It was a lot easier, and faster, to ask direct questions and get knowledgeable answers than wade through potentially thousands of pages of court transcripts. But he was still waiting on other things, too, so time wasn't an issue. Yet.

Knowing Dylan Glithero's wife had divorced him on the grounds of adultery wasn't surprising. He decided he needed to talk to Roslyn Reingold, then considered whether he should just pass the information along to Gannett and let him deal with it.

That triggered the memory of his conversation with JoAnn Weber and a wave of guilt washed over him.

He grabbed the phone and punched in Gannett's number.

The phone rang for a long time without going to voice mail.

Kaye pulled out his cell phone, found Gannett's cell number and called that.

Again, no answer and no voice mail.

Kaye was frustrated. He didn't want to get Gannett in hot water, but he needed to know what was happening with the Weber case.

He again heard JoAnn Weber's voice telling him about her premonition.

He looked up another number and called it.

"Lieutenant Waller, Robbery-Homicide."

"Lieutenant, this is Ben Kaye from West Bureau. How's it going?"

"Can't complain," Waller said. "How're things on your end?"

"Moving along," Kaye replied. "Hey, I called because I've been trying to call Tom Gannett about a case I'm involved in with him, and I can't seem to reach him."

"The Valerie Weber case, right?"

"Yes," Kaye confirmed, glad that at least Waller was on the ball.

"Gannett didn't call and tell you?"

"Tell me what?"

"Well, shit," Waller said. "Gannett's wife filed for divorce and kicked him out of the house. He had to take time off to get his stuff together, find a place to live and figure out what he's going to do."

"How long before he comes back?" Kaye asked.

"Don't know," Waller said. "A couple of the other guys told me he'd told them he might not come back at all if that's what it takes to save his marriage."

"Have you assigned the Weber case to somebody else?"

"Not yet."

"I'll take it," Kaye said instantly.

"You'd do that?"

"Absolutely. I took the complaint about her being beaten right before she was killed, and I've been working with Gannett on background stuff. I talked to the victim's mother just this morning."

"Okay," Waller said slowly. "I'll need to talk to my boss and yours, but I don't see a problem."

"Thanks, Lieutenant."

"Just know that when Gannett comes back, if the case is still open, it rolls back to him, okay?"

Kaye wasn't happy, but replied, "If that's the way you want it, it's okay by me."

Kaye ended the call with a palpable sense of relief. He much preferred being the band leader of a one-man band to playing second fiddle to someone who seemed to have lost the sheet music, and felt the chances of finding Valerie Weber's killer were now in his favor.

He craned his neck to see if the Captain was in his office. No sign of him.

He wrote a quick note.

'Captain: Lt. Waller from RHD will call you. Gannett's out. Weber case is mine again. Kaye.'

He grabbed the Big Boar jacket, left the note in the Inbox on Thompsons's door and headed for the Harley.

Kaye spotted the blue tinted, glass-clad cube of a building just off

Wilshire from three blocks away. It wasn't a skyscraper, even by L.A. standards, where the tendency has always been to build out, not up. The glass cladding made it hard to tell, but Kaye guessed it at ten, maybe twelve, floors.

Shiny, stainless steel capital letters spelled out 'Reingold' in sharp contrast to the matte black pediment that topped the building.

There was a gated parking lot with a manned gatehouse. Kaye rolled up and flashed his ID when the guard slid the window open.

"Official business," Kaye said.

The guard didn't say anything, just raised the bar and let Kaye pass.

The building directory told Kaye that Reingold Capital wasn't the only occupant. There were ten floors, and various businesses, ranging from law firms to insurance companies to a commercial real estate broker occupied offices on the first five floors.

Reingold Capital was listed for the sixth floor with nothing else showing for floors seven through ten. Next to the directory listing, white plastic letters spelled out 'Use elevator #3'.

Elevator #3's first stop was the sixth floor. The doors opened directly into the lobby of Reingold Capital. There was lots of dark wood and leather furniture, deep pile oriental rugs defined the floor spaces and original art hung on the walls.

The reception desk occupied the far wall, on which was the same stainless steel 'Reingold' that topped the building, but on a smaller scale. A young man wearing a conservative, dark suit sat behind the desk and warily watched Kaye approach, his expression telling Kaye that he was trying to decide if he needed to call Security. When Kaye got close, he read the young man's badge. Jeremy.

"You look lost," Jeremy said. "Can I point you in the right direction?"

"This is Reingold Capital, right?"

"It is."

"Then I'm right where I need to be."

"Oh…" Jeremy stammered. "Then, uh, how can I help you?"

"I'd like to see Roslyn Reingold."

"Do you have an appointment?"

"I don't need an appointment," Kaye said, holding up his open badge wallet. "Detective Kaye, LAPD."

"May I ask what this is about?"

"Just tell her I'm here about Dylan."

"You can wait over there," Jeremy pointed to a seating area as he reached for the phone.

"I'm good," Kaye said politely as he put his elbows on the counter and leaned forward.

Glancing nervously at Kaye, Jeremy picked up the phone, punched in a number and waited.

"Ms. Reingold?" he said a moment later. "I'm sorry to bother you, but there's a man – a police detective – here to see you."

Kaye heard a woman's voice on the other end, but couldn't make out what she was saying.

"He says it's about... Dylan," Jeremy said. It wasn't a question and Kaye realized the kid knew who Dylan was.

"What?" The voice was much louder this time and Kaye heard.

"That's what he said."

Another unintelligible sentence from the other end before Jeremy said, "Okay, I'll send him up," and hung up the phone before looking up at Kaye. "Take that elevator," he said, pointing to a different set of doors than Kaye had come out of, "to the ninth floor. Ms. Reingold will be waiting."

"Thank you, Jeremy," Kaye said, pushing off the counter.

When the elevator doors opened on the ninth floor a brunette dressed in jeans and a red blazer over a white t-shirt stood ten feet directly ahead, her feet planted at hip width and her arms folded across her chest.

Kaye looked at her, then let his gaze wander the space. Sharply different than the sixth floor, the ninth looked more like a loft: Open. Plywood floors. Large, flat tables. Overhead lights suspended from the ceiling, and too many big screen monitors to count.

"You wanted to see me?" the woman asked, arms still folded.

"Are you Roslyn Reingold?"

"I am."

"Then, yes," Kaye said, stepping forward and extending his hand. "I'm Detective Kaye, LAPD. I appreciate you making the time to see me."

Reingold at first hesitated, then unfolded her arms and shook Kaye's hand.

Up close, Kaye realized that Reingold's obviously high fitness level made her look younger, and revised his initial estimate of her age slightly upward.

"You told Jeremy this was about Dylan," she said bluntly.

"It is," Kaye acknowledged.

"Come with me."

The center of the space was an office with no walls. A desk, several large filing cabinets, a large tilt-up drafting table and a half-dozen molded plastic chairs sat atop a large, unbound, red carpet remnant.

Reingold took the chair behind the desk, leaving Kaye to choose one of the plastic chairs.

"This looks like a design studio," Kaye said after sitting down. "I thought Reingold Capital was a financial services company."

"We are," Reingold said. "Both private equity and venture capital focused on commercial and industrial real estate. My father founded the company almost forty years ago."

Kaye looked around again, then looked at Reingold.

"I understand your confusion," Reingold said with a smile. "I head up our new division that specializes in negotiated pre-occupancy space planning and build-out."

"I'm going to need more than that," Kaye said, smiling back.

"We acquire financially distressed properties, evaluate them as-built for suitability and function for best-fit core businesses, then solicit the companies that are best matches. We work with them to fine tune the space to the most perfect match possible before occupancy. All they have to pay for is moving their furniture and existing equipment. We then negotiate terms that allow them to amortize their construction expenses over the term of occupancy rather than having to lay out a huge sum of cash-on-hand or borrowing money up front."

"Is it working out?" Kaye asked, intrigued.

"We're growing like gangbusters," Reingold said, smiling again. "Which is good, because it was my idea."

"And you do this all by yourself?"

"No," Reingold replied. "I told everybody to take a break. So, you now have," she glanced at her watch, "eighteen minutes. What's this about?"

"I'm investigating a homicide," Kaye replied bluntly, "and your ex-husband's name came up."

"Dylan?" she asked, clearly skeptical. "You mean, like a witness or something?"

Kaye shook his head and watched to gauge her reaction.

Reingold leaned back, went pale, and clutched the arms of her chair with white-knuckled hands.

"You think Dylan killed somebody?"

"I don't know," Kaye admitted. "I wouldn't call him a suspect at this point, but he is what we call a person of interest, and I have to look into it."

"Holy hell," Reingold muttered, leaning forward again. "I can't believe… I mean, I never… Until about a year ago…" She shook her head slowly and repeated, "Holy hell."

"You're talking about your divorce?"

She nodded. "I was totally blindsided. I thought we had it all. But…"

"How long were you married?"

"Almost ten years."

"Kids?"

"One, a daughter."

"How did you meet?"

"I was working on my Finance MBA at USC," Reingold said. "I had to take a business writing class. Dylan was the instructor, and we, you know, just hit it off. We got married about a year later when I got pregnant."

The guy likes his students, Kaye thought, then asked, "Why did you divorce him?"

"He cheated on me."

"You're sure?"

"Oh, yeah," she said snidely. "I found a phone I didn't know he had and got it open. I couldn't believe the texts – or should I say sexts. They were very explicit. With photos."

"Did you recognize anyone?" Kaye asked.

"The photos weren't of faces, Detective."

"Did you confront him?"

"I did. He denied it, of course," she replied. "So I hired a private investigator. It didn't take him long to bring me photos of Dylan going into a motel with a young woman. A very young woman. I filed the next day."

"Did he contest the divorce?"

"At first, yes," Reingold said. "But after I told him I'd just give him the house in Hancock Park he went along. It was worth it to get rid of him."

That answers Patty's question, Kaye thought.

"Besides," Reingold went on, "I knew it wasn't the first time he messed around, it was just the first time I could prove it."

"He cheated before?"

"Before he went to Grove Charter, Dylan was at Mountbatten Prep in Hancock Park. There were, uh, shall we say 'rumors' about a particular student, and they asked him to resign to avoid a scandal. He denied that one, too, but this time I had him dead to rights."

"Do you remember a name from the sexts?" Kaye asked.

Reingold went into concentration mode for a moment, then looked at Kaye and shook her head. "Sorry, no. I mean, not real names. Just sexy nicknames and stuff. I tried calling the numbers, but nobody ever answered."

"Numbers? Plural?"

"There were two," Reingold said, barely whispering. "How could I have been so stupid?"

"I have another questions that might be tough, Ms. Reingold," Kaye said. "If you're up to it."

Reingold stiffened and nodded.

"Were you aware that your ex had a prior arrest – years before he met you – for sexual battery of a minor?"

Her eyes and mouth flew open and she gasped.

"He never told me that! The lying bastard!"

Kaye could tell she was fighting hard not to cry.

"He was acquitted of the charge," Kaye said, hoping it would help her. "I'm still looking into the case."

"Why would you...?" She looked at him, lost.

"You mentioned photos of Dylan and a young woman going into a motel. Do you still have them?"

"No," Reingold replied. "I didn't exactly consider them keepsakes. I destroyed them after the divorce was final."

"I understand," Kaye said.

"Why would –" She stopped mid-sentence and went pale as a look of horror overtook her. "Oh, my God. You're investigating the murder of an under-age woman, aren't you? Oh, my God!" Her voice broke as she fought back tears.

Kaye sat quietly, letting Reingold compose herself. She took a tissue from a box on her desk, wiped her eyes and blew her nose.

"Sorry," she said, sniffing as she put the tissue away. "I can't believe this. Dylan? I loved him. I had his baby."

"Ms. Reingold, none of this is your fault. Your ex-husband has not been charged with anything. I'm just doing my job."

She was silent for a moment, then glanced at her watch.

"I'm going to have to ask you to leave, Detective." She tried to manage a smile that only half-lit. "My staff will be back soon."

"One more quick question?"

"Sure, why not?"

"Who was the private detective you hired?"

She thought for a moment before answering. "It was the Eliason Agency."

"Thank you," Kaye said, rising to leave.

"Will you let me know, please, what you find out about Dylan?" Reingold asked plaintively. "One way or another?"

"Yes, of course."

As Kaye stepped into the elevator he heard a stairway door open a short distance away and the sound of voices heading into the loft space. The door closed before he saw anyone.

On the way back to the bike, Kaye knew the visit to Roslyn Reingold had been tough on her, but productive for him.

The Eliason Agency principal was one Sonny Eliason, retired LAPD detective. With luck, Eliason would still have the photos in the case records.

As soon as he got to the bike, he searched up the number for the Eliason Agency and called.

"Eliason Agency, this is Sharm. How may I help you?"

"Is Sonny in?"

"I'm sorry, Mr. Eliason is out of town on a case. Can another investigator help you?"

Kaye was impressed. Last he'd heard, Sonny Eliason was a one-man show. Business must be good.

"No, I need to talk to Sonny," Kaye replied. "Do you know when he'll be back?"

Sharm laughed. "If you know Mr. Eliason, you'll know that he won't be back until he gets what he went after."

"Yeah, I remember that about him. I'll try back on Monday. If you talk to him, tell him Ben Kaye called and needs to meet with him. No big rush."

"I'll do that, Mr. Kaye. Thank you for calling the Eliason Agency."

Kaye mentally ran through how Roslyn Reingold's information could help him. If Sonny Eliason still had the photos he'd shown Reingold, and Valerie Weber was identifiable, he'd talk to Kayla Okafor about getting a warrant for Glithero's arrest on statutory rape charges.

That Reingold had found two different numbers on Glithero's phone surprised Kaye. The guy obviously had quite the system going. He wondered if Gannett had gotten around to getting the names of the other female members of Glithero's writing group, but he doubted it. He'd probably need to talk to Holderby about that.

But he was really no closer to tying Glithero to Valerie Weber's murder than he'd been before talking to Reingold. He needed to identify the driver, or at least the vehicle, that had picked Valerie up behind Staples the night she went missing. What frustrated Kaye the most was knowing he had a picture of the white SUV Valerie had climbed into, and its driver; the photo was just too grainy to make out the detail he needed.

That thought made Kaye realize it had been a week since he'd sent the video file from Staples to Digital Forensics. Time to rattle Scott's cage.

He checked the time.

Too late to call today. Monday would have to do.

CHAPTER 14

Kaye threw himself into the '51 Panhead project for most of the weekend.

There'd been a few surprises along the way.

He'd been delighted when he laid out all the parts and pieces to find that the bike was actually an FLF; meaning it had a foot-operated shifter and not the so-called 'suicide shifter' mounted on the side of the gas tank that came on the standard FL model. He'd also determined that the carburetor was the M74-B that was introduced in the middle of the model year production run. That tagged the bike as a later build.

But there were issues, too.

The tin was mostly straight and unblemished, but at some point had been repainted in a two-tone scheme not originally offered by The Motor Company on that model. Kaye wanted an original look, and from the underside of one fender was finally able to determine that the bike had been white when it rolled off the line.

The original Harley emblem was missing from the left side of the gas tank, the speedometer was not original, and somewhere along the line someone had messed with the rear fender struts in order to mount non-standard saddlebags.

Once he bolted the engine down, he discovered he couldn't turn it manually. Since he was already planning a complete tear down, he wasn't going to worry too much about it until he got inside to assess the engine's condition.

And he thought, but wasn't sure, that the cables were wrong for the year and model, so he'd go ahead and replace them with the known, correct cable set.

Still, all in all, he was pleased.

By late afternoon Sunday, from twenty feet away it almost looked like a motorcycle. Kaye knew he could no longer refer to it as the Pan-in-a-Box. It was now the '61 Panhead.

He cleaned up and put his tools away, went inside and changed, then spent two hours punishing himself with a workout that left him so exhausted he barely made it to the shower.

CHAPTER 15

Kaye's first task Monday morning was calling the Medical Examiner's office. He'd awakened with a start during the night with the realization he hadn't yet received the final autopsy report on Valerie Weber.

"This is Dr. Martinek," a woman finally answered after Kaye had spent nearly ten minutes on hold and been transferred multiple times.

"Doctor, this is Detective Kaye from LAPD West Bureau. How are you today?"

"I'm fine, Detective. Just busy. What can I do for you?"

"I understand you did the postmortem on Valerie Weber," Kaye said. "White female, seventeen, her body was found in the Hollywood Reservoir about a week ago."

"I did," Martinek confirmed. "I completed the post last Thursday and sent a copy of the report to your Detective Gannett, with a note to forward a copy to you, as requested by Dr. Archuleta."

"Oh, okay," Kaye said. "That explains it. Tom Gannett has been on leave, and I've taken over the case."

"I did not know that," Martinek said brusquely.

"Not your fault," Kaye reassured her, "I didn't know either until last Friday. When you have a minute, can you please send me a copy?"

"Certainly. I'm sitting at my desk. I'll send It right now."

"Thanks, Doc, and sorry about the communications mix-up."

Kaye gave it five minutes before he opened his email. Martinek had come through and the report was at the top of his Inbox queue.

The first thing listed in the report summary header was Cause of Death. Asphyxiation, likely caused by smothering. The second was estimated time of death, with a window that matched what Tom Gannett had initially told him and Arch had confirmed.

Martinek was, if nothing else, thorough. Because she dictated her findings as she worked, the report narrative began with notes that no physical or developmental abnormalities were noted and that the corpse was consistent with the subject's reported age. In the distinguishing features or marks section Martinek had listed a 2.4 centimeter, roughly heart-shaped *Nevus simplex* on the right side of the back of the neck.

The doctor then noted Valerie's pre-existing injuries and made an estimate of how long before death they had occurred. It lined up with Kaye's impression when he'd first interviewed Valerie and JoAnn Weber.

There were no notes describing peri- or post-mortem injuries, and specifically noted was any lack of indication of recent sexual activity or trauma. Martinek noted that she had taken tissue samples anyway.

Bottom line, Kaye learned, was that Valerie Weber had been a healthy seventeen-year-old until someone had kept her from breathing until she died.

Kaye scrolled to the last page and looked at the Special Notes section.

The first note was that blood had been taken via direct cardiac draw and that toxicology was pending.

The second note made him sit up straight.

"No way," he muttered under his breath.

Valerie Weber had been pregnant at the time of her death, with Martinek estimating the term of the pregnancy at seven to nine weeks.

Kaye instantly grabbed the phone and tried to call Martinek back, only to be told she wasn't available.

He asked for Dr. Archuleta.

"Ben, what's up?" Arch asked cheerfully.

"Hey, Arch, I talked to Martinek about twenty minutes ago and got a copy of Valerie Weber's autopsy report. She was pregnant. Martinek estimated seven to nine weeks."

"You're kidding."

"I wish I was," Kaye said. "I just tried to call Martinek back and couldn't reach her, so I called you. I need to know if she preserved the fetus."

"What do you need?"

"DNA," Kaye replied. "I don't know all the medical ins and outs, but it's possible, right?"

"You mean fetal DNA so you can establish paternity?" Arch asked skeptically.

"Yeah."

Arch was quiet for a moment before saying slowly, "It's not that simple. With a seven, even nine, week gestation period, the fetus isn't really formed, it's just a mass about the size of a soybean, maybe a little bigger, and weighs about a half-ounce. We don't even try to get DNA using amniocentesis until about fifteen weeks. Throw in several days post-mortem and... You get the picture."

"So it's impossible?" Kaye asked.

"Well, it's possible, but… It's called a cell-free DNA test, but it's usually done from the plasma of a living mother."

"Martinek's notes say she got enough liquid blood from a cardiac draw to submit for tox results."

"Hmm, I wouldn't have expected that so long post-mortem," Arch said, "but there are a lot of variables. Her body being in cold water, then the cooler for almost five days may have slowed the decomp process enough for a direct draw to get liquid blood."

"Will the tox screen use all the blood?"

"I don't know the draw volume, so I can't answer that," Arch said, then hesitated before saying, "Look, Ben, even assuming all the dice roll in our favor, cell-free DNA is still cutting edge. No court that I know of has recognized it yet. Plus, roughly half of any fetal strand DNA recovered belongs, by definition, to the mother. You'd never get a match because that DNA combination has never existed."

"What if I have a comparator?"

"Depending on the sex of the fetus, you could, in theory, establish paternity with a slightly less than fifty percent match."

"Exactly," Kaye said. "If half that DNA matches the guy I'm looking at… If nothing else, that gives me statutory rape and motive for murder."

"Do you think you can keep the defense from discrediting the science?"

"Arch, we've gotta try. She was seventeen."

"Look," Arch said, "let me read the full report and talk to Martinek. If the blood from the draw is suitable, or the plasma can be reconstituted, I'll ask around. And you do know that Martinek's estimate of the pregnancy term is right at the lower limit of being able to recover cell-free DNA, right?"

"I didn't, but I still think it's worth a shot," Kaye said.

"The other hurdle," Arch went on, "is that we don't have nearly the equipment in our labs to do that kind of science. It'd have to be done outside, and that would be expensive. The boss would have to okay it, and even then it could take weeks, maybe even longer, to get results."

"Gee, Arch, you sound like you're trying to discourage me."

Kaye heard Arch sigh before the man said, "Okay, okay. I'll see what I can do and be in touch."

Kaye spent the next thirty minutes updating his case file and making notes on his conversations with Martinek and Archuleta. Given Arch's estimate of the time it might take to identify Dylan Glithero as who had impregnated Valerie Weber, he had to hope that something else would break the case first.

He was trying to figure out where to best focus he efforts to find that break when Patty Phillips came through the squad doors, a sheaf of papers in hand.

"Hey, Patty," Kaye greeted her.

"Hi, Detective," she replied.

She grabbed a spare chair, slid it over next to Kaye's desk and sat down.

"What'cha got?" Kaye asked.

"I think I might have found your Trevor guy," she said, handing Kaye the papers. "Officially, he's Trevor Rowell the third."

"Already?" Kaye said as he took and glanced at them. They were obviously screen prints of social media sites.

"Yes," Patty replied, smiling. "You wouldn't think there'd be that many Trevors out there, right? Wrong. But I think I narrowed it down to the right one. Right age, went to the same high school Valerie's biological mother would have gone to at the same time, stuff like that." She shook her head. "It just amazes me what people will share with a world full of people they don't know and never will."

Kaye agreed, which was why he had zero social media footprint.

He perused the pages Patty had given him. Trevor Rowell looked to be about Kaye's age, maybe a few years older, wore a flat top just starting to show stray strands of silver, and a tightly trimmed beard. The man was broad across the chest and shoulders, but was starting to spread a little, looking to Kaye like he could lose a few pounds.

"I'm impressed," he said, glancing at Patty, who smiled.

"Thank you," she said.

"So," Kaye said as he skimmed the pages. "Lives in Camarillo. Convenient. Owns a trucking company. Married. Two kids. All in all, it's pretty bare bones." He looked up at Patty. "Did you run him?"

"I did. Squeaky clean. Not even a traffic ticket."

"Vehicles?"

"I didn't find a single one in his name," Patty said. "All I could think of is that he has everything registered to his business, so I looked. There were dozens and dozens of vehicles, and he's not the sole owner of the company."

"Nobody said it was going to be easy," Kaye wisecracked. "At least you didn't tell me it was a long time ago. I've been hearing that a lot."

"What did detectives do before social media?"

"Ever heard the term 'gumshoe'?"

"In the movies, yeah."

"They wore them because they did a lot of walking and wore out a lot more shoes back then," Kaye said.

"I bet," Patty said, then hesitated before adding, "It's not my place, but Trevor Rowell doesn't look like the kind of man who would kill a daughter he's never even seen."

"Agreed," Kaye said. "Especially a pregnant one."

"Pregnant?" Patty gasped, dumbfounded.

"Yes."

"She was a child! Who would do such a thing?"

"I'm going to find out."

***

It took Kaye well over an hour to make it to Thousand Oaks and find the address he'd located for Trevor Rowell's business.

TRT Trucking occupied a large, tilt-up concrete building adjacent to a ready-mix concrete facility on the north edge of town. It was surrounded by what looked to Kaye to be several acres of asphalt. Two dozen or more tractor-trailer rigs were backed up to large overhead doors on the south side of the building and a line of unhitched fifth wheel trailers were backed up to the edge of the pavement on the east side. Flatbed trailers were liberally sprinkled into the mix. An eight-foot chain link fence topped with three strands of barbed wire encircled the property and the truck entrances were all secured with motorized, rolling gates monitored by video cameras.

Kaye finally found the right driveway and rode around the building to the main parking lot and office entrance. There were almost a dozen vehicles parked in the lot. He noticed that the up-close spots that had 'Reserved' signs were occupied by expensive vehicles, from a vintage Chevy Camaro and Dodge Challenger to a new, white Ford Super Duty dually pickup with oversized rims, a windshield visor, an off-road light bar mounted above that and a black brush guard on the front.

Nice truck. Rowell must use it to haul his toys. Business must be good, he thought idly.

The office building was more design sensitive than the giant mass of gray concrete warehouse. Stucco walls painted light blue were punctuated by tall, narrow, deeply tinted recessed windows. A single door in a brown metal frame, its glass tinted to match the windows, bore white lettering

126

spelling out Trevor Rowell Trucking, Hauling and Cartage and the company's DOT number.

Kaye stepped into a fair-sized office area. Rugs softened the concrete floor and family photos chronicling the company history lined the walls. From the trucks shown in some of the old black-and-white photos, Kaye quickly tumbled to the fact that Trevor Rowell Trucking had been around for quite some time; likely at least three generations.

Three women and two men sat at desks, and all were working the phones.

The woman nearest Kaye looked up, said, "Hey, hold on a sec" to whoever was on the other end, put her hand over the handset mouthpiece and looked at Kaye.

"Sorry, we're not hiring drivers," she said. "Check back in a couple weeks."

"I'm not looking for a job," Kaye said, holding up his ID. "I'm looking for Trevor Rowell."

The woman's eyes got big and she moved her hand off the mouthpiece to speak into it.

"Tony, I'll call you back in a minute." She hung up.

"Is Mr. Rowell in?" Kaye asked.

"Junior?" she asked.

"The third," Kaye replied.

She rolled her chair back, stood up, said, "I'll go get him" and promptly disappeared through a door into the back offices.

She reappeared a moment later.

"He'll be right out," she told Kaye and stood by her desk.

Kaye was aware that the other occupants of the office had gone silent and were now staring at him. He ignored them, keeping an eye on the door that led to the back.

He didn't have to wait long. The door swung open and the man pictured on Patty's social media screen prints stepped out. He pulled the door closed behind him and stared at Kaye.

"I'm Trevor Rowell. Are you sure you're looking for me?"

"I am," Kaye said. "I'm Detective Kaye, LAPD. I just need a couple minutes of your time." He glanced around before adding, "In private."

"Okay, sure," Rowell said. "I can't imagine what I can do to help the LAPD, but come on back."

Kaye gauged Rowell's reaction as genuine and followed the man back through the door and into a nearby office.

"Have a seat, please," Rowell said. "Can I get you something?

Coffee? Soda?"

"No thanks," Kaye said, taking a chair that faced across the man's cluttered desk. As soon as he sat down, he realized he'd chosen poorly. He couldn't see Rowell, only the back of a large computer monitor.

Rowell closed the door and stepped around behind the desk.

"Sorry," he said to Kaye as he grabbed the monitor and moved it aside. "I don't get a lot of guests and I always forget."

"Not a problem."

"What's this about?" Rowell asked as he sat down.

"I'm working an investigation and your name came up."

"My name?" Rowell asked, clearly mystified. "Where did you hear my name?"

"I'd rather not say just yet." Kaye watched Rowell closely.

"Why? What kind of investigation is this?"

"Homicide."

For a brief instant Kaye thought Rowell was going to fall out of his chair.

"I came by to talk to you about Rachel Lowden," Kaye continued. "You remember her?"

"Sure. From high school. What about her?"

"So you went to high school with her?"

"I was two years ahead of her, but, yeah, I knew her," Rowell replied, nodding. Then his expression turned to puzzlement. "I don't understand. I heard Rachel took her own life. Are her parents now claiming someone killed her? If they think it was me, there's no way. I was living in Texas when it happened."

"But you two dated." Kaye said.

"One date," Rowell said. "She asked me to the Sadie Hawkins Dance right before Thanksgiving. I went with her."

"Why did you break up?"

"It wasn't so much that we broke up. I mean, I liked her, but we only went out the one time. I remember that when I picked her up her mom gave me this lecture about the Bible and set a strict curfew when I was supposed to have Rachel home."

"Maybe she was just trying to protect her daughter," Kaye said pointedly.

"From me?" Rowell asked. "Why would she think she had to do that?"

"I heard you had a lot of trouble in school."

"Who told you that?" Rowell laughed. "I was an honor student,

President of my class, lettered in three sports and earned a full-ride baseball scholarship. I played minor league pro ball after college."

"Did you have sex with Rachel?"

"Excuse me?" Rowell protested. "What kind of question is that?"

"A pertinent one," Kaye said stonily. "Please answer it, Mister Rowell."

"We went to a dance," Rowell said. "I was fifteen minutes late getting her home and her dad was literally standing at the curb waiting for us. He was a total jerk and told me not to come around again. Sex? I didn't even kiss her."

"Did you know Rachel got pregnant?"

"No. That must be why she dropped out."

"She had a little girl."

Rowell just looked at Kaye.

"When did you find out Rachel had taken her own life?" Kaye asked.

"Not until I came home from school on break at the end of that summer," Rowell replied. "I'd gone to Texas for incoming Freshman summer ball and they gave us a break before classes started."

"Do you remember who told you?"

Rowell's eyes went blank as he dredged his memory, then shook his head and said, "No. Sorry."

"Mr. Rowell, the big reason I came to see you is to ask if a young woman has recently contacted you, maybe claiming that you were her father?"

Rowell was, as Kaye intended, blindsided by the question.

"Rachel's baby was given up for adoption," Kaye went on. "Her adoptive parents recently told her she was adopted. Her adoptive mother said she didn't take it well and wanted to find her biological parents. Even hinted she had found them."

"Nobody ever… Wait a minute. Why would you ask me about this if you're investigating a murder?" He stared at Kaye, who stayed quiet.

After about five seconds, Kaye saw the light go on in Rowell's eyes and the man sat up straight, a look of horror on his face.

"Oh, my God," Rowell whispered.

"I'm afraid so, Mr. Rowell. A little over a week ago."

"And you think I might have had something to do with it?" Rowell asked.

"I don't have preconceptions, Mr. Rowell, but I have to ask," Kaye replied.

"I understand. But…oh, my God. Wow." Rowell put his elbows on his desk, leaned forward and put his head in his hands for a moment before looking up at Kaye. "Rachel's mother gave you my name, didn't she? I can't believe this. Monica fucking Lowden strikes again."

"Thank you for your time, Mister Rowell," Kaye said, standing up to leave.

On the way back to the Harley, he silently berated himself for crashing the world down on Trevor Rowell's head after all these years.

But Rowell had given him some things he needed to check. It didn't make up for it, but it meant it hadn't been pointless.

Kaye checked the time. He'd planned on going to visit Roshi, but now found himself at the far west end of the Valley. Which meant a long ride into town, then reversing course for another ride home. He decided to visit Kyokoku-Dera first thing in the morning.

He tried to call Captain Thompson, but the call went straight to voicemail and he left a message. Next, he dialed J.J.'s desk, expecting the same outcome.

"Jefferies," came the answer.

"Oh, hey," Kaye said, surprised. "It's Ben. I didn't expect you to answer."

"You caught me by one minute," J.J. said. "What's up?"

"Just checking in. I'm in Thousand Oaks and I'm heading home from here. First, I wanted to touch base on Gaeta."

"Glad you called. We talked to the girlfriend, Crenovitch, a while ago. She was kind of freaked out."

"Why?"

"Turns out she reported a break-in at her place to the Berkeley PD this morning, but nothing was taken."

"Tiger Boys," Kaye said. "Looking for Gaeta."

"Agreed."

"You told her what was going on?"

"We did. She freaked out even more."

"Understandable," Kaye said. "Did she agree not to try and contact Gaeta?"

"It took some convincing by Burke, who, by the way, did a really good job," J.J. said. "She finally talked Crenovitch into staying with some friends for a few days."

"Good," Kaye said. "Did you talk to the gang unit?"

"I did. Some Sergeant named Rivera. He didn't recognize the Tiger Boys right off the top of his head, but told me he'd start nosing around and let me know if he comes up with anything."

"Did you tell him about our conversation with Chen?"

"Yeah, and I asked him specifically not to reach out to her."

"Good call," Kaye said. "And hey, if you see Thompson —"

"I won't," J.J. said. "He left about three to go look at houses. He's wound pretty tight about this whole leaving the department thing."

"That he is," agreed Kaye

"See you in the morning," J.J. said. "Ride safe, shiny side up, all that biker bullshit."

Kaye laughed and ended the call.

***

After he got home, Kaye spent an hour trying to meditate and work out. Concentration was difficult. His conversation with Rowell kept replaying itself in his head. He finally gave up and started fixing some dinner.

CHAPTER 16

Kaye rose early and took a cup of tea out onto the patio to watch the sunrise. The pre-dawn chill precipitated a quick trip back inside for a sweatshirt.

A sliver of new moon hung not far above the eastern horizon. The early flights out of LAX, he thought probably packed with ambitious business travelers trying to somehow beat the time zone game and at least garner a few productive hours in New York, D.C., Atlanta or Miami, were already a constant stream.

The world began to come out of hiding as the sun chased the darkness to the west and the artificial light of humankind, having again done its job of keeping the gremlins and goblins at bay, began to go out.

The ocean was calm, the shore break small enough that all but the most optimistic, diehard surfers would be taking the day off. Gradually the South Bay shoreline emerged and the now darker-than-the-sky hump of the Palos Verdes peninsula rose into view. Minutes later, Catalina Island, barely more than an apparition, began to take shape on the horizon.

Kaye loved this spot and this time of day. He and Amy had spent many mornings here, carefully designing Amy's writing retreat above the garage so it would enhance, not interfere with, the view. They ended up with what was essentially a study-studio apartment that sometimes held Amy captive for days on end as ideas and words, refusing to be interrupted, poured forth onto paper.

The sun crested the eastern horizon, the light instantly dimming the moon while it brought the world's flaws and gritty details into focus.

Kaye sighed, threw the remainder of his tea onto the manicured lawn and headed inside to get ready for his day.

His first stop was a 24-hour florist in Santa Monica, where he bought flowers for Roshi. As he struggled to get them into a saddlebag, he silently hoped they would survive the trip.

When he rolled down the gravel drive toward the temple, things were strangely quiet. There were no monks out early working the gardens, and none walking slowly while they meditated. He parked the Harley near the bottom of the steps and extracted the flowers from the saddlebag. When he turned, Seicho stood at the top of the steps.

"Good morning. No cantaloupe," Kaye said, holding the flowers out for the monk to see. "I brought these for Roshi."

Seicho waited for Kaye as he climbed the steps.

"It is not a good morning, Benkei," the monk said somberly when Kaye was halfway up.

Kaye stopped, at first bewildered by Seicho's comment. Then his mind went blank.

"When?" he managed to whisper after what seemed an eternity.

"This morning just after three," Seicho said.

A tsunami of guilt crashed over Kaye.

I should have come yesterday, but I didn't. I missed my chance to say goodbye.

He dropped the flowers, put his hand to his face and cried.

Seicho came down to where Kaye stood, entwined his arm through Kaye's and silently led Kaye up the stairs and to a bench, where Kaye sat down. When he gathered his wits he heard faint chanting coming from inside the temple and knew it was for Roshi.

"Can I go in?" he asked.

"I'm sorry, Benkei, but not today. Only members of the Order can be inside."

"May I go around and sit in his garden? Please?"

"Of course," Seicho replied. "You know the way?"

"I do. Roshi-sama and I frequently sat *zazen* there."

"I will meet you there shortly."

Kaye rose, descended the steps and followed the path to the gate of Roshi's private garden. He let himself in and sat on one of the curved benches. As he remembered his mentor he watched the koi in the pond, the shadows of the leaves dancing on the garden walls in the early morning breeze, and the myriad sounds of the Universe Roshi had taught him to hear. Tears came again, and he quelled them by controlling his breathing and focusing his concentration on all that Roshi Munan had taught him.

It was almost ten minutes later that Seicho emerged from Roshi's quarters into the garden and approached Kaye, an envelope in hand.

"Roshi Munan left this for you," Seicho said as he held it out. "It was his last act."

"Thank you," Kaye said as he took the envelope.

Seicho left through the garden gate and was lost to sight.

The front of the envelope bore a single kanji character. Kaye couldn't read it, but thought it probably represented Benkei, the name Roshi had bestowed upon him. With shaking hands he carefully opened it.

'Benkei,

Do not mourn. Remember, death is not the end, it is merely a new beginning.

I love you with the love a father has for a son. I will return, *watashi no musuko*, and *Unmei* will bring us together again.

Follow the Path, Benkei. Seek the Truth and the Light, and protect the Innocent now as you did centuries ago.'

The signature was in Kanji.

I should have come yesterday ran through his mind in an endless loop as tears stained the precious goodbye.

CHAPTER 17

It was almost 10:30 a.m. when Kaye walked into the squad room. Things were quiet and Captain Thompson was sequestered in his office working through yet another intimidating pile of paperwork. He hung up his jacket, went to the break room, brewed himself a cup of tea and sat down at the table. Sipping the tea, he gazed out the window and pondered life in general.

Having seen so much death and the often unspeakable things human beings do to each other, and sometimes themselves, Kaye was a bit surprised that Roshi's peaceful passing hit him so hard.

Kaye knew he would need to go to Kyokoku-Dera Monastery and pay his final respects when the time was right.

But he had a murderer to catch first. He gulped down the last of the tea and headed back to his desk.

Roshi's last words of good-bye accompanied him.

He called the District Attorney's office and asked for Kayla Okafor.

"Good morning, Detective," she answered.

"You busy?"

"Not at the moment, but I need to leave for court in a few minutes."

"I'll talk fast," Kaye said. "I wanted to let you know that I spoke to Monica Lowden."

"Valerie Weber's biological grandmother, right?"

"Right. Anyway, Valerie's birth mother, Rachel Lowden, committed suicide not long after Valerie was born, so there's no chance Valerie found her."

"God, what a tragedy," Okafor said softly.

"Yeah," Kaye agreed. "Monica has never gotten over it, but she did tell me who she thought the father was. I tracked him down. He denied it, of course, but I think we can cross him off the list, too."

"Good to know."

"Please pass my thanks along to the Judge for sharing information."

"I'll do that," Okafor said. "Anything else?"

"One thing," Kaye replied. "I've been looking at one of Valerie's former teachers. A guy named Dylan Glithero. I can link them, but I haven't found anything specific to tie him to Valerie's murder. But I might have proof that he's been having sex with underage girls at his school."

"How did you get onto him?"

"He was picking Valerie up after school at Westside Alternative. He teaches at Grove Charter. He was previously charged with sexual battery of a minor, but was acquitted. That's why I went to Orange County."

"And you think he might have picked up where he left off back then?"

"I heard there may be photos that tie him directly to a sexual relationship with Valerie."

"But you don't have them."

"Not yet," Kaye admitted. "Glithero's ex-wife hired a private investigator to prove he was running around on her. The P.I. brought her pictures she says show Glithero going into a motel with a young woman. She also told me he got fired from his former job because of what she called 'rumors' about him and female students."

"Are you trying to locate the photos?" Okafor asked quickly.

"I am. I know the P.I. and I've already called."

"Okay," Okafor said, "if you get your hands on photographic evidence that Glithero was having a sexual relationship with Valerie Weber, that's enough to arrest and question him."

"Tom Gannett already tried to talk to him," Kaye said. "Glithero immediately clammed up and referred Gannett to his lawyer."

"Gannett didn't have photos proving statutory rape, right? He was investigating her murder."

"Correct."

Okafor went quiet for a moment, then said, "Find the photos, if you can, and chase down whatever they give you. If you find evidence of a crime, any crime, committed by this Glithero guy, bring me an arrest warrant affidavit and we'll take it to a judge."

"Will do, Counselor. Thanks."

"Get this guy, Kaye. Please, get this guy."

"I'm working on it."

Kaye hung up and started plotting his next course of action. One thing immediately rose to the top. He picked up his desk phone and made the call.

"Hello," a male voice answered.

"Mr. Weber?" Kaye asked.

"Uh, no, this is Miles."

"Oh, hey Miles. This is Detective Kaye. Is your Mom home?"

"Yeah. Hang on."

Kaye heard the phone being laid down, then heard Miles' voice in the background. "Mom! Detective Kaye is on the phone!"

A moment later, Miles was back. "She'll be right here."

Kaye didn't have time to thank Miles before JoAnn Weber came on the line.

"This is JoAnn," she said, then added, "Hang up the phone, please, Miles."

Kaye heard a click.

"Hello, Detective. What can I do for you?"

"I promised I'd keep you informed," Kaye replied, "and I have some news and information to pass along."

"Did you find out who killed Valerie?"

"Not yet, but I'm making progress."

"What have you found out?"

"I talked to Valerie's biological grandmother. The family did not list Valerie's biological father on the birth certificate to keep him from asserting parental rights, but she pointed me to the man she believed was the father --"

"Oh, please tell me," JoAnn interrupted, "he wasn't some homeless vagrant or anonymous sperm donor."

"No, ma'am," Kaye said, taken aback by the comment. "As a matter of fact, he's a very successful businessman, who told me Valerie had never tried to contact him and that there was no chance he was her father."

"Did you believe him?"

"I have no reason to believe that Valerie, even if she tried, ever found him or that he had anything whatsoever to do with her death."

"How can you be sure?"

"It's my job, Mrs. Weber, which I happen to be reasonably good at," Kaye said. "Even if he is Valerie's biological father, that's not a crime. If I find a link, I'll circle back to him."

"I'm sorry," she said. "I didn't mean to..."

"No need to apologize," Kaye said. "Valerie's biological parents were both high school students, and the mother was, at least in her parents' eyes, simply too young to raise a child. The law," Kaye continued, "seals adoption records until the adoptee is eighteen, which Valerie was not, so not only were the records still sealed, as a minor she couldn't have petitioned the court to see them. Even I wasn't allowed to see them. I had to ask the District Attorney's office for help, and I only got that because of the circumstances of Valerie's death. My conclusion is that Valerie did not find her birth parents, and they couldn't have found her even if they had tried."

"I believe you," JoAnn said softly. "Again, I'm sorry for questioning you."

"You'd make a good defense attorney."

"Gunther and I have been married a long time. Maybe the lawyer thing is contagious."

"I do have one more thing to ask you about."

"Go ahead."

"The final autopsy report on Valerie came in," Kaye said gently. "I hate to do this on the phone, but I need to ask you a difficult question."

"Okay," JoAnn said slowly, and Kaye heard the trepidation in her voice.

"Did you know Valerie was pregnant?"

Kaye heard JoAnn gasp, then begin so say, "No, no, no..." as she broke into sobs.

Kaye let her cry.

After a minute, JoAnn's sobs slowed to intermittent hiccups and gasps, and she eventually was able to ask, "How far along was she?"

"The doctor estimated seven to nine weeks."

"She would have missed a period," JoAnn whispered. "So she must have known, or at least suspected."

"But she never said anything to you?"

"Not a word," JoAnn said, her voice choking up again.

Kaye hesitated before saying, "JoAnn, I can't give you a lot of specifics because the investigation is on-going, but based on what I'm finding I don't think you telling Valerie she was adopted is connected to her death. The chain of events I'm following started before that."

Silence.

"Really?" JoAnn said at last. "You're not just saying that?"

"No, I'm not just saying that. This was not your fault, so give yourself a break. When I make an arrest we'll sit down and I'll give you the whole story. In the meantime, please be patient, and don't share anything I tell you with anyone but your husband."

"Can I ask a question?"

"Sure."

"How did Valerie die?"

"The Coroner listed asphyxiation as the cause of death."

"Oh, God," JoAnn barely whispered. "She knew she was going to die."

Kaye stayed silent.

"Thank you, Detective," JoAnn continued after a moment. "I appreciate you keeping your word and calling me. Detective Gannett still hasn't called."

"Detective Gannett is still out on emergency personal leave."

"Please, keep me updated."

"I will."

JoAnn hung up first, and Kaye thought he heard a second click just as he took the receiver away from his ear.

Kaye spent time updating his case file and notes, then decided to walk around the corner to the local cop deli and get a sandwich. The day had turned nice, so he decided to sit outside to eat. Just as he took his first bite, Amari Burke came around the corner. She instantly homed in on Kaye and stopped outside the wrought iron railing that separated the tables from the sidewalk.

"Mind if I join you?" she asked.

"Not at all."

Kaye covered his sandwich with a napkin and waited while Burke went inside to order. Less than five minutes later, she was back.

"Sorry it took so long," she said, eyeing Kaye's napkin-covered lunch. "You didn't have to wait."

"Not a problem. What have you got going today?"

"J.J. and I caught a string of late-night smash and dash commercial burglaries that happened Sunday night," Burke replied before taking a bite of sandwich.

"What did they get?"

"Clothes and shoes," she replied, her words indistinct around the mouthful of food. She stopped, swallowed, and went on. "We think it was kids – by that I mean not pros – because of what they took."

"Witnesses? Video?"

"Tons of store security video. The morons were too stupid to even cover their faces and they parked their car right in front of the places they hit. We got make and model, but no plate."

"Traffic cams?"

"They're pulling it for us today," Burke said as she crunched a mouthful of chips. "Should be an easy fly ball, unless they were smart enough to pull or cover the plates. But…" She shrugged.

"Anything back from the gang unit about the Tiger Boys?"

"I'm supposed to talk to that Rivera guy at three o'clock."

"Just you?" Kaye asked, curious.

"Yeah, J.J.'s in court on an old Valley case."

"Mind if I sit in?" Kaye asked.

"Hey, the more the merrier. You still working that girl's murder?"

Kaye nodded and said, "Valerie Weber."

"Making progress?"

"Some," Kaye said. "I identified Valerie's birth mother. She died years ago, so..."

"She was adopted?"

"Yeah, and her mom, her adoptive mom, seems to think Valerie located her birth parents and that things went downhill from there. I've got nothing that tells me Valerie found anyone."

"Sounds like a real mess. Good luck."

"Slow and steady wins the race," Kaye said.

"I think Usain Bolt would argue that," Burke said, smiling sideways at Kaye.

The conversation turned to non-work-related subjects. Kaye learned that Burke was married to an architect, had no kids and lived in the North Westchester neighborhood.

"And I'm into Pilates," she said.

"I do yoga," Kaye said.

"You do yoga?" Burke asked, and Kaye could tell she was trying not to laugh.

"Yep," Kaye confirmed. "Started out as injury rehab. It worked, I liked it, I still do it."

"I never would have believed that had I not heard it straight from you. I figured you for a four-hour-a-day weight room guy."

"I don't lift weights at all," Kaye said. "But I struggle with flexibility. That's why I do yoga."

"And you're not married, right?"

"No. My wife died in a motorcycle accident a while back."

"I'm sorry," Burke said, averting her eyes. "I didn't mean to pry."

"You weren't prying," Kaye said. "Natural question from the flow of the conversation. If you'd asked me if I had a girlfriend when you first sat down, that would be prying."

"Oh, God," Burke said, laughing. "I almost asked you that!"

Kaye smiled at her. "We should probably get back to work."

"Ten-four on that," Burke said, getting up and gathering the detritus from lunch. She put the red plastic baskets on the stack already atop the trash receptacle and sucked down the last of her soda before dumping the cup and rest of the paper.

"Thanks for the lunch company," she said when they got back to the station. "My desk, three o'clock?"

"I'll be there," Kaye said and turned to head for his desk.

"Hey, Kaye," Burke said.

Kaye turned around.

"So, do you have a girlfriend?"

Kaye stared at her, but couldn't help grinning.

"Hey," Burke said with an exaggerated shrug of her shoulders, "I'm a detective now. I get paid to pry."

Kaye kept smiling, shook his head, and headed for his desk.

He now had time to kill before the three o'clock call with Rivera. He considered going back through the Valerie Weber file and his notes to see if anything triggered a new idea, link or revelation, but discarded the idea.

Instead he went to the supply closet and grabbed three spanking new legal pads. He put pen to paper and on the first one printed 'WHAT I KNOW I CAN PROVE' across the top. On the second he printed 'WHAT I THINK I KNOW' and on the third 'WHAT I NEED TO KNOW'.

Then he started brainstorming.

He was at if for almost two hours, and when he finally gave up and dropped his pen the results were frustrating. The list of things he still needed to know was far longer than the other two lists combined, and, to his chagrin, the list of what he knew he could prove was woefully lacking. Information he was waiting on would help, but unless Sonny Eliason had an autographed photo of Dylan Glithero going into a motel room with Valerie Weber, or could prove it was Glithero driving the white SUV that had picked Valerie up behind Staples, or had a DNA test proving it was Glithero that had impregnated Valerie, he was pretty much nowhere.

Frustrated, Kaye looked at the time. 2:55 p.m.

Let's go see what we can't *find out from the gang guys,* he thought ruefully as he heaved himself out of his chair and headed for Burke's desk.

She saw him coming and smiled.

"Right on time."

"Well, I had to get something right today," he replied, his frustration showing in his voice.

"Problems?" Burke asked.

Kaye considered the question before answering.

"Not a great day. I'm just impatient, I guess, and want everything tied up in a nice, neat bow I can hand to the D.A. That takes information I'm still waiting on."

Burke looked around to see who else was within earshot, then looked at Kaye and asked, "Can I tell you something?"

"Sure."

"That's my biggest problem with my promotion. In patrol, they send you on a call, you get there, you assess the situation and solve it the best you can. It's like crisis management. You sometimes make somebody happy, but most of the time you piss somebody off, maybe even the person who called 9-1-1. What you can't resolve right then and there becomes somebody else's problem and you move on to the next crisis. At the end of your shift you hang your cop suit in your locker and go home until it's time to come back and put it on again."

"That's a good description," Kaye said. "Sounds like you miss it."

"Now, though, I'm the one the patrol officers wave bye-bye to and the crisis they couldn't solve becomes mine. You wear the detective suit twenty-four seven."

"You're not thinking about asking to go back, are you?"

Burke just shrugged and said, "All change requires an adjustment. And I've never been somebody who was willing to go backwards."

Burke's phone chose that instant to ring.

"Detective Burke," she answered, then listened for a few seconds before saying, "Hey, Sergeant Rivera. Thanks for calling. I've got Detective Kaye here. Okay to put you on speaker?"

Rivera must've said 'yes' because Burke instantly pushed the speaker phone button.

"Hey, Ben, long time no talk to," Rivera said. "How goes it?"

"Can't complain, Lonzo," Kaye replied. "How's the family?"

Burke listened in amazement. She caught Kaye's eye and mouthed, 'You know him?'

Kaye nodded as Rivera said, "Doing great. Luis is still in remission and his doctors say his future looks good."

"Hey," Kaye said, "that's great!"

"Angela and I will never forget what you did for Luis, for us, Ben," Rivera said somberly. "We can never thank you enough."

"Glad I could help, Lonzo. Tell Luis I said hello."

Burke listened to the conversation, her mouth hanging open and her brow furrowed in a 'what the hell' look.

"What can you tell us about the Tiger Boys?" Kaye asked, steering the conversation back to business.

"You know," Rivera began, "I never even heard of them until Jefferies called and asked me about them. I'm glad he did."

"Are they operating in Los Angeles?" Burke asked, leaning toward the phone.

"They're just ramping up," Rivera replied. "But they're not what we're used to thinking about when we think of a street gang."

"How so?" Kaye asked.

"They think of themselves more as consultants," Rivera said. "They meet with the local gang honchos and pitch their connections, their intelligence gathering capabilities and their financial savvy. They're almost like a combination security consultant and asset management outfit rolled into one. Thing is, though, if the prospective client – and I use the term loosely – refuses to sign up the Tiger Boys turn the tiger loose on them until they come around, get with the program, and start paying up. It's the perfect business model. If your prospects are crooks, too, what are they gonna do? Call the cops?"

"Where do they operate now?" Burke asked.

"I called around," Rivera said. "San Francisco is home base, and it looks like they've got a lot of the larger west coast cities covered. They're moving east, too. Phoenix. Vegas."

"You didn't call Lieutenant Chen in Oakland, did you?" Burke asked.

"I did not, per Jefferies' request, which I gotta say I thought was odd."

"We have information that the Oakland PD might have a leak," Kaye said. He went on to tell Rivera about Neil Gaeta's conversation with Tina Magnuson.

"That's the guy who got shot off his motorcycle in Westwood?" Rivera asked.

"It is," Kaye confirmed.

"Fits with what one of the snitches told me," Rivera said. "The hit on your guy was supposed to be a demonstration by the Tiger Boys to show how good their intel is. They even told the shooters what flight the guy would be coming into LAX on."

"Scary," Burke said.

"You're right about that," Rivera agreed. "But the word from our side is that there's a federal task force working to put the Tiger Boys out of business. I just don't know when."

"Hey, thanks Lonzo," Kaye said. "We appreciate your time and input."

"I'll second that," Burke chimed in.

"You're welcome," Rivera said. "And, hey, Ben, let's get together and catch up, okay? Been way too long."

"I hear that," Kaye said. "We'll set something up. Tell Angela and the kids I said hello."

"I will," Rivera said and ended the call.

"Okay," Burke said, turning in her chair to stare at Kaye. "How do you know Rivera? And what kind of help did you give his son?"

"I worked with him a long time ago," Kaye replied. "Not partners, but same Division, same shift. And, miss nosy detective, if you must know, I donated bone marrow when his oldest boy was diagnosed with leukemia."

"You did that? Wow."

"I was a donor match. Not doing it would have been dereliction of duty."

Burke shook her head, then asked, "So what do we do about Gaeta and the Tiger Boys?"

Kaye didn't answer for a moment, then said, "I've got an idea, at least for the short term, how we might break our case, plug the Oakland P.D. leak, if they have one, and get Gaeta home."

"What about the long term?" Burke asked.

"If my idea works, we won't need a long-term plan."

"What's your idea?"

"Let me refine it first. I need to find out when Gaeta is being discharged and talk to Tina Magnuson first."

"Okay," Burke said, shrugging. "Just know you can count on me and J.J. for backup."

"Thanks," Kaye said, standing up, "but you won't be backup, you'll be out front." He turned and walked away.

When Kaye got back to his desk, his voicemail light was blinking.

"Kaye, this is Sonny Eliason. Sharm told me you called looking for me. I'm back in town until about noon tomorrow. Stop by my office in the morning and we'll talk. Oh, and I've moved since I last saw you." Eliason gave him the address. "See you in the morning."

Kaye hung up and was thinking about heading home when his phone rang again.

"Kaye."

"Detective Kaye, this is Lou Ellen at the ballistics lab. I've got the results on the bullet and fragments you dropped off last week."

144

"What did you find?"

"The fragments were useless, except to tell us they came from the same gun as the nearly intact bullet. A Glock nine-millimeter, by the way."

"Did you get anything off the bullet?"

"I was able to get enough that we'll be able to match it to the weapon that fired it, if we ever recover it."

"Thanks, Lou Ellen, I appreciate the call."

"Wait, that's not all. I ran it through the NIBIN system and got a match. The same gun was used three years ago in the homicide of a liquor store clerk in the Valley. It hasn't been on our radar since then. I hope that helps."

"It does," Kaye said. "Thanks."

"I'll send you the report."

Kaye ended the call, leaned back in his chair and smiled.

The first element of his plan for Gaeta had just fallen into place.

CHAPTER 18

Kaye woke early and practiced for half an hour, cleaned up, ate and headed into town. The Station was between home and Eliason's office, so he stopped there first.

There was a phone call he needed to make.

He was earlier than he'd thought he would be and fretted for almost fifteen minutes before he made the call.

It was 8:01 a.m.

Somebody better answer, he thought as he punched in the number.

"Digital Forensics," a woman answered on the second ring.

"Could I speak to Scott?" Kaye asked. "This is Detective Kaye, West Bureau."

"Hold on."

Within ten seconds, a man's voice came on the line.

"This is Scott."

"Scott, Ben Kaye, West Bureau. Where's my video?"

"I'm sorry, Detective Kaye. It's been hell week around here. I spent two days testifying in court, my computer crashed and –"

"Not with my video on it, I hope."

"No, but it took me another two days to get a replacement," Scott said. "Turned out to be worth it, though."

"How so?"

"While I was down we got a new version of the application that does the enhancement and rendering. The results should be even better."

The 'should be' was what Kaye homed in on.

"So what you're telling me is that you haven't worked on it yet?" he asked, his tone communicating more than the question itself.

"No, I have not. I'm still trying to get up to speed on the new application."

"Get it to me as soon as you can," Kaye said.

"I'll do my best," Scott said.

Kaye hung up, spun around and headed for the break room to brew some tea just in time to see Captain Thompson open his office door. He went that way instead, stopping outside the open door and leaning on the frame.

"Morning, Captain."

Thompson looked up and said, "Good morning. What do you need?"

"A safe house."

"What?"

"I need a safe house," Kaye repeated. "I'm not sure exactly when yet. Maybe this weekend, but maybe a few days after that. One day, I hope, because that makes my theory right."

"I'm going to need more than that," Thompson said skeptically.

Kaye explained what he was planning, and why.

"Good idea," Thompson said when Kaye finished. "I'll make some calls and see what I can come up with."

"On this side of the hill, please.

"Agreed. And let me know when the timing is firm."

"Yes, sir."

Smiling, Kaye went back to his desk.

The second piece of his plan for the Gaeta case had fallen into place.

***

Kaye had been halfway expecting to find Sonny Eliason's office in a storefront in an out-of-the-way, maybe a little sketchy, strip mall on a side street.

What he found surprised him.

The Eliason Agency was on the third floor of an office building just one street number off Santa Monica Boulevard in a nice part of town.

His low expectations were again dashed when he walked into Eliason's reception area. When the woman he'd spoken to had said her name was 'Sharm', he'd instantly pictured a gum-popping bleached blonde, nail file in hand, straight out of a 1930s film noir detective movie. Instead, behind the reception desk sat a tastefully dressed and groomed woman, the nameplate identifying her as Charmaine Simons.

She studied Kaye for five seconds before she broke into a grin. "You must be Detective Kaye. I thought Sonny was putting me on when he described you. He didn't tell me you were coming in today."

"That's okay," Kaye assured her. "Is he in?"

"Hell, yes, I'm in," a man's voice boomed from Kaye's left and he turned to see a grinning Sonny Eliason standing in an open door. "I thought that was your voice," Eliason said, stepping forward and opening his arms for a hug. "C'mon, buddy, bring it in. Long time no see."

Kaye wasn't a hugger, but he accepted Eliason's brief bear hug.

"Holy shit," Eliason exclaimed when he let go and stepped back. "You're a bigger chunk of beef than I remember. Still working out, eh?"

"Almost every day."

"And still riding your Harleys, I see," Eliason said, checking out Kaye's attire. "Bet that drives your boss absolutely bat shit crazy."

"We've achieved a sort of détente on that one," Kaye said. "I solve cases, he looks the other way."

"Bet he has a chronic sore neck," Eliason said, laughing, "because as I recall, you close a lot of tough cases."

"Which brings us to why I'm here. I could use your help."

Eliason's expression turned serious. "Come on back," he said, stepping out of the way and extending his hand toward the open door. As Kaye passed, he heard Eliason tell Sharm, "No calls."

Kaye found himself in a common area that served four office doors. Not knowing where to go, he stopped.

"First one on the right," Eliason said. "Come on in. Take a load off."

The office looked like a set from an old Sam Spade movie. Venetian blinds on the window, under which was a credenza with a coffee maker atop it. In front of the credenza was a wooden desk sporting an old time green and brass desk lamp, telephone and desk calendar. The only modern touch was a computer monitor, but Kaye could see neither keyboard nor computer. Two chairs faced the desk, and off to one side was a black, Empire style leather sofa and coffee table.

"I'm impressed, Sonny," Kaye said as he sat down. "Business must be good. How many investigators do you have?"

"Three, plus me," Eliason replied. "And, yeah, business is good. Who'd've thought infidelity was the fourth largest industry in America?"

"Is that all you work? Divorce cases?"

"Hell, no. We also do insurance work, probate, pre-employment, all kinds of stuff. But cheating spouses pay the bills." Sonny shrugged his shoulders. "Shit, I have to turn cases away."

"A cheating husband is why I'm here," Kaye said.

Kaye spent ten minutes outlining the Weber case and his interview of Roslyn Reingold.

Eliason asked a lot of questions and took a lot of notes. Kaye caught himself wishing Tom Gannett had been as thorough.

"You want to see the pictures of Glithero outside the motel, right"

Eliason asked when Kaye finished. "See if the girl's your vic?"

"Exactly."

Eliason nodded, slapped the top of his desk with both hands, stood up and said, "I can do that. Be right back."

He wasn't gone long. Thick folder in hand, he sat down, rifled through the file, pulled several eight-by-tens out of the pile and slid them across to Kaye.

"That Valerie Weber?" he asked.

Kaye leaned forward, spun the photos around and studied them. His heart sank. The photos had obviously been intended to identify Dylan Glithero, not the young woman, whose entire face never showed clearly. But Kaye could tell by her dark hair that she, arm and arm and hip to hip with a smiling Glithero as they entered a motel room, was not Valerie Weber.

"No," Kaye said, glancing at Eliason with disappointment before going back to the photos.

"Well, shit," Eliason said sharply. "But that means the guy must have quite the system going."

"I thought of that," Kaye said. "Can I keep these? If I can identify her as a juvenile, at least I'll have some leverage on Glithero."

"Keep them," Eliason said. "Dates and times are on the back. I've got the digital originals stored on a server."

"Thanks, Sonny," Kaye said, standing to leave and extending his hand.

Eliason stood and reached across to shake Kaye's hand.

"Sorry it was a dry hole," the private investigator said.

"It happens," Kaye said. "Plus, it's another lead."

"That it is," Eliason agreed, then snapped his fingers. "Geez, I almost forgot. Don't know if this'll help you out or not, but the second day I followed Glithero, he drove that girl down to Orange County, the Anaheim Hills, and took her into a gated community."

"Did you get an address?" Kaye asked hopefully.

"No, sorry. He had enough of a lead on me that I didn't get through the gate."

"That's okay," Kaye told the P.I. "Still a good data point. Sonny, I really appreciate the help."

"I'm always glad to help out the Department. Hell, if you guys go out of business, my retirement is toast."

Kaye laughed and said, "See you around, Sonny."

A dispirited Kaye walked back to the bike, mulling over his next moves. What stuck in his mind was Eliason's crack about Glithero having a system going.

Gannett had said the same thing.

Before he stowed the photos in a saddlebag, he studied them again. He needed to know who the young woman was.

It was time to have a serious sit-down with Eilene Holderby.

***

J.J. and Burke walked into the squad room. Both wore smiles as they chatted excitedly. They spotted Kaye and headed his way.

"You want to hear our good news?" Burke asked.

"I could use some," Kaye replied.

"We nabbed our smash and dash crew."

"If you could call them that," J.J. interjected. "High school kids from Encino."

Kaye looked at Burke. "Good call. You thought they were amateurs."

"I wouldn't even call them that," Burke said. "Hobbyists is more like it. They were stupid enough to try and sell the stuff around school."

"Too bad, too," J.J. said. "A couple of them are eighteen. They are now well and truly fucked with a felony criminal record."

"Nobody to blame but themselves," Burke said sharply, and Kaye sensed a disagreement in philosophy between the partners.

J.J. started to say something, but Kaye beat him to it.

"Hey, you guys have a minute to talk about the Gaeta case?"

"Sure," J.J. said instantly.

"Have a seat."

J.J. parked himself on Kaye's short filing cabinet and Burke grabbed a chair and pulled it over.

"Okay," Burke said. "What've you got?"

Kaye laid it out for them and answered all of their questions. Both thought it was a good idea that would keep Gaeta safe, and they worked out specific assignments by location.

"J.J., I know it's technically your case," Kaye said in conclusion. "But I think it'll work."

"Assuming all the pieces come together," J.J. said. "But, yeah, let's go with it. You want to call up north? You've already worked with them."

"If you don't mind," Kaye replied.

"Not at all," J.J. said.

"Okay," Kaye said. "I'll let you know as soon as I find out about a safe house and we'll go forward."

"Sounds good," Burke said, standing up. "C'mon, partner," she lightly jabbed J.J. in the shoulder, "I'll buy you a soda."

Kaye turned back to his monitor just as an email notification popped up.

His pulse quickened when he saw that the sender was Marvin Sunderland and the subject was Trial Transcripts.

'Detective Kaye,

Attached are the transcripts of the proceedings in the Dylan Glithero case you asked about and that of a near-simultaneous trial of another teacher at Moulton High School accused of sexual relations with students. The second transcript was stored next to Glithero's, so I thought I'd forward it along in case you were interested. They are both shorter than I thought they would be, so I don't know if they will be useful or not, but I thought you should make that decision. Both have been scanned in toto and I hope they help. Let me know if I can be of further assistance.

Marvin Sunderland, OCSC Administrator'

Kaye immediately downloaded and saved the files, then replied to Sunderland that he'd received the transcripts and thanked him.

It turned into a long evening.

Sunderland's idea of 'short' was different than Kaye's, but as he read through the Glithero transcript he understood it could have been longer.

The first nugget of information was that the Prosecutor had been Harold Perryman. Glithero had been represented by a Public Defender. The only motion of note was that the Defense had asked the court to reduce the charge against Glithero on the grounds that Glithero was serving as a 'student teacher' and was not a 'teacher' under the meaning of the law. The motion was denied, the Judge calling it an issue for the jury to decide.

Opening statements were predictable and perfunctory. The Prosecution promised to prove that Dylan Glithero was a child molester and the Defense discounted the Prosecution's case, claiming the victim was responsible for the entire situation.

The Prosecution's first witness was the victim, one Lauren Maupin, who, when sworn in, stated her age as eighteen.

Under direct, she denied ever having told Glithero she was eighteen before they began their relationship and admitted that they had never had intercourse.

Under cross examination, she admitted that she had turned eighteen during the course of what she called her 'romance' with Glithero, and, although she never admitted she'd lied to Glithero about her age, the transcript clearly communicated that she was rattled.

The Prosecution's next witness was Detective Sebaly. His testimony was short and sweet. Maupin's parents had called the Sheriff's Office with information that their minor daughter had revealed to them that she was romantically involved with a teacher at her school. Sebaly had interviewed Maupin in the presence of her parents because she was a minor. She gave Sebaly the name of her 'English teacher', Dylan Glithero, admitted there had been sexual activity, but had denied they'd had intercourse. Sebaly then conducted a custodial interview of Glithero, who had cooperated willingly. Glithero admitted that he and Maupin had engaged in mutual masturbation and oral sex, but swore he'd never had sexual intercourse with Maupin and that she'd told him she was eighteen. Sebaly testified that at the end of the interview he placed Glithero under arrest.

Under cross examination, defense counsel had focused on Glithero's responses and attitude during the interview and arrest process. Counsel elicited a response from Sebaly that Glithero had seemed genuinely surprised when he'd told Glithero that Maupin was seventeen, not eighteen.

Glithero took the stand in his own defense, which Kaye found unusual. On direct, Glithero was guided through testimony about his teacher certification status and again admitted that he and Maupin had engaged in various sex acts. But he again denied they ever had intercourse. He also testified that he'd been genuinely attracted to Maupin romantically, and insisted she had told him she was eighteen.

Glithero hadn't wavered under cross examination by the Prosecution. Kaye was surprised Perryman chose to completely ignore the issue of teacher certification.

The Defense then presented a second witness, identified during swearing in as Eugene Calhoun. Calhoun stated his occupation as a teacher at Moulton High School. His testimony consisted of claiming that he'd overheard Maupin tell Glithero she was eighteen. He also characterized Glithero's and Maupin's relationship as anything but secretive, testifying that Maupin followed Glithero around campus 'like a puppy dog' between classes and the two ate lunch together almost every day in the cafeteria.

Calhoun also stood firm under cross.

At the time, there had been no statute barring sexual contact between a teacher and student so long as the student was at least eighteen years of age. Clearly, what Maupin had, or hadn't, told Glithero about her age was the central issue of the trial.

Closing arguments were brief and to the point.

All in all, the trial took a total of only two days.

When Kaye finished the Glithero transcript he hadn't formed a strong impression one way or the other about Glithero's guilt or innocence. But he could certainly understand how a jury, its members in the courtroom and witnessing testimony first hand, had found reasonable doubt where Kaye couldn't from reading a transcript all these years later.

Alone in the squad room now except for the single detective assigned to catch the late night cases, Kaye thought about going home but decided against it. Instead, he took a break and brewed himself a strong cup of tea.

He got his first shock as soon as he saw the summary page that led off the second transcript.

The Defendant's name was Eugene A. Calhoun and he'd been charged with multiple counts of rape, all the victims minors.

Kaye was dumbfounded. Had the Judge in the Glithero trial actually let Calhoun, facing similar charges and known to Dylan Glithero, testify for the defense? Kaye thought that had Glithero been convicted, that alone would have been enough to get the whole thing thrown out on appeal and a new trial ordered.

The Prosecutor in the case was, as Sunderland had remembered, Harold Chilton. Defense Counsel was in private practice.

The cases were as different as night and day, with Calhoun's lawyer inundating the Court with pre-trial motions ranging from change of venue requests to reduction in charges to continuances. Motions were even filed requesting the recusal of the Judge and Prosecutor, both of which were denied. The prosecution filed a motion to bar any testimony related to alleged victims' prior sexual behavior or experience and, over a vociferous protest from the defense, the Judge granted it.

Even the *voir dire* process was contentious, with accusations by the

Defense of a jury packing conspiracy and challenges that several members of the jury were plants for the prosecution, falsifying their identities with the Court's full knowledge and approval. It took days just to select a jury, and Kaye could tell that Judge DeVilbiss was already losing patience with Defense Counsel.

The Prosecution gave a cogent, detailed, logically progressive opening statement, addressing each charge and promising to present conclusive testimony and evidence that the Defendant was guilty of the charges.

Having sat through many trials, Kaye was nonetheless impressed.

Defense Counsel's opening statement was exactly the opposite. His client was innocent, the victim of a conspiracy hatched by disgruntled students and a district administration that had repeatedly and unsuccessfully tried to get rid of Calhoun, at last resorting to this tactic of scurrilous accusations and character assassination. He closed his opener by telling the jury that the person who should be on trial was the Superintendent of the school district.

Kaye searched back to the beginning of the transcript and made a note of the Defense Counsel's particulars, just in case.

Detective Sebaly was the Prosecution's first witness.

Chilton led Sebaly through a carefully constructed, step-by-step case progression. As it turned out, it was something Lauren Maupin, the young woman involved in the Glithero case, had told Sebaly during one of his meetings with her and her parents that had put him on Calhoun's scent.

Chilton had Sebaly paint a vivid picture of how the Detective had eventually uncovered four victims with very similar accounts of how Calhoun had enticed them into circumstances where he had been able to force himself upon them.

Objections by the Defense came fast and furiously, clearly intended to distract the jury and interrupt the chain of testimony. None were sustained.

Kaye also noticed a recurring interruption in the transcript flow wherein the Judge had to halt the proceedings and admonish the Defendant to keep quiet. At one point during Detective Sebaly's testimony, the Judge even threatened to gag Calhoun.

Sebaly was then led through the process of obtaining a warrant for Calhoun's arrest and the actual physical arrest.

When Chilton asked Sebaly for Calhoun's reaction to being arrested, the detective's response was short and sweet. "He demanded his attorney before I could even read him his rights."

The cross examination was brutal and lasted from mid-afternoon of the first day well into the second morning.

As he read, Kaye began to get an appreciation for the Defense Counsel. The man questioned every single detail of Sebaly's responses, often circling back along a different line of inquiry to a previous piece of testimony the Prosecution had used to score with the jury, and again pressing Sebaly if the details wavered one scintilla. He even called Sebaly on the Detective's occasional changes of verbs and adjectives to describe the same action or fact.

This guy wasn't cheap, Kaye thought. *I wonder how a high school teacher affords this kind of legal talent.*

It was when the Prosecutor attempted to present victim testimony that the case began to fall apart.

The first three witnesses were all no-shows, despite being under subpoena.

Kaye also noticed that when Chilton called each one, their names had been redacted because they were juveniles.

At that point the Prosecution requested a recess until the next day in order to find out what the mix-up was. The Defense immediately objected, and the Judge sustained the objection.

But Chilton did get an early lunch break.

When court reconvened, it was entered into the record that the Defendant refused to stand when Judge DeVilbiss entered the courtroom.

Chilton then called his fourth and last witness. The young woman was present and sworn in. Her name was redacted from the record, leading Kaye to conclude she, too, was a juvenile. He glanced down the page and saw that the Recorder had subsequently identified her as 'KS', which he thought must be initials.

Chilton did as thorough a job leading KS through her testimony as he'd done with Sebaly.

In her responses, KS recounted how Calhoun had known she wanted to be a writer or an artist and how he'd made it possible for her to work with the Drama Club on designing and building the sets for the school's Spring production, how he'd continued to ingratiate himself, had ultimately made a sexual advance she had rebuffed, and how he had then, two days before the production was to premiere, raped her in the backstage area of the auditorium.

Defense Counsel was uncharacteristically quiet during KS's

testimony, not raising a single objection when even Kaye, reading it now, thought the Prosecution was leading the witness.

Cross examination, though, was brutal. Counsel did everything possible to undermine KS's integrity and truthfulness. The Prosecution objected regularly, and many of the objections were sustained. At one point the Judge cautioned the Defense about his tactics and admonished him to move on.

But it was the last exchange of KS's testimony that Kaye thought probably sealed Calhoun's fate:

D.C.: Miss [redacted], how do we know you're not just making this up? I mean, the other so-called victims didn't even show up to testify.

D.A.: Objection. Badgering the witness, Your Honor.

J.D.: Sustained. Counselor, restrain yourself to the question only, please.

D.C: Sorry, Your Honor. Miss [redacted] , how do we know you're not just making this up?

KS: Well, if it makes any difference, I got pregnant, and I can't make that up.

There must have been a disturbance in the courtroom, because the Judge repeatedly called for order before warning that he would clear the courtroom if there was another, similar outbreak.

Defense Counsel had objected to KS's answer on the grounds he hadn't been able to question KS on her prior sexual history, thus preventing him from establishing that someone, anyone, else could have impregnated the witness. To Kaye's surprise the Judge sustained the objection and instructed the jury to disregard KS's statement about getting pregnant.

Yeah, Kaye mused. *Like they'll forget she said that.*

The Prosecution declined to re-direct, and KS was dismissed.

Next up should have been medical testimony or supporting witnesses, but Chilton didn't call another witness, instead resting his case.

Defense Counsel asked for an adjournment for the day, telling the Judge it was late and he would prefer to present his case beginning on Monday morning.

The Judge granted the request.

But on Monday, there was no defense and no testimony presented. Instead, it was a discussion between the Judge and both Counsel about plea withdrawals, charge reductions, new pleas, sentence recommendations, and the clearly skeptical Judge grilling Chilton on various aspects of the deal. The Judge at first rejected Chilton's sentencing recommendations out of hand, suggesting to the Prosecutor that he and Defense Counsel try it again. He then adjourned for the day.

What the hell? Kaye thought. *What was Chilton thinking?*

When Court convened the next morning, Chilton presented a different sentencing recommendation. The Judge was still not happy and pointedly questioned Chilton on whether this was the best course of action. Chilton defended the deal, telling DeVilbiss that the victims' families just wanted to put this episode behind them and get on with their lives.

DeVilbiss reluctantly agreed. Previous charges were withdrawn and a new plea of guilty to one count of rape was entered and accepted. But when the sentence was handed down, the Judge, as was his right, deviated from Chilton's recommendation. He tripled the recommended sentence, which led to an outburst from Calhoun, who had to be subdued by Bailiffs. DeVilbiss then conditioned the sentence by allowing parole after two years subject to the findings of the Pardon and Parole Board. He also tempered the Prosecutor's recommendation that Calhoun not be required to register as a sex offender by stipulating that if Calhoun was paroled he would be required to register for a period of time equal to the length of his full sentence, at which time he could petition the Court to have his name removed from the Registry.

The transcript ended with Judge DeVilbiss making it official and adjourning the court.

The Court Recorder, though, still entered the Judge's request to the bailiff to bring the jury foreman to his chambers.

Kaye closed the transcript file, stretched, and checked the time. It was well after midnight and he still had the ride home.

He leaned back and thought about what he'd just read. When he'd talked to Sunderland, even Cox, he'd gotten the impression that the two trials were connected, but now he didn't think so. Glithero and Calhoun weren't co-defendants tried separately. It had been two cases, the timing of the trials probably coincidental.

He wrote a quick note to the Captain to tell him he'd be working in the field in the morning, but should be in by noon, put it in the Inbox slot of the organizer mounted on the outside of Thompson's office door and started gathering the gear he'd need in the morning.

He stopped suddenly, puzzled by something.

The Glithero transcript had been pretty straightforward. The jury had just chosen to believe Glithero, not Lauren Maupin.

But the Calhoun transcript was different. It took Kaye a moment to realize what it was.

KS's testimony.

It had been an almost perfect primer on how an older man could recruit and groom a young girl for sex.

It was a system, and Dylan Glithero now seemed to have an eerily similar system.

Kaye knew he needed to find out if Glithero and Calhoun had worked closely back then and, assuming Calhoun was long out of prison, if the two men had kept in touch.

As he walked to the Harley, he idly wondered what Eugene A. Calhoun, assuming he was still alive, looked like now, and if he drove a white SUV.

CHAPTER 19

It was almost 9:00 a.m. when Kaye, riding the '41 Flight Red Knucklehead, rolled into the Grove Charter visitors' parking lot. He retrieved a file folder from the saddlebag and headed inside.

Mrs. Kowalczyk looked up and smiled when he walked through the office door.

"Good morning," she said. "I didn't expect to see you again after that other detective came in."

"Detective Gannett had a family emergency. The case has been reassigned to me."

"Good. He was very rude," Kowalczyk said. "And I know I shouldn't ask, but are you getting closer to finding out who killed Valerie?"

"Making progress," Kaye said. "I do need to talk to Ms. Holderby, if she's available."

"She is. I'll tell her you're here."

Kowalczyk spun and disappeared into the back office area, reappearing almost immediately.

"Come on through, Detective," she said, reaching under the counter to push the door lock release. "You can go on back."

Even though Holderby's office door was open, Kaye stopped outside and knocked. She looked up, saw him, closed the folder on her desk and set it aside.

"Come in, Detective, and have a seat, please."

Kaye sat in the same chair he'd used on his prior visit.

"So," Holderby said, "I hate to say I hope this is about Valerie Weber, but I don't need any more problems right now."

"It's connected," Kaye said as he reached into his file folder and pulled out half of the photo he'd gotten from Sonny Eliason. He'd trimmed it after deciding not to disclose Glithero's identity unless it became necessary to get the information he needed. He laid the photo on Holderby's desk. "I need to know who this is. I believe she's a student here."

Holderby leaned forward, elbows on her desk, and studied the photo. "Where did you get this?" she asked.

"Sorry, I can't tell you that."

Holderby spun around, rolled her chair next to a large lateral file, opened it, extracted a file and rolled back to her desk. She opened the file and turned it around so it was right side up for Kaye. Clipped to the inside left page was a Student Data sheet, and stapled to the upper left corner of that was a 3"x5" color portrait.

"Audra O'Bannon," Holderby said. "I'm ninety percent sure, but your photo isn't full face, so…"

Kaye compared the two photos and came to the same conclusion. He also noted O'Bannon's date of birth. She was seventeen.

"How long has she been a student here?" Kaye asked.

"She's a Junior now, and came to us as a Freshman," Holderby replied.

Kaye went quiet, considering his options.

"Ms. Holderby," he said finally, "what I'm about to show you has to be kept strictly between us. You can't tell anyone, and there can be no official reaction from the school or the district. It would be premature and jeopardize my investigation if it became public. Will you be okay with that?"

Holderby's expression turned pensive as she studied Kaye.

"Yes," she said. "I can do that. For Valerie."

"Good," Kaye said, deciding to go all in. He reached into his folder and took out the other half of the photo and matched it up to the other photo already on the desk. "Does Audra have a class, or classes, with Mr. Glithero?"

"Oh, my God," Holderby said wearily, slumping back in her chair as she realized the context of the photo.

"This was taken by a private investigator hired by Glithero's now ex-wife," Kaye told her. "When I found out the photos existed, I went looking for them, expecting to find Valerie Weber. But this is what I got."

Holderby looked at Kaye and said, "Audra has Mr. Glithero for English. She's also in his writing group, just like… How can this be?"

"It happens, Ms. Holderby."

She looked at him wide-eyed and asked, "Do you think Dylan… Mr. Glithero killed Valerie Weber?"

"At this point, all I can tell you is that I have found no direct link between Valerie's death and Dylan Glithero. This," he tapped his forefinger on the photo, "just happened to come up, and I have to look into it."

"I understand," Holderby said.

"I am going to need the contact information for Audra's parents," Kaye said.

"Of course. It's there on the face sheet."

Kaye took his paper brains out of his pocket, found what he needed and copied it down.

Before he left the Grove Charter grounds, Kaye walked the teachers' parking lot looking for Glithero's new Highlander. He found it, a USC Trojans decal already on the back window and still bearing a paper plate, and took pictures. Then, just for his own edification, he walked the lot looking for other white SUVs. There were none.

Next stop was the station.

***

Kaye entered the squad room and was headed for his desk when he heard Captain Thompson call his name. He turned to see the Captain waving at him to come to the office.

"What's up, Cap?" Kaye asked, leaning against the door frame.

"I wanted to let you know I got your safe house approved." Thompson held out a piece of paper and set of keys, which Kaye stepped forward and took. "You've got it from noon tomorrow until Monday morning. Let me know if it comes together and I'll take care of the logistics."

Kaye looked at the address shown on the paper. "Perfect," he said. "Thanks, Captain."

Now that he had a safe location lined up, there was only one unknown in Kaye's plan that needed to be nailed down.

He headed back to the '41.

Thirty minutes later he walked up to the nurses' station on Neil Gaeta's floor at Ronald Reagan UCLA Medical Center, showed his ID to the skeptical nurse and asked if Gaeta was still in the same room.

"He is," she replied. "You can go on in."

Gaeta looked much better than he had on Kaye's last visit. Though his broken leg still rested on a pillow, he was in a much more upright position and his color had returned. The only thing still connected was an IV drip.

"Hey," Gaeta said when he saw Kaye, "you're back."

"That I am," Kaye said. "How are you?"

"A lot better," Gaeta replied. "The doc says he'll probably discharge me tomorrow unless there's some kind of problem between now and then. I should be out of here by noon."

"Sounds like you were really lucky."

"That's what the Doc says, too. I'm nowhere near a hundred percent, but I can take it easy someplace else for a lot less money and let them have their bed back."

"That's why I'm here," Kaye said. "What are your plans?"

"I'm going to stay with my old roommate, at least until I'm solid on my crutches and it's safe for me to fly. Maybe another week, tops."

"Instead of your roommate's place, how would you, and him, like to enjoy the LAPD's hospitality at one of our exclusive guest houses for the weekend?"

Gaeta gave Kaye a skeptical look.

"Okay," Kaye continued, pulling a chair over and sitting down. "Here's the deal. The Tiger Boys apparently have an L.A. chapter, and it looks like they knew ahead of time exactly when you'd be coming down to get your bike."

Gaeta instantly connected the dots.

"Sounds like Detective Magnuson was right."

"I agree," Kaye said. "My first priority is your safety. My second, though, is to find out how the information leaked."

"And you have a plan."

"I do," Kaye said, then explained it to Gaeta, who nodded as he listened.

"That's a good idea," Gaeta said when Kaye had finished. "But what do we do if Monday rolls around and nothing has happened?"

"We'll have to assume that the Tiger Boys think you're dead based on the news stories we planted. If that's the case, you and Tina Magnuson will have to sit down and figure out how to go forward once you're back in Berkeley."

Gaeta was quiet for a moment before saying, "You know what's really funny? I wasn't even going to go for a run that morning. I'd worked really late the night before debugging some code and I wanted to sleep in a little bit." He looked at Kaye. "See what discipline gets you?"

"If we believe that tomorrow will be better, we can bear a hardship today," Kaye said softly.

Gaeta looked at him, surprised. "You know Thich Nhat Hahn?"

"I know what my Roshi taught me."

"He must be wise."

"He was," Kaye said. "He died recently."

It was the first time Kaye had acknowledged and shared the news of Roshi's death with anyone, and he found himself wondering why it had been with Neil Gaeta.

"I'm very sorry," Gaeta said softly.

Silence enveloped the two men. It was Kaye who finally broke it.

"All right," he said, standing. "I'll leave it to you to call your former roommate and recruit him. What's his name again?"

"Mike Fisher."

"Got it. And make sure Mike understands that this really isn't optional. He and his family are in danger. I'll be there tomorrow to pick him up, and we'll come get you together."

"He'll understand," Gaeta said. "What about Alina? Can I call her?"

"I'd rather you didn't," Kaye said. "At least not yet. Let's keep the circle as small was possible."

"Makes sense."

Kaye headed for the door, turning around before he left the room. "See you tomorrow."

As soon as Kaye got to the Harley, he made a call to Tina Magnuson.

"Tina, hi. It's Ben."

"Oh, hi. What's up?"

"Are you someplace you can speak freely?"

"I am."

"Good," Kaye said. "Neil Gaeta is being discharged from the hospital tomorrow, and I want to run a flea flicker to try and keep him safe. Maybe even find out if you, or we, have a leak."

"Flea flicker, huh?" Magnuson said, chuckling. "I'm all ears."

"What I need you to do tomorrow, no earlier than noon, is find Chen and tell her Gaeta's out of the hospital and will be staying with his old roommate at the same house where he was hiding when you came down. And do it where other people can hear you."

"You're not using him as bait, are you?" Magnuson asked. "Because if you are, I'm not buying this."

"Not directly," Kaye told her. "The only people in the house will be cops. I'll have everybody else stashed in a safe house I borrowed from our Narcotics and Gang Unit."

"Okay, I get it," Magnuson said. "Good idea. Kills two birds with one stone. Can you tell me where this safe house is?"

"I could, but I'm not going to. I want that to be a choke point."

"Understood. Anything else I need to do?"

"Nope. Just blab around about Gaeta as much as you can, but not until after noon, and maybe we can lure the Tiger Boys out."

"Got it. Keep me in the loop."

"Will do," Kaye said. "Thanks, Tina."

Kaye immediately called J.J.'s cell number.

"Jefferies."

"J.J., it's Ben. Are you at the station?"

"Yeah."

"Is Burke there?"

"Not right this instant, but she's in the building and should be back in a minute. Why?"

"Neil Gaeta's being discharged tomorrow," Kaye said. "I need to sit down with you both and finalize our plans. Can you hang out until I get there? Shouldn't be too long."

"We'll be here."

Kaye fired up the '41 and headed for the station. When he walked into the squad room J.J. and Burke were both already parked close to his desk.

"We have a 'go'?" Burke asked.

"We do," Kaye said as he sat down. "Gaeta gets discharged tomorrow morning. I'm going to pick up his roommate before I pick him up and take everyone to the safe house together. I'd like you both to meet me at the roommate's house so the roommate, Mike Fisher, can meet you before he leaves you alone in his house for the weekend."

"The entire weekend?" J.J. asked.

"I know," Kaye said, "but I don't think it'll come to that. I've already talked to Magnuson and she's going to chum the waters up north when the time is right. If anything is going to happen, my guess is it'll be tomorrow night."

"I sure hope so," J.J. said. "I'm supposed to take my wife to the Hollywood Bowl on Sunday."

"You'll make it," Kaye assured him. "If it's still quiet on Sunday morning, we'll call it."

"What about relief?" Burke asked. "Back-up? Food?"

"The Captain said he'd take care of it when we had a firm timeline," Kaye replied. "He's my next stop."

"Where will you be?" J.J. asked.

"I'll be at the safe house," Kaye replied. "I can't leave Gaeta and Fisher uncovered in case there's more going on here than we know and things really go in the toilet."

"Okay, then," Burke said dramatically, rolling her eyes. "I guess I'll go home and tell my husband I'm spending the weekend with another man." She giggled.

"I'm not saying a word to my wife about you," J.J. blurted, then laughed.

When J.J. and Burke went their separate ways, Kaye headed for Thompson's office. The two sat and hammered out the logistical details for Kaye's operation.

"I'm not good with Jefferies and Burke not having back-up outside and close by," Thompson said. "What if these Tiger Boys show up in force?"

"I don't think they will," Kaye said. "But if we have a couple extra bodies, that's a good idea. Just tell them not to make themselves too obvious."

Thompson gave Kaye a look and said, "I have done this a time or two, you know."

"Did I say that out loud?" Kaye said, smiling as he stood up. "Sorry… Doctor Thompson."

"Very funny, Detective. I hope my laughter isn't too loud for you."

Back at his desk, Kaye started organizing his priorities. One downside of his plan was that it essentially took him off the Valerie Weber case until Monday, and there was one thing he really needed to chase down first.

He grabbed the phone and called the Weber residence.

"Hello," JoAnn answered.

"Mrs. Weber, Detective Kaye."

"Oh, hello Detective. Are you calling with news?"

"In a way. I was wondering if I could stop by in a while and talk to you."

"Of course," JoAnn said. "I'll be here, but I'm not sure what time Gunther will get home."

"That's okay. If he's there, that's fine, but he doesn't need to be."

"I'll see you when you get here."

***

Kaye rolled up and parked the '41 just as Miles Weber turned into the driveway. He waited for Kaye to walk up the sidewalk to the front door.

"Cool motorcycle," Miles said, staring at the '41. "What kind is it?"

"Harley-Davidson," Kaye replied.

"I've never seen a Harley like that," Miles said.

"That's probably because it was manufactured before your grandfather was born."

"No shit? Really?" Miles asked excitedly. "Where'd you get it?"

"A friend gave it to me," Kaye replied as memories of Cynthia and Michael Graham flashed through his mind. "I restored it."

"That is too cool," Miles said. "Mind if I check it out?"

"Sure, but don't touch, okay? It's a lot different than the new ones."

"I'll keep my hands in my pockets, I promise. Hey, come on in first and I'll tell my Mom you're here."

Miles opened the front door and stood aside as Kaye entered. Then, without closing the door, he walked to the bottom of the stairs and shouted, "Mom, Detective Kaye is here."

"I'll be right down," JoAnn's voice came from upstairs.

"You can go in and sit down," Miles said to Kaye.

"Thanks, Miles. Remember, hands in pockets."

Miles smiled broadly and went out the front door, closing it this time.

As Kaye walked into the front room, he saw Miles bee-lining it down the sidewalk to the '41.

"Sorry to keep you waiting," JoAnn said from behind Kaye, causing him to spin around. She had a look of nervous anticipation on her face, and her hands were clasped.

"No problem," Kaye said. "I've been here about five seconds."

"Do you have news?" The hands started twisting.

"Some, but there's something I have to ask you first."

"Of course. Shall we sit down?"

JoAnn stepped around him and sat down in the same spot on the couch she'd occupied when Kaye had delivered the news of Valerie's death. Kaye opted for an arm chair across the coffee table.

"Didn't Miles come in?" JoAnn asked, looking around.

"He's out looking at my motorcycle."

"That kid is motorcycle crazy," JoAnn said with a laugh. "He's been pestering us for months to buy him one."

"Has he taken a riding course?"

"He did, and passed the test to get an endorsement. But Gunther won't hear of it. He told Miles that when he finishes school and gets a job with health insurance, if he still wants a motorcycle he can buy one for himself."

"Sounds reasonable to me," Kaye said.

"Enough about Miles," JoAnn said. "How can I help you today?"

"I wanted to ask you about Valerie's adoption."

"Oh," JoAnn said, her eyes going wide. "Of course. I'll answer the best I can."

"Thank you," Kaye said. "Did you adopt Valerie through Social Services?"

"No," JoAnn replied. "We went through a private agency."

"Do you remember the name?"

"Um… It was… Sunshine Adoptions? Sunbeam Adoptions?" She hesitated. "Something with Sun in it. I'm sorry, it was so long ago."

"That's okay," Kaye said. "Do you remember where it was?"

"Van Nuys."

"Do you remember who your case worker was?"

"I don't remember her name," JoAnn said. "But she was very nice. Guided us through the entire process."

"Did the agency have a child for you to adopt when you first contacted them?"

"They did not. And, honestly, it doesn't work that way, or at least it didn't back then. We had to apply, go through a background investigation, pay all kinds of fees upfront – it was very expensive – and then wait."

"How long did you wait?" Kaye asked.

"Almost six months."

"Do you remember when the adoption was finalized?"

"October seventeenth," JoAnn said instantly, hesitated a beat, then added the year.

"When you filed the original report on Valerie's beating, you gave the officers July eleventh as her date of birth. Is that right?"

"Of course it's right," JoAnn said, indignation creeping into her voice. "We have a birth certificate. The agency assured us it was the date on the original, which was then sealed, and the new one was issued with us listed as her legal parents. Why would you ask me that? Is there some kind of problem with the adoption?"

"I'm just cross-checking, Mrs. Weber."

"Is that 'no', there's no problem?" JoAnn asked. "Or 'yes', there's a problem?"

"There's no problem that I'm aware of," Kaye replied.

"Well, there's a problem I'm aware of, Detective," she said angrily. "And you're it. You can't seem to find whoever killed my daughter and now you're questioning me. I think I'd like you to leave."

Kaye stood and headed for the door.

"I'm sorry if I upset you," he said before he pulled the front door open. "Thanks for your time. I'll stay in touch."

JoAnn stood stock still, arms folded, glaring at him with tear-filled eyes.

Miles was heading up the sidewalk as Kaye headed down.

"Your bike is awesome," Miles said. "How much would one like that cost?"

"Depends," Kaye said absently, still thinking about JoAnn. "If you can even find one, there are a lot of variables."

"How much would you sell that one for?"

"I wouldn't sell it. It means too much to me."

"Even for a million bucks?" Miles asked.

"Not even for a million bucks," Kaye replied, then added, "Hey, Miles, do me a favor and go check on your Mom to see if she's okay. I think I upset her. Tell her I'm sorry."

"Huh?" Miles said, taking a moment to process what Kaye had said. "Oh, okay, sure." He hurried up the sidewalk, took the four steps to the porch in one bound and opened the door.

Kaye heard him shout, "Mom!" before he turned and headed for the million dollar '41.

CHAPTER 20

Kaye drove the pickup to work. He bagged a few provisions and went first to the safe house to drop them off and reconnoiter the house and neighborhood.

He drove slowly down the street, searching for the house number Thompson had given him. It was the last house on his left before the street turned right and paralleled the tall concrete barrier separating the neighborhood from the Santa Monica Freeway. Tall Eucalyptus trees that anchored the landscaping on the other side towered above the wall, casting a hodgepodge of shadows on the pavement as he circled the block.

The house was a boxy, 'T'-shaped two-story, the second floor obviously an add-on. The edge of the concrete driveway butted up against the freeway barrier. A six-foot wrought iron fence, the vertical pieces close enough together to keep out everyone but Gumby and arrow tips to discourage climbing, extended from the barrier across the front of the house to a common corner post shared with the house next door. Arrivals would first need to get inside the fence in order to get to the front door.

There was no enclosed garage, but the second story addition, supported by stout metal columns, extended over the driveway to create a double-depth carport accessible only through a locked gate in the wrought iron fence. In front of the carport, on the concrete apron near the freeway barrier, a taller column was topped by a good-sized streetlamp.

Not bad, Kaye thought as he let himself in and walked the property. Limited access, good protection, no windows on the freeway side of the house and only one easily blocked access point for vehicles.

The back yard was separated from the neighbors by a six-foot chain link fence that extended all the way across the back to the freeway barrier.

There were a couple of vulnerabilities, if whoever wanted to get in was determined enough. Someone with help and the right equipment could scale the barrier from the freeway side, using the buffer landscaping for cover, and Kaye guessed the distance from barrier to the closest rooftop to be about eight feet. He knew he could easily make that jump. The far back corner of the lot on the freeway side had a six foot stretch of fence that was accessible from the next street over without entering the neighbor's yard, and from there the back door, which was actually on the side of the house, was accessible.

Kaye let himself in.

Not the Four Seasons, he thought as he looked around, *but it'll do for a couple nights.*

Kaye did a cursory walk-through of the house. Upstairs bedrooms would do to house Mike Fisher and his family, depending on who he brought with him. Given his crutches, the stairs would likely be an obstacle for Gaeta, but the small powder room tucked under the stairs meant he could stay downstairs with Kaye.

Five minutes later he was headed off to meet J.J. and Burke.

***

Two unmarked LAPD units, one silver and one white, were parked outside Mike Fisher's place when Kaye rolled up.

He knocked lightly on the front door, then let himself in. J.J., Burke and two casually dressed men Kaye wouldn't have pegged for cops had they not been wearing belt badges and sidearms all stood together in the center of the living room. A man Kaye assumed was Fisher sat on the couch watching TV, a blue backpack on the cushion next to him. The man saw Kaye, turned the television off and stood up.

"Mike Fisher," he said, extending his hand. "You must be Detective Kaye. I thought Neil was exaggerating, but…" He smiled lopsidedly.

"Nice to meet you, Mr. Fisher," Kaye said, shaking hands. "Thanks for agreeing to do this."

"Call me Mike. And no thanks is necessary. Neil and I go way back. I'd walk through fire for him."

"You two roomed together in college?" Kaye asked.

"We did. Three years."

"Are you a computer guy, too?"

"Hardly," Fisher said with a laugh. "I'm a photographer."

"Really?" Burke spoke up, looking around the room. "Are any of these your work?"

"Not all of them," Fisher said modestly. "Just a few. No artist wants a house full of his own work."

"Wow," Burke said, "You're good."

"Thanks."

"You and Neil make unlikely friends," Kaye said. "Artist and computer guy."

"Don't sell Neil short," Fisher said. "He's a creative genius, he just uses zeroes and ones instead of lenses or pigments."

"Never thought of it that way," Kaye admitted, then turned to the two officers he didn't know. "And you guys are…?"

"Tito Salazar," the shorter, heavier man introduced himself.

"Will Schroeder," the other man said.

"And you work where?" Kaye asked.

"Gang unit," Salazar answered. "Lonzo's our boss."

"I appreciate you coming out," Kaye said. "What's your plan?"

"We just stopped by to meet everybody face-to-face so we don't shoot each other later," Schroeder said, smiling. "Then we're gone until it gets dark. When we come back we'll be in a different ride and find a good spot close-by where we can watch without being obvious."

The West Bureau squad detectives and the Gang Unit detectives spent a couple minutes exchanging cell numbers and confirming radio frequencies, then Salazar and Schroeder took their leave.

"Nice to meet you guys," Salazar said on the way out. "Nothing personal, but we hope we don't see you again soon." He grinned and pulled the front door closed behind him.

Kaye turned to Fisher. "Have you talked to Neil today?"

"I have," Fisher said, nodding. "He said the doc put in the discharge order, the nurse has been through the check-list with him, and he can leave whenever he wants to after," he glanced at his watch, "right about now."

"Who all's coming?" Kaye asked. "Don't you have a wife and child?"

"It's just me," Fisher replied. "My wife and daughter went to her mom's place for the duration. I figured it was safer."

Kaye turned to J.J. "You all set?"

"Ready as we'll ever be," J.J. replied. "You're not planning on walking Gaeta out the hospital front door, right?"

Kaye smiled. "I've got to make a phone call before I can answer that."

"Let us know when you get to the safe house," Burke said.

"Will do," Kaye said, then turned back to Fisher. "Let's go. We don't want to keep the man waiting."

***

171

Traffic was lighter than Kaye had anticipated and they made it to the hospital in good time. Before he looked for a parking place, he found a spot to pull over and grabbed his cell phone.

"Hey, it's Ben," he said when the call was answered. "Did you get a chance to spread the word?"

He listened for several seconds, then said, "Good. Thanks. I'll let you know what happens,"

He ended the call and saw a bewildered look on Fisher's face.

"The game is officially on," he told Fisher. "Now all we have to do is wait."

He found a parking place not too far out, and he and Fisher headed upstairs.

"Why don't you go tell Neil we're here," Kaye said as they approached the nurses' station. "I'll be right there."

"Okay," Fisher said and headed down the hall.

When Fisher was out of earshot Kaye leaned in and asked the nurse, "Has anyone else been interested in Mr. Gaeta this morning? The press, relatives, anybody?"

The nurse glanced down and checked a call log. "Not that showed up here," he said. "We don't give out patient information over the phone, anyway, so…"

"That's what I thought. Thanks." He headed for Gaeta's room.

The hospital wouldn't budge on their policy that discharged patients were taken to the exit in a wheelchair, but Kaye did convince the staff member not to use the main entrance, and to wait inside with Gaeta and Fisher until he brought the truck around. Even then, he took a circuitous route through the parking lot, keeping his eye out for suspicious vehicles, looking particularly for any with two occupants that looked to be killing time. He saw nothing out of the ordinary.

Gaeta was still on crutches and Fisher stayed close to make sure his friend didn't take an untimely tumble. Gaeta went into the back seat so he could stretch out his leg.

"Where're we going?" Gaeta asked, making eye contact with Kaye in the rearview mirror.

"The Four Seasons," Kaye replied, smiling into the mirror as he started the truck.

"Sounds good to me," Gaeta said sarcastically. "Probably a lot cheaper than the place I just checked out of."

Fisher snorted and twisted in his seat to look at his friend. "No joke," he said. "And the food's probably better, too."

Kaye took several alternate routes and evasive actions as they headed for the safe house, keeping a close watch for any possible surveillance. He concluded that if anyone was tailing them, it had to be at least a three-car team and he doubted even the Tiger Boys had those kinds of resources.

At least he hoped they didn't.

"Stay in the truck," Kaye said as he pulled into the driveway and stopped outside the gate.

"I don't know," Gaeta deadpanned as Kaye got out. "The Four Seasons in The City looks nicer than this."

"Don't let it fool you," Kaye teased back. "Very hush hush, geared for celebrity types that want to avoid the paparazzi."

"And the guys with guns," Fisher chimed in.

Kaye grinned at Fisher and said, "There is definitely that."

Fifteen minutes later the truck was locked under the carport and Gaeta was settled on the living room couch watching TV. Fisher had taken his backpack upstairs and called his wife to check in. When he came back down he cornered Kaye in the kitchen.

"No way Neil can do those steps," he said quietly so Gaeta wouldn't overhear him. "I see one couch. Where will you sleep?"

"I'll be fine," Kaye replied. "Besides, even if Neil was upstairs, I'd be down here keeping an eye on things."

"But you're expecting the bad guys to try my house, right?"

"I hope they don't try either place, but, yeah, that's the plan," Kaye said. "We should have a nice, boring evening."

"Okay, just let me know if there's anything you need me to do."

"Thanks, Mike."

Fisher went back to the living room to keep Gaeta company and Kaye called J.J.

"It's me," Kaye said when J.J. answered. "How's it going?"

"All quiet on the decoy front," J.J. replied. "Your end?"

"Same here. Nothing suspicious at the hospital or on the way here."

"Did you talk to Magnuson?"

"I did," Kaye confirmed. "She put the word out right on time."

"So now we just wait."

"Yep," Kaye said, checking the time. "How's Burke doing?"

"She's just hanging out. Said to tell Fisher he's got a great video game system."

Kaye chuckled. "I'll pass it along. Just tell her not to break anything."

J.J. laughed.

"Call me if anything happens, and text me in an hour if everything's quiet," Kaye reminded him.

"Will do."

It turned into a long evening.

Kaye got a text from a bored J.J. every hour, and about a half-hour after dark he got a call from Salazar reporting that he and Schroeder were on station outside Fisher's house, had checked in with J.J. and would stay until J.J. cut them loose.

Fisher took charge of caring for Gaeta, organizing the medications and making him comfortable on the barely long enough couch, getting him what he needed and helping him up and down when the need arose.

For his part, Kaye patrolled the house, checking the outside and fretting, mostly because he thought somebody had to. He would much rather have been at Fisher's, lying in wait for the Tiger Boys instead of being the babysitter, but his was the one-man job and he hadn't wanted to break the nascent partnership bond between J.J. and Amari Burke or crush Burke's confidence by pulling her from her first potentially dangerous assignment.

Just after 11:00 p.m. Fisher woke Gaeta and gave him his medications. Gaeta, his leg propped on pillows, went back to sleep almost immediately.

"I'm going to bed," Fisher then told Kaye. "Neil can't take any more prescriptions until morning. He can have aspirin or anything OTC if he needs something. If you hear voices upstairs, it's just me. I'm going to call my wife and say goodnight."

"Got it," Kaye said. "I, and the LAPD, can't thank you enough for doing this."

Fisher shrugged and said, "Hey, it's Neil," then headed up the stairs.

Kaye turned off all the exterior lights, let himself out the back door and did another lap around the house without going outside the fence. He was surprised by the level of ambient noise produced by the freeway traffic and was glad to be living where he lived. He stood in the darkness at the corner of the house farthest from the freeway and watched the neighborhood for a few minutes.

One car came down the street and turned into a driveway several doors up on the opposite side and Kaye watched the occupants get out and go inside. He saw no other cars, walkers with or without dogs, joggers, nothing.

Right on schedule his phone lit up with a text from J.J.

'Hope it's more exciting there than it is here.'

'It's not, and I'm good with that', he answered.

'Yeah, probably better than the alternative. I'll check
  back in an hour.'

'I'll be here.'

'Oh, for the record, Burke is not a night person. LOL'

Kaye wandered around for a few more minutes before heading inside. He turned the carport light and back porchlight back on, left the front porch lights off, then went to the living room to check on Gaeta.

Sleeping like a baby, he thought enviously. *With a broken leg.* The envy dissolved.

Two overstuffed chairs flanked the living room couch, facing the space that had been occupied by a coffee table until Fisher dragged it aside to make things easier for Gaeta. Kaye sat down in the one that basically faced the front door and leaned his head back against the cushion.

Why so jumpy? No Tiger Boys here. I'm babysitting. Lighten up.

The noise that woke him was metallic, or at least he thought it had been once he was awake. He listened carefully, but the sound didn't repeat. All he could hear was Gaeta's quiet breathing. Thinking maybe it had been Fisher opening or closing the refrigerator door, he got up and walked quietly to where he could see into the kitchen, dimly lit by the range vent hood light.

No Fisher.

Maybe the upstairs bathroom door.

He turned and went to the stairs, stopping at the bottom to listen.

Nothing.

Check it.

He started upstairs just as his phone lit up.

'All quiet here. U?'

'Stand by.'

'???'

'Stray noise. 0'

'Let me know.'

'10-4'

He continued up the stairs and saw light seeping from under the bathroom door.

While he stood watching, he thought he heard the noise again, fainter this time, and the light under the door disappeared.

He waited for Fisher to come out, but the door stayed closed.

He glanced back over his shoulder and saw that the downstairs was completely dark. The light in the kitchen had gone off.

Shit!

He knew what the noise was.

He grabbed his phone and punched in 9-1-1.

"What's your emergency?" the dispatcher asked.

"This is Detective Kaye, West Bureau," he whispered, then gave her his badge number and location. "I need assistance, Code Three. Plainclothes officer on site. Repeat, plainclothes officer on site."

"Ten-four Detective. Please stay on the line."

"Can't do that," he said tersely, hearing the sound of the back doorknob being twisted. "I'm about to have intruders." He drew his Kimber.

The dispatcher said nothing to him, but he heard her broadcast.

Then to Kaye she said, "Cavalry's coming, Detective."

Kaye ended the call and silenced his phone as he descended as quietly as possible, stuffing the phone under the cushion of the chair he'd been sitting in.

Raising the Kimber to chest level in a two-hand grip, he shuffle-stepped toward the kitchen and stopped just short of entering. He listened for the sound of the knob turning, but heard nothing.

Where are the goddamn sirens?

He turned and stepped quickly to the front window and peered through the small opening between the drapes and the wall. The light on the post outside the carport was off, but he could see working lights on other houses.

Power's been cut.

Pistol ready, he took a position where he could cover Gaeta and both doors.

Just as he heard the first, faint sound of an approaching siren, it was drowned out by the sound of breaking glass upstairs. He abandoned his position and quickly crossed the living room to the stairs, going up only far enough to get a clear field of fire down the hallway. With only a small movement of his head he was also able to see the living room down and behind him.

He hadn't been on the stairs for five seconds when he heard the door to Fisher's room open and saw Mike step partway into the hall and look around.

At the same instant another figure stepped partway through the door of the bedroom between the top of the stairs and where Fisher was standing. Both arms were extended downward at a forty-five-degree angle, hands clasped.

Fisher saw the other figure first, shouted, "Ben!" at the top of his lungs before starting to retreat into the bedroom.

Kaye saw the second figure spin toward Fisher and the hands start to come up.

"Mike, get back!" Kaye shouted as he raised the Kimber.

Fisher froze, stunned.

Kaye's shout also distracted the intruder, who started to spin toward Kaye and raise his hands, arms straight. Kaye saw the pistol.

Just before Kaye fired twice, he registered the sound of breaking glass coming from the kitchen.

The intruder in the upstairs hall managed to squeeze off one shot before crumpling to the floor.

Kaye spun and leapt down to the living room floor, ducking his head to gain clearance. He ended up in a half-crouch and stayed there.

Another intruder, this one with a flashlight and only partly visible from Kaye's position, stood just outside the kitchen in a spot where the dining room and living room were visible. The intruder extended the flashlight, it's beam settling on Gaeta, and in its dim glow Kaye could see the gun braced against the back of the hand that held it.

His hearing dulled by the shots fired in the narrow stairway, Kaye thought he heard a siren, much closer this time, as he raised the Kimber and fired again.

The flashlight wavered and the figure disappeared back into the kitchen.

Kaye saw movement and looked at the couch. Neil Gaeta was bolt upright, and even in the darkened room Kaye could see his wide-open eyes. He held a finger in front of his lips to tell Gaeta to stay quiet as he crab-walked toward the kitchen, pistol ready. He hadn't gone far before he could see the flashlight beam shining at an angle that told him it was laying on the floor. Another step and he made out a foot at the end of a motionless leg. As he watched, the foot moved and then pulled back out of sight.

A sound caught his attention and he spun toward the stairs, ready to fire again, and saw Mike Fisher standing partway down, bending down to see into the living room. Kaye, keeping a wary eye on the kitchen, held out his hand, palm toward Fisher, to tell the man not to come down any farther.

Fisher nodded, used his right hand to point back over his shoulder, then used his left hand to make a slashing movement across his throat.

One down, one to go, Kaye thought, nodding at Fisher.

Kaye could now hear multiple sirens rapidly approaching. He heard the sound of a vehicle parked out front start, then accelerate hard up the street away from the freeway.

"Game over," Kaye said to whoever was in the kitchen. "Your buddy's dead, you're down, and I think I just heard your ride leave without you. Toss your gun out where I can see it and crawl out into the dining room.

"I can't, I'm shot," a male voice answered.

"I certainly hope so," Kaye said darkly. "But you're not dead. Yet. I saw you move. Toss the gun and crawl out, hands empty."

"I can't," the voice repeated, defiant this time. "My leg don't work."

"You don't throw with your foot. Toss the gun, then roll onto your stomach and put your hands straight out to your sides."

"Okay, okay, just don't shoot me."

Too late, moron, Kaye thought. Before he could say anything else, the windows on the front of the house lit up with the glare of spotlights and a voice came over a megaphone.

"This is the Los Angeles Police Department. The house is surrounded. Detective Kaye, if you are able, call Dispatch now. You have thirty seconds."

Kaye considered his options before carefully back-stepping, pistol still trained toward the kitchen, until he was able to grab his phone from under the chair cushion. He again dialed 9-1-1.

"This is Detective Kaye," he whispered to the dispatcher that answered, again giving his badge number and location. "I have units standing by outside. I have one suspect dead and one down, still alive. No other injuries. A vehicle left here northbound just before the units arrived. I don't have a description. The situation is stable, but unresolved, and I can't get to a door without exposing myself to an armed suspect. I need a few minutes."

"Ten-four, Detective. I'll relay the information to the Sergeant at the scene. Can you stay on the line?"

"I can leave the call open, but I need my hands."

"That's fine."

Kaye put the phone on the coffee table near his previous vantage point as he listened to the dispatcher relay information to the units outside. As his sight angle improved, he saw a blue steel pistol under one of the chairs around the dining table.

"Detective?" The dispatcher came back on the line.

"I'm here," he said.

"I put out a BOLO on the possible vehicle, but it's pretty thin. The scene commander says he'll stand by for another five minutes before he calls SWAT."

"That should be enough. Tell them not to shoot me when I open the front door."

"I already did."

Kaye ended the call and listened for sounds from the kitchen, hearing nothing.

"I'm guessing you heard most of that," he said loudly. "We've got about four minutes before this is out of my hands. What's it gonna be?"

"I'm lyin' on my stomach, just like you told me to. I give up, man."

Cautiously, Kaye moved toward a spot from where he'd be able to see into the kitchen. He knew he'd be momentarily backlit when he crossed in front of one of the windows, but there was nothing he could do about it except by ready.

Don't let him have another gun.

The suspect was prone on the kitchen floor, arms straight out to his sides and hands empty. Kaye holstered his pistol, moved in, handcuffed the man and did a quick search for other weapons.

This isn't a man. He's just a kid.

"Where are you hit?" he asked after the kid was secure.

"My hip," the kid said through gritted teeth.

Kaye reached out, grabbed the kid's flashlight off the floor and used it to examine the wound. It was bleeding, but would wait for paramedics.

"In case you were wondering, you're under arrest. Lie still," Kaye ordered. On the way to the front door he grabbed the pistol from under the dining room chair, made it safe, and tucked it into his waistband. He unlocked the front door, stood to one side, pulled and let it swing wide open.

"Sergeant, this is Detective Kaye," he shouted. "I'm Code Four, one in custody. I need an ambulance and a coroner."

"Step outside, Detective, hands above your head," a voice shouted, no megaphone this time.

Kaye sat the flashlight on an end table and complied. He was immediately bathed in light. "I've got one dead upstairs and one wounded and handcuffed on the kitchen floor," he said. "The other two are friendlies."

"We're coming in," the voice said.

"Please do," Kaye said, then turned around and went back inside, grabbing the flashlight again.

Neil Gaeta, his eyes wide, was as white as the sheet that now lay on the floor.

"You okay?" Kaye asked as he drew back the curtains to let some light in.

Gaeta nodded and managed to croak, "Yeah, I think so."

Two uniformed officers stepped through the front door and surveyed the scene.

"There's a prisoner cuffed on the floor in there," Kaye said, pointing to the kitchen. "You can keep an eye on him for me, but don't move him until the medics take a look at him."

"Yes, sir," one of them said as they headed for the kitchen.

Kaye bounded up the stairs. The other shooter, his sightless eyes staring at the ceiling, lay halfway in the hallway and halfway in the bedroom with the broken window. From the looks of things, both of Kaye's shots had found center mass. He found the dead man's gun underneath one leg, made it safe, and slid it into his waistband next to the other one.

"Mike," he said loudly as he knocked on the back bedroom door, "you can come out. We're all good."

Fisher opened the door a crack and peeked out. "You sure?"

"Yeah, the troops are here."

"Neil's okay?"

"A little pale," Kaye replied. "Like me, probably." He smiled, turned around, and went back downstairs.

The Sergeant in charge, his name badge proclaiming him to be 'Simmons', was standing in the living room.

"First things first," he said to Kaye. "Did a vehicle flee the scene right before we got here?"

"Yes," Kaye told him. "I heard somebody haul ass out of here about then. Why?"

"Two units have a suspicious vehicle stopped about a mile from here. Silver Expedition, tricked out, custom wheels. One occupant too stupid to slow down and remember to turn his lights on."

"Arrest him and impound the vehicle. In the inventory search have them look for weapons."

"You're sure?" Simmons asked skeptically. "Solid PC?"

"Yeah," Kaye said. "The vehicle description matches what the suspects were driving when they shot him," he pointed to Gaeta, "the first time. They came to give it another try."

"Sounds good to me," Simmons said, then stepped away to radio the units on the stop and give them instructions.

Two medics, kits in hand, came through the front door and stopped to take stock of the scene before heading for Gaeta.

"Not him," Kaye told them, noticing Mike Fisher now collapsed in one of the armchairs. "The guy on the kitchen floor. GSW to the hip and, yeah, he's under arrest."

"You got more light than this?" one of the medics asked.

"No," Simmons spoke up, "the power's been cut. Just do the best you can with what you've got."

Kaye watched the organized chaos expand exponentially as more resources arrived over the next couple of minutes. He went and leaned against the wall, took out his cell, and called J.J.

"Are you guys okay?" he asked as soon as Jefferies answered.

"Quiet here," J.J. replied. "How are you? We heard what happened."

"Already?" Kaye could hear Burke in the background, asking rapid-fire questions J.J. ignored.

"Yeah," J.J. said to Kaye. "Salazar and Schroeder heard dispatch put out the officer needs help call and recognized the address. They came in right away, just in case."

"But no sign of Tiger Boys?"

"Nothing at all."

"Well, shit," Kaye muttered. "That's not good. Somebody knew Gaeta would be here, not there."

"Somebody's got a leak," J.J. said. "And it looks like it might be us."

CHAPTER 21

Kaye was at the scene until almost 5:00 a.m., dealing with the deputy coroner, the shooting team, and working closely with the forensics team on evidence collection. He tagged the two guns he'd recovered and turned them over to the team supervisor with instructions to get them to the ballistics lab as soon as possible.

His last task was arranging new accommodations for Gaeta and Fisher, which he solved by taking them to the Marriott in Beverly Hills and checking them into a suite until Monday.

Gaeta was too exhausted to stay awake through most of the process, but Fisher protested when he saw Kaye take a credit card out of his wallet to pay.

"I'll get reimbursed," Kaye assured him, not really caring if he did or not. "And it's worth it. Nobody but me will know where you are. Stay in the rooms and order room service. I'll be in touch on Monday."

Fisher was smart enough to have figured out that something had gone very wrong and simply told Kaye, "Thanks. I'll take care of Neil."

From the Marriott Kaye went back to the station and made phone calls. The wounded kid from the safe house was out of surgery and doing fine, except for being in the prisoners' ward. Sergeant Simmons gave him the specifics on the arrest of the Expedition driver, and that the man had been carrying when they hooked him up.

"He's also a convicted felon," Simmons added. "So you've got a firearms possession charge to work with, too, if you need it."

Three guns, Kaye thought. With luck, one of them will match the bullet taken out of Gaeta after the first shooting.

His last duty before going home was touching base with J.J. and Burke.

"Anything out of the ordinary?" he asked J.J.

"Nada. Quiet as a church on Monday. I cut Salazar and Schroeder loose a little after three. Hope that was okay."

"Why don't you and Burke go home, too," Kaye said.

"Sounds like a plan. Are we back tonight?"

"No, there's no point. By now somebody's figured out their guys screwed up, and they don't know where Gaeta is."

"Where'd you put him?"

"Privileged information."

J.J. laughed. "Good idea. What do we do about the security breach?"

"I don't know yet. We'll talk about it Monday. Have a nice weekend, what's left of it."

"Will do," J.J. said. "And, hey, Ben?"

"Yeah?"

"Nice work. Glad you're okay."

"Thanks. Get some sleep."

Kaye took his own advice, thinking on the way home, maybe for the first time ever, that he was glad he'd driven the truck. He was exhausted to the point where he wasn't sure he could have ridden home safely.

He slept deeply and dreamt vividly of sitting *zazen* with Roshi, each a student pondering the unanswerable koan of the Buddha's Zen. When the meditation ended, though, Roshi very uncharacteristically chose not to launch into a discussion of insights or breakthroughs.

Instead, he simply asked, "Benkei, are you happy?"

"Happiness, like all things, is transitory," Kaye replied in true Zen form.

Roshi laughed and clapped his hands.

"No, Benkei! A simple question. Are you happy?"

"In what way, Roshi-sama?"

Roshi laughed again. "Have I failed by wrongly teaching you that life is a riddle, a question to be answered with yet another question? It is not a trick question. Does your life bring you joy? Do you laugh with friends? Do you love?"

Kaye was nonplussed. This was not the Roshi he knew, and didn't know what to say.

"You clap with one hand, Benkei. I hear nothing."

Kaye tossed in his bed and moaned softly. When he settled, Roshi remained, staring intently at him.

"I am...content," Kaye told his mentor.

"Contentment and happiness are not the same things," Roshi said softly.

Kaye sat quietly for a moment, trying to decode this new approach.

"Is not the absence of unhappiness, happiness?" he finally asked.

"No, it is not," Roshi said. "Do you remember the koan of the master who filled a potential student's cup but continued to pour, spilling it everywhere?"

"I do. When the man protested, the master told him his mind was already too full to learn and sent him away, the message being that the man must return with an empty mind if he wanted to learn."

"Very good. It is a very powerful lesson," Roshi said. "But there is a real-life lesson there, too, if one thinks deeply in a more practical sense."

"What is that?" Kaye asked.

"A man must drink. A genuine thirst cannot be slaked with an empty cup."

Kaye tossed and moaned again, but still Roshi remained.

"Do not go thirsty on your journey through this life, Benkei, simply because the destination you seek is a waterfall. Destinations are not always reached."

"How can I be happy?" Kaye asked.

"I cannot answer that for you. I can only tell you that, in the truest sense, you cannot enjoy the rustle of the leaves when there is no wind, or detect the fragrance of the rose after its petals have fallen, if you have not first felt the wind blow through the forest or smelled the rose at its height."

"I think I understand," Kaye said uncertainly.

Roshi stared at him, then asked, "Do you know Rumi?"

"No."

"He was a great poet, philosopher and Sufi mystic of the thirteenth century. Some call him the Buddha of Islam. Do you know what he said of Buddha's Zen?"

Kaye shook his head.

Roshi looked deeply into Kaye's eyes and said, "Maybe you are searching among the branches for what only appears in the roots."

Kaye, unable to withstand Roshi's gaze, broke eye contact and looked down.

When he looked back up, Roshi was gone.

In his place sat Kaye's deceased father, wearing his dark blue factory uniform, the patch embroidered with his name – Matthew – above his left breast pocket, grinning like the cat that caught the canary.

"Good advice, Ben," Matthew Kaye said. "Stop and smell the roses."

The vision of his father faded into the deep as Kaye began to float toward the glittering surface of wakeful reality.

When he broke through, his dream, like those of most, was already half-forgotten.

CHAPTER 22

First thing Monday morning Kaye went looking for Captain Thompson, but the boss wasn't in his office.

Frustrated, Kaye changed tacks, called the lab and asked for Lou Ellen in firearms and ballistics.

"Lou Ellen, hi. Detective Kaye, West Bureau."

"Good morning, Detective," Lou Ellen said. "What can I do for you so bright and early?"

"You remember our conversation last week about the bullet you looked at that came from the shooting on Wilshire in Westwood?"

"Sure," she replied. "The Gaeta case. What about it?"

"Friday night here was another attempt on Gaeta's life," Kaye said. "The bad guys didn't get away this time. I recovered two handguns and Patrol recovered one. I did the paperwork to have them tested and compared, and I'm calling to ask if you would bump them up the list."

"Why?"

Kaye explained the situation, what he needed, and why. "If the guy bonds out before I get results, I'll probably never find him again."

"I think I saw the test requests when I got here this morning," Lou Ellen said slowly as Kaye heard the sound of papers being shuffled. "Yeah, here they are. Came in Saturday." She paused, then added, "I don't have the guns yet, though. Let me track them down and I'll get on it as soon as I can."

"That's all I can ask," Kaye said. "Thanks, Lou Ellen."

Kaye's next call was to Tina Magnuson in Oakland.

"Hi, Ben. What's up?"

Kaye related Friday night's events.

"Holy crap," Magnuson said. "And this all happened at your safe house, not the old roommate's place?"

"That's right."

"That's not good," Magnuson said. "Where's Gaeta now?"

"I've got him stashed. Proprietary information."

Magnuson was silent for a moment, then said, "Probably a good thing. Got any ideas on how the safe house location got blown?"

"Not yet," Kaye replied. "My Captain set it up, and he's not in yet. I'll start digging as soon as I talk to him."

"Anything I can do on this end?"

"You can tell me who else you told about the safe house."

"Hey, hold on just one minute," Magnuson protested. "I did exactly what you asked me to do. Nothing more, nothing less. Period. So don't go accusing me because you have a security problem."

"So you didn't say anything to anybody?"

"I did not," Magnuson said firmly.

"Leave a note, a doodle, anything, on your desk?"

"No, I... Oh, shit," Magnuson muttered. "I might have, damn it. But, Ben, it would've been a scribble that didn't mean anything to anybody else. Besides, you didn't give me the address, remember?"

"That's right, I forgot," Kaye said. "But somebody not only knew about the safe house, they got the address, too. In very short order."

"I'll dig around on my end," Magnuson said, "and I'll pass along anything I come up with."

"I'll start looking into it down here. By the way, how's the Li trial going?"

"Testimony wrapped up last Friday. Closing arguments start this morning and the jury should have it by Wednesday, maybe sooner depending on jury instructions."

"You think Gaeta could come home?"

"I think... maybe he should wait for a few days," Magnuson replied, then lowered her voice. "A little bird told me there might be a deal cut on the Li Case."

"And you think Gaeta's safety could be part of it?" Kaye asked.

"My little bird would neither confirm nor deny that."

"We can always hope," Kaye said. "I'll be in touch."

"Thanks for the call, Ben. Glad you're okay."

Kaye leaned back in his chair, mentally castigating himself for insulting Magnuson by forgetting he hadn't given her the safe house address. To him, that meant it had been leaked from inside the LAPD.

Not a comforting conclusion.

Movement caught his eye and he turned to see the Captain heading for his office. He waited briefly, then got up and followed.

"Morning, Captain," he said from the open door as the boss shrugged out of his suit jacket and hung it up.

"That it is," Thompson said tersely. "Happens every day after the sun comes up." He turned and glared at Kaye. "What do you want,

Detective?"

Taken aback, Kaye considered saying 'nothing' and retreating, but changed his mind.

"I need to talk to you about Friday night."

"I heard about that," Thompson said as he sank into his desk chair. "From the Chief. This morning. That and other things."

"Oh," was all Kaye could say.

"Oh? What's that supposed to mean?"

"It explains your rotten mood."

The Captain practically slammed his elbow down on the desk and rubbed his chin while staring at Kaye.

"I'm not in a rotten mood, Detective," he said obsequiously. "If you have pertinent Department business to discuss, please step into my office, have a seat and we'll talk. Otherwise, get the hell out." He smiled.

Kaye walked in and sat down.

"I need to know," he said, "who you talked to at the Gang and Narcotics unit about the safe house."

"Lieutenant Lenoir."

"Did you explain to him that the operation was confidential?"

The glare again, this time accompanied by a clenched jaw.

"Detective Kaye," Thompson said at last, "I'll spare you the embarrassment of listening to my response to your asinine question. If that's all you needed, get out."

"Yes, sir," Kaye said, rising to leave.

He was almost to the door when Thompson said, "Kaye", and he turned around.

"The son of a bitch broke his word," Thompson said bitterly. "Postponed the test and still had the balls to ask me to stay on."

"I'm not surprised," Kaye said.

"I've wasted time and am right back to square one."

Kaye didn't know what to say. "Captain," he said at last, "I'm probably not the best source for career advice, but, honestly, I think this all boils down to one question only you can answer."

"And what, pray tell, might that be?"

"I think you have to decide, rank or no rank, if you want to be the cop with a doctorate, or if you want to be a Professor who used to be a cop."

Thompson stared at him yet again and said, "Very clever, Detective. Is that one of those Zen riddles? Did that guy Roshi teach you how to do that?"

Kaye bit back his first response and said, instead, "Yes, he did."

"Well, I'll take it under consideration."

Kaye turned again to leave.

"Oh, and Kaye?"

"Sir?"

"Two things," Thompson said. "You've already been cleared on the Friday night thing, so keep doing what you do."

"Good to know," Kaye said, careful to keep his voice neutral. "And?"

"When you find out who leaked that address, bring me their head on a pike. It'll be my going away present to the Chief."

Kaye smiled. "I'll do that, Captain."

Kaye returned to his desk and saw an email notification on his monitor.

It was from Arch.

'Ben; Sorry, but the M.E. denied my request on the Valerie Weber DNA test. Said it was too expensive and too iffy just to establish paternity without more evidence linking it to the killer. He seemed to think it might just be something Weber's parents want, maybe for a civil action, and said that's not our job. I'll preserve the samples. If you get a solid link to a suspect, let me know and we can try again. Sorry. Arch.'

Kaye typed and sent a short reply.

'Arch, thanks for trying. I'll let you know if I come up with anything else. Ben.'

He checked the time, leaned back, and planned out the rest of his day. The first order of business was yet another phone call.

"Lonzo Rivera," the Gang Unit Sergeant answered.

"Lonzo, Ben Kaye. Got a minute?"

"Sure. You calling about Friday night's shit show?"

"I am" Kaye confirmed. "First, though, thanks for sending your guys to help."

Rivera laughed. "Yeah, to the wrong place."

"Not your fault. But that's why I'm calling. I talked to my Oakland PD contact and she swears she didn't breathe a word about the safe house to anyone. In fact, she reminded me that I never gave her the address in the first place."

Rivera was silent for a moment, then muttered, "Fuck me."

"Yeah," Kaye said. "My first thought, too. I talked to Thompson this morning. He told me it was Lieutenant Lenoir that set it up."

"Lenoir's a stand-up guy. I don't see —"

"I'm not saying he's the leak," Kaye interrupted. "But I've got to start someplace and his name came up first."

"You want me to transfer you to him?"

"No, I want to talk to him in person. Is he usually in the office?"

"Ninety percent of the time, yeah. He's here now."

"Okay, I'll try and get over there this afternoon," Kaye said, then hesitated a second before continuing. "And, hey, Lonzo? Don't mention to Lenoir that I'm stopping by."

"Jesus, Ben, you sound like Internal Affairs. You sure you don't want to just hand this over to them?"

"I do not. I had to shoot two guys, Lonzo, and I want to know who burned me."

"That I understand. Stop by my desk when you get here, okay?"

Rivera hung up without waiting for a response.

Kaye checked the time again and felt like the morning had gotten away from him. He decided to handle the Marriott over the phone instead of in person. Ten minutes later he'd paid for two more nights and updated Gaeta and Fisher on the situation. Neither was the least bit unhappy about a couple more days of hotel cable and room service.

One more call to make.

"Hello," a female voice answered.

"Hello," Kaye echoed. "May I speak to Mrs. O'Bannon, please?"

"This is Elise O'Bannon."

"Mrs. O'Bannon, my name is Ben Kaye. I'm a detective with the LAPD." He gave her his badge number and call back verification information.

"What can I do for you, Mr. Kaye?"

"I'm investigating an incident involving a student at Grove Charter, and your daughter's name came up. I was hoping to set up a time when I can stop by and talk to you and your husband."

"Audra's name came up in a police investigation?" O'Bannon asked. "There must be some sort of mistake."

Great, Kaye thought. *Another one of those parents.* He said, "Audra's not in trouble, Mrs. O'Bannon, but my information, which I consider reliable, is that she may have some knowledge of the incident I'm looking into. She might not even know what she knows, if that makes sense."

"Can you be more specific?"

"Not on the phone, Ma'am," he replied. "When would be a good time for me to stop by?"

"Uh…let me think," O'Bannon said slowly. "My husband is out of town and won't be back until –"

"I can speak with just you," Kaye interjected.

"Oh, okay," O'Bannon said. "Do you want to come by later today? Audra has an after school activity on Mondays, so she won't be home until later."

"I can be there by four."

"Do you need the address?"

"I have it. I'll see you at four this afternoon. If things change, I'll give you a call. And thank you."

Another time check, and Kaye began to wonder why he was doing it. He'd never been clock conscious before, at least as far as he remembered. Working by the clock was hardly the nature of the job. Some days were eight hours, some were twenty-four. You got done what you needed to get done, and if that inconvenienced someone, too bad for them.

He grabbed the Big Boar jacket and headed out.

After a brief stop at one of his favorite food trucks for a couple tacos, he headed for the Gangs and Narcotics Unit headquarters, found a parking place and headed inside.

Lonzo Rivera must have been watching for Kaye, because he was waiting just inside the door.

"Hey, right on time," Lonzo said, smiling as the two shook hands.

"You have news?" Kaye asked.

"Maybe," Lonzo said. "I poked around a little bit, and one of our P.A.s remembered taking a call a little after noon on Friday. The caller asked for Lenoir by name and the P.A. put her through."

"Doesn't that happen a lot?"

Rivera shrugged. "We all have direct numbers for our snitches and almost nobody calls the main number and asks for the brass by name. It was unusual enough that the P.A. remembered it, but it could be nothing. Could've been his mother and she forgot his number." Rivera laughed.

"Is he in?"

"Yeah."

"Care to introduce me?"

"Sure. Come on."

Rivera led Kaye deeper into the offices, stopping outside an open door and knocking on the door frame.

"What is it, Sergeant?" Kaye heard a voice he assumed was Lenoir.

"Sir, Detective Kaye from West Bureau is here," Rivera replied. "He'd like to talk to you, if you have a minute."

"Is this about the cluster fuck last Friday night?" Lenoir asked.

"I believe so, sir."

"Okay, send him in."

Rivera turned, stepped aside and motioned Kaye forward.

Kaye stepped into the office, giving Rivera a nod of thanks as he went by.

"Have a seat, Detective," the man behind the desk said, neither standing nor introducing himself. Had it not been for the nameplate on the desk, Kaye wouldn't have known who he was about to talk to.

He sat down and waited.

Lenoir finished signing some papers and looked up, "Sorry about that. Paperwork is out of control. Now, what can I do for you?"

"I'm looking into what happened last Friday night," Kaye replied, "and Captain Thompson told me he worked with you on setting up the safe house."

"Yes," Lenoir acknowledged. "He and I worked out the details. And you should know, Detective, that I've asked Internal Affairs to look into this. If we have a security problem, we need to plug it."

"Agreed," Kaye said. "I don't mean to sound insubordinate, Lieutenant, but did you share the safe house location with anyone? Inside or outside the unit or the department?"

"Why would you ask me that?"

"Just trying to be thorough, sir."

"Detective, your reputation precedes you. You don't work for me, but I would recommend that you follow protocols, let the system work, and see what IA comes up with."

"Not gonna happen," Kaye said bluntly. "When three guys show up at what's supposed to be a secure location and try to kill me, I'm not about to follow protocols and let the system work, because the system is only interested in finding somebody to point the finger at. I want the bad guys, not a scapegoat."

Lenoir stared at Kaye. "I see your point," he said finally. "Fill me in on what happened before Friday."

Kaye gave Lenoir the entire chain of events, from his arrest of Neil Gaeta at the Oakland PD's request to Gaeta being shot off his motorcycle on Westwood Boulevard to his plan to lay a trap for the suspects. The only thing he held back was Tina Magnuson's name.

"Solid plan," Lenoir remarked. "Should've worked."

"But it didn't," Kaye pointed out, staring at Lenoir, who broke eye contact. "Lieutenant," he went on after an awkward silence, "who else did you talk to?"

Kaye didn't think Lenoir was going to respond, so he said, "Sir, if we can nail this down before Internal Affairs gets rolling on it, we'll both be better off. Who'd you talk to last Friday afternoon?"

Lenoir leaned forward, put his elbows on his desk and rubbed his face.

Kaye knew the man was weighing his career options.

Lenoir put his hands down and looked at Kaye. "I talked to Lieutenant Chen at the Oakland PD gang task force."

"Did she call you, or did you call her?"

"She called me."

"Why? Do you know Chen?"

"Yeah. We met a couple years ago when we worked together on a legislative study committee in Sacramento. We've kept in touch."

"And you're sure it was Chen on the phone?"

"I have no reason to think it was anyone else," Lenoir replied. "It sounded like her. She called me by the right name – I use my middle name. She asked about my family, said we needed to get together. It was as much about catching up as it was about your operation. She had all the details of your set-up, by the way."

"Except the address of the safe house." Kaye took a chance.

Lenoir nodded and echoed Kaye. "Except the address of the safe house."

"And you gave it to her."

"I did," Lenoir confirmed. "Chen said, 'My task force needs Neil Gaeta and I'm responsible for his safety. I need the safe house address for the record, in case I have to cover my ass'. That's a direct quote."

"So it was Chen, not you, that brought up the safe house?" Kaye asked.

"Yes, I'm sure of it. I didn't mention it, she specifically brought it up."

"What did you do after you spoke to her?"

"I had Sergeant Rivera detail two of his people to the false target house in case the bad guys showed up there."

"I wondered about that," Kaye said. "What time did Chen call you?"

"I think, maybe, just before one? A little earlier, maybe?" Lenoir replied. "I remember Rivera coming back almost right away and telling me his people were on site at the decoy location."

"Do you still have the number she called from?"

"No," Lenoir said gloomily. "It came to me as a transfer."

"You said you've kept in touch with Chen. So you must have her contact info."

"I do. It's on my personal cell, in my locker."

"Go get it," Kaye said.

Lenoir rose and left the office, returning a moment later with his cell phone. He sat down, tapped on the home screen, then read to Kaye what he had for Chen's contact numbers.

"The first number sounds familiar," Kaye said. "I think it's the Oakland PD internal number."

"Want me to call her?" Lenoir asked.

"No," Kaye said quickly. "Let's keep her in the dark for now. It could've been Chen that called you, and she played you. Or it could've been someone close to her that got your information and used it. If it was her, we don't want her to know we're suspicious. If it wasn't her, we don't want her to start setting off alarms all over the place."

"Doesn't matter now," Lenoir said resignedly. "I violated secure operations procedures. Internal Affairs is going to nail me to a cross."

"Which is exactly why I came to see you," Kaye said. "Because that's where they'll stop. Look, as far as I'm concerned, we are now working this case together. Do a write-up of our conversation and possible leads. Might help you with Internal Affairs. I'll talk to one of my contacts at Oakland PD and see if we can track down what's going on." He rose to leave.

"Thanks, Detective. Keep me informed, please."

"Hell, yes," Kaye said, smiling. "Partners talk. I'll send you the case number."

Lenoir smiled.

Lonzo Rivera was waiting for Kaye when he walked into the outer offices area.

"Did you get something?" Rivera asked.

"I've got somewhere to start," Kaye said, slowing down but not stopping.

"That's all you're gonna give me?" Lonzo said, keeping pace.

"Lonzo, come on. You know how this works."

"You're right. Sorry." Rivera stopped and watched Kaye walk out the door.

As soon as he got back to the Harley, Kaye took out his cell phone and called Tina Magnuson.

"Hey," he said when she answered, "are you someplace where you can talk?"

"Hold please," Magnuson said officiously. Kaye then heard her tell someone, "Hey, I've gotta take this. Be right back."

A moment later, she came back on on-line. "Hey, Ben, what's up?"

"Just talked to Lieutenant Lenoir in Gangs and Narcotics. Guess what?"

"I'll play. What?"

"He told me Chen called him on Friday, not long after you put out the word, and asked for the safe house address."

"You're kidding!"

"I wish I was," Kaye said. "Turns out they know each other professionally, so he gave it to her."

"Oh, my God," Magnuson said. "So Chen is our leak?"

"Not so fast," Kaye said. "I'm not convinced it was really Chen that called."

"What makes you think that?"

"Couple of things. Unfortunately, there's no record of the originating number."

"What do we do now?" Magnuson asked.

"Do you know a friendly judge that would give you a warrant for Chen's cell phone records?"

"I do. I know Chen's department number, but not her personal number."

Kaye pulled out his notes. "Try this," he said, then read off the number Lenoir had given him.

"Got it," Magnuson said. "I'll try and run them down and have something for you as soon as I can."

"Let me know. Thanks, Tina."

Kaye stashed his phone, fired up the Harley and headed for his next destination. It wasn't nearby, and he wanted to be on time.

CHAPTER 23

Just before four o'clock Kaye rolled past the O'Bannon residence. It was a beautiful Craftsman style home on a double lot. Broad steps led from the sidewalk up to the main yard level. A second set then led up to the deep, covered front porch. The driveway passed through an arch built into the facade to reach the garage in the back.

He kept going, swinging into a cross street to park, grabbed what he needed from the saddlebag and headed for the house.

He rang the doorbell, which he noted was equipped with a video camera. The door opened a few seconds later. A woman Kaye guessed as mid-40s, dressed in yoga pants and a baggy sweatshirt, her hair pulled back in a ponytail, looked askance at him.

"You're Detective Kaye?" she asked, her breath a bit ragged.

"Yes, ma'am." He handed her a business card. "I'm a few minutes early. Sorry if I interrupted your workout."

"I just finished."

"May I come in?"

"Of course," she said, stepping back and holding the door wide open as Kaye stepped into the foyer. "I'm Elise O'Bannon."

Kaye shook her hand and looked around. Lots of woodwork and built-ins, hardwood floors, high ceilings with carved moldings, and a large fireplace with a stunning tile surround separating it from glass-fronted bookcases topped by stained glass clerestory windows.

"Nice place," he said, meaning it.

"Thank you. It's taken us fifteen years to restore it, but it was worth it. Please," she gestured and started for the living room, "come, sit down."

Kaye took a seat in a wooden chair with leather cushions and O'Bannon sat on the sofa, her hands clutched in her lap.

"Now, what can I do for you, Detective?"

"As I said on the phone," Kaye began, "I'm investigating a case involving a student at Grove Charter and your daughter's name came up."

"Came up?" O'Bannon asked, her eyes narrowing. "In what

context?"

Kaye reached into the file folder he'd carried in, pulled out the photo he'd gotten from Sonny Eliason and handed it across to O'Bannon, who glanced at it, laid it on the coffee table, looked at Kaye and said, "Okay, so?"

"Do you recognize the man in the photo?"

"Yes," she replied instantly. "That's Mr. Glithero, Audra's literature teacher and…writing mentor, I guess you'd call him."

"And that is Audra, correct?"

"Yes," she confirmed. "May I ask where you got this photograph? A school outing?"

"No, ma'am," Kaye replied. "It was taken by a private investigator hired by Mr. Glithero's now ex-wife."

"Why would…?" O'Bannon started to ask before she hesitated and looked down at the photo. She snatched it up with her right hand and stared at it, her left hand going up to cover her mouth as she inhaled sharply. "Oh, my God, they're at a motel."

"Yes," Kaye said. "Normally I wouldn't make this my business, but Audra is a minor and Mr. Glithero is her teacher. If she is, and I believe she is, having a sexual relationship with Dylan Glithero, he's committing a crime. And that is my business."

O'Bannon stared at the photo, her eyes glazed and her expression blank.

"What about Audra?" she asked at last. "Is she in trouble?"

"Not with us, Mrs. O'Bannon. From the LAPD's perspective, she's the victim of a sexual predator."

Finally, she looked up and asked nervously, "Where does this go from here?"

"I'd like to talk to her," Kaye replied. "And I'd like to have a female detective present. We're not allowed to talk to a minor without a parent present unless they give us consent. In this case, I think you should be present."

"I'd like to be there."

"I thought you would."

"Do we have to go to the police station?"

"No," Kaye assured her. "We can do the interview here if you prefer."

"I would," O'Bannon said, nodding. "And this may seem an odd request, but…"

"Go ahead."

"Can we do this before my husband gets back? I'd like to know exactly what's really going on before I have to tell him about it."

"Of course," Kaye said. "Let me make a couple quick phone calls and see if tomorrow works."

"I'll be right back," O'Bannon said, then rose and walked from the living room through the dining room before turning out of sight. She had barely disappeared when Kaye heard her choke back a sob.

His first call was to Amari Burke. He explained what he needed, then heard her ask J.J. what their schedule looked like tomorrow afternoon. He couldn't make out the reply, but she came back and said, "I'm good. Set it up."

He then called Kayla Okafor, hoping she was still in her office.

She was. "What can I do for you, Detective?"

"I need maybe an hour of your time tomorrow morning," he said. "I need to ask you one quick question first."

"What's the question?"

"Has a defendant named Rogelio Leandro made bail yet?"

"You do know you could call the jail and get that information, right?"

"I know," Kaye replied. "But I'll end up talking to fifteen people and be on hold for fifteen minutes, and right now's not a good time for that."

"Hold on," Okafor said, and Kaye heard the soft clatter of her keyboard. "Is this the guy that was stopped leaving the scene of your shooting incident Friday night?"

"It is," Kaye confirmed. "You heard about that?"

"Kaye, everybody heard about that."

"Is Leandro still in custody?"

"Uh, yes, he is. Bail set at two million, cash. He'll be there for a while."

"Would your office be willing to make a deal with this bozo if he helped us, and maybe the Oakland PD, plug security leaks?"

"We could talk to him."

"I want something from Leandro, but I need leverage to get it, if he even has it," Kaye said. "You being there gives me instant credibility."

"Well, looks like tomorrow's your lucky day," Okafor said. "I had a motion argument on my calendar for tomorrow morning, but it was continued about an hour ago. Does nine work for you?"

"Nine it is," Kaye said. "At the jail. Thanks, Counselor."

Kaye ended the call just as Elise O'Bannon, her eyes red and a box of tissues clutched in one hand, came back into the room.

"I'm sorry," she said as she sat down.

"You don't have to apologize, Missus O'Bannon. I understand."

"Thank you." She hesitated before asking, "So…tomorrow?"

"Yes," Kaye replied. "Any time after noon would work for me and Detective Burke."

O'Bannon thought for a moment before asking, "How about three? Audra usually has her writing…" She stopped. "I don't think she'll be going to that anymore. I'll pick her up early."

"Thank you, Mrs. O'Bannon," Kaye said as he stood up. "I'm sorry to bring this to your doorstep." He took a business card from his pocket and handed it to her. "Call me if anything changes."

"I will. And you don't need to apologize, either, Detective. This is the kind of thing every mother dreads, but needs to know. I actually appreciate you letting me know what's happening."

Kaye took his leave and walked back to the Harley.

The first order of business was to call Burke back. It went to voice mail and he left her a message that he'd meet her at the squad at 2:00 p.m. tomorrow.

He was about to pull away when a movement down the block caught his eye. A deep red Toyota SUV had turned the corner beyond the O'Bannon house and was headed in his direction. Two doors before the O'Bannon's the Toyota pulled to the curb and stopped. The passenger door opened and someone got out, but Kaye couldn't see who it was. The Toyota then continued in his direction. As it passed, he recognized the driver.

Dylan Glithero.

He looked back down the block and saw a young woman, backpack slung over one shoulder, make the turn from the sidewalk toward the O'Bannon's front door.

Audra O'Bannon.

After school activity, indeed, he thought ruefully.

CHAPTER 24

Kaye arrived at the jail thirty minutes early for his meeting with Kayla Okafor and headed downstairs for the property custodian's office.

"Morning, Harry," he greeted the man behind the cage.

"Hey, Detective Kaye," Harry responded. "Long time, no see. How's tricks?"

"Can't complain. Nobody listens anyway."

"Ain't that the truth." Harry chuckled. "What can I do for you?"

"You're holding a guy named Rogelio Leandro. I'm meeting with him and a rep from the D.A.'s office in a few minutes. I need to know if there's a cell phone in his belongings."

Harry frowned. "You know I can't let you look at it, right? Not without a warrant or a release signed by the prisoner."

"I know," Kaye replied. "I just need to know if he even had one on him when he was booked. If not, it'll be a short meeting."

Harry nodded knowingly. "When was Leandro booked in?"

"Early last Saturday morning."

Harry turned to the computer and busied himself before looking at Kaye, saying, "Be right back," before turning and disappearing into the seemingly endless rows of shelves stacked with plastic bins.

He wasn't gone long.

"There's a cell phone in Leandro's stuff," he said as he walked back to the counter, grabbed a form and slid it under the cage to Kaye. "Have him sign that and it's all yours."

"Thanks, Harry." He spent a couple minutes filling out the form so it only needed Leandro's signature, then headed back upstairs. He got to the ground floor just in time to see Okafor push through the main entrance. She saw him and headed his way.

"Good morning," she said, looking Kaye up and down. "You look spiffy today. I think this may be the first time I've seen you in a coat and tie outside of court."

"I've got an interview later today with a juvenile female and her mother. I didn't think the biker thing would work."

"Must be important."

"If it goes well, I'll be picking up Dylan Glithero."

"You got the pictures?"

"I did, and I've identified the girl."

"Obviously it wasn't Valerie Weber," she said.

"No, but she has almost the identical history with Glithero that Valerie did."

"I hope it turns out," Okafor said. "So, fill me in on why we're here this morning."

Kaye laid it out for her, from his original arrest of Gaeta, the Tiger Boys, Peter Li, and on through the incident at the safe house.

"I want the call history off Leandro's phone," Kaye said in conclusion. "He had to have been in contact with someone who's been feeding him information."

"Why not just get a warrant?" Okafor asked.

"That gives me the phone, but not access to it. Who knows what kind of security he has. I want to make it worth his while to surrender the phone and open it for me."

"Good idea, as long as he didn't delete it before his arrest."

"Won't know unless and until we see the phone, which we need to do before we offer a deal."

"It's a good idea," Okafor said. "I looked up his charges. If he's smart, he'll roll instead of spending the rest of his life in prison."

"Well," Kaye said, "let's go see what Mister Leandro can do for us."

They checked in with the jail desk and told the officers what they needed. They were directed to the right floor, and, after checking weapons, to an interview room.

The entire hallway side of the room was glass, and Rogelio Leandro, clad in an orange jumpsuit, was already seated at a table bolted to the floor. His ankles were shackled and a chain that passed through a heavy eye bolt fastened to the tabletop was looped through the chain of his handcuffs.

The jailer let them in. "Buzz," he said, pointing to a button in the inside door frame, "when you need to get out."

Leandro didn't even turn his head when they entered. He finally looked at them when they took seats across from him, but didn't say anything.

Okafor led off. "Mr. Leandro, I'm Assistant District Attorney Okafor, and this is Detective Kaye of the LAPD."

"I know who he is," Leandro muttered and looked at Kaye. "What do you want from me, pig?"

"Your cell phone," Kaye said easily as he laid the form Harry had given him on the table.

Leandro snorted in derision. "I give you nothing, man. I do, I'm a dead man."

"Tiger Boys?" Kaye asked.

Leandro just shrugged, but answered the question by breaking eye contact.

"If you don't," Kaye said, "you're still dead. I'll get a warrant, get the phone, then spread the word you cooperated."

"And," Okafor spoke up, "you get nothing from me. You're looking at multiple counts of conspiracy to commit murder, one count of felony murder, convicted felon in possession of a firearm and enough misdemeanors to choke a horse."

"Plus," Kaye added, "if the gun you had matches the ballistics of the gun used to shoot Neil Gaeta off his motorcycle, you're on the hook for that, and probably a store clerk out in the Valley." He paused, then added, "Think hard, Rogelio. Don't make a stupid mistake just to show us how tough you are."

"My gun won't match nothing," Leandro said, squirming in his chair. "I didn't shoot that guy."

"But you were there, right?" Kaye said pointedly. "Too bad for you the guy behind you is in the car business. He even told us what brand of custom wheels you run on your ride. Pull up your right sleeve."

"What?" Leandro protested. "Why?"

"Just do it," Kaye ordered.

Leandro grumbled, but reached over and pulled up his right sleeve until it bunched at his elbow.

No tattoo.

"I believe you," Kaye said. "You didn't shoot the guy on the motorcycle. So, you letting us look at your phone, or what?"

"Sounds to me like I'm fucked if I do and fucked if I don't." Leandro looked away and squirmed again.

"Rogelio," Okafor said sympathetically, "you just don't get it, do you? Yes, you are fucked. Either the Tiger Boys turn you into garden mulch or my boss sends you to prison for life. Thing is, if you help us out, my boss just might settle for a quickie instead of the full monte." She paused, then winked at Leandro and added, "Who knows, either way it's probably good practice for when you're inside."

A surprised Kaye glanced sideways at Okafor and bit his tongue to keep from smiling.

"Plus," Okafor went on, "you should know we didn't get all dressed up just for you. If you don't help us out, from here we go to the hospital and talk to the kid Detective Kaye shot. What do you think he'll tell us? Then we bury you, instead."

"Davie Boy ain't dead?" Leandro asked, his eyes bouncing from Okafor to Kaye and back.

"If Davie Boy was who came in through the back door," Kaye said, "yeah, he's alive. The upstairs guy?" He shook his head slowly and thought he read a smirk in Leandro's eyes. "Friend of yours?"

Leandro stared at him and Kaye knew the man was making his decision.

"No friend of mine," Leandro muttered at last. "Fuckin' Tiger Boys. Piss on 'em. They think they own everybody now."

"What are you going to do, Rogelio?" Okafor asked. "I'm prepared to drop the felon in possession of a firearm charge just for signing the form. After that, everything depends on what's on your phone."

Leandro studied her. "You sure you're a lawyer?"

"I'm sure," Okafor told him. "What makes you ask?"

"You ain't even advised me of my rights."

Okafor laughed. "Rogelio, we're only required to advise you of your rights if we want to question you about a crime and use your answers against you in court. We're just asking to borrow your phone for a few minutes. No jeopardy attaches to you."

"You sure?"

"I'm sure."

Leandro studied Kaye for a moment, then looked at Okafor and smiled.

"Can I borrow a pen?"

"Right choice, Rogelio," Okafor said, smiling as she extracted a pen from her pocket and held it out where he could reach it.

It was decided that Kaye would retrieve the phone and Okafor would remain and start talking deal with Leandro.

"Can I see you outside first?" Kaye asked her.

"Sure," she replied, standing up and looking at Leandro. "Be right back."

Kaye buzzed and the jailer came and opened the door. They stepped into the hallway and Kaye pulled the door closed behind them.

"What?" Okafor asked.

"As part of your negotiations, see if you can get him to agree to talk to Lonzo Rivera, one of our gang unit guys," Kaye said softly. "Leandro could be either a great actor or not a real Tiger Boys fan. Maybe he'll give us some good intel."

"I'll try. Now, go get the phone before he changes his mind."

The jailer let Okafor back inside and Kaye hustled back down to the property room.

Harry acted surprised that Kaye had gotten the signature, but nonetheless had the phone on the counter waiting. To Kaye's surprise, it wasn't a burner. He cosigned the form in front of Harry and told him he'd have the phone back as soon as he could.

"Don't sweat it," Harry said. "We've got a paper trail."

Back upstairs, the jailer let Kaye back into the interview room.

"Are we good?" he asked Okafor as he sat down and put the phone on the table.

"We're good," Okafor replied.

"Pass code?" he asked Leandro.

"My face," Leandro said, smirking.

Kaye pointed the phone's camera at Leandro and reached around to touch the bottom of the screen. When he turned the phone around, the home screen was open. He immediately disabled the screen lock and security settings, made a note of the phone's number, then went to the call history. It went back several weeks.

He looked at Okafor and nodded. Then he went to Contacts. There weren't a lot, and most of them were nicknames, valuable nonetheless because of the associated numbers and email addresses.

He used his phone to take photos of everything back to before Neil Gaeta had been shot in Westwood.

Leandro and Okafor chatted while he worked.

The last thing he did was enable the security settings and screen lock, close the home screen and held it up for Leandro to see.

"Just like I got it," Kaye said. "Only your face can open it. It'll be back in the property bag."

Leandro nodded, then looked at Okafor. "Hey, you ever want to check out that whole sex with the D.A. thing, look me up, huh?"

An angry Kaye started to reach for Leandro, but Okafor stopped him with a curt shake of her head.

"It's okay," she said, then turned to Leandro. "*En sus suenos, gilipollas.*"

Leandro scowled, but held his tongue.

"I'll be in touch with your legal representation as soon as I know who it is," Okafor continued. "You'll do some time, Rogelio, but, depending on what Detective Kaye gets from your phone, we'll make it as short and easy as possible."

Leandro just nodded.

On the way out, Kaye asked, "Did he agree to talk to Lonzo Rivera?"

"He did," Okafor replied. "He really seems to hate the Tiger Boys. Why would he help them?"

"Because they don't take 'no' for an answer, even from inside."

"Well, I hope you got what you needed."

"Won't know until I can sort it all out."

"Let me know," she said as they parted ways in the main lobby.

"Will do, Counselor. Thank you."

He went back downstairs and returned the phone to Harry, then headed back to the station and started working through the photos he'd taken of Leandro's phone.

He started by entering the calls from the phone's history into a spreadsheet in the order they were listed. It was repetitive, time consuming work and Kaye was glad he hadn't gone back any farther than he had.

By the time he'd finished, he was bleary-eyed. The spreadsheet had hundreds of rows. But it was a mishmash of random data that told him almost nothing. He stared at it for a moment trying to figure out where to go, then reached for his desk phone and punched in an extension number.

"Patty Phillips."

"Hi, Patty. Detective Kaye. You got a few minutes? I need some help with a spreadsheet."

"I can do that," she replied. "Can you give me about ten minutes?"

"That works. I can use a break."

"Okay, see you in ten."

Kaye hung up and headed for the break room. Nine minutes and one vending machine protein bar later he returned, a half-full mug of hot tea in his hand. He'd barely sat down when Patty came in.

"Hi," she said, smiling. "Haven't seen you for a while."

"Been busy."

"I heard about what happened. I'm glad you're okay."

"Thanks, Patty. It could've been a lot worse."

"I heard that, too," she said seriously, then changed the subject by asking, "So, what are you working on?" as she scanned Kaye's monitor.

He explained how he'd hoped Leandro's phone would lead him to whoever had betrayed his safe house location. "But I'm at the end of my skill set in terms of trying to manipulate all the data."

"Ideally, what would you like to end up with?" she asked.

"Ideally? How about separate lists of incoming, outgoing and missed calls, sorted by area code, the number on the other end, date and time, contact information and their current addresses and criminal histories."

She looked sideways at him.

"Hey," he said, "you said *ideally*," and laughed.

"You had me worried there for a second," she said, then studied what Kaye had so far. "Okay, I think we can do almost everything, and if you give me some time I can probably get some addresses and records. Scoot over a little bit."

He did, and Patty rolled in and went to work. She started sorting and cutting and pasting at a pace Kaye soon gave up trying to follow.

And she still had time to chat.

"Are you making progress on finding Valerie Weber's killer?" she asked, glancing at Kaye for a second before focusing again on the spreadsheet.

"A little bit," he replied. "Not enough to make an arrest yet."

"You'll get him," she said, paused, then, eyes still on the spreadsheet, asked, "Do you know if she ever found her birth parents?"

"She didn't." Kaye explained about the sealed court records and Valerie being a minor. "I talked to Trevor Rowell, the guy you found for me. He knew Valerie's mother, but said there's no way he was Valerie's father and that she never came looking for him."

"You know," Patty said as she manipulated the now multiple spreadsheets, "there are websites out there where adopted or abandoned kids and their biological families try to find each other." She glanced at Kaye again. "No lawyers or courts involved. Don't know how, or if, they work, but they're out there."

"I did not know that," he said as he watched her work her magic. "Wouldn't have helped in this case. Valerie's mother died when Valerie was still an infant."

Patty's hands froze as she turned to look at Kaye. "Oh, my God. The world can sure be a terrible place."

"That it can."

"One more question?"

"Sure." He expected another inquiry about the Weber case.

"Do you want your lists sorted ascending, or descending?"

"Oh," Kaye said, surprised. "Uh, put the most recent on top."

"Will do."

Thirty seconds later, the nearby printer came to life as Patty stood up. She grabbed sheets out of the tray and sat back down as she handed them to Kaye.

"There you go, Detective. I saved the electronic copies in your documents folder and named them Leandro's Phone, one, two and three."

"That's it?" Kaye asked, feeling suddenly incompetent.

"That's it," Patty confirmed. "I also emailed them to myself, and I'll see who I can match up to some of the numbers and pull up their records. No promises, though."

"Thank you, Patty. I really appreciate your help."

It didn't take him long to figure out which pages were which. He started with Incoming calls. There were over two hundred of them.

This guy must live on his phone, he thought as he began to study the list.

Most of the calls had originated in area codes associated with the Greater Los Angeles metro area. He just glanced at those, figuring that the information pipeline likely originated in the Oakland area. If there was a multiple link phone tree involved he'd never be able to track it.

To his chagrin, there wasn't a single call from the 510 area code, which covered most of the east side of San Francisco Bay, including Oakland. He grabbed the outgoing call sheets. Leandro hadn't made a single call to the 510.

Shit, he cursed inwardly. *Am I looking at the wrong phone? Maybe the dead guy?*

He instantly knew Leandro was an actor. If the dead man upstairs was a Tiger Boy, why was he inside to do the dirty work while Leandro sat outside, warm and cozy in his ride?

He kept at it, though, knowing that if he had to repeat the process, at least he'd be able to get the dead guy's phone without a signature.

There were several area codes he didn't recognize. 206 was Seattle, and it got his attention because Leandro had gotten a call from there the very morning he'd helped Magnuson and Horton arrest Neil Gaeta at the gas station off I-10. 209 turned out to be the portion of central California around Stockton. 267 was Philadelphia and 279 was Sacramento.

When he finally got down to 925, he had to look it up and did a double take. It covered portions of Alameda and Contra Costa counties inland from the Bay. Leandro had received several calls from a 925 number, one of them coming on the day Neil Gaeta had been released from jail after testifying against Peter Li. The last had come in last Friday afternoon. The times seemed random.

He grabbed the outgoing call list and went to area code 925. Four outgoing calls to the same number that had called him; the first on the first day covered by the spreadsheet, the last not long after receiving the call on the day Gaeta was released from jail. He checked the times and sat up straight.

Each outgoing call had been made at precisely the top of an hour.

To Kaye, that clearly meant a pre-arranged system.

"Got'cha," he muttered to himself. "Now, who the hell are you?"

He was tempted to call the number and see who answered, but decided against it. Based on what he'd learned thus far, the Tiger Boys had a solid intelligence network and he didn't want whoever it was to get spooked. Plus, he'd give good odds that the number was probably a burner and probably not turned on except at prearranged times.

He grabbed the desk phone, checked the department directory and punched in a number.

"Lenoir," the Gangs/Narcotics Unit Lieutenant answered.

"Lieutenant, Ben Kaye. How are you?"

"Hangin' in, Detective. Internal Affairs will be here to talk to me at three. Ask me again at four."

"I've got some information for you."

"Your case number?" Lenoir asked.

"Crap, I forgot," Kaye said. "I'm sorry." He checked his case log and gave Lenoir the number. "There's more."

"I'm listening."

Kaye gave Lenoir the quick rundown on interviewing Leandro and what he'd gotten off the phone. "I don't think it was Chen that called you, but I'm willing to bet that whoever did either knows Chen or is somehow connected to someone who does. That's how they knew so much about you. I'm also convinced the intel leak is in Oakland, not with us."

"That's good news," Lenoir said.

"It is, and hopefully it'll soften the blow from IA. Slap on the wrist instead of dagger to the heart."

Lenoir laughed.

"If I could," Kaye went on, "I'd be there at three, but I've got to interview a potential witness in a homicide. I do have a suggestion, though."

"Go ahead."

"Call Chen and ask her point blank if she called you. And tell her not to tell anyone else that you called. At this point you've got nothing to lose, and you might get some new information."

"Good idea," Lenoir said. "I'll call her."

"One more thing. As part of his deal with the D.A., Leandro agreed to talk to Lonzo Rivera."

"Lonzo told me," Lenoir said. "It's all set for tomorrow."

"Tell Lonzo to be careful," Kaye said. "Leandro made out like he hates the Tiger Boys, but I think he might be one."

"What?"

"Think about it. If Leandro was a local, like he wants us to believe, why would he be talking directly to a Tiger Boys source in the Bay Area? I think he was running things, and told us the dead guy was a Tiger Boy to throw us off."

"Then why would he give up his phone so easily?"

"He knows he's going down," Kaye replied, "and he wants as soft a landing as possible. Plus, he has a weakness."

"What's that?" Lenoir asked.

"He thinks he's always the smartest person in the room."

Kaye wished Lenoir good luck with IA and ended the call. He considered calling Tina Magnuson and relaying what he'd gleaned from Leandro's phone, but thought better of it. He didn't know who the 925 area code number belonged to. He'd wait to call her, and, like Gaeta's whereabouts, keep the phone info to himself for now.

He glanced at the clock and saw it was later than he thought. He called Burke's cell phone.

"Hey, where are you?" he asked when she picked up.

"We just pulled into the station," she replied. "Where are you?"

"In the squad. I'll be right down. You can drive."

CHAPTER 25

It was 2:55 p.m. when Burke pulled the unmarked silver Explorer to the curb in front of the O'Bannon residence.

While en route, the two had discussed how to approach the interview, agreeing that a key element would be to avoid anything that might suggest to either Elise or Audra O'Bannon that Audra had somehow done something wrong or created her own problem.

"Wow, nice house," Burke said as she shut down the unit and leaned forward to get a better look out of the windshield.

"Wait until you see the inside," Kaye told her, then opened the door and stepped out.

Elise O'Bannon must have been watching for them, because she opened the front door as soon as they topped the front steps. Kaye could tell she was wound pretty tight.

"Afternoon, Mrs. O'Bannon," he said cordially, stepping forward to shake her hand. "This," he pointed, "is Detective Amari Burke."

"Nice to meet you, Detective," Elise said, nodding.

"My pleasure, ma'am," Burke said, also shaking Elise's hand. "Thank you for letting us come into your home. It's very beautiful."

"Thank you. Please come inside. Have a seat in the living room. Audra's upstairs. I'll get her."

"You weren't kidding," Burke whispered to Kaye. "This place is gorgeous."

"Elise said it took —" Kaye started to say before he heard footsteps coming down the stairs.

Elise followed an obviously reluctant Audra, dressed in jeans and a baggy sweatshirt, her hair pulled back into a ponytail, into the living room. "Sit there, Audra," she said tersely, pointing to the chair nearest the sofa where Kaye and Burke sat.

"Mom, what is this?" Audra demanded. "What's going on?"

"I'll let the detectives —" Elise started to say.

"Detectives?" Audra asked, her eyes going wide and the color draining from her face.

"Yes, Audra, detectives from the LAPD. They need to talk to you."

"About what?"

"They'll explain," Elise said sharply, then turned to Kaye. "I've decided to let you talk in private. If you need me, I'll be in the study." She turned back to her daughter. "Tell the truth, Audra. They're here to help you, not get you in trouble."

A shocked Audra watched her mother disappear around the corner beyond the staircase, then turned to Kaye and Burke with a deer-in-the-headlights look.

"Audra, I'm Detective Kaye," he introduced himself, "and this is Detective Burke."

"You can call me Amari if you like," Burke said, smiling.

"What's this about?" Audra had the same nervous habit her mother did; hands twisting in her lap.

"We're investigating a case involving a Grove Charter student and your name came up," Kaye replied.

"You're not in trouble, Audra," Burke said softly.

"That's right," Kaye said. "But we think you might know something about what happened, and might not even know it."

"Okay," Audra said, her voice more confident. "I'll help if I can."

"Do you know Valerie Weber?" Kaye asked.

"I did," Audra replied. "She doesn't go to Grove Charter anymore. I think she goes to Westside now."

"She did," Kaye said, watching for any reaction to his use of past tense. There wasn't one.

"Are you investigating Valerie? What did she do?"

"She didn't do anything," Kaye said bluntly. "She was murdered."

Audra gasped. "What happened?"

"That's what we're trying to figure out," Burke said. "Did you have classes with Valerie when she was at Grove Charter? Do you know if she had a boyfriend? Enemies? Any problems?"

"I had an English Lit class with her, and we were in an after-school group together," Audra said, "but we didn't really hang together, so…" She shrugged.

"The after-school group," Kaye said. "Would that be Mr. Glithero's writing seminar?"

Audra nodded. "Yeah."

"And you're still in the group, right?" Kaye asked.

Audra nodded again.

"When you were in the group with Valerie, did you ever notice anything unusual or different about Valerie and Mr. Glithero's interactions?" Burke asked.

"What do you mean?" Audra asked.

"Did they get along?" Burke replied. "Was Mr. Glithero tougher on her than he was on anybody else? Easier, maybe? Did Valerie give him a hard time? Anything like that?"

"Uh, not that I noticed."

"How about the other members of the group?" Kaye asked. "Did they all get along with Valerie?"

"Yeah, I mean, nobody hated her or anything like that," Audra said. "She was real quiet. Mr. Glithero thought she had talent. He almost never criticized her work."

"Did he criticize everyone else?" Burke asked.

"Maybe criticize isn't the right word." Audra backtracked. "I mean, it's his job to teach us, and constructive criticism is part of that, right?"

"It is," Kaye agreed. "Does Mr. Glithero provide you with constructive criticism?"

"Sometimes," she replied, her voice hardening. "Dylan…" She stopped and her face flushed. "Mr. Glithero says I'm a much better writer this year."

"You call your teacher by his first name?" Burke asked.

"Sometimes," Audra said defiantly. "We all do. He says it's a peer relationship, not a student-teacher one."

"But you just said it's his job to teach you, and offer constructive criticism," Burke pointed out. "I'm confused. What, exactly, is the nature of your relationship with Mr. Glithero? Dylan."

Audra blushed deeply and twisted her hands together even more tightly.

Kaye and Burke glanced at each other and Burke dipped her chin ever so slightly.

Kaye reached into the file, pulled out the photo from Sonny Eliason, turned it around so Audra could see it and asked, "Do you call him Dylan when he takes you to motels?"

Audra stared at the photo, her mouth open in shock. "Where did you get that?" she at last managed to ask, her voice barely above a whisper.

"That's not important," Burke said softly. "What is important is that you explain to us what's going on, and how it started. And, Audra, remember, you are not in trouble, okay?"

"Why are you asking me this?" Audra blurted. "What does it have…" She stopped and her eyes went wide. "Oh, my God! That's it!

211

You think Dylan murdered Valerie! That's insane. He's kind and gentle and…" She stopped again and just stared at them.

"Audra, are you and Mr. Glithero having sex?" Burke asked.

"It's not like that!" Audra protested.

"What is it like?" Burke asked. "And, Audra, remember, you're still a minor. The law sees you as a victim, not as a criminal in all of this. Especially because Dylan Glithero is your teacher."

"Does my Mom know about…that?" Audra pointed to the photo from the motel.

"She does," Kaye replied. "You should also know that I saw Mr. Glithero drop you off down the block yesterday afternoon. Your Mom does not know that."

"Audra, please tell us how all this started and what's going on," Burke said. "We want to help you and we're trying to protect you."

"Dylan killed Valerie, didn't he?" Audra asked softly as a tear rolled down her cheek.

"We don't know that yet," Kaye said.

"That's why we need to know about your relationship with him," Burke said. "Will you tell us? Please?"

Audra looked plaintively at Burke, then glanced furtively at Kaye before looking back at Burke.

"Do you want to talk to me alone?" Burke asked.

Audra nodded. "Please."

"Do you want your Mom to be here?" Burke asked. "If she wants to be, we can't keep her out, and it might be a good idea."

"Okay," Audra whispered.

Burke turned to Kaye. "You got a legal pad? I left mine in the unit."

Kaye slid a pad out of the file and gave it to her. "I'll go tell Elise to come in."

He escorted Elise back to the living room. When Audra saw her mother, she burst into tears. Elise quickly crossed the room and put her arms around her daughter.

Kaye caught Burke's eye and mouthed, 'I'll be outside'. She nodded in acknowledgement as he turned and headed for the front door.

It was nearly an hour later when the front door opened and Burke stepped out. She turned and hugged both the O'Bannons before heading for the unit and Kaye.

"Well?" Kaye asked when Burke had settled into the driver's seat and handed the file to him.

Burke held the steering wheel with a death grip and stared out the windshield for a moment before answering. "Classic set-up. Glithero offered her something she really wanted, which was to get published, and she fell for it. It took me a while to get her to admit she and Glithero were having consensual sex. But she thinks the other guy drugged and raped her."

"The other guy?" a bewildered Kaye asked.

"Read the statement," Burke said wearily. "Right now I just want to get back to the station, write this up, then go home and hug my husband."

"That bad?"

Burke looked at him and he saw murder in her eyes. "I'd love to get my hands on those guys."

***

It was getting into the evening when Burke finally headed home. She'd been very quiet while she wrote the report summary of her interview with Audra O'Bannon. Kaye had left her alone while he tried to figure out a way to uncover who was behind the 925 area code number in the East Bay. The only advantage, if it could be called that, was that he knew Leandro's outgoing calls always happened at the top of the hour. He needed to figure out a way to make that work for him.

Once Burke was gone, he pulled Audra O'Bannon's statement from the case file and read it.

It was what Burke had relayed to him, except in Audra's words and much more graphic. Glithero had enticed her into signing up for a summer writing group, but it seemed she was the only one in it. After a couple weeks he'd told her about a friend of his who could get her published, offered to introduce her, and from there the progression was textbook. When things got out of control, Glithero had convinced her she was the one who would get in trouble, so she should keep her mouth shut. The friend, a man she knew only as 'Art', had pushed her around and threatened her. Audra said she'd kept quiet to protect her and her family's reputation.

Art must be the guy who lives in Anaheim Hills, Kaye thought.

Kaye was simultaneously dumbfounded and enraged, instantly understanding Burke's anger. It was a classic grooming set-up. Entice the target with something they want, string them along, manipulate and cajole them into giving you what you want, then blame them for everything.

He spent the next two hours writing an arrest warrant affidavit to support a litany of charges against Dylan Glithero.

On the way home he tried to keep his mind off Glithero by pondering how to best track down the 925 area code number owner. As distracted as he was, he came up with one idea that, with some refinement and the right timing, might just work.

He flashed back to his early days as a detective and advice his more experienced partner had given him.

"Always try to eliminate the obvious suspect first. If you can't, it means the son of a bitch probably did it."

He smiled. It might work, it might not, but either way it was worth the effort.

As soon as he walked into the house he turned into the kitchen, picked up the phone, dialed the Marriott and asked for Gaeta's room.

"Hello." Kaye recognized Mike Fisher's voice.

"Hey, Mike. It's Ben. How's it going?"

"Neil's a lot better. He's talking about trying out for the crutch Olympics. But we're both getting cabin fever."

"I figured," Kaye said. "That's why I called. If you're comfortable leaving Neil on his own for a day or two, you can go on home."

"Really?" Mike asked skeptically.

"Really," Kaye echoed. "You'll be safe."

"What about Neil?"

"I'm working on a plan to get him home safely. Might take a couple days to put it together."

"Have you found out what went wrong last Friday?" Mike asked, and Kaye heard the doubt in the man's voice.

"Making progress," Kaye replied. "That's actually part of the plan to get Neil home, too."

"Okay, I trust you."

"Can I talk to Neil?"

"He's in the shower. I'll fill him in."

"Great, and Mike, thanks for all your help on this. Neil's lucky to have you for a friend," Kaye said. "Tell him I'll be in touch soon."

CHAPTER 26

At 7:45 a.m. Kaye was waiting in the hallway outside the Office of the District Attorney.

Five minutes later, Kayla Okafor got off the elevator.

"Uh-oh," she said, coming to a halt when she saw him. "I hope this isn't bad news."

"Not at all," Kaye said, holding up the affidavit. "I'd like you to take a look at this before I go to a Judge."

"I can do that." She stepped around him and slid her key into the lock.

"Are you always the first one here?" Kaye asked.

"Hardly. Lots of people get here before I do. But we don't officially open until eight, so we leave the door locked."

She was right. The office was already a buzz of activity.

"Okay," she said after they'd settled in her office. "What've you got?"

Kaye didn't say a word, just handed her the affidavit. She looked at him, puzzled.

"Just read it," he told her.

She did. As she progressed, Kaye saw her eyes narrow, then her jaw started to clench and her lips pursed into a tight line. When she finished, she held the affidavit in both hands and stared at it before finally looking up at Kaye.

"Don't change a damn word," she said angrily, then punched the intercom button on her phone. "Leslie, could you come in for a second?"

"I'll be right there," a woman's voice answered, and a moment later Leslie entered the office.

"Who's on warrants this morning?" Okafor asked her.

"Judge Franklin has it until noon."

Okafor held out the affidavit and said, "Would you make me two copies of this, please?"

"Of course," Leslie said. She grabbed the affidavit and left the office.

"Isn't Franklin the judge you asked about Valerie Weber's adoption file?" Kaye asked after the door was shut.

"He is. And I want him to read every word of this. You'll get your warrant."

"And I can multi-task," Kaye said, half-smiling.

"What? Care to explain?"

"Not yet."

"Okay," Okafor said slowly. "Keep me in the loop?"

"Of course," Kaye replied just as there was a knock on the door.

"Come," Okafor said loudly.

Leslie entered and handed the affidavit and two copies to Okafor, who thanked her before handing the original back to Kaye.

"No shortcuts on this one," she said. "Wrap him up so tight he'll never see the light of day again. And find that Art guy."

"That's the plan," Kaye assured her as he rose to leave.

As he crossed the lobby toward the building's front doors his cell phone buzzed.

It was Tina Magnuson.

"Hey, Ben, how's it going?"

"Making progress. What's up?"

"I thought I'd call and let you know Peter Li was found guilty."

"Good. Justice prevails."

Magnuson laughed. "Well, sort of. As soon as the verdict was rendered and sentencing set, the State relinquished custody to the Feds and they made a deal to keep him out of the gas chamber."

"You mentioned that possibility," Kaye said. "You also mentioned that a guarantee of Gaeta's safety might be part of the deal."

"It was, and it is," she said. "If anything happens to Neil, to Alina, or their families, the Feds turn him back over to us and he goes to Death Row."

"Good to know. Neil's chomping at the bit to get home." As soon as he said it, Kaye had an idea. "Hey, how about this? I've got to go to Ukiah to do an interview on another case I'm working. I'll bring him to you and you can give him the nitty gritty personally."

"I think that's a grand idea," Magnuson said. "When did you have in mind?"

"Friday, say around two o'clock? That'll leave me enough daylight to make it to Ukiah."

"Let…me…see," Magnuson said, obviously checking her calendar. "Yeah, two on Friday works for me. See you then?"

"We'll be there," Kaye replied. "And if anything changes I'll let you know."

It was a short walk to the Courthouse and twenty minutes later Kaye stepped into Judge Franklin's chambers.

"Good morning, Detective," Franklin greeted him and motioned him to a chair opposite his. "Have a seat."

"Good morning, Your Honor," Kaye said as he sat down.

"What've you got for me?"

"Applications for an arrest warrant and search warrant," Kaye replied, setting his affidavit on the desk.

"What charges?"

"Forcible rape, statutory rape and sexual assault of a minor with prostitution enhancement."

"And the search warrant?"

"I want the suspect's DNA."

Franklin studied him for a moment, then said, "Raise your right hand." A moment later, Kaye was sworn in and a pensive Franklin had started looking over the affidavit.

"How old is the victim?" the Judge asked.

"Seventeen now, Your Honor, but I believe I can establish she was sixteen when this all began. The suspect is a teacher at the victim's school."

Franklin reached up and started rubbing his forehead while he read the affidavit.

"Who's the original complainant?" the Judge asked without looking up.

"It didn't come to me as a complaint," Kaye replied. "I discovered the situation while investigating the murder of another juvenile female, who previously attended the same school and also took classes from the suspect."

Franklin peered over the top of his reading glasses at Kaye. "Do you believe your suspect in this case also killed the other juvenile?"

"He's a person of interest, Your Honor. At this point I don't have anything solid to tie him to the murder, but the girl who was killed was pregnant. I need to see if Glithero's DNA is a match, or not. It may prove culpability, or it may be exculpatory."

"This arrest warrant wouldn't happen to be a fishing expedition to get Glithero's DNA for the homicide case, would it?"

"No, sir," Kaye said emphatically. "The victim in the case was groomed, compromised, manipulated and coerced before she was convinced she was to blame. It's the classic pedophile progression. There's a second suspect, whom she says beat her to keep her quiet, but all I have now is a first name, no positive ID."

"Okay," Franklin said slowly, then went back to the affidavit. A couple of minutes later he looked up at Kaye. "Here's what I'm going to do. I'll sign the arrest warrant, but I think the search warrant is redundant and could cast doubt on your motives here. I understand the connections and your desire for Glithero's DNA, but I honestly don't think the warrant would stand." The Judge studied him for a moment before adding, "You are certainly aware that you can get the DNA post-arrest. Why bring this to me at all? You could've done this electronically through the District Attorney's office. Would've saved you your morning."

"I know, Your Honor. But I needed to see you about something else, too."

"And what might that be?"

"The Valerie Weber case."

Franklin froze, and Kaye could tell from the look on the Judge's face he was searching his memory.

"Oh, yes, I remember," he said after a moment. "That's the young woman Ms. Okafor inquired about. The adoptee, right?"

"Yes," Kaye said, and saw the expression on Franklin's face change.

"Is that the homicide that might be tied to Mr. Glithero?"

"It is, Your Honor," Kaye replied. "I need to see the full adoption file."

"Why?"

"There are…inconsistencies I need to run down."

"Inconsistencies? Such as?"

"I'm hearing conflicting things from different people. I'd like to be able to separate truth from fiction."

"Well," Franklin said thoughtfully, "the adoptee is deceased."

"So is her biological mother."

"When did she die?"

"Shortly after Valerie was born. It was ruled a suicide." Kaye shrugged.

Franklin leaned back in his chair and drummed the fingers of his left hand on his desk, his eyes unfocused.

"Okay," the Judge said, leaning forward. "First, I'll grant the warrant for Mr. Glithero's arrest. You can legally collect his DNA at the time of arrest. On your way out, ask my clerk for an adoption record access form. Even though the adoptee is deceased, we'll follow protocols. Fill out the form; I recommend before you leave; and give it back to her along with your email address. I'll sign it. It might take a few days for it to process through the Administrator's office, but as soon as it does we'll send you the file. Anything else?"

"No, Your Honor," Kaye replied, standing. "Thank you."

"Thank you for your good work, Detective. Makes my job easier."

Back in the outer office Kaye asked the clerk, Lois, for the form. It took him twenty minutes to fill it out, including a summary of why he was asking for access.

"I'll be in touch," Lois said when he handed it back to her.

***

Kaye spent a good part of the afternoon catching up with documentation on the O'Bannon and Weber cases. While he worked, it dawned on him that he hadn't spoken to JoAnn Weber for a while. He called her home number and got no answer. When he tried her cell it went straight to voicemail.

"Mrs. Weber, it's Ben Kaye. I called to update you on your daughter's case. I am making progress, but it's been slow. I'm still narrowing it down and waiting on other information I've requested. Bureaucracy moves slowly, but don't give up on me. I will find whoever killed your daughter. Thank you, and feel free to call me if you have questions."

Less than ten seconds after he hung up, his phone rang. He picked it up, expecting it to be JoAnn Weber.

"Mrs. Weber, thanks for –"

"Kaye, it's Lenoir." The Gang/Narcotics Lieutenant interrupted.

"Oh, sorry L.T. What's up?"

"I wanted to let you know I called Chen. You were right. She didn't call me."

"I didn't think so, but I wasn't positive," Kaye said. "Without being too nosy, how'd it go with IA?"

"Not as bad as it could have," Lenoir replied. "A week off without pay and removed from the Captain's promotion list for one year."

"Ouch."

"Yeah, that's the one that hurt. I actually had my eye on your boss's job. I heard he was leaving."

"The rumor's going around," Kaye said, keeping his voice noncommittal. Lenoir didn't say anything, so Kaye continued. "I have more information on the leak. You got a pencil?"

"I do."

Kaye told Lenoir about Leandro's phone records and the 925 area code number.

"Nice work," Lenoir said. "That's good intel. Any ideas on how to find out who it belongs to?"

"One," Kaye replied. "But it's a longshot." He went on to tell Lenoir about Peter Li being convicted and his subsequent deal with the Feds. "At least Neil Gaeta shouldn't have to live his life looking over his shoulder."

"Well, that's something. Hey, gotta run. Keep after 'em, Detective."

"You, too, L.T."

He kept after the paperwork, mostly because it kept him at his desk, near his computer. He had his email Inbox open and kept looking to see if the arrest warrant for Dylan Glithero had shown up. He was about to pack it in for the day when J.J. came into the squad.

"Where's Burke?" he asked.

"She took a sick day," J.J. replied and shrugged. "No specifics provided."

"Well, I'm glad you happened to come in. What's your Friday afternoon look like?"

"Nothing comes to mind." He sat down on Kaye's filing cabinet. "What's going on?"

Kaye told J.J. about Peter Li's conviction and deal, and about taking Gaeta back to Oakland before going on to Ukiah.

"You want me to go with you?"

"No, but there's something I need you to do from this end while I'm there," Kaye replied, then laid it out.

"Okay, I get it," J.J. said, smiling. "Yeah, I can do that. Think it'll work?"

"I don't know," Kaye admitted. "But it's all I've got right now, and given the circumstances I'm not going to spend a whole lot more time and energy chasing it."

"Agreed." J.J. nodded. "Not our problem."

The two talked shop for a few minutes, then decided it was time to call it a day. When Kaye turned to shut down his computer he saw the email from Judge Franklin's clerk. The subject line read 'Glithero Warrant' and a file was attached. He saved it, then opened and reviewed it, looking for possible 'gotchas' that the Judge may have thrown in. He didn't see anything obvious. When he got to the bottom he was pleased to see that Judge Franklin had entered a bond amount rather than leaving it to an arraignment magistrate that wouldn't be familiar with the details of the case to possibly set only a token amount.

It was going to cost Dylan Glithero a cool half-million to get out of jail.

He printed the warrants and checked the time.

Dressed as he was, he'd need a uniformed officer to go with him to collect Glithero, and he'd have to deal with transporting and booking his suspect.

Reluctantly, he decided that Glithero would have to wait until tomorrow to go to jail.

CHAPTER 27

In anticipation of picking up Dylan Glithero, Kaye wore slacks and a sport coat, and drove the pickup. His first task after arriving at the station was to call Neil Gaeta, who was thrilled when Kaye told him they'd be going North the next day.

"You sure you're ready?" Kaye asked. "It's most of the day in the car."

"I'm beyond ready," Gaeta said. "I've already talked to the Doc. He cleared me and referred me to a doctor in Berkeley. Just tell me what time I get paroled."

Kaye laughed. "Yeah, must feel like that. I'll pick you up at six-thirty tomorrow morning."

His next call was to Eilene Holderby at Grove Charter.

"Good morning, Detective," she answered cheerfully. "What can I do for you?"

"I need to know if Mr. Glithero has a free period during the day today."

She checked, and told Kaye that yes, Glithero had an open period starting at 11:15 a.m. "May I inquire as to why you're asking?"

"I need to talk to him," was all Kaye said.

Holderby was quiet for a moment, then asked, "Would it help if I had him in my office waiting for you?"

"It wouldn't hurt."

"And," she asked cagily, "should I arrange for someone else to cover his next class, just in case?"

"That might be prudent, Ms. Holderby," Kaye replied. "See you at eleven-fifteen."

Kaye updated case files and printed several copies of the Glithero warrants. As he reviewed them yet again, he had an idea. Turning to his computer, he put together a quick email.

'Arch,

I'd like to take another run at getting the cell-free DNA test on Valerie Weber's blood. I have an arrest warrant for rape, statutory rape and other charges for

222

a suspect in another case, and he's the guy I've been looking at on the Weber case. Same M.O.; young girl, student of his, etc. Only difference is this victim is still alive. After the arrest I can collect his DNA. I need to know if this is the guy who impregnated Weber.
Ben'

He re-read the email several times, trying to decide if he was over- or under-selling his request. Finally, he just sent it. He trusted Arch.

***

It was just after 11:00 a.m. when Kaye pulled the unmarked unit into Grove Charter. He didn't bother with the visitors' lot, choosing instead to park at the curb outside the main entrance. He'd hardly gotten out of the car when a bell rang and students suddenly appeared everywhere as they changed classes.

He decided to wait for the next bell and the empty hallways it signaled.

When the 11:15 a.m. bell rang the swarm disappeared almost as suddenly as it had materialized, and only a few tardy stragglers remained. He headed for the office.

Mrs. Kowalczyk was waiting for him.

"Good morning, Detective Kaye," she said somberly. "Ms. Holderby is waiting for you." She buzzed him through.

He stopped outside the closed door of Holderby's office, knocked twice, then opened the door and let himself in. Holderby was behind her desk and Dylan Glithero sat in the chair Kaye had occupied on his last visit.

Glithero turned at the sound of the door opening, saw Kaye, then turned and glared at Holderby.

"What's going on, Eileen?" Glithero said, his voice flat.

"Dylan, this is Detective Kaye. He asked me to arrange this meeting so he could talk to you."

"About what?" Glithero demanded angrily.

"He'll fill you in," Holderby replied. She looked at Kaye. "Detective, have a seat."

"That won't be necessary," Kaye said, his eyes fixed on Glithero. "Are you Dylan Glithero?"

"I am. Tell me what this is about."

"Can you confirm your date of birth and current address for me, please."

Glithero gave Kaye the information.

"Dylan Glithero, I have a warrant for your arrest. Please stand up and –"

"On what charge?" Glithero demanded. He stayed seated, his hands clamped to the chair's arms, as his eyes bounced between Kaye and Holderby.

"Rape, statutory rape and sexual assault of a minor," Kaye replied. "Now, stand up and put your hands behind your back."

"Who is it I'm supposed to have raped?" Glithero demanded, making no effort to rise.

"The victim's name is Audra O'Bannon."

"Did you know about this?" Glithero spat at Holderby.

The Principal stuttered, making a gesture of futility. "He asked for a meeting. I…"

"One more time, Mr. Glithero," Kaye said murderously. "Stand up and put your hands behind your back. If you don't, I'll do it for you."

"This is bullshit," Glithero protested as he stood up, turned his back to Kaye and put his hands together behind his back.

Kaye handcuffed him. While still holding the cuff hinge he advised Glithero of his Miranda rights.

"Do you understand your rights as I've explained them?" he asked when he was done.

"Goddamn right I do," Glithero blustered. "All I've got to say is I want my lawyer."

"Works for me," Kaye said. "Let's go."

He steered Glithero around the chairs and guided him to the door, nodding his thanks to a still-stunned Eileen Holderby as he went by.

Keeping one hand wrapped around Glithero's upper right arm, Kaye led him to the main entrance. He reached out and pulled the door open, and as it swiveled he caught a fleeting glimpse of a figure reflected in the glass. He turned to look.

Thirty feet away, stock still in the middle of the hallway, his eyes wide and his mouth hanging open, stood Kenny Vaughan.

***

Three hours later, after booking Glithero and obtaining a DNA sample, Kaye returned to the squad room.

Glithero hadn't uttered a word to Kaye during the entire process, speaking only to answer direct questions from the booking officer. To Kaye, the man's silence and attitude seemed rooted in smug confidence rather than fear or concern.

And that worried Kaye.

What does he know that I don't, he kept asking himself. He had no answer.

He tried calling Kayla Okafor, but she was in court. He left a message with her paralegal to pass along that he'd arrested Glithero, and the bond details from the warrant.

Then he carefully documented Glithero's arrest and booking in the case file. As he worked, it suddenly dawned on him that if he intended to be in Ukiah the day after tomorrow to talk to Greg Sebaly, he should probably check with Sheriff Merritt first. He cussed himself out as he made the call.

"Merritt," the Sheriff answered.

"Sheriff, Ben Kaye from the LAPD. How are you?"

"I'm well, thank you."

"Hey," Kaye said, "I know it's short notice, but I was hoping to come up there on Saturday to talk to Detective Sebaly. I have to be in Oakland tomorrow, and it would really help me out if I could just make one trip. Would that work?"

"I'll make it work," Merritt replied. "I told Greg you were looking into Glithero and he got really excited. I know he'd love to talk to you."

"I'm planning on being in Ukiah by late Friday evening, so if early Saturday works best for you and Sebaly, that's okay with me."

"How about nine on Saturday morning?"

"Where should I go?"

"Just come to the Department. We'll go together."

"Sounds like a plan," Kaye said. "Thanks, Sheriff. See you Saturday at nine."

Kaye sat and worked out the logistics for the weekend. Timing was critical for his meeting with Tina Magnuson, but, either way, it shouldn't take long. From Oakland to Ukiah was about two hours. He called and made a motel reservation, just in case, knowing that if things went according to plan and he got out of Ukiah by mid-afternoon, he could make it home that evening.

CHAPTER 28

Neil Gaeta was packed, ready, and excited when Kaye knocked on the hotel room door at 6:30 a.m. Any misgivings Kaye had about taking Gaeta home vaporized as he watched the man navigate the suite on his crutches at an astonishing pace.

"Only one problem," Gaeta said when they were ready to go.

"What's that?" Kaye asked.

"Would you mind carrying the suitcase?"

Kaye laughed. "I think I can handle that."

By 7:00 a.m. they were checked out and on the road.

With one stop for gas and food in Ventura, it was just shy of 1:30 p.m. when Kaye took the 6th Street exit off the 880. A block from the Oakland PD headquarters he swung into a restaurant parking lot.

"I need to make a couple calls," he told Gaeta.

"Don't hurry on my account," Gaeta said with a smile.

The first call was to Tina Magnuson.

"Hey, Tina, we're almost there," he told her. "Okay if we're a few minutes early?"

"Sure. Come on up. Third floor."

His next call was to J.J.

"Hey, it's Ben. You ready?"

"I am," J.J. replied. "Are you there?"

"Close enough. Remember the sequence?"

"I wrote it down," J.J. assured him.

"Let's hope this works," Kaye said and ended the call.

At a quarter to two, Kaye and Gaeta were ushered into the Detective Squad room on the third floor of Oakland PD headquarters. Magnuson saw them and came to meet them.

"Neil, it's great to see you," she said as she gave Gaeta a hug made awkward by his crutches.

"Good to see you, too, Tina," Gaeta said. "Without Detective Kaye, I wouldn't be here."

"That's what I hear." She turned to Kaye. "Thanks, Ben. And thanks for bringing him home."

"My pleasure."

"Have you filled Neil in on what's happened?"

"I thought I'd let you do that," Kaye replied.

"Absolutely," Magnuson said.

She led them to a cubicle large enough to hold two desks, the chairs situated so the occupants' backs would be to each other. A tan leather bomber jacket hung over the back of one chair. Several other chairs were lined up outside the desk area against the panels between Magnuson's cubicle and the adjoining spaces.

"Grab a couple of those, will you?" She asked Kaye, pointing at the chairs as she stood aside to let Gaeta through.

Kaye grabbed two chairs. It would be crowded, but it would work.

"Tom's supposed to be here in a sec," Magnuson said, "but let's get started."

She had barely begun to bring Gaeta up to date on all the happenings in the Peter Li case when Tom Horton walked in.

"Sorry I'm late," Horton said as he sat down in the chair holding the bomber jacket. "Hey, Neil, you're looking good." He reached out and shook Gaeta's hand.

"So, as I was saying," Magnuson said as she launched back into her narrative.

Kaye watched the clock.

Magnuson was still filling Gaeta in on the details of Li's deal with the Feds when Kaye heard a barely discernible ringtone coming from somewhere nearby.

He checked the clock again. Two o'clock, straight up.

The sound persisted. It took Kaye a moment to realize it was coming from the inside pocket of the bomber jacket hanging on Horton's chair.

"Do you need to get that," he asked Horton, interrupting Magnuson and staring into the man's eyes.

"That?" Horton asked nervously. "Uh, no, it's okay. That's my wife's ringtone. I'll call her back." He turned to Magnuson and said, "Sorry. Continue."

She did.

Kaye listened and watched the clock.

One minute after the phone in the jacket had stopped ringing, it started again.

Horton ignored it.

"Tina, excuse me," Kaye said, interrupting Magnuson and turning to Horton. "You should probably get that. It might be important."

Horton stared back at Kaye and said, "Ignore it."

The phone kept ringing.

"You really should answer that," Kaye said bluntly. "Leandro might have important news for you."

"Who?" Horton asked, and Kaye saw worry flash in the Oakland PD detective's eyes.

"Rogelio Leandro," Kaye said. "You know, your contact with the Tiger Boys."

"What?" Magnuson blurted, stunned.

"There's your leak," he said to her, pointing at Horton.

"My partner? That's impossible! Tom?" She looked at Horton, who stayed quiet.

"Get the phone," Kaye told her. "I can tell you the number those calls came from. It's another detective I work with. We got the number off a phone belonging to Rogelio Leandro, who we popped right after the shootings at the safe house."

"I don't have to sit here and listen to this bullshit," Horton snarled and stood up.

"Pretty clever, actually," Kaye said to him. "You knew enough about Chen to get a woman to call one of our Lieutenants that knows Chen and pretend to be her. That's how the Tiger Boys got the safe house address."

"Get out of my way," Horton demanded and tried to brush past Kaye.

He may as well have been trying to move a cement truck.

"Sit down," Kaye said menacingly. "And if you so much as look at your sidearm I'll feed it to you."

Kaye thought for a moment that Horton was going to challenge him, but he saw the expression in the man's eyes change from defiance to defeat.

"Sit down," he repeated.

Horton stepped backwards and collapsed into his chair.

"You miserable son of a bitch," Magnuson hissed. "We've been partners for three years. How could you?"

"I had no choice," Horton said weakly.

"No choice?" Magnuson exploded. "You're a cop, goddamn it! You only had one choice!"

Horton stared at her. "They sent me pictures of my kids getting off the school bus a half-block from my house. What was I supposed to do?"

"Tell them to fuck off! Report it! Get protection!" Magnuson half-shouted. "Oh, my God!" She stood up and put her hand on the butt of her pistol.

By now, others in the squad room were gathering near the cubicle, watching and listening.

"Stand up," Magnuson savagely ordered Horton.

"Tina, please," Horton begged.

"Stand up!"

Horton stood up, head down and shoulder sagging.

"Hand me your pistol," Magnuson ordered. "Use your left hand, and butt first or I'll shoot you myself."

Horton complied, dropping the magazine to the floor before handing the weapon to Magnuson.

"I should cuff you…" Magnuson started to say, then stopped and glared at the crowd now surrounding the cubicle. "For fuck's sake, don't just stand there!" she shouted. "Somebody go get Chen and the Captain!"

Two men detached themselves from the group and hurried off in different directions.

"Show's over," she said wearily to those who remained. Then, to Horton, "Sit down. And give me your badge. You're done."

Kaye waited until Chen and Magnuson's Captain showed up, then filled them in on the chain of events surrounding the phone sting.

The Captain listened intently. The whole time Chen looked at Horton with daggers in her eyes.

"That's about it," Kaye concluded. "And I'm not trying to defend him," he looked at Horton, "but Leandro told me the Tiger Boys don't take no for an answer." He saw Chen nod slightly. "They would've killed his kids without a second thought."

"We'll look into it," the Captain said. "Thank you, Detective Kaye. Nice work."

Two uniformed officers appeared, handcuffed Horton and led him away.

"Oh, my god," Magnuson said as she collapsed into her chair when it was just her, Kaye and Gaeta. "I never would've thought…"

Kaye looked at her with a half-smile. "Well, to tell you the truth, I was worried it was going to be you."

"No way," Gaeta spoke up. "She's the one who warned me."

"Standard diversion," Kaye said with a shrug.

Magnuson looked at him and shook her head. "Either way, I think we're done here. Neil, hang on for a few minutes and I'll take you home."

She looked at Kaye. "Can you hang around and have dinner later, Mr. Suspicious?"

"Sorry, but I've got to be in Ukiah tonight for an early interview tomorrow on a homicide I'm working."

"I owe you both dinner," Gaeta said. "As soon as I can walk, it's on me for all of us."

Goodbyes were said and Kaye headed for the pickup.

When he was beyond the worst of the traffic, he made two calls. The first was to Kayla Okafor. It went to voice mail.

"Counselor, Detective Kaye. Oakland PD just identified their intel leak thanks to what we got off Rogelio Leandro's phone. You're good to go on a plea deal."

The second call was to a very grateful Lieutenant Lenoir.

CHAPTER 29

The beautiful small towns strung along Mendocino County's wild, rugged coastline and the locally produced world-class wines capture most of the region's attention. Ukiah, the County Seat, lay well inland, bisected by Highway 101.

The Sheriff's Office and County Jail complex vaguely reminded Kaye of Westside Alternative as he turned off Low Gap Road into a parking lot ringed with one-story buildings and barbed wire topped chain link fences. He found a spot posted Visitors Only, parked, and headed inside.

"Can I help you?" asked the deputy behind the glass-fronted reception counter.

"Good morning," Kaye said, handing her his badge wallet. "I'm here to see Sheriff Merritt. He's expecting me."

She glanced at the ID and handed it back. "The Sheriff told me you'd be coming in. Hold on a sec. I'll let him know you're here."

"Thank you."

He turned to survey the lobby. It was small, with one large window covered by a narrow-slat Venetian blind that hung lopsided, but succeeded in cutting the glare off the shiny linoleum floor. Molded black plastic chairs lined two walls, and above them was the seemingly obligatory gallery of County Sheriffs past.

No politicians here. Yet. Kaye thought as he scanned the portraits. Mendocino County had eighty percent the land area of L.A. County, but only one percent of the population. It was exactly what Sebaly had said he was looking for.

"Detective Kaye?" A gruff voice from behind him brought Kaye back to the present. He turned to see a large, burly man in uniform standing in the open double doors that led to the offices.

"That's me," Kaye said and headed that way. "Sheriff Merritt, I presume. And, please, call me Ben."

The two lawmen shook hands and Kaye was surprised that Merritt's hand was almost as big as his.

"Nice to meet you, Ben. Come on back."

Merritt's office was a careful balance between ceremony and function. Against the wall behind the large oak desk were gold-edged American and California flags, the narrow wall space between them displaying Merritt's awards and credentials, and photos of him posing with dignitaries and celebrities. One entire wall was bookshelves filled to overflowing with volumes on criminal law and procedures, penal codes and hardbound Federal and California Supreme Court decisions. Before Kaye could sit down, Merritt had to remove a stack of folders from one of the chairs in front of his desk.

"Pardon the mess," Merritt said. "I'm trying to get our records fully digitized and sometimes I think I bit off more than my budget, or my sanity, can chew."

"Don't worry about it. There are a lot of days I couldn't tell you what color the top of my desk is. Comes with the territory."

"You want some coffee or something?"

"I'm good, thanks."

Merritt studied Kaye for a moment before saying, "I really didn't expect you to come all the way up here. The Glithero case is ancient history, and given Greg's condition, well…"

"Dylan Glithero isn't ancient history to me," Kaye said. "I arrested him day before yesterday."

"Really? You solved your homicide?"

"No," Kaye replied. "Rape, among other things. A seventeen-year-old student of his."

"Greg will be tickled to hear that," Merritt said. "That case haunts him."

"I've got a couple of those myself."

There was a moment of awkward silence, broken by Kaye.

"When we spoke on the phone you said Deputy Sebaly had been shot in the line of duty."

"Correct."

"What happened? I saw an old news story, but it didn't have many details."

"He walked into an armed robbery in progress at a convenience store up in Willits." Merritt saw the look on Kaye's face and added, "It's a little ways north of here on one-oh-one. Anyway, he got the guy who was about to execute the clerk, but didn't know the other guy in the store was an accomplice, not a customer. Greg got him, too, but not until the guy shot him. He lived, but he's in a chair and his speech center was damaged."

"Is he," Kaye paused, searching for the right word. "Coherent?"

"Oh, yeah," Merritt said instantly. "Mentally, he's all there. Sharp as a tack. He uses a computer to communicate. I contract with him for all our digital forensics, if that tells you anything."

"Got it. Where can I find him?"

"He doesn't live far from here. If you don't mind, I'd like to go with you. I'll drive."

"How about I follow you, in case you get hung up or called out?"

Merritt chuckled. "That'll work."

Less than ten minutes later, Kaye pulled his pickup to the curb behind Merritt's department pickup in front of a well-kept, single story house. A ramp led from the driveway outside the single car garage door and made a ninety degree turn to the porch. The front yard landscaping was lush and potted plants were everywhere.

"Does Sebaly live alone?" Kaye asked as they approached the front door.

"No," Merritt replied. "He lives with his wife and daughter."

"I guess I pictured him as single."

"He was when I hired him," Merritt said. "And full disclosure, he married my baby sister. You can talk to Greg privately. I just came along to visit."

Kaye suddenly understood why Merritt was so protective of Sebaly.

They reached the porch. The entry door was open. A dark-haired woman in jeans and a sweatshirt stood behind the screen door and pushed it open when she saw Merritt.

"Hey, Gary," she said, glancing at Kaye. "What's going on?"

"Hey, Katy," Merritt replied. "This is Ben Kaye from the LAPD. He needs to talk to Greg."

The woman started to say something, but Merritt stopped her. "I've already talked to him about it. He knows we're coming."

"Then come on in," she said easily, holding the door wide open and stepping out of the way. "Welcome, Mr. Kaye. Greg's out on the patio." She pointed to an open sliding glass door on the back side of the house. "Go on back."

"Please, call me Ben," Kaye said. "And thank you."

"I'll go with him and say hi to Greg," Merritt said and led the way.

They navigated to the back door. Outside, Kaye saw a man in a wheelchair, his back to them, pulled up to a table, working intently on some potted plants.

"Hey, Greg," Merritt announced their presence as he slid the door open. "I brought Detective Kaye to talk to you."

Sebaly spun from the table. He wore sweatpants, slippers, a t-shirt under a light jacket and an Oakland A's baseball cap. He waved at them to come on out.

"If you'll excuse me," Merritt said to Kaye, "I'm going to go visit with my sister." He turned and went back into the house.

Sebaly eyed Kaye and put aside the plant – some kind of cactus, Kaye thought – he'd been working on. Then he picked up a computer that was on the table, put it in his lap, held up one finger in a 'just a minute' gesture, opened the computer and began typing furiously.

"Welcome." A digital voice came from the computer. "It is nice to meet you. Thank you for coming. Please have a seat."

"My pleasure," Kaye said, choosing an Adirondack chair only a few feet from Sebaly. "And that is astounding."

Sebaly smiled lopsidedly and began typing again. "Thank you. It is much faster than waiting for me to try and talk and much easier to understand."

"You type pretty fast," Kaye observed.

Sebaly smiled again as his fingers worked. "I write my own macros. I can say many things with only a few keystrokes." His fingers worked again, longer this time. "Complex sentences take time."

"I'll remember that."

Sebaly typed some more and Kaye leaned forward to watch the screen. He realized that the software anticipated sentence structure and that the computer started 'talking' even before Sebaly stopped typing.

"You are here to talk about Dylan Glithero."

"I am," Kaye replied. "I should probably start by telling you I arrested Glithero day before yesterday for statutory rape."

Sebaly's smile was not artificial as he worked the keyboard. "That does not surprise me. Please begin by telling me about your case and how Glithero came to your attention."

Kaye spent thirty minutes going through every aspect of the Valerie Weber case, from her assault and initial interview with her and her mother, to his arrest of Glithero on unrelated rape charges involving Audra O'Bannon. He knew from the Orange County trial transcripts that Sebaly was an astute investigator, so left nothing out and included his impressions and suppositions.

"But you still have no witnesses or forensic evidence to connect Glithero to Valerie Weber's murder."

"Just a gut feeling," Kaye said.

"Gut feelings are not admissible in court."

"Too true. I know Glithero couldn't have known I was looking at him, but he still managed to stay one step ahead of me until Detective Burke convinced Audra to give us a statement."

"That is because he has been there before. Did you read my reports on the case?"

"I tried," Kaye replied. "After Glithero's acquittal his lawyer got an order from the Court commanding the Sheriff's office to destroy them. If it weren't for the child abuse exception, I would have never even known about his arrest."

"Not his lawyer. Eugene Calhoun's."

"What makes you say that?"

"Glithero had a public defender. Calhoun had major legal counsel. His family has money."

"Calhoun would do that for Glithero?"

"Calhoun was Glithero's supervising teacher. They became good friends. Brothers in crime. And sin." Sebaly laughed.

"I saw that Calhoun testified for Glithero in Glithero's trial," Kaye said. "I couldn't believe the Court would allow that."

"That is what friends, and good lawyers, are for." Sebaly smiled again.

"So, let me ask you," Kaye said carefully. "Do you think Glithero was guilty?"

"I did when I arrested him and did when the trial started. But the victim was terrible on the stand. I think she really cared for Glithero. Plus, there was Calhoun's testimony. I was not happy with the verdict, but I understood it."

"Based on what you knew then, do you think Glithero is capable of murder?"

Sebaly's hands went still as he thought about the question. Finally, he started typing.

"I would have said no back then. Now I cannot say. But Gene Calhoun certainly would have been."

"His name hasn't come up in connection with this investigation."

"You said in your summary when we started that there is another suspect in the O'Bannon case."

"There is," Kaye confirmed. "All I have is a first name, and I haven't started digging yet."

"What is the name?"

"Art."

Sebaly's hands went still again as he stared at Kaye. Slowly, he started typing again.

"Eugene Arthur Calhoun."

Kaye was stunned.

"Did you read the case reports?"

"No," Kaye admitted. "When I went to your old department to look into Glithero, I'd never heard of Calhoun. I did hear there was a...scandal involving teachers, but I didn't hear the name Calhoun until the Court Administrator, without a request from me, sent me Calhoun's trial transcript after finding it stored right next to Glithero's. He thought I might be interested. I read through it, but... I missed it."

"Understandable."

Kaye sat quietly, mentally berating himself for what he knew was a mistake.

"Gene Calhoun was, is, a despicable human being." Sebaly's computer intoned. "I knew he raped more young girls than he was charged with. I believe he paid parents to keep their daughters quiet."

"But he was found guilty and put away."

"I cannot take credit for that. Only one victim had the courage to testify, against her parent's wishes."

"K.S."

"Yes. I remember that her first name was Kathy, but my injury has robbed me of her last name after all these years. She was a very brave young lady. The Prosecutor tried for a plea deal, but the Judge saw through it and I'm sure her testimony had a lot to do with it."

"I read that in the transcript," Kaye said. "Why would the prosecutor do that?"

"It was complicated. The public seemed to think that Glithero and Calhoun were co-defendants because they were both teachers at the same school, but they were not. Separate cases. When Glithero was acquitted, there were protests outside the courthouse."

"I heard that."

"I believe that the prosecutor in Calhoun's case, whose name was Chilton, got nervous when Glithero was acquitted. His case against Calhoun was tenuous at best given that only one victim testified. Chilton's boss wanted a conviction one way or another."

"It sounded to me like he was willing to give away the store to get it," Kaye said.

"Chilton was not like that. He was a good prosecutor. His boss bullied him into it. That is why he quit after the trial, even though the Judge ignored the sentencing recommendation."

"What happened after that?" Kaye asked. "I heard there was an internal investigation."

"There was. I was cleared of any wrongdoing. But I had had enough. To me, being investigated was a giant vote of no confidence and an attempt by Chilton's boss to pin his failures on me. So I quit."

"I understand," Kaye said. "I will tell you that just from reading your testimony in both trials, you did a great job on the investigations. One thing I don't get, though, is why the trials were held at pretty much the same time."

Sebaly shrugged, then typed.

"Another political misread by the District Attorney. And pressure from Calhoun's lawyer. He saw the opportunity to tilt the field in his client's favor. Had Kathy not come forward to testify, Calhoun would have walked, too."

Kaye sat silent, pondering how politics and miscalculations seemed to have a way of getting in the way of truth and justice.

"You should check the sex offender registry for Calhoun. As I recall, he was ordered to register. They will have his current address, or at least they should."

"I'll do that. Is there anything else you can tell me about Calhoun I should know? Like where he did his time?" Kaye asked.

"I believe he was remanded to Lancaster, but I don't know if he was ever transferred, or how much of his sentence he actually served. He was a very devious individual, even back then. I can only imagine what his time in prison did to him. If you want more insight into his behavior and motivations, read my case reports. He was convicted. They should still be on file."

"Thank you very much, Detective Sebaly," Kaye said as he stood up. "I appreciate you taking the time to talk to me, and I really appreciate your insights. I'm truly sorry about what happened to you."

Sebaly's hands flew over the keyboard.

"Do not feel sorry for me, Detective Kaye. A hazard of the job we all face. Because I came here I have a beautiful wife and daughter. I would not trade them to be an Olympic sprinter. One more thing."

"What's that?"

"You already have Glithero. Get a conviction. Now catch and convict Eugene Calhoun. He belongs in prison."

"That's the plan." Kaye shook Sebaly's hand and took his leave.

"Did you get what you needed?" Merritt asked when Kaye got back inside.

"I did," Kaye replied. "Thank you."

"I'm glad he could help," Katy said.

"Me, too," Kaye said as he reached into his pocket, grabbed a business card and handed it to her. "If you ever need anything...Anything at all...you call me." He turned to Merritt. "I'm going to take off from here, if that's okay."

"Sure," Merritt said, shaking Kaye's hand again. "Let me know how this turns out, so I can tell Greg."

"I will, Sheriff. Thanks again."

As Kaye drove south he planned his next moves, intending to track down Eugene Arthur Calhoun. The Department of Corrections might be a good place to start. If nothing else, he needed a recent photo to show Audra O'Bannon. He also wanted to take another run at Dylan Glithero. A weekend in jail is often a very effective attitude adjustment mechanism.

CHAPTER 30

After a weekend in the pickup, the '61 Duo Glide was a welcome transportation change on Monday morning.

He was busy updating and closing the Gaeta case file when Captain Thompson came in, saw him, detoured to his desk and leaned casually against the filing cabinet.

"I heard you found the leak in the Oakland PD," the Captain said. "Nice work."

"I did," Kaye said. "One of the detectives that came down when we hooked Gaeta, if you can believe that."

Thompson shook his head and said, "It happens. Cops are human, too. At least it was one of theirs and not one of ours."

"Agreed. Lenoir was happy."

"I bet."

"Sorry I didn't bring you the head," Kaye said, smiling. "You'll have to find a different present to give the boss when you celebrate leaving."

"I still haven't decided," Thompson said, his expression turning sour. He tapped his knuckles on the filing cabinet. "Carry on, Detective. Again, nice work."

Kaye, glad he wasn't in Thompson's predicament, watched the Captain walk to his office. Since Amy's death the job had lost a lot of its luster and he often thought about quitting. He'd even taken a leave of absence and gone to Colorado to help a former colleague, now a Chief of Police, solve a particularly unusual case. But then there would be a bright moment, like saving Neil Gaeta's life and uncovering an informant in the ranks. Those brought back his old enthusiasm, even if only temporarily.

With a sigh he changed the status of the Gaeta case to 'Closed by Arrest', saved the file and reached for his phone. A minute later he was connected to Kayla Okafor.

"Good morning, Counselor."

"Detective Kaye, good morning. What can I do for you?"

"I was thinking of going downtown and taking another run at Dylan Glithero this morning," he replied. "Over the weekend I talked to the

Orange County detective that arrested him way back when. With what I know now I might be able to –"

"Save your breath, Detective," Okafor interrupted. "Glithero posted bond Friday morning. His attorney reached out to this office and specifically told us, and by inference you, to stay away from his client."

"You're kidding. His bond was a half-million. Who posted it?"

"His attorney bonded him out. Certified funds, the source was not disclosed."

Calhoun. It has to be, he thought. "I think I know where the money came from," he told Okafor.

"Doesn't matter where it came from. It only matters that it belongs to the Court if Glithero fails to appear."

"It matters to me," Kaye said. "I know who the other guy is in all this, and I heard he has money."

"I feel your pain, Detective, but posting someone's bond is not a crime."

Kaye ended the call just as he heard J.J. and Burke's voices as they came into the squad. They were having a spirited discussion on the next steps to take on a case. J.J., as the senior partner, would prevail, but Kaye was encouraged to hear Burke standing up for her two cents worth. It meant she was finding her footing as a detective.

"Hey, Ben," she said when she saw him.

"Hi guys," Kaye responded.

"It worked!" J.J. exclaimed, high-fiving Kaye.

"It did. Thanks for your help."

"Who was it," J.J. asked.

"Horton," Kaye replied.

"Wait…" J.J. said. "Wasn't he Magnuson's partner?"

"He was," Kaye confirmed.

"Holy crap!" Burke exclaimed. "Did they arrest him?"

"They did." Kaye filled them in on what had transpired.

"What happens now?" J.J. asked.

"His career is over," Kaye said. "After that, I don't know. The Tiger Boys went after his family to get leverage on him, so it'll depend."

"Jeez," Burke muttered. "What a mess."

"How'd the trip to Ukiah work out?" J.J. asked.

"Good," Kaye replied. "Got all kinds of insights and intel. Now I just need to chase it all down."

"Good luck," J.J. said. Then, to Burke, "Well, partner, shall we?"

"I guess," Burke said with a huge sigh. "Never a dull moment." Before she turned to follow J.J. she winked and grinned.

Kaye leaned back in his chair, chagrined. With Glithero on the loose, his morning was suddenly free. He opened his email and found a reply from Arch, timestamped late Thursday.

'Ben, the boss approved the cell-free DNA analysis on the Weber case. I'm taking the sample to the lab first thing in the morning and I'll try and twist their arm on results. I'll let you know as soon as I have something. Thanks. Arch.'

Next, he navigated to the law enforcement portal for the State Pardons and Parole Board. Despite trying several alternate spellings, he was unable to find Eugene Arthur Calhoun. To him, that meant Calhoun had either already cleared parole, or had served his entire sentence and been released.

He considered his options, then grabbed the phone.

"Lieutenant Adamson, please," he asked the Orange County deputy that answered.

His call was transferred and a moment later Adamson answered.

"Lieutenant Adamson, this is Detective Kaye, LAPD. We spoke in your office recently about Dylan Glithero."

"I remember," Adamson said. "How's the case going?"

Kaye told her he'd arrested Glithero late last week, but the girl involved in that case wasn't his homicide victim.

"I also tracked down Detective Sebaly," he added. "He had another, very similar case involving another teacher at almost the same time, and that defendant was convicted. I have reason to believe that individual might also be connected to my current case."

"What's the guy's name," Adamson asked instantly.

"Eugene Arthur Calhoun."

He heard the tapping of the keyboard before Adamson spoke.

"Got him. What do you need?"

"His date of birth and current address from your sex offender list."

Adamson gave him the DOB, then said, "Uh...hmm... Calhoun isn't on our sex offender list."

That told Kaye that Calhoun had served his entire sentence, then successfully petitioned the Court to have his name expunged from the list. To Adamson he said, "I read the trial transcript. It was a circus. There is one more thing you could do for me, if it's possible."

"What's that?"

"Sebaly told me I should read his reports on the Calhoun case to gain insight into the guy. Since Calhoun was convicted, I assume your office still has them?"

"We should," Adamson said, then went quiet for a moment while Kaye listened to the keyboard. "Yep, looks like we have them, but they're not digitized."

"Can I get copies?"

"You can," Adamson replied. "You'll need to go to our website and fill out a records request form. Make sure you use the law enforcement officer page, or they'll send you a bill. They'll find them, print copies and send them to you. I have to warn you, though, they're old enough it could take a while."

"Ah, bureaucracy," Kaye said.

"Amen to that." Adamson chuckled. "But at least we still have them. It was a long time ago."

"I've been hearing that a lot lately," Kaye said ruefully. "Thanks, Lieutenant."

Kaye immediately went to the OCSD website and filled out the records request form. It didn't take long. The page acknowledged his request, but gave him no indication how long it might take.

Next he dialed Patty's extension.

"Hey, Detective. What's up?"

"Can you look up a driver's license for me?"

"I can do that," Patty said. "Who are we looking for?"

"The guy's name is Eugene Arthur Calhoun." He gave Patty the particulars he'd gotten from Adamson. "He should have a rape conviction in Orange County about the same time as Dylan Glithero's arrest back then. If you find him, run a history for me, please."

"If I find him, would a photo line-up help?"

"Yeah, it would, now that you mention it."

"Okay, I'll see what I can do."

"Thanks, Patty."

He'd barely hung up when the phone rang.

"Already?" he asked, expecting it to be Patty.

"I'm sorry," a woman's voice said. "I'm trying to reach Detective Kaye."

"This is Detective Kaye. My fault, I thought you were someone else. How can I help you?"

"This is Lois, Judge Franklin's clerk. I wanted to let you know that the release of the Weber adoption file was approved. I have it, and you can come by and pick it up anytime."

"Thank you, Lois. I'll stop in and get it."

"The Judge also wanted me to warn you that the file is, uh, a bit of a mess."

"How so?"

"You'll see."

He grabbed the Big Boar jacket and headed for the '61. On the way, he reflected again on how important information flow was to what he did. After his initial interview with the Webers, he'd figured the case would be a slam dunk. Ex-boyfriend, or maybe the jealous ex of a current boyfriend, maybe a rivalry of some sort. If he'd had the same volume of information flow then that he was getting now, he thought Valerie Weber might still be alive.

After a quick stop for a sandwich he headed to the Courthouse and picked up Valerie Weber's adoption file. Lois was at lunch, but the envelope was waiting for him. He sat on a bench in the hallway and skimmed through the file. There was a lot of information, most of it pertaining to the background check on the Webers, and he knew he'd need to dedicate a chunk of time to go through it more closely.

On the way back to the '61, his cell phone buzzed. Caller ID said 'Lab'.

"Kaye."

"Detective, this is Lou Ellen in firearms and ballistics. I have some results for you on the weapons you wanted tested."

"What did you come up with?"

"On the weapon tagged as 'downstairs' I was able to match the serial number to a burglary report in Encino from last year. But I pretty much came up empty on ballistics. I also came up completely empty on the gun recovered from the Rogelio Leandro arrest." She paused. "But on the 'upstairs' weapon we hit the jackpot. It was a ballistics match to the bullet recovered from Neil Gaeta, and it matched the store clerk homicide in the Valley last year. The serial number had been filed off, but I was able to raise it and match it to a gun store burglary in Bakersfield four years ago."

"Which means it could have passed through a lot of hands since then," Kaye said.

"Exactly," Lou Ellen agreed. "But at least we know it was the gun used to shoot Neil Gaeta, and it's off the street now."

"True. And the guy who was carrying it is also off the street."

"Sounds like a dead end to me," Lou Ellen said, then quickly added, "No pun intended, Detective. Sorry."

"Don't worry about it," Kaye said. "Would you email a copy of your findings to me?"

"I can do that," Lou Ellen said.

Kaye sat on the '61, wondering if he should go back to the station or go see JoAnn Weber to brief her on Valerie's case. When he thought about it, he realized he didn't really have anything to tell her until he had the DNA results. Everything else had turned into the O'Bannon case, which he couldn't reveal to her.

Please let the DNA test work, he thought, knowing that without it he had nothing to tie Dylan Glithero to Valerie Weber outside their student-teacher relationship.

"Well, shit," he muttered to himself. "Back to the barn."

***

When Kaye pushed through the squad room doors he nearly ran over Patty Phillips as she was leaving.

"Sorry, Patty," Kaye said. "Guess I could pay attention."

"That's okay. They should put windows in these doors. Plus, I was looking for you. I found a driver's license for Eugene Calhoun. The issue date is fairly recent." She paused for a second before adding, "And the address is in Orange County."

"Anaheim?"

"Newport Beach. I checked, and it's on one of the islands in the harbor. This guy must have money."

That doesn't fit with what Sonny told me about the gated community in the hills, he thought. To Patty he said, "I think you're right."

"And I left the photo line-up on your desk," she said. "Call me if you need anything else."

Kaye found the folder containing what Patty had come up with. The Orange County arrest and conviction was the only entry on Calhoun's criminal history, which made sense considering the man had spent a goodly chunk of his life in prison. He studied the license photo and the photo array.

Doesn't look like a monster, but he is one, he thought. *They should make guys like that wear signs.*

He put everything back in the envelope and picked up the phone.

"Hello," a woman answered.

"Elise O'Bannon, please. This is Detective Kaye, LAPD."

"Hello, Detective. This is Elise."

"How are you, Mrs. O'Bannon?"

"Okay, I guess," she replied. "Under the circumstances."

"And Audra?"

"Hard to tell, honestly. She refused to go to school after you and Detective Burke were here. But once the word got around that you had arrested Mr. Glithero, she went back. She's supposed to meet with the Principal today."

"Glithero made bail on Friday," Kaye told her.

"Doesn't matter. I was told he's been indefinitely suspended from his teaching duties."

"Good to know. The reason I called is that I think I've identified the man Audra called 'Art'. If it's convenient, I'd like to stop by later and show Audra some photos."

"You mean like a line-up?"

"Exactly."

"That would be fine. We'll be here."

"Thank you, Mrs. O'Bannon. See you around five?"

"Five works. Thank you, Detective."

Kaye hung up and leaned back in his chair. Assuming Audra identified Calhoun, which he thought was a lock, he'd have a warrant for Calhoun by midday tomorrow and hopefully have him in handcuffs by the end of the day.

But the address thing niggled at the base of his certainty.

He pushed that aside, picked up the phone again and called JoAnn Weber.

When she answered he identified himself and immediately apologized for upsetting her on his last visit.

"You don't need to apologize, Detective," she said. "Miles talked some sense into me. It was mostly my fault. Can we just start over?"

"We can do that," Kaye said. "I thought I'd call with an update on the case."

"Good news, I hope," she said, and Kaye heard the trepidation in her voice.

"Actually, yes. I have a primary suspect in Valerie's death. I'm still connecting all the dots, but I'm waiting on DNA test results. If they come back like I think they will, it should be enough to get an arrest warrant."

"Who is it?" she asked instantly.

"His name is Dylan Glithero. He's –"

"Mister Glithero the teacher?" Weber blurted. "Oh my God! How did you…?

"I tied the white SUV that had been picking Valerie up after school to him. I also have video of a white SUV picking Valerie up where she parked her car on the night she went missing. I'm still waiting on enhanced video, but I should be able to make a driver identification when I get it."

"Is that why you asked me about our cars? A white Toyota?"·

"Yes, ma'am," Kaye replied. "Glithero's arrest last week was on other charges involving an underage girl at Grove Charter. I'll know more when the DNA results come back and I get the video."

"Audra," JoAnn Weber barely whispered.

"Excuse me?" Kaye asked, not sure he'd heard her correctly.

"The other girl. Is her name Audra?"

"How do you know that?"

"Audra was in Valerie's classes and writing group with Mr. Glithero when she went to Grove Charter," she said. "They didn't get along."

"In what way?" Kaye asked.

"Who knows? High school girls."

"When did the problems start?"

"Valerie and Audra were on-again, off-again starting in Junior High. 'Frenemies' is probably the best way to describe their relationship. But it seemed to get worse during Valerie's last year at Grove Charter. She was always complaining that Audra spread lies about her and tried to undercut her."

"Do you think Audra had anything to do with Valerie getting in trouble and having to change schools?"

"I hadn't thought of that," JoAnn said. "I thought all that had to do with us telling her she was adopted. But, maybe."

"Okay," Kaye said. "Might not have anything to do with what happened, but I'll poke around a little bit and see if there's a connection. Is there anything else I can do for you, Mrs. Weber?"

"Catch Valerie's killer."

"I'm working on it."

Kaye checked the time. He still had about an hour before he had to leave for the O'Bannon's.

He decided to use the time to take a closer look at Valerie Weber's adoption file. It didn't take him long to figure out why Judge Franklin had warned him.

Valerie, nee Crystal Lowden, hadn't been born in a hospital. It had been an unattended home birth, which kicked in an entirely different set of rules with which Kaye was only passingly familiar. He set the file aside and went to the State's website to research what was required and how to decipher the file.

It was so convoluted that he lost track of time.

"Call it a day, Detective." Captain Thompson's voice brought him back to the present.

"Huh?" he said, looking up.

"Go home," Thompson said. "Beat some traffic."

He looked at the clock and mentally kicked himself, repeatedly.

"G'night, Captain," he said as he reached for the phone. "I'm not far behind you."

He called Elise O'Bannon, told her he was running late, apologized, and told her he was on the way.

He grabbed the Big Boar jacket and the folder Patty had assembled. Three steps from his desk he spun around, went back, scooped up the adoption file and headed out.

He rode hard to make up time and managed to make it to the O'Bannon's only a few minutes late.

"I'm so sorry," were the first words out of his mouth when Elise opened the door. "I got caught up in something else."

"That's okay. Come on in. Audra's in the living room."

Trailed by Elise, Kaye headed for the now-familiar living room.

"That's quite the jacket," Elise said from behind him. "I didn't figure you for an outlaw biker."

"Hardly," Kaye said, laughing. "It's a keepsake from my younger days. I still wear it to honor friends."

"Well, it's beautiful," Elise said as she brushed past Kaye and sat down in the armchair next to Audra. "My husband would love it."

Kaye took a seat on the couch.

"I've already told Audra why you're here," Elise said, looking at Audra, who nodded.

"You want me to look at some pictures?" Audra asked Kaye.

"That's right," Kaye replied, then went through the standard photo line-up advisement and warnings. "If you see the man you know as Art, please point him out." He passed the line-up array to Audra. "And take your time."

Audra took it and began to study it. Kaye could tell she was concentrating and stayed quiet. It was over a minute before she spoke.

"I'm sorry," she said, handing the array back to Kaye, "but I don't recognize any of these men."

"Audra, are you sure?" Elise asked.

"Yes, Mom, I'm sure." She turned to Kaye. "None of those pictures are Art."

"That's okay," Kaye said. "Remember what I told you before I showed you the pictures." He tucked the array back into the folder. "Do you mind if I ask you a couple more questions?"

Audra glanced nervously at her mother before looking back to Kaye. "Uh, sure, I guess."

Kaye studied Audra intently before asking, "Do you remember when and where you first met the man you know as Art?"

"I don't remember exactly when," Audra replied, "but I met him for the first time when Dylan took me to his house in Orange County."

"Do you remember which city you went to?"

"Uh..." She hesitated. "Not really. I don't know very much about Orange County."

"Was it near the ocean?"

"No," Audra replied instantly. "It was more, like, in the hills someplace."

Kaye tried to figure out how that fit with what he knew about Gene Calhoun. "And you're sure it was Art's house?"

"Pretty sure," she said. "I mean, I didn't go through his mail or anything, but he had a studio set up and he knew where stuff was, so..." She shrugged.

"Was it in a gated community?"

"Yeah, it was. I remember Dylan had to put a code in before the gate would open."

"Audra, do you remember talking about Valerie Weber the last time I was here?"

"Yes," Audra said softly. "What happened to her is horrible."

"Did you get along with her?"

Audra hesitated and looked at her mother.

"Whoa," Elise said, "stop right there. Audra had nothing to do with what happened to Valerie Weber. This was supposed to be about showing her the pictures."

"Sorry," Kaye said. "I didn't mean to imply –"

"Exactly what *did* you mean to imply?" Elise interrupted angrily.

"I wasn't trying to imply anything," Kaye said. "It's a legitimate–"

"No, it's not," Elise interrupted again, launching herself from the chair. "That line of questioning has nothing to do with what happened to Audra. Whoever you thought this Art person was, well, obviously you're wrong. I think you should leave."

Kaye stood up and took the photo array from Audra. "Thank you for your time," he said politely. "The District Attorney's office should be in touch." He headed for the door.

That went well, you moron, he thought as he swung over the '61. *So, Art, who the hell are you?*

***

He stopped on the way home and got takeout. When he stepped through the back door his generally bad mood resulting from the epic fail with Elise and Audra O'Bannon wasn't helped by walking into the big, empty house.

Why bother? he asked himself as he looked around. *I can go anyplace I want to go, do anything I want to do. What's the point?*

That triggered memories of Roshi, who so often had told him he was following his intended Path.

I'm not Benkei anymore. I'm plain old Ben Kaye. No more mojo.

The thought deepened his growing depression. Suddenly he recalled one of his last conversations with Roshi after the two had sat *zazen* together.

"Roshi," he'd asked, "do you ever wish you'd done something else with your life?"

Expecting simply another question in response, as was Roshi's wont during a lesson, Kaye had been surprised when the old monk's face went blank before he looked down. Kaye instantly regretted asking the question. When Roshi looked up, moisture glistened in his eyes as he stared into nothingness.

"There was a girl in the camp," he'd barely whispered. "Mizuki. Beautiful moon. And she was beautiful beyond belief. We were young, but I loved her. I have always…" His voice broke and he looked down again. "She died of cholera," he managed to croak before falling silent.

"I'm sorry, Roshi."

The apology seemed to bring his mentor back.

"For asking the question? Or for hearing the answer?"

Always the teacher, Kaye remembered thinking. But his response was, "For causing you pain."

"Pain and doubt are life, Benkei."

"Does that mean that lack of pain and lack of doubt are death?"

Roshi had stared hard at him, then curled one corner of his mouth in a half-smile.

"Not death, Benkei," he said as he effortlessly pushed himself to his feet without putting a hand down. "*Nakara*," the old monk said softly before he walked away.

Kaye had had to look it up. The closest match he found in Western thought was Purgatory.

Get over yourself and do your job, he told himself. *That's what they pay you for.*

He grabbed the bag of takeout and a Guinness, picked up Valerie Weber's adoption file and went to Amy's above-the-garage refuge to escape the loneliness.

What he found in the file kept him up most of the night.

CHAPTER 31

A dead-tired Kaye rolled the Road King into the station parking lot just before 8:00 a.m. As soon as he got to the squad room, he shrugged out of the Big Boar jacket, fetched himself a strong cup of tea and called Kayla Okafor.

It went to voicemail.

"Counselor, it's your favorite detective calling again. I need to talk to somebody in your office that handles Child Protective Services cases about the finer points of the law. This is about the Valerie Weber case. Call me, please. I'll be in the office. Thanks."

He busied himself with paperwork, including a list of questions for Okafor, while he waited for a call back.

Amari Burke came in about fifteen minutes after he'd left the message for Okafor.

"How goes the O'Bannon case?" she asked after pleasantries were exchanged. "Did you find that Art guy yet?"

"I thought I did. Eugene Arthur Calhoun. Note the middle name. He, Glithero and high school girls go way back. Calhoun's done time."

"But Audra didn't pick him out?"

"Nope."

"She's lying," Burke said matter-of-factly. "What's next? Want me to talk to her?"

"I don't think it would help," Kaye replied. "The D.A. says she can be compelled to testify, but—"

"Yeah, but you need an ID from Audra for the PC to arrest the guy in the first place. Can't put the cart before the horse."

Kaye shrugged again. "What're you gonna do?"

"She probably couldn't pick him out because he had his pants on," Burke said, laughing. "You need a picture of his, uh, you-know-what. Preferably in battle dress."

"I thought you were on Audra's side?" Kaye said. "You wanted to get your hands on the guy. What happened?"

"Nothing," Burke said. "I'd still love the opportunity to ten ring the guy, but I can still see the humor in the situation." Her expression changed. "I've got to. Otherwise, some of this stuff eats me up."

"I hear that," Kaye said. "Oh, I also found out that Audra and Valerie Weber were classmates, but not exactly friends."

"Really?" Burke asked. "You think there's any chance Audra got involved with Glithero because she knew Valerie was, and wanted to one-up her?"

"It crossed my mind. But when I tried to go there, Elise threw me out."

"Oh, yeah," Burke said sarcastically. "The ever present 'not-my-kid' parental response."

Kaye smiled. He'd heard it a thousand times over the years.

"Where's J.J.?" he asked.

"Dentist," she replied, making a face. "Be a little late."

Kaye's phone chose that instant to ring.

"I've got to take this," he said, reaching for the receiver.

Burke nodded, waved and headed for her desk.

"Thanks for calling me back," he said when he answered.

"It sounded important," Kayla Okafor said.

"It is."

"Okay," she said. "You're on speaker, and I have Sandi Nelson here with me. She works child welfare cases and should be able to answer your questions."

"Hi, Detective," a woman said.

"Morning, Ms. Nelson. Thanks for making yourself available."

"Not a problem. Kayla's already given me the basics of your case. How can I help?"

"There were some things I ran into during the investigation that bothered me, so I got a warrant for the adoption file and went through it last night. I have some questions."

"I understand," Nelson said. "Between Kayla and me, we should have some answers. But let me start out by asking you a question."

"Okay."

"Was Valerie adopted through the State, or through a private agency?"

"Private," Kaye replied, then gave her the name and address he'd found on letterhead in the file. It was close to what JoAnn Weber had told him, but not exact.

"I've never heard of them," Nelson said, "but that was a long time ago. Now, tell me why you found it necessary to get a warrant for the file."

"I tracked down the biological grandmother and the man she claimed was Valerie's biological father. By the way, her birth name was Crystal Lowden. The man I talked to said it wasn't possible for him to be the father."

"He denies they ever had sex, right?" Nelson said.

"Exactly," Kaye replied. "And he says he didn't know she was pregnant until after the baby was born."

"Is he listed on the birth certificate?"

"He is not," Kaye told her.

"It's not at all unusual for a young man to deny responsibility for a child he's fathered inadvertently," Nelson said. "Horrible way to put it, I know, but it fits. It often comes down to denial or eighteen years of child support payments."

"Could be," Kaye admitted. "But my impression was that he was telling the truth, and there were enough discrepancies between what the grandmother told me and what he told me about the situation, and what the adoptive parents told me, that I wanted the file to get a solid timeline."

"Let me ask you this, then," Nelson said. "Why not just talk to the baby's biological mother? Surely her mother, the grandmother, knows where she is."

"She's deceased," Kaye said. "Which brings up the first inconsistency in the file I don't understand."

"What's that?" Nelson asked.

"When I found the birth certificate I learned that Crystal Lowden wasn't born in a hospital. The certificate says Home Birth at the top. What can you tell me about how that works?"

"How long ago was this again?" Nelson asked.

"Almost eighteen years."

"Wow," Nelson said. "By then a home birth was a rare occurrence, except maybe in rural areas. Is there a midwife or RNP listed on the certificate?"

"There is not," Kaye said. "Is that a legal requirement?"

"I don't think so, but I'd have to check the in-force statutes for that time. But, like I said, home births were rare by then. You've already told me the father's name isn't listed. What about the mother's name?"

"Her name was Rachel Lowden, and, no, she's not listed," Kaye said. "The word 'deceased' is written on that line, which begs the question… How is that possible?"

"There could be at least two things going on," Nelson said. "One is that Rachel Lowden died in childbirth. Another is that she died shortly after the child's birth and the cause of death was determined to be complications of giving birth, and the home birth certificate wasn't issued until after either of those things occurred. If Rachel Lowden died in childbirth, her death certificate should be included in the adoption file."

"It's there," Kaye said. "It lists COD as incident to childbirth, which raises another glaring discrepancy."

"How so?" Nelson asked.

"Rachel's mother and the man I interviewed both told me Rachel took her own life."

"You'd have to ask the Medical Examiner's Office about that," Nelson said. "Is there a court hearing transcript in the file?"

"No," Kaye replied. "But there is a notarized statement from Rachel's parents, Leon and Monica Lowden, attesting to their relationship to the child and surrendering all future claims and rights."

"That's changed," Nelson said. "Current law requires a hearing."

"You said a minute ago that the birth certificate could have been issued after Rachel died, even if she didn't die in childbirth," Kaye said. "How would that work?"

"In home births, the law requires that the medical professional present complete the necessary forms and notifications, just as if the birth had taken place in a hospital," Nelson replied. "In a case like this, with no medical professional present, the law allows up to one year for parents of unattended home-birthed babies to file for a birth certificate."

"A year?" Kaye was astounded.

"It can be longer," Nelson said. "But even back then, I'm pretty sure the law required a court hearing if over a year had passed."

"How is the date of birth verified?" Kaye asked. "I mean, it sounds like it could just be made up."

"It's the date declared by the parents," Nelson said, "or, in this case, the grandparents."

"So it could just be made up," Kaye said flatly. "Nobody checks."

"Ben," Okafor spoke up, "didn't you tell me that one of your concerns was conflicting information on the date of birth?"

"That's one thing I want to straighten out," he replied. "But I didn't know how this all works. Knowing the Lowdens had a year to declare a date of birth helps explain the problem, but the day the Webers celebrated as Valerie's birthday doesn't fit with what I'm finding."

"There should also be an Amended Birth Certificate in the file listing the adoptive parents, the child's declared new name and the same date of birth shown on the home birth certificate – whatever that might be in this case," Nelson said, and Kaye heard frustration in her voice.

"It's here," Kaye said. "But the DOB is different."

"Really?" Nelson sounded surprised. "That's extremely unusual. What's the discrepancy?"

"Exactly two months after the DOB on the original certificate, which apparently could have just been made up."

"That sounds like a data entry error to me," Okafor said.

"I don't know," Kaye responded. "August would be entered zero-eight, October is one-zero. That's not a typo, that's a major oversight."

"Sandi, is there any way to check that?" Okafor asked.

"You can try Vital Statistics, but it's a long shot. I mean, you're already in possession of the same documents they have. If this young woman was still alive, she and her adoptive parents could try to chase it down, but it would be expensive. With her biological mother deceased, the father undetermined and the adoption agency closed, you're talking pretty much impossible."

"Thank you, Sandi," Kaye said. "I really appreciate your help."

"Glad I could help," Nelson said. "Call me directly if you have other questions."

"Will do," Kaye said, then added, "Kayla, can you stay on the line for a minute?"

"Sure," Okafor said.

Kaye heard Nelson and Okafor exchange thanks and talk about having lunch together some time soon, then he heard a door close.

"I'm back," Okafor declared. "What did you need?"

"I wanted to let you know that yesterday I showed Audra O'Bannon a photo line-up that included a photo of the guy I was positive was Art, based on former association with Dylan Glithero."

"Yeah, and…?"

"She couldn't pick him out."

"What?"

"Said the guy we want wasn't in the photo array."

"Are you convinced?" Okafor asked.

Kaye thought about it for a few seconds. "I'm not sure. I also heard that Valerie Weber and Audra O'Bannon didn't get along, but when I tried to ask Audra about that her mother shut down the interview and threw me out."

"Very interesting," Okafor mused. "We can always subpoena Audra and compel her testimony, even though she's a minor."

"Waste of time," Kaye said. "No jury will ever buy that a woman can't identify a man she's been having sex with for, what, months, maybe longer?"

"Unless," Okafor said slowly, "she has a damn good reason not to."

***

After talking to Okafor and Nelson, Kaye considered his options. Unknowns bothered him tremendously during any investigation and, dead or not, the confusion over Valerie/Crystal's date of birth was a giant unknown. The kind that concealed motive.

With a sigh he turned his attention back to the adoption and case files on his desk and started going through them again, searching for something he might have missed, or for which the context of his understanding might have changed with information gathered since.

Kaye's desk phone rang.

"Detective, this is Scott in Digital Forensics."

"Hey, Scott," Kaye said, "I thought maybe you quit. I hope you're not calling to tell me you don't have my video."

"Nope," Scott shot back, "I'm calling to tell you that it's finally done. I just emailed you the file."

"Great," Kaye said as he opened his Inbox. The email from Scott, with the file attached, was at the top of the unread messages list. "Got it," he confirmed.

"Sorry it took so long," Scott said. "But I think the results were worth it. The new version AI algorithms let me do a decent, but not huge, upscaling and the pixel interpolation was much better than it was with the old version. One warning."

"What's that?"

"Even though the early part of the video was in color because of available light, once it gets dark it can still only record in black and white. The software can interpolate colors based on pre-existing data, but courts won't accept it as evidence, so we disable that function. Don't make assumptions about what color things are, like the car itself, the driver's hair, stuff like that, unless you see them before it got dark."

"Got it," Kaye acknowledged. "And thanks, Scott."

Kaye opened the file and instantly saw the improvement in clarity. He still couldn't read the license number on the back of Valerie Weber's Mini, but he could tell it was a California plate. He fast-forwarded to just before the vehicle that picked Valerie up arrived, then let the video run at normal speed. He saw the lights of the approaching vehicle, watched as Valerie, bag in hand, got out of her car and disappeared under the overhanging tree as she headed for Valleyheart Drive, saw the approaching lights stop, then move again several seconds later.

When the vehicle entered the gap between the trees where the driveway cut Valleyheart, Kaye paused it. He clicked forward one image at a time, stopping when the driver was centered in the frame.

"Shit," Kaye muttered, leaning back. "So much for that."

Scott had been right. The image was much better than the original. Even in just gray tones, it was good enough that Kaye knew it wasn't Dylan Glithero behind the wheel.

Back to square one.

The driver was, Kaye thought, a white male, but he looked older and heavier than Glithero. The ball cap created a deep enough shadow that the top half of the driver's face was pretty much a black blob.

Who the hell is that? Kaye wondered as he studied the image closely. Scott's warning about gray scale now made him uncertain the vehicle was even white. In fact, it now seemed to be several different colors because of the shadows created by the trees between the streetlight and the vehicle. It could be silver, or any light, less saturated tone.

He started mentally cataloging how the driver might fit into the chain of events as he knew them. Relative? Father of a friend? He immediately dismissed those as possibilities. After all, Valerie Weber had ended up dead. It was much more likely that the driver had some connection to Dylan Glithero.

Another teacher, maybe? When it hit him, Kaye rolled his eyes and smacked himself in the forehead. Then he dug into the O'Bannon file and grabbed the printout of Gene Calhoun's driver's license and held it up next to the frozen video frame.

You're on a roll, Kaye. Oh for three.

The driver of the SUV wasn't Calhoun, either.

He closed the video file and saw yet another email notification on the screen. It was from Arch, and the subject was 'DNA'.

'Ben,

Talked to the people at Genome Labs. They think they've isolated enough cfDNA from Valerie Weber's samples to do comparisons. I've already talked to Nadia Mehrabi in the FSD lab and asked her to call my contact at Genome. Call her to discuss what you need. Hope this works out.

Arch

P.S. Boss says to have your checkbook ready, just in case...LOL'

Kaye immediately picked up the phone and called Forensics Services. He'd worked with Nadia Mehrabi before and she'd testified in several of his cases over the past few years.

They spent a few minutes catching up, then the conversation turned to business.

"Genome Labs has already sent me the data I need," Mehrabi told him. "Just to confirm, you want their results compared to the sample collected from," she paused briefly, "Dylan Glithero, your suspect in a rape case."

"Correct," Kaye confirmed.

"And your interest is in establishing or eliminating possible paternity."

"Yes."

"Now, the sixty-four-dollar question," Mehrabi said. "If it's not a match to Glithero, do you want me to run it through the system?"

Kaye thought about it for a few seconds. "Might as well. Who knows, lightning strikes, right?"

Mehrabi laughed. "Yes, it does. I'm running the Glithero samples today. I should have an answer for you before you go home."

"Thanks, Doc."

Kaye hung up and leaned back.

Well, that's progress, he thought, hoping for a match. He knew in the back of his mind, though, that if it wasn't, in all likelihood he'd have to cross Dylan Glithero off his suspect list unless and until he came up with something else.

Thinking about Valerie Weber took his mind back to Rachel Lowden. The whole home birth thing and varying dates still bugged him. What if it wasn't forgetfulness or clerical error? What if it was purposeful? Who would do that? And why?

"Earth to Detective Kaye." Captain Thompson's voice penetrated his concentration. "Come in, Detective Kaye."

Kaye spun his chair to see a smiling Thompson standing just a few feet away.

"Wool gathering, Detective?"

"No sir. Just got word that I should have DNA results on the Weber case today, and I was trying to figure out Plan B in case I'm wrong."

"Speaking of Plan B, you got a second?"

"For you, Cap, anytime."

Thompson snorted derisively before turning and heading for his office.

"What's up?" Kaye asked as he sat down opposite his boss.

"I wanted to let you know." Thompson smiled. "I've decided I'd rather be Professor Thompson than Captain, or even Commander Thompson, the cop with a Ph.D."

"Good for you," Kaye said sincerely. "I think that's the right choice. Did you find a house?"

"Not yet. But we've done some, shall we say testing, and we're expanding our search area."

"That's great. Something will turn up."

"And when you see your Roshi – that's the right word, right? – please tell him we appreciate the sage advice." Thompson grinned. "Even if it was second-hand."

"I'll be sure to pass it along."

CHAPTER 32

Five frustrating minutes later, Kaye grabbed the Big Boar jacket and headed out. He didn't have anywhere specific to go, he just needed to not be in the squad room for a while.

The deli was close enough, and the parking scarce enough, that he walked around the corner to get a sandwich. He tried to enjoy his sandwich and the nice day.

But his thoughts kept drifting back to Rachel Lowden.

Finally, he gave up, bolted down the rest of the sandwich, drained what was left of the iced tea and walked back to the station. He didn't go in, just went straight to the Harley. He fired it up and headed downtown, rolling hard on the throttle to vent his frustration.

Thirty minutes later, he bypassed the Central Records counters used by the public on the first floor of Department Headquarters, keyed in the door entry code and went inside to the intra-department records request counter.

"Good afternoon, Detective," said the smiling PA behind the counter. "What can I do for you?"

"I need to get my hands on an old report," he replied. "It would probably be classified as an unattended death or suicide."

The PA's brow knit as he digested Kaye's request. "I don't suppose you have a case number?"

"I do not. The victim was one Rachel Lowden." He spelled out the name, provided a general time window and the Lowden's address in Northridge.

"I can do a quick check while you wait, if you want," the PA said. "That was –"

"A long time ago." Kaye finished the sentence. "I know. But see what you can find."

"Will do. I believe the call records are digitized into the system, but I don't know about the reports."

"I'll wait."

The PA scurried off and sat down at a computer terminal. About ten minutes later he stood up and headed back to the counter. Kaye went to meet him.

"Detective, I found several calls to that address in the time frame that matches, all involving the last name Lowden."

"Really?" Kaye asked, surprised. "What kinds of calls?"

The PA handed him a sheet of paper. "These are the numbers. The reports are all archived downstairs if you want to go look them up. Sorry, but I don't have access to the archives from my terminal."

"That's okay. I can find them."

"Have you been downstairs before?"

"Oh, yeah. I know the way. Thanks for your help."

The basement of the building was one massive records archive, containing documents and reports dating back decades. The department had finally embraced the digital age, but the decision had been made that the expense of speeding up the retrieval of records that might never be searched for wasn't a good return on investment. While some had been converted to microfiche way back when, there was still a lot of paper.

The space always reminded Kaye of a massive library in a fantasy movie, with row after row of tall shelves, interrupted only by the columns that held up the building above, stacked with look-alike boxes full of records. Each row had a master index of dates and report number ranges at each end, and every box was labeled with its specific content range.

There was a long-standing joke in the department that a rookie officer from a long-ago Academy class was occasionally seen wandering aimlessly through the space, unable to find his way out.

Kaye opted to go to the staff desk and get help. Over the years he'd figured out that the staff was about equally divided between older, retired librarians from academia and young PAs putting in their time and hoping for a station assignment. He approached a silver-haired woman whose name tag told the world she was Margaret.

"Good afternoon," she greeted him. "What can I help you with today, Detective… Kaye, isn't it?"

"Yes, ma'am," he said and handed her the list the PA upstairs had given him. "I'd like to review these incidents."

Margaret tilted her head up and looked at the list through the bottom half of her bifocals. "My, these are quite old." She glanced at Kaye, then back at the list for a few seconds before saying, "Wait here, please."

She turned and disappeared into the stacks. Less than five minutes later she returned, holding a bulging, 8.5" x 11" manila envelope and two spools of microfilm. She first noted the item numbers of the microfilm rolls on the desk log, then asked Kaye for his badge number and wrote it in the log, too. She then wrote them on the back of the manila envelope, and he noted that his was the first and only name on the page.

"Please return everything to me when you leave," Margaret said. "Have you searched microfilm before?"

"I have," Kaye told her.

"You can use that reader," she pointed, "when you're ready."

"Thank you, Margaret."

He decided to search the microfilm first. He loaded the first spool and browsed the internal index.

He had no problem locating the reports. The first two were noise complaints, one week apart. Kaye assumed from the reporting party address that neighbors of the Lowdens had called them in. Each time, responding officers had restored the peace and the narratives were short and sweet: No argument or resistance by Leon or Monica Lowden, residents, and no sign of domestic issues. Both promised to keep it down. Alcohol was noted as a probable contributing factor.

Sounded to Kaye like noisy parties and neighbors disgruntled they weren't invited.

He spooled through to the next incident number on the list, expecting to find yet another noise complaint. What he found surprised him. The original call had been placed by Leon Lowden, reporting a juvenile female runaway. A unit had been dispatched, then cancelled when Mr. Lowden had called back and reported that his daughter had returned home safely and there had simply been a misunderstanding. Based on the date, Kaye guessed Rachel would have been fourteen, maybe fifteen.

He changed to the next spool and found the next report. It was another noise complaint by a neighbor, dated some five months after the ones he'd just checked. But this time there was a notation of a possible domestic disturbance. Two units were dispatched. The reporting officer noted that Monica Lowden appeared to have a fresh bruise on her face, but she insisted her husband had not struck her. She was partially disabled and had fallen down. No arrest was made. Alcohol was again noted as a probable contributing factor.

He found two more runaway incident reports, both withdrawn by Leon Lowden.

After re-boxing the microfilm spools, Kaye moved to an empty table and turned his attention to the envelope.

It was the record of Rachel Lowden's death investigation, and the first thing that Kaye focused on was the date of the report. It was three weeks *before* the date recorded on Crystal Lowden's Certificate of Home Birth.

The report itself was pretty straightforward. The call to 9-1-1 had come from the Lowdens' phone number. The caller was female. The dispatcher had sent medics first, then the sector patrol unit.

Rachel Lowden had been found in the bathtub, already deceased, by her mother. The patrol unit had requested detectives and a coroner. Leon Lowden arrived home approximately twenty-five minutes later. Detectives Capell and Manning had arrived just after Mr. Lowden.

Kaye read through their on-scene investigation notes and the statements they'd taken from Leon and Monica Lowden. Both mentioned that their daughter had recently given birth, was suffering from post-partum depression and had been receiving counseling after a previous suicide attempt. An infant girl was present in the house. No counselor's name was listed.

The tentative conclusion, pending autopsy, was suicide.

Kaye next studied the photos taken and related notes made by the detectives. Rachel Lowden was nude, sprawled in the bathtub, which contained approximately nine inches of water. Her right arm dangled over the edge of the tub. Blood had run down the outside of the tub and puddled on the tile floor. The water in the tub was deep red from blood, and Detective Capell had recovered a single-edge razor blade from the bathroom floor directly under the victim's right hand.

Deep, incised lacerations were present on the inside of both arms just above the elbows, and both wrists had superficial lateral incisions with little evidence of blood.

A brief note was found on the dresser in the victim's bedroom by Leon Lowden. Kaye searched for and found it in the file. It read: 'I can't go on like this. I want my baby and I can't have her'. He examined the note closely and saw what he thought might be a small spot where some sort of fluid had been blotted off the surface.

The Medical Examiner's report essentially confirmed the on-scene conclusion. Cause of death was exsanguination resulting from deep wounds on both arms just below the medial epicondyle of the humerus, resulting in the severing of both the anterior and posterior ulnar arteries. Due to the lack of bleeding, the wrist wounds were deemed superficial and likely inflicted after the cuts to the elbows.

Probably couldn't hold on to the razor blade anymore, Kaye thought.

But he was confused by the contradictory causes of death between the ME's report and the death certificate. How did a young woman cutting her arteries with a razor blade and bleeding out in the bathtub become 'Causes incident to childbirth' when it had, impossibly, happened three weeks before the declared birth date of the child? Had someone determined that Rachel Lowden's depression was the root cause driving her to suicide? If so, who? The report didn't say. Nor could he find any reference to forensic testing of the possible fluid spot on the note.

He finished reviewing the report and took it, and the microfilm boxes, back to the desk.

"Did you find what you were looking for?" Margaret asked.

"I did, thank you," Kaye replied, then held up the report. "I'll need to take this with me."

"Oh," Margaret said, surprised. "Yes, of course." She reached under the counter and came out with the inevitable form. "Just fill this out and sign it, please."

Ten minutes later Kaye had stowed the report in a saddlebag and headed home.

CHAPTER 33

Between the dense fog and a multi-vehicle accident where Pacific Coast Highway turns inland and morphs into eastbound I-10, it was almost nine when Kaye pulled the pickup into the station parking lot. Others must have been having commuter problems, too, because the morning head count was low.

Amari Burke was there and saw Kaye come in.

"Please tell me you didn't ride a motorcycle today," she said, making a face. "It's bad out there."

"Not today," he told her with a smile. "Fog, more specifically the drivers of cars on foggy days, is one of the things I avoid."

"Sounds like a good policy to me."

"Haven't seen much of you and J.J. for a couple days," Kaye said. "What's going on?"

"We've been working late. Some guy is roughing up hookers, and I mean way past just paying extra for the bruises. We're dedicating today to the scourge of all police officers."

"Field interview cards," Kaye said knowingly. "Good luck with that."

As if on cue, J.J. pushed through the doors into the squad room, saw Burke and came over.

"Well, partner, you ready for an exciting day?"

"Oh, yeah, always," Burke mugged.

"Morning, Ben," J.J. said. "Hey, if you've got nothing else to do, we can use you."

"Sorry," Kaye said, not trying to hide his smile. "My to-do list is full. You'll have to soldier on without me."

"Thanks, buddy," J.J. said with a chuckle. "I'll remember that."

"Come on," Burke said, grabbing J.J.'s sleeve. "The sooner we start, the sooner we finish."

She pulled J.J. away as he looked back over his shoulder at Kaye with a 'help me' look.

Kaye smiled as he watched them go, then turned to organizing his day. He hadn't been at it long when his desk phone rang.

"Kaye."

"Ben, hey, it's Arch."

"That's not what my caller ID says," Kaye joked.

Arch laughed. "I'm on my personal cell. This fog is a killer."

"What do you need, Arch?"

"I'm curious about what you heard from Mehrabi about the cell-free DNA."

"I haven't talked to her yet. I got hung up downtown yesterday afternoon."

"Must've been a major hang-up," Arch said. "I figured you'd be camped outside her door."

"I'll call her this morning."

"And let me know? I'm anxious to get this science into court. Could be huge."

"I'll let you know," Kaye promised, then had a sudden idea. "Hey, Arch, I need a favor."

"Another one?" Arch's tone was leery.

Kaye quickly filled Arch in on his hunt for background on Valerie Weber and Rachel Lowden, including the death investigation report he'd found in the archives.

"It just bothers me," he said. "If I bring you the file, any chance you could take a look at it? Maybe find anything your office might still have and review it?"

"I suppose I could do that," Arch said slowly. "Do you have a deadline?"

"No. Take all the time you need. Like I said, it's background, and it was a long time ago."

"Okay, get it to me and I'll take a look."

"Thanks, Arch."

Kaye reached out and pushed the disconnect button, then dialed the Forensic Science Division. After being transferred twice and put on hold, Nadia Mehrabi finally picked up.

"Doctor, this is Detective Kaye."

"Well, hello Detective. I tried to call you yesterday. Twice."

"I heard. I'm sorry. Sometimes duty calls, and when it does I have to answer."

Mehrabi laughed. "That's a good way to put it."

"What did you find out on Valerie Weber?"

"Doctor Archuleta brought me the outside lab's results on Weber's samples," Mehrabi replied. "They'd already produced a mapping of both

Weber's DNA and the cell-free DNA obtained from her blood, so my part was easy. I ran it against the sample from Dylan Glithero."

"And?" Kaye asked anxiously.

"There was no match. Dylan Glithero was not the father of Valerie Weber's baby."

"You're certain?"

"Absolutely. There was zero match with Glithero. Weber's DNA was a textbook match to the cell-free DNA, as I would have expected. The science is solid. Sorry it's not the result you were hoping for."

"You don't have to apologize, Doc. It is what it is."

"I hope you don't mind, but since the fetal DNA didn't match Glithero I went ahead and submitted a qualified request to the system. If the father's DNA is on file, we should get a hit."

"That would've been my next question," Kaye said.

"Might be a little longer than usual because of the request type," Mehrabi said. "I'll let you know when I hear."

"Thanks, Doc."

Kaye ended the call, leaned back and took his frustration out on his chair. Had it been a living thing, it would have suffered two badly broken arms.

Shit, he cursed silently. *What am I missing?*

***

One phone call and an hour later he pulled the pickup to the curb in front of the Weber residence. It was time to eat a little crow. And he wasn't looking forward to it.

JoAnn Weber showed him into the living room.

"Is there anything I can get you, Detective Kaye?" Her voice was polite but frosty.

"No, thanks. I'm fine."

She perched on the arm of one of the chairs. "You said on the phone you had news. Have you finally made an arrest in my daughter's murder?"

Kaye took a deep breath. "No, I haven't. In fact, I'm in the position of basically having to start over with the investigation."

"Excuse me?" she said sharply.

"The other day I told you I was focusing on Dylan Glithero, one of Valerie's –"

"And you said you were waiting on DNA to confirm he killed Valerie," Weber interrupted.

"It wasn't Glithero's DNA," Kaye said. "He was not the father of the child your daughter was carrying. I also had our digital forensics team enhance the video from Staples that showed Valerie being picked up there the night she disappeared. Glithero was not the driver of the vehicle. I'm sorry."

JoAnn Weber went from defiant to crushed in about two seconds. "Who was it?"

"I don't know yet," Kaye admitted, "but I will keep looking." He paused before adding, "I would like to confirm one thing with you, if it's okay. And I am not trying to insult you."

Weber looked at him, defeat in her eyes, and said, "Go ahead."

"To be perfectly frank, Mrs. Weber, I found irregularities in Valerie's sealed adoption file," Kaye said, then hastily added, "Not involving you or your husband. In the paperwork around the agency and birth parents. There are multiple dates of birth on multiple forms, and the timeline doesn't work. The head of the family law division at the District Attorney's office thinks it could be a clerical error. I don't think so."

"The date of birth we gave you when we filed the original report is what's on the birth certificate we have," Weber said flatly. "I'll show it to you if you'd like to see it."

"That won't be necessary," Kaye told her. "I confirmed it. But it… bugs me, if that makes sense. What I need to ask you is if, back during the adoption process, there was ever any doubt about Valerie's real date of birth? Was the agency evasive, or not forthcoming? Paperwork problems? Anything out of the ordinary?"

"Not that I recall, but I can ask my husband," she said, then stared at Kaye for what felt to him to be a long time before she said softly, "I never should have told her she was adopted. This is all my fault. You'll never find the person who actually did it, because the truth is I killed her, just as sure as you're sitting here now."

"Mrs. Weber, I –"

"I know what you told me, Detective. It's your job to tell me I didn't do it. But you're wrong about that, too."

The 'too' stung. "I'm not giving up, Mrs. Weber. I'll do everything I can to find whoever killed Valerie."

"I'm sure you will," Weber said evenly. "Now, if you'll excuse me, I have somewhere I need to be."

"Of course," Kaye said, rising. "I'll keep you informed."

"Thank you. Good day, Detective."

Kaye let himself out and went back to the truck. He sat there for a couple minutes, replaying his conversation with JoAnn Weber, trying to think of ways he could've softened the blow.

Bottom line, there wasn't any way to do that. JoAnn Weber's daughter was dead. It was his job to catch her killer, and so far he had failed miserably.

Movement caught his eye and he turned to see JoAnn Weber's car backing down the driveway. At the same time, Miles Weber opened the front door and stepped out onto the porch.

Miles and his Mom exchanged waves and JoAnn drove off down the street. Instead of going back inside, Miles came down the front steps and headed toward Kaye. As Miles rounded the front of the truck, Kaye rolled down his window.

"Hey, Miles," he said when the boy stood by the truck. "Sorry, no bike today. Too foggy."

"That's okay," Miles said, putting his hands in his pants pockets and shuffling nervously. "That's not why I came out."

"Oh?"

"Yeah. I, uh… I was in my dad's den, you know, working on a project proposal for one of my classes." He paused and looked away as he continued. "I didn't mean to eavesdrop, but I could hear you and my mom talking. I think there's something you should know."

"What might that be?"

Miles shuffled some more before looking Kaye in the eye and saying, "Valerie already knew she was adopted before Mom and Dad told her."

"Really?" Kaye kept his voice even. "Do your parents know that? Is that why they told her? To be upfront about it?"

"I don't think they knew that Valerie knew. I mean, I heard them argue several times about whether they should even tell her or not."

"How do you know she knew?"

"She told me."

"Did she tell you how she found out?"

"Yeah."

"Want to share that with me?"

"Oh, uh, yeah, sure," Miles blurted. "I mean, it's not like it's privileged information or anything, I guess."

Kaye stayed quiet, waiting. Miles got the hint.

"Val had a biology class her Freshman year and they did a unit on genetics. Somewhere along the line she figured out there weren't any other redheads in any of the pictures of Mom and Dad's families. I mean,

269

none, not even cousins or anything. She even asked me to help her dig up old family stuff just so she could check it out. She went back pretty far.

"One day she came to me and told me she didn't believe she was descended from the Weber family or the Hoffman family – that's my mom's maiden name – so she figured she must've been adopted.

"I told her I thought she was loony, but she showed me the paper she did for her biology class. She got an 'A' and told me the teacher loved it. Then she showed me the DNA ancestry test she'd mailed in that she thought confirmed it. I told her it didn't make any difference if she was adopted, but she wasn't so sure."

"Miles, did you tell your Mom and Dad this?"

"Val asked me not to."

Kaye considered what Miles was telling him in light of what else he knew.

"I assume Valerie had her own computer, right?" he asked.

"Yeah, we both have laptops for school. Val took hers almost everyplace she went. Used to joke about great writers always needing a way to keep track of great inspirations."

Kaye instantly thought about Amy. Hers had practically been surgically attached.

"Do you know if she took her laptop with her the last time she left?"

"It's still on her desk in her room."

"Do you think I could borrow it?" Kaye asked carefully.

"I don't know," Miles said slowly.

"You don't have to give it to me," Kaye said. "If you do, I'll give you a receipt and I promise I'll bring it back in the same condition it's in now."

"I know my Mom and Dad haven't touched it since..." Miles said, his voice trailing off. "I think they still hope she'll just show up, and this has all been a giant fuck up. I doubt they'd even miss it."

"I don't want it to be a secret, Miles. You can show them the receipt. If they get upset I'll bring it back right away."

Miles thought about it for a bit, then said, "That sounds fair. I'll go get it." He turned and hustled up the sidewalk.

Several minutes passed. Kaye used the time to draft a basic receipt he could give Miles, leaving blanks where he could fill in the laptop's specifics.

Miles emerged from the house, a small black backpack in hand.

"Here you go," he said, handing it through the window to Kaye, who promptly took out the laptop and opened it to get the particulars to finish filling out the receipt, which he signed and handed to Miles before putting the laptop back in the pack.

"It's not the official form, but it's good. One more question?"

"Sure."

"You don't happen to know her password, do you?"

"No, sorry."

"That's okay. We've got people for that," Kaye said. "And Miles, you make sure you tell your Mom and Dad I have this." He held up the backpack. "If they get upset, they can call me and I'll bring it back. I promise I won't throw you under the bus."

"Okay," Miles said, smiling.

"And when you tell your parents about the computer, tell them Valerie figured out she was adopted before they told her. I don't know about your Dad, but your Mom's really beating herself up about all this. It wasn't her fault. She needs to know Valerie already knew."

Miles nodded. "Okay, I'll tell them."

Kaye started the truck and watched Miles go back up the sidewalk and into the house before he pulled away. He got to the end of the block, made the turn and pulled over to the curb again, leaving the truck running. He removed the computer from the backpack and started checking all of the pockets and compartments.

In an inner, zippered compartment obviously intended to hold pens and pencils, he found a yellow sticky note, folded in half and stuck together. It had nothing written on it.

Why would she... he wondered. Using a fingernail, he carefully pried the sticky edge apart and unfolded the paper.

Okay, there's no way in hell that's a coincidence, he thought as he stared at the note.

On it was the word 'crystal', followed by a sequence of five numbers, printed in pencil.

Kaye knew they weren't random. They were the date of birth listed on Crystal Lowden's certificate of home birth.

CHAPTER 34

The official epicenter of Los Angeles County health care is the County-USC Medical Center and the collection of clinics, schools and agencies that surround it. One of those is the County Medical Examiner's Office. It occupies a stately, old brick building reminiscent of a New England university on the western side of the vast, sprawling health campus. The fog had long since burned off, but it still took almost an hour to make it through traffic across town to the East Side.

Kaye pulled in off Mission, swung past the front entrance and ended up finding a parking spot on the ground level of the adjacent parking structure.

He'd called ahead to let Dr. Jaime Archuleta know he was on the way, and found Arch in his office.

"Hey, Ben," Arch greeted him when he walked in. "How goes the battle?"

"I'm losing," Kaye said as he sank into one of the chairs in Arch's small office. "The cell-free DNA didn't match my suspect, and he wasn't the guy driving the car that picked Valerie Weber up the night she disappeared. So I'm basically starting over."

"Did Mehrabi run DNA in the system anyway?"

"She did. Now it's wait and see."

"That's too bad," Arch said. "I really wanted to get cell-free DNA science into a court room."

"I really wanted to get my killer into a court room." Kaye retorted.

"Point taken," Arch said. "You wanted to show me something?"

"I do," Kaye confirmed, handing Rachel Lowden's death investigation file across the desk.

Arch opened it and his eyebrows raised as he looked at Kaye. "Who is this?"

"Rachel Lowden, Valerie Weber's biological mother," Kaye replied. He laid out what he'd found in Valerie's adoption file and why he'd decided to do some deep digging. "If you have the available time, I'd appreciate it if you'd go through the medical aspects of the investigation and see what you think. Anomalies, exclusions, contradictions, things like that."

"Why?" Arch asked, looking up from the file.

"Mostly because that woman's mother and an ex- boyfriend from high school, whom the mother said was Valerie Weber's biological father, both told me Rachel Lowden committed suicide. The death certificate lists 'causes incident to childbirth'."

"Have you checked hospital records?"

"That's part of it, too," Kaye said. "Valerie was an unattended home birth. Somehow, between the time she was born and the time she was adopted, the timeline says that the mother killed herself before the baby was born. I don't think that works."

"Could've been contemporaneous," Arch noted. "Would fit the COD."

"I don't think so. I'm talking sizable differences."

"Hmm…interesting," Arch muttered, as much to himself as to Kaye, as he continued skimming through the file. "Okay," he said, looking up at Kaye, "first thing you should know is that families sometimes put a lot of pressure on us not to list suicide as a cause of death. They don't want the stigma, but they do want the insurance check. Sad, but true. If this woman had recently given birth, was under treatment for depression or several other variables, the childbirth link could have been a courtesy. A perfectly legal courtesy."

"But you will take a look at it?"

Arch's answer came slower than Kaye would have liked.

"Sure, I'll take a look at it. With any luck I'll be able to dig up the post report, if there was one." He looked at Kaye. "Don't expect much, okay? Seems pretty cut and dried to me, at least at first glance."

"Thanks, Arch."

"One more question."

"Shoot."

"Where's Rachel Lowden's body?"

"Uh…" Kaye stammered. "No idea. I don't know if she was buried, cremated, or what. Should I find out?"

"You might have to. If there was an autopsy, it'll tell me where the body went. If there wasn't one, you might have to do some digging." Arch smiled broadly. "A little pathologist's joke there. Get it?"

"I got it," Kaye said, smiling as he stood up. "Let's hope it's not necessary."

***

Another near-hour of heavy afternoon traffic delayed Kaye's return to the station. When he entered the secure parking lot he saw several civilian employees already heading for their cars.

He grabbed the backpack Miles Weber had given him and hustled inside, but instead of heading for the squad room he went looking for Patty Phillips.

"Got a minute?" Kaye asked, perching on the corner of her desk without waiting for a reply.

"Sure," Patty replied, eyeing the backpack Kaye held. "What do you need?"

He held up the backpack. "This computer belonged to Valerie Weber. Remember the conversation we had about websites where adopted kids and parents that gave up their babies could try to find each other?"

"I do," Patty said. "I'm surprised you do. I didn't think you were listening."

"Ouch," Kaye said. "Anyway, I have strong reason to believe that Valerie may have found her biological family, and I know she didn't do it through the courts."

"And you think she found somebody on-line?"

"I do," Kaye said. "Her brother told me she figured out she was adopted before her parents told her. And I found this in the backpack with the computer." He handed the yellow sticky to Patty.

Patty looked at it, then at him, confused.

"Valerie's given name when she was born was Crystal Lowden. And the numbers are the date of birth on her original birth certificate."

"Holy cow!" Patty said incredulously. "She found them!"

"You're a lot more computer savvy than I am," Kaye said as he held up the computer. "I don't know for sure if that's the current password, but could you see if you can get into this and go through it to see what you can come up with? Maybe whoever told her she was born Crystal Lowden?"

"I can do that," Patty said, taking the computer. "I can't promise I'll do it tonight…"

"I don't expect you to do it tonight," Kaye said. "Whenever you get to it will do."

"Sounds good to me."

"If the password doesn't work, or you run into security you can't get past, leave it alone and I'll take it to the lab. But I think it's worth a try, and I won't have to wait weeks to find out what, if anything, it can tell us."

"I'll get on it first thing tomorrow."

"Thank you, Patty."

***

When he walked into the house, Kaye was again assailed by thoughts of loss and loneliness, and couldn't even bring himself to turn on the lights. He changed clothes in the dark and returned to the garage and the sanctuary it offered.

He tinkered with the '51 Panhead for a while, but it wasn't yet ready for reassembly. He'd been playing with the idea of increasing the engine displacement from the original near-74 c.i.d. to 80, and was still searching parts availability to make sure it was feasible before having any machine work done.

He went upstairs to Amy's retreat, only to find an empty refrigerator.

Probably a good thing, he thought. *Anything still in here would have been a hazardous waste site by now.*

A sudden whim hit him. He rolled the '41 Knucklehead out and headed for Paradise Cove.

After a bite to eat at the beach-side cafe he walked to the end of the pier. It was a place he frequented when something – sometimes he wasn't even sure what – weighed on his mind. Tonight, though, he knew what was bothering him.

His life.

What had happened? Was he losing his drive, his touch? There no longer seemed to be a goal. When Amy was alive, they'd been a binary star system, existing independently but inexorably dependent on each other for stability and continuity. Then, in the blink of an eye, she was gone. But not completely. Her scent still lingered in the house, though he was no longer convinced he wasn't just imagining it. The artwork she loved still hung on the walls. The antiques she treasured still held strategic spots in the house. Even the pots and pans she loved still nested in cupboards, waiting but seldom, if ever, feeling the heat of a burner.

Her mother had come and taken all of Amy's clothes, telling Kaye it was to spare him the heartache of going through them. But he doubted her motives. He and Amy's parents had never gotten along. Amy had often tried to convince him he was imagining things, but Kaye also remembered the thinly-veiled reproach for the fact they'd remained childless. At one point Amy's father, Charles, had taken Kaye aside and quietly suggested they consider adoption. Not long after that, he'd come home from a shift to find a beaming Amy holding a positive home pregnancy test, then, three weeks later, telling him she'd lost the baby.

After Amy's death her parents had obviously blamed him and soon cut off all communication. To them, he no longer existed.

As Kaye gazed out over the Pacific, he remembered Monica Lowden's grief over losing her daughter and granddaughter and lamenting that there was never another. He understood. No child meant no glimmer remained of the other star, no new point in space upon which one could anchor an orbit and go on.

Just a black hole, its inescapable gravity swallowing all light.

CHAPTER 35

Kaye overslept. Not because he'd been overtired, but because it had been almost 3:00 a.m. the last time he remembered seeing the clock on the nightstand. Still, he didn't hurry. There was fog again, although nothing like yesterday, and he figured that if he gave the sun a little time to work he might be able to ride.

Which he did.

He got to the station, went to the break room and brewed himself a cup of tea, then sat and went through the Dailies.

When he returned to his desk an email notification pop-up was on the screen. He opened and read the message, and his pulse quickened.

'Call me ASAP. Got a hit on your DNA. Mehrabi.'

He grabbed the phone, called FSD and asked for Mehrabi. She picked up almost immediately.

"Doc, this is Detective Kaye. Just got your email."

"Thanks for calling so quickly, Detective," she said. "We got lucky and got a match on the fetal DNA from Valerie Weber. A former long-time guest of the Department of Corrections. Got a pencil handy?"

"Go ahead."

"Okay, the match is to a guy named Eugene A. Calhoun."

"Calhoun?" Kaye echoed, and added, "Are you kidding?"

"No, Detective. Eugene A. Calhoun," she confirmed. "You're familiar with him?"

"He's on my radar in another case involving underage girls."

"Well," Mehrabi said, "the match is so close that even considering the Birthday Problem, I'd testify in court that Calhoun impregnated Valerie Weber."

Kaye went quiet and pondered what Mehrabi was telling him, leading her to ask, "Detective, do you have questions?"

"Not right now, Doc," he answered. "That's all I needed."

"Call me if you need anything else."

"Will do, Doc, and thanks."

He immediately called ADA Okafor.

"I've got about two minutes, Detective," she said after Kaye identified himself. "What's up?"

"I just got the report from FSD on the fetal DNA from Valerie Weber. It matches a guy named Eugene Arthur Calhoun –"

"Arthur?" Okafor interrupted. "As in Art from the Audra O'Bannon case?"

"I doubt there are two of them," Kaye told her. "I have an address down in Newport. I need an arrest warrant."

"Forward the FSD report to me immediately," Okafor said. "I'll take it to Judge Franklin myself as soon as my meeting is over. He already knows enough of the background that he'll give us a statutory rape warrant based on the DNA. We can add or amend charges later if we need to."

"How long, you think?"

There was a brief pause before Okafor answered. "Give me until, say, one-thirty? I'll text you."

"That works," Kaye said. "Thanks, Counselor."

"Gotta go," Okafor said quickly, and she was gone.

Kaye leaned back in his chair. There was no chance he was going to just enter the warrant for Calhoun into the system and hope a cop somewhere happened to bump into the guy and run him. He wanted to hook Calhoun up personally, the sooner the better.

He wracked his brain, trying to remember anyone he might know from the Newport PD, but came up empty. He looked up the main non-emergency number and called. A woman answered and asked what he needed.

"My name is Ben Kaye. I'm a Detective at the LAPD West Bureau. I need to speak with one of your Detectives, please."

"One moment," she said and put him on hold.

He waited almost two minutes, amused that the hold music was Dick Dale surf guitar.

"Jim Whitman," a voice finally said. "How can I help you?"

Kaye went through the introduction again, this time giving Whitman his badge and call back numbers.

"What do you need?" Whitman asked brusquely.

"I'm waiting on a warrant for one of your locals on a Statutory Rape charge that may also be connected to a homicide. I'm planning on heading down there this afternoon to find the suspect and thought I'd check in as a courtesy to see if I need one of your guys to go with me."

"I appreciate that," Whitman said, his tone softening. "We'll send a patrol officer with you to make the arrest. What's the suspect's name and address?"

Kaye gave Whitman Calhoun's name and the address off Calhoun's driver's license.

"Are you sure?" Whitman asked skeptically. "That's not exactly a low rent neighborhood, even for down here."

"That would fit what I know about him," Kaye said.

"Okay," Whitman said slowly, "how about this? When your warrant is confirmed, come to the department and ask for me. I'll go with you."

"Do you know Calhoun?"

"I've been looking while we've been talking," Whitman replied. "We've got nothing on the guy."

"My ADA says she expects to have the warrant signed by about one-thirty. I'll be there when I know for sure."

"Works for me," Whitman said. "See you then."

Kaye checked the clock and mentally organized his timeline. Two hours, say, to make it to the NBPD headquarters and connect with Whitman. Find Calhoun's address; half an hour?

Just go, he told himself. *Knock on Whitman's door when you hear from Okafor.*

Captain Thompson was at his desk dealing with the usual mountain of paperwork when Kaye knocked lightly on the open door.

"Come in," the Captain said, then looked up. "Yes?"

"I wanted to let you know I'm heading down to Newport," Kaye said.

"Why?"

"FSD matched DNA from Valerie Weber to an ex-con friend of Dylan Glithero, and that's where he lives. The DA's office is getting a warrant, and I've already talked to the locals."

"Good hunting," Thompson said, nodding.

Kaye headed south. He'd never been to the NBPD headquarters, but it wasn't hard to find. It was a sizable, two-story, white building screened by lush landscaping and surrounded by luxury condos, banks and high-end car dealers. Signs directed drivers to the nearby Fashion Island Center.

Kaye pulled into the public parking lot, shut down and checked his phone. Nothing from Okafor yet. He looked across Santa Barbara Drive, spied a deli/coffee shop tucked into the plaza behind Chase Bank and decided to wait there.

An iced tea and turkey sandwich later his phone lit up with a text alert. It was from Okafor.

'Franklin signed the warrant. It's attached. Good luck finding Calhoun.'

He tapped on the file icon and scanned through it. One count of Statutory Rape, day or night service, and, like Glithero, a half-million-dollar bail.

The guy will bond out before I finish writing the arrest report, he thought angrily. But there was nothing he could do about it.

The NBPD lobby was crowded. Both desk officers were dealing with people, another half-dozen sat in chairs against the wall, and still more stood alone or in small groups waiting their turn. Kaye navigated his way to a spot near one of the desk officers, took out his badge wallet and palmed it. The officer saw him, stopped talking to the person he was dealing with and eyed Kaye.

"The line starts back there," the officer said. "Wait your turn."

Kaye held up his badge wallet and let it flip open. "Ben Kaye, LAPD. I'm here to see Detective Whitman. He's expecting me."

"Oh, okay. Hang tight. I'll let him know you're here," the officer told Kaye, then told the person already standing there, "Just a second," and picked up the phone.

Kaye found a spot against the wall and waited. It was only a couple minutes before the security door behind the desk opened and a tall, slender man in slacks, dress shirt and tie stepped partway into the lobby and looked around. Then he turned and said something to the desk officer, who pointed at Kaye. The man's gaze swept over Kaye, then he looked back at the officer.

Kaye read the officer's lips. "That's him." He pushed off the wall and walked toward the man, who was now watching him.

"Detective Whitman?" He held out his hand. "Ben Kaye."

"Jim Whitman," the man said as he shook Kaye's hand. "Come on back."

Whitman led Kaye down a long hallway and turned into an office. Three desks and at least that many filing cabinets, almost all of which did double duty as shelves holding various electronic devices, occupied the cramped room. A window overlooked the department parking lot and the Porsche dealership beyond the high concrete block wall.

"Grab that one," Whitman said, pointing to one of the desk chairs as he sat down. "Did your warrant come through?"

"It did," Kaye said. "I have an electronic copy on my phone."

"That'll work," Whitman said, then spun around, grabbed a business card off his desk and handed it to Kaye. "Forward it to that number and I'll print copies."

Kaye forwarded Okafor's text, and two minutes later Whitman had printed off multiple copies.

Whitman looked it over and said, "Half a million on Statutory Rape? You must really want this guy."

"I do," Kaye said. "What started out as a young girl telling her mother she got beat up at school has turned into a homicide tied to a case from almost twenty years ago."

"You think this Calhoun is your killer?"

"He had motive. The girl was pregnant and turned up dead. The fetal DNA tagged Calhoun as the father."

"You got his DNA?"

"It was in the system. He did time on that old case I mentioned, pretty much the same situation back then, minus the homicide."

"Really?" Whitman asked. "Not often an ex-con makes it good enough to live at the address you have."

"Is it a pricey neighborhood?"

Whitman laughed. "Everything here is pricey. But this address isn't a neighborhood, it's an island in the harbor. Well into eight figures for the cheapest address there." He paused, then said, "You know, I think we should take a uniform with us on this. Instant credibility with security." He picked up his desk phone and punched in a number. "Hey, it's Whitman. Is Sergeant Wareing in the building? Good. Have him come to my office, please." He hung up.

The two detectives talked shop for a few minutes before a burly cop with a tight flat top haircut appeared in the door.

"Hey, Andy, come on in," Whitman said. "Ben, this is Andy Wareing. Andy, Ben Kaye, LAPD."

"Nice to meet you," Wareing said to Kaye before asking Whitman, "What's up?"

"Detective Kaye has asked for our help serving an arrest warrant," Whitman replied. "Under the circumstances, I thought your presence would be beneficial."

"What circumstances?" Wareing asked, eyebrows raised.

"Linda Isle," Whitman said.

"Seriously?" Wareing asked, smiling. "What's the charge? Insider trading?"

"Statutory rape," Kaye said. "Possibly connected to a homicide."

"I'll explain later," Whitman told Wareing. "Right now, let's go see if we can find this guy. Ben, you ride with me. Andy, follow us in a marked unit, okay?"

"You got it. I'll be waiting," Wareing said, then turned around and disappeared down the hallway.

A few minutes later Kaye and Whitman, in an unmarked car, followed by Wareing in a marked patrol unit, headed down Jamboree Road toward the ocean. They crossed Pacific Coast Highway, went down the hill, turned right on Bayside and wound generally westward along the edge of the harbor. Kaye caught occasional glimpses of the water between the houses lining Bayside and it looked like boats outnumbered houses five to one.

After about a mile, Whitman made a left off Bayside and almost immediately had to stop at a guard shack manned by an armed private security officer.

Whitman rolled down his window and flashed his badge. "Official business."

The guard didn't say anything, but stepped back into the shack. Seconds later, the gate started to rise.

"Thanks," Whitman said as he drove forward. Kaye watched Wareing follow without stopping.

Almost as soon as they cleared the gate they crossed a narrow bridge. Kaye was impressed by the houses lining the water and the vessels tied up at private docks.

Whitman saw him looking. "Welcome to Linda Isle, home to the one-percenters of the one-percenters."

It didn't take long to locate the address. Kaye's first thought was how a guy with Calhoun's history managed to live in a place like this. The house was pure white, modern architecture and it was hard to tell where the landscaping ended and the house, which was more like a pavilion, began. The drive was circular, going around a large, spreading tree that shaded the entire area.

Whitman stopped in front of a tall wrought iron gate, beyond which Kaye could see a Zen garden to rival anything at Kyokoku-Dera monastery. Beyond that was a magnificent set of wooden doors carved into the image of a tall ship under full sail.

Wareing rolled to a stop behind them.

The gate was secured and had no visible keypad or card reader, but did have a video camera. A small panel on one side had what Kaye decided was a good, old-fashioned doorbell button. He leaned sideways and pushed it.

A moment passed before a male voice said, "Yeah, what do you want?"

"Newport Beach Police," Whitman replied, holding his badge up to the video camera. "Open the gate, please."

"I'm sorry, I don't think I can do that."

"Can't, or won't?" Whitman asked evenly.

"I need to see some better identification," the voice said.

With that, Wareing stepped forward into the camera's field of view and glared up at the lens.

"This good enough for you, wise guy?" he said forcefully. "We have a warrant. Either you open up and let us in or I'll drive my patrol unit through your gate, your garden, and your spectacular front doors. I'll count to three. One…"

The lock on the gate buzzed and the gate slowly swung open.

"Nice work," Kaye said to Wareing in a low voice.

When they were halfway through the garden the bow section of the tall ship swung inward. A young man stood there waiting. Kaye guessed him at maybe twenty-one and he projected the quintessential look of the SoCal beach lifestyle.

"What's this about?" the kid asked bluntly when they reached the door. He didn't step aside to allow them to enter.

"We're looking for Eugene Arthur Calhoun," Whitman said. "This is his house, correct?"

"Well, sort of," the kid replied nonchalantly.

"What does that mean?" Whitman asked, his voice taking on an edge.

"I don't think that's any of your business," the kid retorted.

"Okay, look," Kaye said, stepping close to the kid and holding up his badge. "I'm Detective Kaye, Los Angeles Police Department. I have an arrest warrant for Eugene Arthur Calhoun, who has told the State of California under penalty of perjury that he lives at this address. I don't care who owns the house, I care if he's here, or not."

The kid smiled. "Uncle Gene uses this as his home address, but he's not here now."

"Where is he?" Kaye asked.

"I don't really know," the kid said, shrugging. "Could be anywhere."

"Narrow it down," Kaye said bluntly. He, too, was losing patience.

"Let's see," the kid said, putting his finger on his chin and pretending to think. "Gee, uh, New York? Maui? Maybe Lake Como or Buenos Aires? Or Dubai. Yeah, he could be in Dubai. Our family owns lots of real estate and my uncle travels quite a bit since… Well, for the last couple years or so."

"Since he got out of prison, you mean," Kaye said.

"Where he never should have been in the first place," the kid shot back.

"When did he leave?" Kaye asked.

"Ah, finally, a cogent question with a definitive answer," the kid said sarcastically. "Uncle Gene left at noon last Friday."

"But he didn't say where he was going?" Whitman asked.

"I already answered that," the kid said flatly, staring at Whitman.

"How did he leave?" Kaye asked.

"Our driver took him to the airport," the kid replied. "And before you ask, I should tell you, we don't fly commercial." He smiled.

Kaye turned to the Newport cops. "We're done."

"Don't you want to search the house?" Wareing asked.

"Come right on in," the kid said, stepping aside.

Kaye looked at the kid, then turned to Wareing and said, "Waste of time. I'll make sure the warrant's in the system and start turning over rocks."

"You're sure?" Whitman asked.

"I'm sure," Kaye confirmed, then turned to the kid and said, "Thanks for your time."

The kid didn't say anything, just shut the door in their faces.

Back at NBPD headquarters Kaye thanked Whitman and Wareing, fired up the Harley and headed for the Bureau.

By the time he got to the squad room it was late enough that he checked his messages and email, didn't find anything that couldn't wait, spent a few minutes confirming Calhoun's warrant was in the system, and headed home.

After a workout and light dinner, he parked in his favorite patio chaise and surveyed the world as it went by. He'd decided on the way home that Eugene Calhoun's departure hadn't been a coincidence. Dylan Glithero had likely called Calhoun from jail on Friday morning to warn him that Audra O'Bannon had talked and the cops were on the way, and Calhoun had repaid Glithero by posting the bond before skipping town.

He also thought it would be a waste of time to try and find Calhoun at any of the family's properties in the USA, even if he could manage to compile a list. Interstate extradition was a simple matter.

He felt almost certain Calhoun had fled to a foreign country, and while Kaye wasn't intimately familiar with extradition treaties and processes, it was probably a country that either had no extradition treaty with the U.S. or a country where sex with a sixteen-year-old wasn't a crime.

But even List Treaty countries wouldn't harbor a murderer, and while he was nowhere near proving Eugene Calhoun had killed Valerie Weber, he didn't know for sure that Calhoun *hadn't* murdered her. He considered calling his contact at the FBI office in Los Angeles and asking for their help, but dismissed the idea.

Keep digging, he told himself. *If it's there, I'll find it.*

CHAPTER 36

It started as one of those throwaway days all cops, especially those that work nights, detest.

After putting on a coat and tie, and driving the pickup, Kaye ended up spending most of the morning camped on a bench outside a courtroom at the Foltz Justice Center. It aggravated him for two reasons. One, he wasn't the primary detective on the case, he'd been more of an extra, just-in-case presence on the arrest team, and, two, though he was never subpoenaed by the Prosecution to testify, they asked him to be there, again just-in-case, and he didn't know he'd wasted his time until court broke for lunch and the bailiff informed him he could go home.

It was almost one o'clock when he finally made it to the squad room. He hung up the sport coat, plopped into his chair and stared at the blank computer monitor.

Okay, what now? He again found himself in wait-and-see mode while others were doing the digging he couldn't do, and it didn't help his mood.

He needed to find Eugene Calhoun, but didn't know where to begin. Based on the house in Newport and the list of places the smartass kid had run off, Calhoun had obviously never lived on just a teacher's salary.

Then why become a teacher? He instantly remembered an old hunter's adage his father had often repeated. 'A wise hunter already knows where the game is.' Young girls go to high school. Fertile ground for Calhoun's type of hunting.

The family wealth also explained Calhoun's legal talent at his Orange County trial.

The family.

Kaye went to the internet and started searching. It took some time to find what he was after. One of Eugene Calhoun's paternal ancestors had been an enterprising merchant in Central California during the Gold Rush, building a food services and supply empire from a single dry goods store. Because the company was private there were no financial disclosure requirements, but Kaye had no problem believing that the Calhoun family was probably worth well into the billions of dollars.

Easy enough to avoid extradition, he thought. *Just buy a small country.*

There wasn't enough public information about the company to yield any worthwhile hints as to where Calhoun may have gone and it didn't take Kaye long to decide he was wasting his time.

He was reaching for the squad room door when it was pushed open from the outside and he found himself face-to-face with Dr. Jaime Archuleta.

"Arch, what are you doing here?"

"I came to see you," Arch said, lifting a hand to show Kaye the file he was carrying, "about this."

"Is that the Rachel Lowden file?"

"It is."

"That was fast."

"What can I say?" Arch smiled. "You want me to leave and come back tomorrow?"

"Very funny. Follow me."

"Okay," Arch said after they'd both sat down. "I went through this last night and, well, let's just say a few things bothered me. So this morning I dug up the autopsy report, and a couple of other things bothered me."

"Start from the top," Kaye said.

Arch nodded. "It really wasn't any one thing specifically, it was more a combination of things. Like the fact that there wasn't much water in the tub. Everybody thinks they'll bleed out faster if they hold their cuts underwater. Clotting is chemical, not wet or dry. Running water slows it down a little, but unless the water in a tub is over about a hundred and fifty degrees it has no effect. And nobody, I mean nobody, sets their water heater that high. Besides, the water wasn't even deep enough for her to submerge her elbows.

"The victim also had long hair. In the photos, the last five or six inches of her hair was wet, but it wasn't in the water. How does that happen?

"But the biggest thing that bothered me is that it was a seventeen-year-old girl. Getting both concurrent ulnar arteries is tough, but she managed to do it on both sides?"

"The parents told the detectives she was in counseling for depression," Kaye pointed out. "And she left a note."

"I know," Arch said. "Look, the best way for me to describe my impression is this. If you're in the front row of the theatre you get a good, close-up view of the actors, sets, costumes, everything. If you're thirty rows back, you're not seeing the same show. Maybe they weren't looking hard enough. I mean, open and shut, right? Girl bleeds out in the bathtub, razor blade on the floor directly under her hand. Parents say she's being treated for depression and, oh, by the way, here's her suicide note. Let sleeping dogs lie, right?"

"You think the scene might have been staged?" Kaye asked.

"I don't know," Arch replied, his exasperation clear. "I wouldn't testify to it in court, but..." He shrugged his shoulders and raised both hands, palms up. "We're the guys in row thirty now, and things look...different. We have to ask questions."

"Did you find anything in the autopsy report?"

"The only thing was a notation of a fresh contusion to the side of the head, which the examining pathologist attributed to the edge of the bathtub." Arch shrugged. "And with those injuries, I'm supposed to believe she fell into the bathtub and her head hit first? Oh, and I found out the body was cremated, so you won't have to dig any deeper."

Kaye went quiet, mulling over what Arch was telling him.

It was Arch who broke the silence. "Ben, why did you want me to look at this?"

"Because I had the same reaction to the photos," Kaye told him. "Investigation by the book, note and all, but when I looked at the photos I kept expecting someone to yell 'Cut!' and then somebody else would walk into the shot and the girl in the tub would stand up, put on a robe, and leave."

"Was there any physical evidence found at the scene?" Arch asked.

"The razor blade found on the floor and the note in the victim's bedroom."

"See! That's what I'm talking about," Arch said. "The right arm is hanging out of the tub, and the razor blade is on the floor, right where you'd expect it to be. Think about it, though. The blade has to be in her left hand to cut her right arm, and vice versa, right? If she dropped the blade from her right hand, that means she had to have cut her left arm last. With the degree of injury already sustained to her right elbow, I highly doubt she could have pulled that off."

"Determination, maybe?" Kaye posited.

"I guess," Arch said, then went quiet for a moment before adding, "I have to say, if Rachel Lowden had been embalmed and buried instead of cremated, I'd be asking for an exhumation order. Just to make sure."

"After all this time?"

"You'd be surprised," Arch said as he stood up. "I'd better get going, let you get out of here, too."

"Thanks, Arch."

"It's what I do. Don't hesitate to call if there's anything else you want me to look at."

Kaye stayed at his desk, slowly going through the Lowden file again. He didn't recognize the names of either detective that had handled the investigation, but, like he'd told Arch, the whole thing was done by the book, right down the line.

There'd been no blood except Rachel Lowden's at the scene. No sign of forced entry into the house, although Monica Lowden had broken down the bathroom door after returning from shopping to find Rachel in the tub. Monica told the detectives that she'd heard Rachel's favorite music playing inside the bathroom, Rachel hadn't answered her frantic calls to open the door, and after she finally got in she found her daughter's favorite scented candles burning on the vanity counter.

Let it go, he told himself. *She killed herself because she was guilty about giving up her baby. Case closed.*

***

Takeout in hand, Kaye got home early enough for a quick workout and to sit *zazen*. It was the first time since Roshi's death and he struggled mightily, his concentration crumbling under the weight of his memories of his friend and mentor.

After cleaning up, he reheated the takeout. It was a mild, pleasant evening and he went outside to eat. The ocean was calm as darkness consumed the light, serving to accentuate the seemingly inexhaustible stream of aircraft departing LAX.

He sat there for hours, empty bags and paper containers stacked next to the chaise, his mind drifting back and forth between worries and pleasant memories.

He smiled at the memory of Amy giving the realtor a Come To Jesus lecture after the man had insulted them by telling them he didn't think a teacher married to a cop could afford this house.

But what if Rachel Lowden was murdered? Who gets justice for her?

"Jesus, Kaye," he muttered aloud, "give it a rest."

Unwilling to face the empty house, he slept above the garage.

CHAPTER 37

There was a note from Patty on his desk when Kaye got to the squad.

'I need to show you something. Call me when you have some time available. P.'

He called Patty.

"Good morning," he said when she answered. "You need to show me something?"

"I do."

"Valerie's computer, maybe?"

"Yes. Give me about fifteen minutes and I'll be up." She hung up.

He went to the break room and brewed a cup of tea. On the way back he grabbed the Dailies off the bulletin board and took them to his desk.

Business as usual, he thought as he thumbed through them. *Good thing crime is good for the budget. And promotions. And better retirements.*

Less than a minute after hanging the Dailies back on the board Patty pushed through the squad room doors and beelined for Kaye's desk. Valerie Weber's computer was cradled in the crook of her left arm.

"Hi," she said as she dragged an empty chair over and sat down.

Kaye eyed the computer and asked, "Did you get in? Find something interesting?"

"Oh, yeah." She grinned like a Cheshire cat as she opened the computer. "I can't wait to show you."

Patty put the computer on the desk and started to move her chair so she could get to the keyboard. "Scoot over," she said absently. "I'll drive."

"Yes, ma'am," Kaye said with exaggerated politeness as he followed orders.

"Sorry," Patty said quickly, glancing sideways to see if Kaye was smiling. He was. "First of all, the password you found worked. I went through her history," she continued, "and found quite a few sites that claim to help reunite everyone from biological parents and children to long-lost lovers. Some are obvious scams and some are just fronts to sell DNA kits, but some of them are legit.

"I was able to figure out she'd set up account profiles on two of the sites, but I couldn't log in because I didn't have the passwords."

"Patty," Kaye said, "this is a girl who carried her password around with her. Surely she —"

"She did," Patty interrupted. "I finally found a username and password file buried in a system directory. Voila, I'm Valerie Weber. I could even see her cloud storage, including her email."

"Good work," Kaye said.

"Interestingly enough, there were no social media accounts or passwords on this computer. I'm guessing that's because teenagers don't use the big platforms, they tend to gravitate toward the newer, less commercial ones. But, at any rate, no social media."

"She probably had all that on her phone," Kaye commented.

"That's what I was thinking, too," Patty said. "But I was able to log in to those sites as her and go through her messages. Detective, she messaged with two individuals, one on each site, for quite some time. Then one of them disappeared after telling Valerie she was wasting her time and should stop looking."

"Really?" Kaye said, surprised. "Why would someone have an account on that kind of site and then tell people that?"

"Good question," Patty said.

"Was the user male or female?"

"I can't be sure, but I'd guess a woman. The username was G-E-N twenty-nine, which I thought was odd, so I checked. There was already a J-E-N twenty-nine, so… Probably another Jennifer."

"And Valerie stopped communicating with this person?" Kaye asked.

"Yes. She continued messaging with the other person for several months, then quit going to the site completely about eight months ago."

"She either found somebody, or she gave up," Kaye said. "How long had she been looking?"

"The accounts were created about eighteen months ago," Patty said. "Based on the messages I found, I don't think she gave up. I think Valerie found one of her birth parents, or at least she thought she did."

"What's the username?" Kaye asked.

"Matt eighteen fourteen," Patty replied and handed Kaye a piece of paper. "That's the username and website URL."

Kaye glanced down. Matt1814. "Maybe a bible verse?"

"I thought of that, too," Patty said. "I looked it up. Matthew eighteen, verse fourteen, is about the loss of a child. I don't think that's a coincidence."

"Sounds like regrets to me," Kaye said.

"Could be. Here, let me show you."

She typed the URL in and hit enter.

The page came up, and Kaye was astounded.

"Holy cow," he said. "Scroll down."

There were hundreds and hundreds of posts, all from people seeking lost or separated family members, lovers or friends, dated in just the last ten days, and thousands of older ones.

"You went through all of those?" He asked Patty.

"Didn't have to," she replied. "Watch this."

She moved the cursor to an icon on a bar near the top of the page and a Your Profile menu box dropped down. She clicked on it and a login box appeared.

Kaye watched her type in Valerie's username and shook his head.

LilLostRedhead.

Patty checked her notes and typed in the password.

Valerie Weber's quest for her biological family filled the screen.

The page was in two columns. Topping the narrower left column was a blurry photograph of Valerie Weber, which Kaye thought looked at least a year or two old. Beneath it was Valerie's 'Personal Ad'.

'My parents have never told me, but I think I'm adopted. Why? Because I'm the only redhead I can find on my family tree going back as far as I can search, and my biology teacher says DNA doesn't work that way. I'm almost sixteen, 5'7" tall, born in Los Angeles County and I was born with one distinctive feature that my real parents would know about. If you think you might know who I really am, please message me.'

The double-wide right-hand column was Valerie's message board.

"Everyone with a user account can see your profile," Patty said. "But only the logged in user can see their own message board."

"She didn't post much of a profile," Kaye observed. "Her D.O.B. is only the month and year, and I don't think that's even right."

"I think she was being careful," Patty said. "There are a lot of predators working these sites."

"Wonderful," Kaye said sarcastically.

"The messages are in descending order of receipt date – newest on top," Patty said as she scrolled down, eventually ending up at the bottom of the list.

"When was her first message from Matt eighteen fourteen?" Kaye asked.

"It wasn't until about six months after she signed up," Patty replied as she watched the screen and scrolled up. "Ah, here it is."

Kaye leaned in and read the message.

'I know someone who is searching for a young woman born in the San Fernando Valley in the same month/year as you. She had red hair when she was born and was given up for adoption as an infant. I think we should meet in person and talk, someplace public, your choice, and bring whoever else you want to bring with you so you feel safe. I also live in the Los Angeles area.'

"What did she write back?" Kaye asked.

"It took her a pretty long time to answer," Patty said, scrolling up.

"She was probably scared," Kaye said.

"I think so, too. Oh, here," she pointed at the screen.

'I don't know about meeting. I don't have anyone else I can bring. Can you tell me your real name and what my real name is?'

The response from Matt1814 came fairly quickly.

'I understand your reluctance to meet. Believe it or not, this is scary for me and my friends, too. I don't think it's a good idea to share names until we're sure about this. It might just confuse you more.'

At least whoever this Matt eighteen fourteen is, he isn't a total creep," Patty said.

"We don't know for sure it's a 'he'," Kaye reminded her. "And they could just be being careful not to overplay their hand."

"Hadn't thought of that."

Valerie's next message to Matt1814 was short and to the point.

'In my public profile I said I was born with one distinctive feature. If you think I'm who you're looking for, tell me what that is. Otherwise, this conversation is over.'

Matt1814 didn't answer for almost two weeks. Kaye tried to imagine Valerie's stress level during that time. Finally, she got a response.

'Okay, my friends' daughter was born with a small, almost heart-shaped birthmark on the right side of the back of her neck, right at the hairline. I won't message you again unless I hear from you first. I hope you find who you're looking for.'

Kaye leaned back in his chair and went quiet.

Patty turned and looked at him. "What's wrong?"

"Valerie Weber's autopsy report said she had a two-point-four-centimeter-wide *nevus simplex*, a birthmark, on the right side of the back of her neck."

"That was it," Patty said. "That's how she knew." She scrolled upwards, through the past toward the present, pausing at a message from Matt1814. Embedded in the message was a photo of a smiling young woman holding an infant.

Kaye instantly recognized the mother as Rachel Lowden. The message was simple. 'This is your mother, Rachel, holding you. Your name is Crystal Lowden.'

Valerie replied the same day. 'She's not a redhead.'

Matt1814 replied within 24 hours. 'Your father has red hair.'

It was two days before Valerie messaged again. This time she also sent a photo, more a close-up than her profile picture. 'I want to meet my birth parents. This weekend.'

Matt1814's reply was swift. 'You are the spitting image of your mother. Name the place and time.'

Valerie responded the same day. 'Two o'clock Saturday at the inverted fountain plaza on the UCLA campus.'

Matt1814: 'I'll be there with flowers for the beautiful girl with red hair, lost no more.'

"And that was the last message between them on this site," Patty said. "They must have met, hit it off, and started another line of communication."

"Agreed," Kaye said. "And I think the whole friends thing is a ruse. She wants to meet her parents and the reply is 'I'll be there'? Doesn't jibe."

"I didn't notice that. But it could also mean that Matt eighteen fourteen knows Valerie's biological mom killed herself and doesn't want to tell her, at least not like this."

"Could be," Kaye said. "Sounds like we need to find out who Matt eighteen fourteen is."

"Agreed," Patty said, then hesitated. "I'm not sure I know how to do that."

"I'll take it from here. Thank you, Patty. I appreciate your great work on this, and I'll pass that along to the Commander."

Patty was quiet for a moment, then said, "I met her, Detective. I didn't know her, but I met her. This feels personal."

"I hate to say you get used to it," Kaye said, "because you really never do. You just have to learn to…compartmentalize, if that makes sense."

"I guess," Patty said, sighing deeply. "I'd better get back downstairs. Let me know if there's anything else I can do to help." She stood and headed for the door.

Kaye shut down Valerie's computer and turned to his. He went to the web and ran a 'whois' on the domain name from Patty's note. It was owned by an LLC with an address in Pasadena.

Shouldn't be too tough, he thought. *At least it's not in Romania or Singapore.*

He bent to the task of writing a request for a prosecutorial subpoena that would compel the website owners to disclose any and all information relevant to the username Matt1814. It would only be the first step in the digital trail, and Kaye hoped Matt1814 wasn't computer savvy enough to have taken steps to conceal his or her identity.

He was careful to construct the case summary so it could be copied and pasted into the next application, if needed.

When he was satisfied, he picked up the phone and called Kayla Okafor. No answer. He called the main office number and asked for her, only to find she was in court and would not be back in the office until Monday.

"I'll be there," Kaye said and hung up.

CHAPTER 38

Kaye's timing was perfect. He'd just gotten off the elevator when he saw ADA Okafor come out of the stairwell door at the end of the hallway. They met outside the door to the office.

"Good morning, Detective," Okafor said as she put her briefcase under her left arm and rummaged in her purse for her keys. "How was your weekend?"

"Great," Kaye replied. "Spent it working on a bike restoration."

"Oh? No trip to...where is it...Santa Ynez?"

Kayla Okafor never asked Kaye directly about Auggie McMaster, just seeming to prod once in a while to see if the status quo had changed.

"Not this weekend," Kaye said, answering the question without giving any details.

Kaye followed Okafor to her office, where she put her briefcase on her desk and dropped her purse on the credenza behind it.

"You want coffee?" she asked Kaye.

"Sure, I'll take a cup. Black, please."

"Be right back. Sit, please."

She left, returning a few moments later with a mug in each hand and handing one to Kaye.

"Okay," she said as she sat down. "I'm not surprised to see you. I assume you got the phone calls, too."

"Phone calls? I'm here about a subpoena for some digital evidence in the Weber case."

"You didn't get calls from Elise O'Bannon or an attorney named Vickers last Friday?"

"No."

"Lucky you," Okafor said, then took a sip of her coffee. "Mrs. O'Bannon called to, as she put it, inform me that she and her husband had discussed it and decided they did not want this office pursuing charges against Dylan Glithero for his relationship with Audra. Said they just wanted to move on and not further traumatize their daughter."

"Why am I not surprised?" Kaye said sarcastically. "Did Elise mention anything about Calhoun? Whose family, by the way, is worth a very large fortune."

"She did not," Okafor replied. "But the word must've gotten around, which leads to the second call. Gerald Vickers, Attorney at Law, counsel to the Calhoun family."

"What did he want?"

"Apparently, whoever's cage you and the Newport Beach Police rattled called and told him what was going on, so Vickers called this office to demand a copy of the warrant and affidavit and to inform us that Mr. Calhoun, whom he said was currently out of the country, denies any and all charges, and is, in fact, innocent and wrongfully accused."

"Calhoun's nephew," Kaye said. "First-class knucklehead. He must've called Vickers."

"Vickers didn't say. But he asked me questions about the case."

"Did you answer them?"

"Of course," Okafor said. "I have to, Detective. But he did not ask about forensics and I did not volunteer the DNA results on Valerie Weber. Vickers assumed that the alleged victim was Audra O'Bannon, and he was enough of a jerk that I didn't correct him. He can find out during discovery."

"Where does all this leave us with the O'Bannon case?" Kaye asked, already knowing the answer.

"Unfortunately, pretty much dead in the water," Okafor replied. "Unless you want to put Audra on the stand as a hostile witness and we take our chances."

"Waste of time," Kaye said. "If I had to guess, I'd say the Calhoun family made it worth the O'Bannons' while not to pursue the case. Seems to be Calhoun's pattern."

"But you can't prove that."

"No."

"We can still get Calhoun on the Weber warrant. The DNA speaks for itself."

"We hope," Kaye said. "Cell-free DNA is still pretty new science."

"No time like the present," Okafor said. "The warrant is active and when Calhoun is arrested, we'll charge him and put him back in prison."

"If he's ever arrested. The guy's protected by a fortress built of money, the ramparts manned by high-priced legal talent."

Okafor studied him for a moment, then said, "You sound discouraged."

"I guess I am," Kaye admitted. "To think this all started with a mom bringing her daughter in to complain she'd been beaten up at school. I told her it would be easy. Didn't turn out that way, and I'm not exactly her favorite detective these days."

"Stuff happens," Okafor said, leaning forward, putting her elbows on the table and clasping her hands together. "It's our job to figure out exactly what stuff happened and whose stuff it is. Sometimes the pile's just bigger and stinkier than we thought it was. But it's not our stuff. Right?"

"That's what they pay me for," Kaye said with a sigh. "Which brings me to why I'm here."

"Fill me in."

Kaye laid it out for her, starting with getting his hands on Valerie Weber's computer, then what Patty had uncovered.

"I've got the domain owner's information," he said in conclusion. "I need a subpoena for the account information on Matt eighteen fourteen."

He handed Okafor the application, which she quickly scanned.

"Shouldn't be a problem," she said when she looked up. "They're even in our County. You want one of our guys to serve it, or do you want to?"

"Probably better if it came directly from this office."

"I agree," Okafor said, nodding. "I'll fast track this and have it drawn up right away. With luck, we'll serve it today, tomorrow at the latest."

"Thanks, Counselor," Kaye said, rising to leave. "Let me know when you get the return. This is only step one."

"Will do."

On the ride to the station Kaye thought about how quickly the Calhoun family had circled their wagons and acted to start putting up barriers. The kid at the house had to have called Vickers, or one of his associates, before they'd even gotten off the island. And it seemed obvious to him that Vickers had talked to Eugene Calhoun before he called Okafor.

A question suddenly popped into Kaye's head.

How does a guy with that much juice end up serving his entire sentence?

It had been obvious to Kaye when he'd read the Orange County trial transcript that Calhoun had a top-notch defense. If the Judge hadn't ignored the prosecutor's sentence recommendation, Calhoun might have done his time in County and never seen the inside of a State prison. As it turned out, Calhoun's lawyers had probably been pounding on the

298

Pardon and Parole Boards doors from day one, trying to get their client out.

Why didn't Calhoun make parole?

As he pulled into the station parking lot, he knew one thing: He needed to know more about Calhoun's time in the slam.

It might give him some insight into how to find the guy now.

Back at his desk, the first thing he did was look up the number for the Pardon and Parole Board in Sacramento. He navigated the convoluted electronic menu and eventually connected to a live human being.

"Pardons and Paroles, this is Jackie. How can I help you?"

Kaye identified himself, then said, "I'm looking for the Parole Board hearing transcripts for a prior inmate named Eugene Arthur Calhoun. He served his sentence in Lancaster, had several hearings, but was never recommended for release. I'm curious to know why."

"Do you have a date of birth, or his inmate ID number?" Jackie asked, and Kaye could hear the soft tapping of a keyboard in the background as he gave her Calhoun's DOB.

"Okay, here we are," Jackie said after a brief wait. "Eugene A. Calhoun, matching DOB… Detective, is there a specific hearing you're interested in? There were four."

"Four? Really?"

"Yes, sir. Four." She gave him the date range.

"Can I get them all?"

"Of course. Do you want paper or electronic format?"

"Electronic will work."

Jackie then asked Kaye a series of questions, obviously filling out a request form.

"All right, that should do it," she said at last. "I'll forward this to the right people and you should have these in your inbox within forty-eight hours. Anything else, Detective?"

"That's all I need. Thanks, Jackie."

Four hearings and no release. Kaye knew there could be a multitude of reasons. The transcripts would tell him. He hoped they'd also yield the names of Calhoun's supporters, who might now know where the man was.

He checked the time and decided to go grab lunch. He walked around the corner, ordered the Chef Salad special, then parked at an outside table. It was a glorious day, but the slight chill reminded Kaye that winter – or at least Southern California's reasonable facsimile thereof – was not far off.

He ate at a leisurely pace, people watching and thinking about the Weber case. Like he'd told Okafor, what he'd first thought would be a slam dunk had turned into quite the can of worms. Worms didn't bother him. Not being able to find the can opener did. He thought about Valerie's almost desperate attempt to find her biological family and realized he couldn't relate. Why would people spend that much time and effort to find people who'd never really been in their lives, often by choice?

There had been lots of posts on the site by people just looking for old friends or sweethearts, especially from their high school days. He couldn't relate to that, either. High school had been an unpleasant experience for him, and his first crush hadn't known he was even alive.

He eventually found his way back to the station and spent some time updating the Weber case file and going over it, again, looking for things he might have missed.

He didn't find anything.

It wasn't really quitting time, but Kaye felt dead-ended. An option suddenly popped into his head, so he grabbed the Big Boar jacket and headed out.

The gate at Kyokoku-Dera Monastery was open, which for some reason Kaye took as a good omen. He idled the bike down the gravel drive, stopping as usual at the crest of the small rise that overlooked the grounds. The view was still stunning, but Kaye thought the flowers were a little less vivid and the branches a little droopier, as though, they, too were in mourning for Roshi.

The flat stone was still next to the main temple stairs, and after Kaye swung off the bike he turned to see a smiling Seicho standing on the top step.

"Greetings, Benkei," Seicho said and bowed slightly. "I wasn't sure we would see you again."

"I wasn't sure you would, either, to be honest. I came without an offering. I always brought Roshi a cantaloupe."

"His favorite," Seicho said. "But do not worry. I'm allergic."

"Good to know," Kaye said, half-smiling.

Seicho came down the steps. "Let's take a walk," he said, then went around Kaye and took the path toward the pond.

Kaye caught up and walked at Seicho's side.

"So," the monk asked, "why did you choose to come today?"

Kaye had to think about it.

"I don't think I chose the day as much as the day chose me."

"Explain, please."

Kaye tried. Fading memories of past good times. Difficulties at work. A growing unease with his life in general.

"I feel like I've lost direction," he said in closing. "And I miss Roshi."

"I, too, miss him," Seicho said softly. "Are you sitting *zazen*?"

"Not really. I'm too distracted."

Seicho stopped. "You have the cause and effect reversed, Benkei. Distractions should not preclude *zazen*. *Zazen* will soothe distractions."

"It's not that simple right now."

"It is never simple," Seicho said, hesitated for two beats and asked, "Where are we, Benkei?"

"Kyokoku-Dera Monastery," Kaye replied instantly.

"More specific, please."

Kaye hesitated briefly before answering. "On the path to the pond."

"Are we moving?"

"No, not right now."

"Yet we are still on the path, are we not?"

"Yes," replied Kaye, suppressing a smile and knowing he'd been outsmarted again.

"What if the pond is not our ultimate destination?" Seicho asked. "Are we on the wrong path?"

Kaye hesitated again. "I don't know. Perhaps the path continues beyond the pond."

Seicho smiled. "Very good." He raised his hands out to his sides and gestured at their surroundings. "We work diligently to smooth this path, both for our guests and our own walking meditations. But life is not so simple. Sometimes there are stones upon which we trip. Sometimes there is mud through which we must slog." He hesitated for a moment before adding, "And sometimes we realize that the pond is not our final destination, which will only reveal itself farther down the path. *Zazen* is your work to do in order to more easily crush the stone and dry the mud. You must do the work, Benkei, in your practice and in your life."

Tears came to Kaye's eyes as he looked at Seicho. "Thank you, Roshi-sama," he said softly, bowing slightly.

"You honor me, Benkei-bo."

That evening Kaye sat *zazen* for almost a half-hour. It wasn't his most successful session ever, but it was far from his worst. Afterward he spent an hour on a strenuous workout, which buoyed his spirits even more.

CHAPTER 39

There had been a time when smaller cities and counties viewed penal institutions as prized economic development tools, based on the belief that if you built it, they – meaning jobs – would come. In some parts of the country that philosophy still prevailed.

But when an area is already booming, finding out the State plans to build a maximum-security prison in your neighborhood usually brings protests, not celebrations, from local residents and their Chamber of Commerce.

Such was the case in the town of Lancaster when the State announced plans for such a facility in the high desert north of Los Angeles. After some give-and-take, during which the State did most of the taking and Lancaster most of the giving, it was finally agreed that the prison would be built. But not inside the city limits, and the word Lancaster would not be part of its official name.

But that's what people called it, because that's essentially where it was. So much for give and take.

The ride was more direct from home than it would become by going to the station first, so Kaye called Captain Thompson to let the boss know he wouldn't be in the station until later that day, if at all.

Thompson had been less than pleased.

"Why waste a day going all the way up there?" He'd asked Kaye. "You got a warrant for the guy, let it work."

"Just a couple things I want to check, Captain," Kaye had countered. "I've already called, so they know I'm coming."

Thompson had grudgingly acquiesced, which was good for Kaye. He was going, with or without the boss's approval.

He left before daylight. It was a long ride before he rolled up to the main gate. One guard stayed inside the guard post, keeping watch. Another emerged, eyeing Kaye skeptically until he held up his badge wallet.

"Detective Kaye, LAPD," he announced. "I'm here to see Deputy Warden Mendez. He's expecting me."

The guard outside did a double take and said, "Oh, okay, we were expecting you," before turning and signaling his partner to open the outer gate. He turned back to Kaye. "Nice bike, Detective. Pull through and wait for the inside gate to open. Are you armed?"

"I am."

"You'll have to surrender your weapon out here. Pick it up when you leave."

"I can do that. Thanks."

It took almost fifteen minutes for Kaye to complete the entry security process. When he was finally ushered through the last automatic steel door into the prison itself, he was met by a short, mustached man in a blue pinstripe suit.

"Detective Kaye? I'm Luis Mendez, Deputy Warden. Welcome."

"Thanks, Warden," Kaye said as they shook hands. "I appreciate you taking the time to see me on such short notice."

"Not a problem. Let's go to my office."

Kaye followed Mendez through another security door and down a short hallway cleverly disguised as a concrete tunnel. Mendez stopped and keyed a code into a pad mounted next to a door. Kaye heard the lock click, then Mendez opened the door and stepped aside to let Kaye go in first.

The office looked like Mendez lived in it. A microwave, dorm-sized refrigerator, coffee maker and large flatscreen monitor all occupied the space. The walls held photos of Mendez with several California Governors and Attorneys General, as well as photos of a woman and three teenagers.

"So, Detective," Mendez said as he busied himself pouring a cup of coffee, "you're interested in a former inmate, correct?"

"I am," Kaye acknowledged. "Eugene Arthur Calhoun. He did time for statutory rape with special circumstances."

"I remember Calhoun," Mendez said as he sat down. "Crap, I'm sorry. I don't get enough company to keep my manners sharp. You want a cup?"

"No, I'm good. You remember Calhoun? Was he a problem?"

"On the contrary," Mendez said. "Hardly heard a peep out of the guy while he was here. But I sure as hell remember his lawyers. Drove me out of my mind with complaints about conditions, food, yard time, you name it. It always got worse in the months leading up to Calhoun's parole hearings, like they thought they could be such assholes we'd let Calhoun out just to get rid of him, and them."

"That's one reason why I'm here," Kaye said. "Calhoun's family is loaded. I read the trial transcript and the State's sentencing recommendation, which was ignored by the Judge. Calhoun ended up here. I got curious about why he was never paroled."

"What's your current interest in Calhoun? I mean, you're not doing research for a book, right? Because if you are, I can't talk to you."

"Nothing like that," Kaye assured the Warden. "I've got another statutory rape warrant out for him, but he's in the wind. I'm hoping I might find some leads on where he might be. I heard he fled the country, but you know how it is. Check all the boxes."

"Indeed," Mendez said. "Sounds like your primary interest might be visitor logs and cellmates."

"And why he was never paroled."

"I can't really help you with that. Other than providing space and security, those hearings belong to Pardon and Parole. We don't even attend them. You can get transcripts from Sacramento."

"Already put in the request."

"But I can help you with the other things." Mendez spun his chair to a position in front of his keyboard. "I'll pull up the visitor log first."

Kaye waited while Mendez brought up the data.

"Okay, kind of what I expected," the Warden said after a bit. "Mostly confidential meetings with his lawyers. Some family — at least the last names are Calhoun — for the first couple of years, then it tapered off."

"Is that the norm?"

"With family, yeah, which is too bad. The lawyers not so much. Billable hours, you know, plus travel. Most of our guests don't have those kinds of resources."

Mendez looked back at the screen and kept slowly scrolling through the spreadsheet. Kaye watched, saw Mendez stop, scroll back in the opposite direction, then reverse directions again.

"That's odd," Mendez muttered, obviously talking to himself, not to Kaye.

"Did you find something?" Kaye asked, curious.

"I'm not sure," Mendez said, his attention still on the screen as he rapidly scrolled back and forth through the spreadsheet. He stopped suddenly, minimized the open spreadsheet and opened another record. He spent several minutes looking through it before turning to Kaye.

"I think our database may be corrupted," he said flatly.

"How so?"

"Because I'm finding visits from a family member of one of Calhoun's cellmates in Calhoun's record."

"Could just be a data entry error," Kaye speculated. "Same cell number, maybe, and the wrong name was selected?"

"I don't think so," Mendez said, shaking his head. "A lot of the visits are after the cellmate was given a compassionate release for terminal cancer. The docs gave him less than six months to live, so we let him go home to his family to die."

"What was he in for?"

"Armed robbery and one count of felony murder."

"So he was a lifer," Kaye said.

"Basically, yes," Mendez confirmed. "He was no youngster when we cut him loose, but he'd have been here a lot longer if he hadn't gotten sick. But I've still got to figure out why these visits are on…" His voice faded as his attention went back to the monitor.

"Was the last name similar to Calhoun?"

Mendez glanced at Kaye and made a face. "No. Dobson, first name Sharon."

Dobson? Kaye's mind raced. "Does it note how she's related to the cellmate?"

"The family box is checked, the notation says daughter," Mendez replied as he peered at the screen.

"How often did she visit?"

"Uh, it says here," Mendez said slowly as he scanned the screen, "she visited Calhoun's cellmate regularly right up until the time he was released. Then, at least according to this, she visited Calhoun multiple times over a six-month period, starting about a month after Dobson was released up until about four months before Calhoun got out." Mendez looked at Kaye and added, "Interesting, the visits were always on a Monday."

"Not to talk out of turn, Warden, but that doesn't sound like a mistake to me. Sounds like scheduled meetings. How long ago was the last one?"

"Almost two years ago."

"What was the cellmate's name?"

"Royal Duane Dobson," Mendez replied, and kept talking as he leaned back so Kaye could see the photo on the screen.

Kaye didn't hear a word Mendez said after 'Dobson'. His chest tightened, his ears roared with the sound of pounding blood, his breathing turned rapid and shallow, and his vision started to blur. Time was suspended.

"Detective Kaye, are you all right?" Mendez's voice finally cut through the fog.

"I'm sorry," Kaye managed to say as he was jolted back to the present. "I guess I got distracted, but I'm okay."

But he wasn't.

Royal Duane Dobson was the drunk who'd run over and killed Amy.

CHAPTER 40

Kaye was still shaking when he stopped for gas in Lancaster before heading back to Los Angeles.

No way, he kept telling himself. *It can't be. It's not possible.*

But it was. Roy Dobson's face was forever etched in his memory, along with the images of a torn, broken and bleeding Amy lying in the road waiting for an ambulance while he begged her not to go, not to leave him. And the last words he ever whispered to her.

"I love you Ames."

The rest was history. Disobeying orders and tracking down Dobson, with full intent to tear the man to pieces, then instead simply handcuffing and turning him over to the local police. He'd been suspended, then walked away from the case, not caring if he ever laid eyes on Dobson again or what happened to the man.

No way. It can't be. It's not possible.

He took a break at the gas station, getting something to drink and a sandwich, then sitting to gather his wits. It took nearly a half-hour before he felt confident he could safely make the ride to the station.

It was nearly 4:00 p.m. when he dragged himself into the squad room and collapsed into his chair. He hadn't been sitting long when he heard Captain Thompson's voice behind him.

"How'd it go?"

Kaye spun his chair around. "Okay, I guess. Calhoun was a model prisoner, but the Deputy Warden said his lawyers were hounds from hell."

"Money makes the world go 'round."

"That it does."

"I didn't mean you…" Thompson sputtered. "I don't see…"

"I know, Cap. Don't worry about it. Besides, I'm a lot of zeroes away from being in Calhoun's neighborhood."

"Did you come up with anything solid?"

"Maybe," Kaye said, deflecting the question. He wanted to chase it first.

"Okay," Thompson said. He started to turn around, then stopped. "I almost forgot. Deputy DA Okafor is looking for you."

"I'll give her a call. Thanks, Cap."

Thompson stood and studied Kaye. "You sure you're okay? You look, well, I hate to say it, but you look like hell. Are you sick?"

"I'm fine," Kaye said. "Just not a good day. I may bag it after I talk to Okafor, if that's okay."

"Your call," Thompson said. "Not an issue for me."

Kaye watched his boss walk back to his office, thinking about how much his relationship with Thompson had improved since he'd first joined the squad, and remembered what an Idaho cop who'd gotten between him and Thompson had said.

"Sounds to me like he'd like to make a lampshade and footstool out of your hide."

With a wan half-smile he spun back around, picked up the phone and called Okafor.

"I heard you were looking for me," he said when she answered.

"I am," she confirmed. "I've got news about that Matt eighteen fourteen user account. They don't tie personal information to user account names because the site is free, but they did give me the IP addresses."

"Addresses, plural?" Kaye asked. "That doesn't sound like it'll be easy to trace. Could even be public places, like coffee shops or libraries."

"It's not as bad as it sounds," Okafor said. "I don't pretend to understand this stuff, but the techie I talked to said there was a pattern. Initially the addresses were random, like public places. But when Matt eighteen fourteen started communication with Valerie Weber, it was the same address from then on out."

"Were they able to tell you who owns it?"

"They did, sort of. Not the person, but they were able to tell from their routers which service provider was directing the traffic to the site."

"Then we should be able to track it."

"I'm way ahead of you," Okafor said, and Kaye could hear the smile in her voice. "Our office has a designated contact in the provider's L.A. service center, just for cases like this. I've already spoken to her and emailed her the subpoena. She said she'd have the account information by tomorrow, latest."

"That's good news," Kaye said. "Strong work, Counselor."

"Don't thank me until we have a name. It could still turn out to be Joe's Anonymous Internet Café."

"Then I go get Joe's video security footage."

"Bingo," Okafor said. "You going to be around tomorrow?"

"Not first thing in the morning," he replied. "I've got something to check. Thanks again for bird dogging the tech stuff for me."

"Talk to you tomorrow."

Kaye leaned back in his chair and pondered his next move.

"Screw it," he muttered, standing up and grabbing the Big Boar jacket. He headed for Thompson's office. "Cap, I'm headed out," he said from the open door.

Thompson looked up. "Sounds good. Get some rest. Hey, how'd it go with Okafor?"

"We might finally have a solid lead in the Valerie Weber case. We'll know tomorrow. Oh, and I've got to go to Orange County in the morning."

"Okay, keep me in the loop. Now, get out of here."

Kaye was glad to oblige.

CHAPTER 41

It was mid-morning when Kaye rolled into the visitor's parking lot at Moulton Junior High. He'd berated himself on the ride down, thinking he was probably wasting his time, but he wanted to check something that he hoped might help him find Calhoun.

After parking the Road King he encountered locked doors on both the school's main entrances. One had a sign that read 'Ring Bell For Entry' and he pushed the button next to the door. Almost immediately an armed security guard approached and, without opening the door, asked what Kaye wanted.

He showed his badge and ID and the guard opened the door.

"I need to talk to someone in the office," he told the guard.

"Come on in."

"Where's the office?"

"Just follow me," the guard said. "I'll show you."

It wasn't far. Several women were working at desks behind the counter and one rose when she saw the security guard open the door for Kaye.

"How can I help you?" she asked, a quizzical look on her face as she glanced at the guard.

"My name is Ben Kaye. I'm a detective with the LAPD. I'm working a current case that connects back to this building when it was Moulton High School, and –"

"That was a long time ago," the woman said.

"So I've been told," Kaye said, smiling. "Long story short, I was hoping you might have old yearbooks from the high school days."

"What years?"

Kaye gave her a date range.

"I know we don't have them in this office. You could talk to Mrs. Marsh in our media center. She would know if any were kept, and where they might be."

"How do I find Mrs. Marsh?" Kaye asked.

The woman gave him directions, then reached under the counter. "You'll need to wear this," she said, handing him a sizable, green laminated badge with 'Visitor' printed in black on both sides. It had a loop to go over the wearer's head. "Tells everyone you're official."

"Got it," Kaye said, putting the loop around his neck.

When he walked into the media center there was no sign of anyone, so he went to the central counter and waited. A minute later a woman, a stack of books cradled in one arm, emerged from a door on the far wall and headed his direction.

"You must be the policeman. I'm Mrs. Marsh."

"And you must be psychic," Kaye said, smiling.

"Hardly. Norma from the office called while you were on your way." She shifted the books into her hands and put them on the counter. "Told me you were looking for these. They're dusty, but..."

"Not a problem," Kaye said, looking at four volumes of the Moulton High School Lancers yearbooks. The top one was the first year he'd asked for.

"Use any of the tables you like," Mrs. Marsh said. "You've got about twenty minutes quiet time before the next bunch of students shows up."

"Thank you."

Kaye took the stack and went to the nearest table. He flipped quickly through the book to get some idea of how it was organized. Only the Senior class portraits were in color. Everything else was black and white.

He went first to the Activities section and found the Drama Club page. Most of the page was a group photo and he wasn't surprised to see that the Advisors were Mr. Calhoun and Mr. Glithero. Without knowing Calhoun had done time, Kaye would not have guessed that the man pictured had aged into the man whose driver's license picture he'd found in the system. He actually had to read the caption to pick out Dylan Glithero, who looked more like a fresh-faced student than a student teacher.

He scanned the student names in the caption. None had the initials K.S.

He went to the next book and again found the Drama Club page, with almost the same picture as the previous year. Dylan Glithero was the person in the picture that looked to have grown up the most. Again, no Drama Club member with the initials K.S. was in the photo.

He went to the Junior class section. There was no portrait of a student with the initials K.S. between Brian Sabathia and Amanda Taylor. Puzzled, Kaye went to the next year and looked. K.S. wasn't in the Drama Club photo or Senior class section. As he'd expected, the Drama Club now had two different advisors.

It suddenly made sense to Kaye. The scandal surrounding the Calhoun and Glithero cases surely must have had a major impact on K.S. and her family, maybe enough for her to drop out, or for her family to move. Or she could have simply chosen not to pose because of the circumstances.

He thought he might have missed something, so he went back through the Faculty section of each yearbook looking for anything that might give him insights into Calhoun's likes, personal life, anything relevant. He found nothing.

Probably wouldn't have made a difference, he thought. *Prison changes people.*

He finished just as the media center doors opened and a class filed in. Mrs. Marsh appeared out of nowhere.

"All done?" she asked, noting the closed and stacked yearbooks.

"Yes, ma'am," Kaye said, standing up. "Find what you were looking for?"

Kaye thought for a moment, then said, "Not really, but that's not necessarily a bad thing."

***

Not willing to pass up an opportunity to find Calhoun, he decided to take the long way, along the coast through Newport Beach, back to the station. He took I-5 south to the PCH exit in Capo Beach and, on a whim, rode past the old Harley Charlie's location. It was still gone, erased for the sake of tire tread, and a fresh wave of nostalgia washed over and saddened him.

What did you think? He thought, angry at himself. *It's not going to grow back.*

At Jamboree Road he turned left, went down the hill to Bayside and around to the Linda Isle guard shack.

Despite his badge and ID card, the guard gave him a hard time.

"You're not a local," the guy said. "I don't think I have to let you in."

"I was here not long ago with two Newport cops," Kaye reminded him. "You let me in then. Remember?"

"Yeah, still —"

"Look," Kaye interrupted. "You got kids? A daughter?"

"Yeah. Why?"

"I'm looking for a guy with an address on this island who likes little girls. I've already gotten a warrant for his arrest. He wasn't here last time, but I was down here for something else and came by on a whim to check."

"A child molester?"

"Yes, a child molester," Kaye said. "How about this. Let me in, and if the guy is home, I'll sit on him, call Detective Whitman and wait for him to come make the arrest. That work for you?"

Without a word the guard reached out, pushed the button, and the gate went up.

Once over the bridge Kaye pulled over and stowed his Kimber and ID in one of the saddlebags. He grabbed the black knit watch cap from the windshield bag and pulled it down low, almost to his eyebrows.

There was a bright red Porsche 911 Carrera 4s Cabriolet parked in Calhoun's driveway. Kaye pulled in behind it and shut down. He walked slowly to the front gate, knowing he was on video surveillance, and tried to open it before standing there looking befuddled. He made sure to turn around and check the driveway so whoever, if anyone, was watching would be sure to see the Big Boar colors. When he turned back around, he acted as though he'd just discovered the doorbell, pushed it, then stood there, hands in pockets, hoping the same knucklehead kid didn't answer the door.

A long moment later, a woman's voice came through the intercom.

"Leave or I'm calling the police."

"Uh, wait, please," Kaye said hesitantly. "I'm looking for Gene. Gene Calhoun. Does he live here?"

"Who are you?"

"My name's Benny. Benny LaPlante, from, uh, Lancaster."

"How did you get this address?" She was clearly skeptical.

"Gene gave it to me, "Kaye said. "You know, when we were inside together. I did him some favors and he told me that if I was ever in a bind I could, uh, look him up."

Things went quiet for a few moments before the woman spoke again.

"Come to the front door," she said as Kaye heard the sound of the lock disengaging.

He stepped through the entry garden and waited outside the carved sailing ship doors.

A minute passed before the door opened. A beautiful young woman, easily six foot four, her close-cropped hair dyed gold, and an almost-not-there bikini under a sheer white coverup, looked Kaye up and down.

"You're a friend of Gene's?" She was clearly skeptical.

"Yeah," Kaye replied, trying to sound nervous as he purposely ogled the woman. "Uh, is he here?"

"Where did you say you know him from?"

"Lancaster."

She stared at him, then smiled. "Benny, you want me to turn around so you can see the whole package?"

"Uh, no… I mean…" Kaye stammered and looked away. "I'm sorry. I didn't mean, you know, to be rude."

"It's not rude, Benny. I'm actually flattered. Would you like to come in?"

"I don't want to bother you. If Gene's not here, I mean."

"He's not here at the moment," she said, "but you're welcome to come in and wait. I'm sure we can find some way to pass the time."

"Will he be back soon?"

"Maybe," she said, shrugging and smiling. "He went sailing with some friends this morning."

"Oh, okay," Kaye said, shuffling some more. "Hey, I can just come back later."

"Are you sure?"

Kaye looked her up and down again. "Am I sure? Not by a longshot, gorgeous, but… my old lady… I just can't, you know?"

"I understand," she said sympathetically. "You don't know what you're missing, but good for you for being true."

"Would you maybe do me another favor? Instead of… You know."

She grinned. "I'd be happy to."

"Don't tell Gene I stopped by. I'm embarrassed enough already, having to ask for help, you know?" Kaye shrugged and made a face. "Things are kind of, uh, flexible in my life right now, and if I don't make it back for a while, well, I don't want Gene to be pissed at me. You understand, right?"

"I do," she said. "Nice to meet you, Benny. And just so you know, you're wait time would've gone on Gene's tab." She smiled and shut the door in Kaye's face.

Kaye half-smiled on the way back to the bike.

Eugene Calhoun was still in town. If the beautiful party favor kept her word, they might have a shot at nabbing him after all. Before he left the island, he called and left a message for Whitman.

CHAPTER 42

It was mid-afternoon when he made it back to the squad room. He went by Thompson's office to tell him what he'd found out about Calhoun's whereabouts, but the room was closed and dark.

He'd barely settled into his chair when his phone rang. He recognized Okafor's number.

"Afternoon, Counselor. What can I do for you?"

"Where have you been, Detective? I've been trying to call you since lunch."

"I went to Orange County, which I remember telling you yesterday I was going to do."

"You did," Okafor said. "You also said you'd be back by noon."

"Got me there," Kaye admitted. "But I was late because I stopped by Eugene Calhoun's house. Unfortunately, he wasn't there. He was out sailing with friends."

"What?"

"That's what I was told."

"By whom?" Okafor asked testily.

"I don't know her name," Kaye said. "But I think she works for Calhoun, maybe in some kind of on-call capacity, if you get my drift. Anyway, what's so important?"

"I got a return on the subpoena to the Internet Service Provider on the IP address used by Matt eighteen fourteen."

"Let me guess," Kaye said. "Calcutta public library."

"Hardly," Okafor said. "You are not going to believe it."

Kaye waited for the next shoe to drop, but Okafor said nothing.

"Are you going to tell me, or do I have to guess?" he asked finally.

"Are you sitting down?"

"Yes, Counselor, I'm sitting down."

"Leon Lowden of Northridge, California."

Kaye was stunned. "Say that again?"

"I knew you wouldn't believe me," Okafor said gleefully. "Matt eighteen fourteen is none other than Leon Lowden, Valerie Weber's maternal grandfather."

"You're absolutely certain?"

"My contact told me 'five nines', whatever that means," Okafor said. "They said that IP address belongs to the… whatever they call it, router, gateway, whatever… on the account billed to Leon Lowden at the same address in Northridge that's on the tax records. Who else could it be, right?"

"Zeros and ones don't lie," Kaye said. "Gotta be him."

"Does that give you something to work with?" Okafor asked hopefully.

"I'd say," Kaye replied. "Might need two of me."

"Then you'd better get started. Let me know if I can do anything else."

"Will do. And nice work, Counselor."

I'll be damned. Leon Lowden, he thought. *Really?* He shook his head and started making a plan.

He'd barely gotten organized when he saw Captain Thompson hustling in his direction.

"Good, you are here." Thompson said. "I just ran into the Watch Commander downstairs. He's looking for you. Said you didn't answer his page."

"I didn't hear it. I was on the phone with the DA's office," Kaye said. "Does he need to see me?"

"No, you're needed at Grove Charter."

"For?"

"A shooting," Thompson said grimly. "The first on scene said the Principal asked for you by name." He held out a set of keys. "Take an unmarked. Code three."

"Any more details?" Kaye asked, snatching the keys and grabbing his jacket.

"They also requested a coroner."

"Thanks, Cap." Kaye practically ran out of the squad room.

The key fob told him what unit it was and in short order, lights flashing and siren blaring, Kaye was in headed for Grove Charter. Even then, it seemed to take a long time to get there.

He shut down the siren as he approached the visitors' parking lot driveway. One marked unit, its overheads still flashing, was parked near the front door.

Where is everybody? He wondered as he turned in.

He parked, got out and headed for the front door. He was only halfway there when the door opened and a clearly distraught Mrs. Kowalczyk stepped halfway out.

"They're all in the faculty parking lot," she shouted, pointing to the far side of the school. Then she disappeared back inside.

Kaye decided it would be faster to get there on foot than by driving and took off at a near sprint.

Several more marked units, an ambulance and an LAFD pumper truck were clustered in the faculty parking lot. As Kaye got closer he saw two uniformed officers working to try and keep a small group of students away from the scene. He headed toward them.

"Who got here first?" he asked when he was close enough.

"Goodreau and Pope," one of the officers answered, pointing.

Kaye kept going. He knew Frank Goodreau by sight and spied him not far away, talking to one of the paramedics.

He wove his way through the parked cars to the knot of cops and fire department personnel. As he rounded the front of a silver pickup he saw a tarp-covered body lying on the asphalt between two parked cars. He stopped, suddenly registering that one of the vehicles was a red Toyota Highlander with a Trojans decal on the back window. Its driver door was open.

No way, he thought as he moved forward again.

Goodreau saw him and came to meet him.

"Hey, Detective Kaye," Goodreau said. "Thanks for coming. The Principal specifically asked for you, so…" He shrugged.

"Not a problem," Kaye said, looking down at the tarp. "Do we know what happened?"

"Oh, yeah. Some kid walked up to a teacher as the guy was about to get into his car and emptied a pistol into him."

"Do we know who the shooter was?"

"Yep," Goodreau said, nodding. "Damnedest thing. We found him leaning against the back of the red Toyota when we got here. The gun was on the ground, the slide locked back."

"Witnesses?"

"At least twenty, and they all know the shooter. Knowing kids today, somebody probably got it on video on their phone."

"Did you get a name?" Kaye asked.

"Kenny Vaughan," Goodreau said. "All he would say was 'He deserved it. He killed her' over and over."

"Where's Kenny now?"

"In the Principal's office with Pope and school security."

"Is Crime Scene on the way?"

"Didn't think we'd need them with that many witnesses and an admission."

"Call 'em anyway," Kaye said. "Gotta check the boxes, right?"

"I'll get them here."

Kaye stepped over to the corner of the tarp, leaned down and lifted it up. He saw exactly what he was expecting and turned to Goodreau. "Victim's name is Dylan Glithero. He is, or was, a teacher here."

Glithero was on his back, his eyes still open. As he took photos, Kaye couldn't help but think Glithero looked surprised.

"You know the guy?" Goodreau asked.

"I was working a case and his name came up."

"A homicide," Goodreau said, connecting the dots.

Kaye nodded. "Glithero wasn't the killer, but it turned out he had a thing for high school girls."

Goodreau whistled softly and shook his head. "Got him killed."

"You did call the Coroner, right?"

"Yes, sir. They called right before you got here and said they were still about ten out. Should be here any time."

"Okay, good," Kaye said. "I'll be in the office if you need me."

"Roger that."

Kaye didn't sprint this time, sorting out how best to approach Kenny Vaughan.

It'll be easier for us and harder for him if he's eighteen, he thought. *Please don't let him be eighteen.*

Mrs. Kowalczyk, thoroughly frazzled, saw Kaye come in.

"They're all in Ms. Holderby's office," she said. "Door's open. Just go on back."

"A question first," Kaye said, "since Kenny's in there. What was Mr. Glithero doing on campus? I thought he was suspended."

"Because all the charges were dropped, he was allowed to come back. Today was his first day." She stopped and got a strange look on her face. "And his last, as it turned out."

Kaye nodded and headed for Holderby's office.

Eilene Holderby sat at her desk, her red-rimmed eyes staring vacantly straight ahead. Kenny Vaughan was handcuffed to a chair in the corner, staring at the floor. Officer Pope stood between Kenny and the door, although it probably wasn't necessary. A burly man Kaye had never seen before stood off to one side, just behind Holderby. His shirt proclaimed him to be Security.

"Ms. Holderby," Kaye said to get her attention, "are you all right?"

319

"I honestly don't know, Detective," she replied, and Kaye could tell she was struggling not to cry.

"And you are...? Kaye asked the man standing behind Holderby.

"Ollie Manley," the man replied. "District Security."

"Okay," Kaye said. "Thanks for your help, Mr. Manley. We'll take it from here."

A look of relief crossed Manley's face as he nodded and left the room.

"Officer Pope?"

"Yes, sir?"

"Why don't you go out and help Officer Goodreau wrangle forensics and the coroner," Kaye said, then looked at Kenny before asking Pope, "Did you search him?"

"I did," Pope confirmed. "All he had on him were his car keys."

"Okay, and you can take your cuffs with you. Kenny and I know each other."

Pope removed the handcuffs and headed outside. Kaye stopped him. "Officer, I want a tight lid on this. No information released to the media, period. Feed them the whole active investigation, next of kin line. Got it?"

Pope nodded. "Yes, sir."

Kaye slid a chair over, positioning it so he could see both Kenny and Holderby.

"Kenny, look at me, please," he said as he sat down.

Kenny slowly looked up.

"How old are you?"

"Seventeen."

Kaye turned to Holderby. "Have you tried reaching his mother?"

Holderby nodded. "I haven't been able to."

"Are you prepared to act *in loco parentis*?"

"Of course," Holderby replied.

Kaye nodded and turned to Kenny. "Kenny, do you understand that you're under arrest?"

"Yeah."

"Do you understand that you can be tried as an adult, even though you're not eighteen?"

Kenny shrugged. "It is what it is."

"I need to read you your rights."

"Why? Half the school saw me do it."

"It's procedure," Kaye said. "Think of it as my version of the scientific method. Other people are going to check my work and I want it to stand up to peer review."

"Oh, okay," Kenny said. "I get it."

Kaye recited the standard Miranda warning and Kenny said he understood.

"Will you answer my questions?" Kaye asked.

"Excuse me," Holderby spoke up. "Kenny, I don't think you should say anything right now. Let some people have a chance to help you first."

"Why?" Kenny said. "Like I said, a lot of people saw me do it. I'm not proud of it, but I'm not sorry, either. If I have to go to jail, I'll go to jail."

"You admit to shooting Mr. Glithero?" Kaye asked pointedly.

Kenny nodded. "Yeah. He deserved it."

"Why did he deserve it?"

"Because he killed Valerie," Kenny replied. "I mean, that's why you arrested him, right? I saw you."

Oh my God, Kaye thought as he stared at Kenny.

He decided he was done. He had witnesses and an admission. Now was not the time to crush Kenny by telling him that no, Dylan Glithero hadn't killed Valerie Weber, and he still didn't know who had.

"Kenny, you'll have to come with me," Kaye said as he stood up.

"I know," Kenny said as he stood up.

"I have to handcuff you. Remember, scientific method, okay?"

"Yeah, sure." Kenny turned around and put his hands behind his back and Kaye put the cuffs on.

"Is your car parked here at school?" Kaye asked.

"Yeah."

"Is there anything in it I should know about? Another gun, more bullets, anything like that you want to tell me about?"

"Oh, no, nothing like that. Just my books and homework. You can search it if you want."

"I don't think that will be necessary," Kaye said. "Is it locked up?"

"Always."

Kaye looked at Holderby. "Is it okay to leave the car here until his mom can make arrangements to pick it up?"

She nodded.

"All right," Kaye said, grabbing Kenny by the arm. "Let's go."

As Kaye guided Kenny to the door, Eilene Holderby looked at him, mouthed 'thank you' and finally surrendered to the tears.

CHAPTER 43

The parking attendant must have recognized Kaye. As soon as he started the turn from street to driveway, the guy in the shack raised the gate and waved him, astride the '41 Flight Red Knucklehead, into the visitor's parking lot outside Reingold Capital.

The same snappily dressed young man sat at the 6th floor reception desk. If he recognized Kaye, he wasn't about to acknowledge it.

"Can I help you?" he asked when Kaye approached the counter.

"Good morning, Jeremy. I need to see Ms. Reingold."

"Do you have an appointment?"

Here we go again, Kaye thought. *Kid's a slow learner.* "Police business, remember? I don't need an appointment."

"I'm sorry, she's busy."

"Interrupt her," Kaye said brusquely.

"I —"

"Interrupt her," Kaye repeated, his tone now deadly as he put his elbows on the counter and leaned over. "If you say no, I'll leave. But you go with me. In handcuffs. Got it?"

"All right. All right. Jeez," the kid said as he picked up the phone.

Kaye stayed leaned over.

The kid stared at Kaye as he spoke into the phone. "I'm sorry to interrupt you, but that Detective is here again. He needs to see you, and won't take no for an answer." He listened for a moment, then said, "I'll send him up." He listened again for a second, then said, "Oh, okay."

"Thank you," Kaye said, pushing off the counter. "I know the way."

"She's coming down," the kid said quickly.

"You'd better hope so."

A minute later, Reingold stepped off the elevator, saw Kaye and headed toward him with an exasperated look on her face.

"This better be important," she said as she stopped in front of Kaye. "I have three very important potential clients upstairs and —"

"Is there someplace we can talk?" Kaye interrupted.

"What's wrong with right here?" she demanded.

"I think a little privacy would be best." He glanced sideways at the kid behind the desk, obviously all ears.

"Outside. Follow me," Reingold said sharply, spinning on her heels.

Kaye followed her down a hallway, around a corner and through a door to an outside terrace garden.

"Okay," she said to Kaye when they were outside, "what's so goddamn important today?"

"I think we should sit down."

"I don't need to sit down, Detective. I need to get back upstairs."

Kaye took a deep breath. "I'm sorry, Ms. Reingold, but I have to inform you that your ex-husband, Dylan Glithero, was shot and killed yesterday afternoon."

Reingold stared at him uncomprehendingly, then went deathly pale. Kaye saw her eyelids start to flutter as her eyes started to roll back. He reached out and caught her by the arms. He felt her sag momentarily, but she recovered and he held on while she regained her balance.

Kaye looked around, then guided her off to one side of the door, helped her sit down on the edge of a concrete planter, then sat down next to her. Her eyes were wide open as she stared blankly, gently rocking back and forth, her hands clasped in her lap.

"Can I get you something?" he asked. "Water? Anything?"

She shook her head and barely managed to say, "No, I'll be all right."

Kaye waited.

"What happened?" Reingold finally asked softly.

"A student confronted him after school in the Grove Charter parking lot and shot him multiple times. He died at the scene."

"It was about that girl, wasn't it?" she whispered.

"Yes."

"Did Dylan kill her?"

"No, Roslyn, he didn't kill anybody," Kaye replied. "I saw the photos your private investigator showed you. The girl in them was not the girl who was killed."

"Then why would...?" She let the question hang.

"It's complicated," Kaye said, "and I'm still trying to sort it all out. But word got around the school about my investigation and the boy who shot Dylan must have drawn his own wrong conclusion."

Because I made a mistake flashed through Kaye's mind.

"Did you catch him?" she asked.

"We did. He just put down the gun and waited for our officers to get there. He admitted it."

"What'll happen to him?"

"He's still a juvenile," Kaye said. "But the law allows him to be tried and sentenced as an adult for the murder."

"Oh, God," she whispered. "What a tragedy."

Kaye stayed quiet, expecting Roslyn to stand up, signaling an end to their conversation.

Instead, she looked up at him and said, "I should have told you this before. There's this guy, a friend, if you can call him that, of Dylan's. I only met him once, but he –"

"Gene Calhoun," Kaye interrupted. "Sometimes goes by Art."

"You know about him?"

"I do," Kaye told her. "In fact, I knew about him before I came to see you the first time, so don't beat yourself up for not mentioning him."

"He's a real creep."

"I haven't had the pleasure of meeting him," Kaye said. "But I have an active warrant for him, and I'll find him."

"Thank you."

"I'm sorry for coming here to deliver this kind of news. But it's something that will be all over the news today and I didn't want you finding out like that."

"I appreciate that," she said. "Have you notified anyone else in the family?"

"I have not. Honestly, I don't even know where to start looking for them."

"I'll call them, if that's allowed."

"That's fine with me, as long as you're okay with being listed under next of kin notification in my report."

"Sure. Why not?" She stood up, unconsciously reaching back and brushing off the seat of her pants. "Well, I'd better get back to it. Clients are waiting. Thank you, Detective. I can't imagine being in your shoes."

"Not my favorite part of the job," Kaye admitted. "And please tell the young man inside I'm sorry for being such a hard ass. But sometimes it's part of the job description."

"He'll understand." She smiled wanly. "He's my nephew."

"I'll find my own way out," Kaye told her.

She turned and Kaye watched her walk back inside.

Glithero sure married up, he thought. *Too bad he couldn't keep his zipper up.*

***

324

When Kaye walked into the station he didn't go upstairs. Instead he headed directly to Patty's desk.

"Good morning," Kaye said as he grabbed a chair and sat down. "Got a minute? Or two, maybe?"

"Sure. What's up?"

"I think we may finally have something solid on Valerie's murder, and I need your help."

"Did you find out who Matt eighteen fourteen is?" she asked expectantly.

"I did. Leon Lowden."

Patty's eyes went wide. "Valerie's real grandfather?"

"That's where the Internet Provider that owns the IP address sends the bill."

"I'll do whatever I can."

"Let's start with a driver's license." Kaye gave her Leon's approximate age and the address in Northridge.

Patty went to work. With the name and address it didn't take long to pull up Lowden's license, complete with picture.

Could be the guy, Kaye thought as he stared at the picture and recalled the image from the video from behind Staples.

Leon Lowden was a big man. Almost sixty, six foot two and two thirty, with a bull neck, square jaw, thin lips and a nose that looked to have been broken at least once. Lowden was balding on top and the sides were cut close.

What Kaye saw were the listed hair and eye colors.

Red and hazel.

"Patty, I need you to dig deep on this guy. School, military service, job history, where he works now, churches, organizations or clubs, anything and everything you can find."

"Got it," Patty acknowledged. "Want a 'vehicles registered to' right now?"

"Good idea. Go ahead."

In seconds, Patty had pulled up the data. The Lowdens owned two vehicles: The Ford Expedition Kaye had seen when he'd gone to see Monica, and a two-year old VW Tiguan. White.

Jackpot, Kaye thought. *This is the guy.* He looked over Patty's shoulder and wrote down the Tiguan's plate number.

"Keep digging," he told Patty. "Keep me posted on what you come up with."

"Will do, Detective."

Kaye headed upstairs and went to make himself a cup of tea. On the way back to his desk he grabbed the Dailies. They were pretty much business as usual. When he was done scanning them they went back on the board.

Back at his desk, he felt idle, trying to think of something he could do on the Weber case other than wait for Patty. He thought about calling JoAnn Weber and briefing her on his progress, but decided against it. He'd already disappointed her several times. He'd talk to her when he had Valerie's killer locked up.

He went through the case file again, making certain it was up to date.

He finally got around to opening his email, and sat up straight, staring at the screen. The top item in his inbox was from the State Pardons and Parole Board and the subject was The Files You Requested.

Kaye opened it. Four files were attached, each titled Eugene A. Calhoun Parole Hearing, followed by Calhoun's inmate number and the hearing date. He mentally matched the hearing dates to what he remembered from the trial transcripts. Calhoun had waited two years for his first hearing, then had one every three years after that until being released.

He opened the file with the earliest date. It was *pro forma*, with the date, time, place, names of Board members present, inmate's and inmate's attorney's names. Meetings were generally brief and somewhat perfunctory, with the Board members having reviewed the inmate's history beforehand. No inmate family members were allowed in the hearing room. Victims of the inmate's crime were allowed to speak, but only one was allowed in the room at a time, and not all of them got a chance to speak.

The transcript was exactly what Kaye was expecting. Calhoun led off with an impassioned plea for release, saying he was a changed man, he'd learned his lesson, he'd already paid a steep price, and if the Board would see fit to grant him parole he guaranteed they wouldn't regret it.

Calhoun's attorney, the same that had defended him at trial, spoke next, essentially giving the Board a statistical argument comparing Calhoun's crimes and subsequent sentence to across-the-board State records for similar cases. In Kaye's mind it could've been summed up in one sentence: You should parole my client because you've paroled others that fit the same profile, and if you don't I'll make your lives a legal hell.

Normally, a hearing report ended there.

But one of Calhoun's victims had appeared, unaccompanied, before the Board.

Kathleen Shaeffer, 19, and a resident of Lake Forest, California.

Shaeffer? K.S. is Kathleen Shaeffer? Kaye thought, stunned by the coincidence.

Ms. Shaeffer's statement was brief and concise.

"Eugene Calhoun raped and impregnated me while I was still in high school. He was sent to prison, and now, after only two years, wants you to release him. Because of problems with the pregnancy I was sentenced to life without the possibility of being a mother. If you release this monster on parole, he'll do it to another young girl because that's who he is. Thank you."

Parole was denied and the next hearing was set for three years hence.

Kaye re-read Shaeffer's five sentence statement again. He remembered her statement under cross examination that she'd ended up pregnant. Apparently she had lost her ability to bear children after Calhoun raped her.

He opened the next file. It was dated almost three years to the day after the first one. He compared the composition of the Board to the first hearing and saw that the member names were different.

This time, Calhoun claimed to have found Jesus and was now leading a Bible study group in his cell block. If the Board would see fit to grant parole he promised to spread the Gospel to an even larger audience on the outside.

He also noted that Calhoun had a different attorney.

Two strikes and you're out, he thought. *Too bad when the client is worth billions.*

The lawyer was different, but the argument was essentially the same except that he claimed Calhoun's family had forgiven him, would welcome him back into the family business, and the taxpayers of the State of California could stop supporting Eugene Calhoun.

Kathleen Shaeffer, now 22 and living in Laguna Hills, had again appeared and made the exact same statement to the Board she'd made three years prior.

Parole was again denied and another hearing scheduled for three years later.

The third file was virtually a carbon copy of the first two. Kaye noticed that one member of the Hearing Board from three years prior was also on this Board.

Calhoun again made his argument, but even in print Kaye detected an underlying anger and resentment for not yet being released.

Calhoun's lawyer, different again this time, made the same fundamental arguments made by her predecessors, but then also appealed to the Board that enough was enough and presented statistics to prove it.

Kaye scanned down to the Victim Testimony section, sat bolt upright and stared at the page on the monitor.

What the...Hell? Kaye's mind raced.

Amelia Shaeffer, 25, had appeared and made the same statement that had been made twice before.

Kaye was dumbfounded. When had Kathleen Shaeffer become Amelia Shaeffer? Amy Shaeffer? He leaned forward, put his left elbow on the desk, his left hand to his forehead, and stared at the screen without seeing it.

He slowly regained his composure and let his eyes drift down the page. There was an additional note below the witness statement.

'Commissioner Robertson pointed out that the name of the victim that appeared to testify was inconsistent with that shown on the two previous hearing transcripts. Upon questioning, Ms. Shaeffer explained to the Board's satisfaction that she had legally changed her name after the last hearing, three years ago, because she feared for her safety and was tired of the notoriety and publicity still surrounding the Calhoun case.'

Parole was again denied and a new hearing date set for three years in the future.

Kaye put his head in both hands and stared at the screen, his thoughts swirling.

She would've told me. It must be another Amelia Shaeffer. It's got to be. My Amy was pregnant. She lost the baby, but she was pregnant. It's not my Amy.

Robotically, Kaye opened the final hearing transcript.

It was different. At the last minute, Calhoun had refused to appear. Instead, yet another lawyer was allowed to read Calhoun's statement to the Board.

'I'm tired of wasting my time. You'll never release me as long as that Shaeffer bitch shows up and lies to you about me. Her medical problems are not my fault. I'd rather just finish my time, get out of here and never have to deal with you idiots again. Go to hell.'

The attorney was quick to point out to the Board that the last sentence were his client's words, not his.

Amelia Shaeffer, 28, and residing in Los Angeles, was present to testify, but was excused and the hearing adjourned without action.

Once he closed the transcripts, Kaye's logical mind began to reassert itself. He knew from driver's license searches that there was no such thing as a truly unique name, especially in a State of almost forty million people. It certainly wasn't that much of a stretch that Kathleen Shaeffer, concerned for her safety and welfare, had randomly chosen Amelia as her new first name. Maybe her grandmother, or other beloved relative or friend, had been named Amelia.

Sure, Kathleen could have changed her name to Amelia. Sure, she could have lived in the same general parts of Southern California. It was a big place.

But Kaye didn't believe in coincidences. Especially when they lined up in a row and laughed in his face.

Could Kathleen Shaeffer, teenage rape victim, have grown up to be the woman he'd married?

Yes.

Was it plausible?

Not to him.

Until he considered that the man who'd crashed into and killed Amy Shaeffer was the former cellmate of Eugene Calhoun, the convict repeatedly denied parole because of Kathleen, then Amelia, Shaeffer.

Kaye's mind still spun. He assessed, then reassessed over and over, what he knew, always reaching the same conclusion.

Eugene Calhoun had paid Roy Dobson to exact his revenge on the woman who'd kept him in jail.

The only coincidence had been him catching the Valerie Weber case.

He desperately hoped he was wrong.

***

After a brutal workout, which he'd hoped would take his mind off things, Kaye ate a light dinner and sat out on the patio, trying to figure out what to do to salvage his sanity.

Deep down he wanted to track down Gene Calhoun and tear the man to pieces with his bare hands. But he'd felt the same raw emotion with Roy Dobson and hadn't been able to do it. After all, at least according to Roshi, he was Benkei the peace maker, not Yoshitune the Warlord.

He needed to talk to someone, get some advice.

He grabbed his cell phone and punched in a number.

"Why, hello, Benjamin," the familiar voice of his mother answered. "This is a nice surprise."

"Hi, Mom. You got a minute? I need some advice."

"I've got all the time you need."

Kaye laid it all out, starting with his first and only interview of Valerie Weber, the general course of his investigation, the startling revelations of his prison visit and the contents of the parole hearing transcripts.

"And I don't know whether to believe it or not, or what to do," he concluded.

"Lord Almighty," his mom whispered, then went silent for a moment. "Okay, first, son, you need to find out for sure if Kathleen Shaeffer was the same person as Amy. Have you tried to track down her, or her parents?"

"Not yet."

"You need to do that. If you can find Kathleen Shaeffer and look her in the eye, then you'll know. I mean, yes, it looks like they could be one and the same, but you really don't know for absolute certain. I can't even remember how many times I've heard you say 'don't collect evidence that fits your suspect, find the suspect that fits your evidence'. Right?"

"True," Kaye said. "I still have several things I need to track down and see if they correlate."

"That's what you need to do, Ben. If Kathleen Shaeffer is not your Amy, then Amy's death was God's will, not an act of pure evil."

"There's another side to this, too, Mom."

"What's that?"

Kaye took a deep breath. "If Amy really was Kathleen first," he hesitated to keep his voice from breaking, "then the whole part of our marriage about having kids and raising a family was a lie. She knew it couldn't happen, but she never told me."

"Oh, Benjamin, don't think like that. There could be lots of reasons Amy never conceived. In fact, I remember she did get pregnant once, right?"

"She told me she did. Then she told me she lost the baby, so who knows?"

"Don't assume the worst, son. Lots of women suffer miscarriages. It's not their fault."

"I know," Kaye said. "it's just that…"

"I understand. But you can't jump to conclusions. Find the evidence. Is there anything else, any place else, you can look at that might tell you for sure?"

"I'm still waiting on some old reports," he replied. "They're internal, so they shouldn't be redacted like the transcripts were."

"There you go," she said. "Wait for the reports and see what else you find out."

"I will."

"In the meantime, catch whoever killed that little girl. Are you getting close?"

"I think so. I have a computer user and his address that I can tie to the victim. I haven't talked to him yet, but that's next on my list."

"How's your love life?" she asked out of the blue. "You still seeing... Auggie, right? The wine girl?"

Kaye laughed. "Gee, Mom, you don't remember her name?"

"Benjamin, please don't tease me about my memory," she said and Kaye heard the hurt in her voice. "After what your father went through, it scares me."

"Sorry, Mom," Kaye said softly. "I didn't mean to hurt you."

"I know. It's okay."

"But to answer your question, no, I'm not still seeing Auggie."

"What happened?"

"We just had a heart-to-heart and decided now was not the right time for us," Kaye replied. "She got a terrific opportunity that takes up most of her time and I'm always busy."

"That's too bad, son. You deserve to be happy. If there's one thing I still don't understand about the whole Buddha thing it's why there's so much focus on everybody being unhappy."

"It's not about being unhappy," Kaye said patiently. "It's recognizing the source of unhappiness and dealing with it."

"I guess," she said. "Either way, if Auggie is the one, call her. Don't let her get away. Got it?"

"Got it, Mom. I'll let you go. Thanks for listening, and for the advice."

"Anytime, and please let me know what you find out about Amy."

"I will. Love you."

"Love you, too."

CHAPTER 44

Kaye made it to the station early and immediately started brainstorming on how to pursue Leon Lowden. He wanted to avoid talking to Lowden for the first time in the presence of his wife, but that would be tough if Patty couldn't come up with where he worked. He didn't want to pressure Patty. She didn't officially work for him any more than she worked for anyone else in the Bureau, but he compulsively checked his email all morning, and every time the squad room doors opened he quickly turned, hoping it was Patty.

He grabbed the printout of Lowden's driver's license and pulled up the Staples video, hoping he could draw a definitive conclusion that it was Lowden who had picked Valerie up the night she disappeared. But the lighting and the driver's baseball cap, pulled low, kept him from being a hundred percent certain.

He went back to the beginning of the video and went through it one click at a time, looking for anything he might have missed. His first thought was that the driver's build was right, unlike when he'd disqualified Dylan Glithero as the driver simply because Glithero wasn't big enough. When the white SUV cleared the overhanging tree, he paused the video and examined the frame. The driver's left forearm was visible, resting on the door because the window was down. In the original video, he'd noticed a smudge, but hadn't been sure if wasn't simply a product of the lighting and shadows. This time he looked closer. He clicked forward and the forearm was gone.

Probably drives right-handed, but changed hands when Valerie got in the right side of the car.

He clicked back and enlarged the image until it began to pixelate, reduced it slightly, and took the magnifying glass out of his desk.

It's a tattoo, he concluded. *And it's good-sized.* He couldn't manipulate the image to get detail, but was convinced the 'smudge' was a good-sized, symmetrical tattoo on the driver's left forearm.

That's where military guys get ink, he thought. *Wonder if Leon's a vet?*

He reached for the phone to call Patty. Just as he touched the handset, it rang, displaying Patty's extension.

"Perfect timing," he said. "I was just about to call you."

"Really?" Patty said. "Then you can go first."

"I don't know where you are on Leon Lowden, but would you put finding out if he served in the military on your list?"

"I can do that. In fact, I was calling you about him."

"You got something?"

"I do," she replied. "To be honest, I'm not finding a lot, but I did search some of the professional connection sites and found out what he does and where he works. Got a pencil?"

"Shoot."

"He's an engineer. Consults on project management and sells heavy construction equipment, things like graders, bulldozers, paving systems, stuff like that. He works out of an office in Sylmar." She gave him the address and name of the company. "I can't find anything else on the company name, which is LCEC, like a headquarters someplace else, so I'm thinking maybe he owns it. You can look at his profile on the site if you want to." She gave him the URL.

"Good job, Patty. Thank you."

"You're welcome, Detective. I'll let you know right away if I come up with anything else."

Kaye immediately pulled up the website and found Leon Lowden's profile page.

It was short on personal information and didn't include a photo. He read through it carefully and concluded it was more of a professional credentials and competence verification for potential clients than anything else. No resume was posted, leading Kaye to believe Lowden wasn't a job seeker. He did learn that Lowden had a BSCE degree from UCLA and was a registered Professional Engineer in the State of California.

He searched up the company name and found a website. It was professionally done and listed Lowden's offered services, along with many testimonials from satisfied clients. Kaye thought about filling out the Contact Form to try and draw Lowden out, but decided against it. He had an address.

"Hey, you got a minute?" Captain Thompson's voice penetrated his concentration.

Kaye spun his chair around. "Yep. What's up?"

"Let's go in my office."

When they were seated, Thompson started. "The University has thrown me a curve ball."

333

"Uh-oh."

"Yeah. They've informed me that they've been planning on expanding their criminal justice and public policy classes to their satellite locations, and have decided that adding me to the instructor roster is the perfect time to do that."

"Don't they have campuses, or at least offer classes, from the Valley all the way down into Orange County?"

"They do," Thompson replied, nodding.

"And," Kaye said as the pieces fell into place, "they want you to commute to every one of them."

Thompson nodded again. "It's a damn good thing we didn't commit to a house convenient to the main campus."

"What are you going to do?"

"I told them that what they were asking me to do was not consistent with what they offered me in terms of workload and compensation, and I would have to reconsider."

"Did they respond?"

"They understood, or at least they said they did." Thompson shrugged. "But I get the feeling they think they have me over a barrel, and I don't like getting bent over, if you know what I mean."

It was Kaye's turn to nod. "I hear that. What about the Chief's offer of a command staff job?"

"I think that ship has sailed."

"Wow," Kaye said softly. "What are you going to do?"

"I've already got some other irons in the fire, just in case."

"Let me know if there's anything I can do to help."

"Thank you, Detective." The Captain changed the subject. "Anything solid on the Weber case?"

Kaye ran it down, leaving out any reference to the old cases, Gene Calhoun, Roy Dobson or Amy.

"The biological grandfather?" Thompson asked, shaking his head in wonderment. "Just when you think you've heard and seen it all."

"Don't know for sure yet," Kaye said, "but looks like it might be heading that way."

"Okay, keep me posted."

Back at his desk, Kaye busied himself by not accomplishing anything other than hanging out, hoping Patty would waltz in and hand him the keys to the kingdom of Leon Lowden's deepest, darkest secrets.

Eventually his stomach reminded him he hadn't eaten in a while and he walked around the corner to grab a bite. As he ate and people watched he tried to refine a strategy for approaching and questioning Leon Lowden. The worst thing that could happen would be that the first word out of Lowden's mouth would be 'lawyer', so he finally opted for the other end of the spectrum.

Surprise was sometimes a very effective technique.

***

At first Kaye thought he'd written the address down wrong. In his mind he was looking for an equipment yard, with maybe a small pre-fab metal building to house the office and staff. What he saw instead was a sleek, three-story office building designed to look like a giant piece of black and white sedimentary rock.

There was no sign out front and the only legible lettering on the front doors was the street number required by the fire department. It matched what Patty had given him.

He found a place to park the Harley and went inside. There was a tenant directory on the wall just inside the vestibule door that solved the mystery. The building housed maybe fifteen different tenants, including a dental practice, a marketing company and a real estate appraiser. Kaye located LCEC on the directory and headed for Suite 302.

The plaque on the door explained everything. Lowden Construction and Engineering Consulting. Under that was Leon Lowden, PE.

That door opened into a reception-slash-waiting area containing a desk, a small sofa and several bookshelves. Photographs of major construction projects in progress adorned the walls. Beyond, Kaye could see a larger office off to his left, and a conference room was to his right.

The young brunette at the desk looked askance at Kaye when he walked in.

"Are you lost?" she asked.

"Don't think so," Kaye said as he held up his badge. "Detective Kaye, LAPD. I'm looking for Leon Lowden. Is he here?"

"Not at the moment," she said hesitantly and glanced at the wall clock. "But he's due back any minute if you'd like to wait."

"Thank you." He took a seat on the sofa.

He was surprised how busy the young woman stayed just answering the phone and confirming office appointments and site visits. It was obvious that Leon Lowden logged a lot of miles, not all by car.

He'd waited almost fifteen minutes when the door opened and Leon Lowden, briefcase in hand, walked in.

"Noreen, would you –" Lowden said before he read the look on Noreen's face, stopped mid-sentence and turned to see Kaye.

"He's here to see you, Mr. Lowden," Noreen said quickly. "Detective Kaye, LAPD."

Lowden studied Kaye for a moment, then said, "I would have guessed that. You talked to my wife, what, a week or two ago?"

"That was me," Kaye confirmed as he stood up. "I'd like a few minutes of your time, Mr. Lowden."

"Sure," Lowden said. "Can you give me a minute first?"

"Certainly," Kaye replied.

Lowden turned back to Noreen and finished relaying instructions, then walked around her desk and into his office.

Kaye waited.

Lowden appeared less than a minute later.

"Come on in, Detective."

Kaye went in.

"Sorry about that," Lowden said as he sat down behind his desk and gestured at the chair opposite. "Now, what can I do for you?"

Kaye surveyed the office as he sat down. In addition to the desk and chairs, there was a large computer station with multiple monitors and large format printers.

"I'm investigating the murder of a young woman named Valerie Weber," Kaye replied, extracting his pen and notebook from his pocket.

"Sorry," Lowden said. "I don't know a Valerie Weber."

"You would have known her as Crystal."

Lowden sat up straight and stared at Kaye. "You mean the baby my daughter gave up for adoption?"

"I do."

"My wife said you came by to ask about Rachel. You told her the girl was trying to locate her birth parents."

"That's correct, Mr. Lowden. When was the last time you saw Crystal?"

"What?" Lowden blinked in surprise. "The last time I saw Crystal?"

"That was the question, sir."

"I haven't seen her since the day we surrendered her to the adoption agency when she was an infant," Lowden said matter-of-factly. "Why would you ask me that?"

Kaye ignored the question. "And where was Rachel when Crystal was turned over?"

"You know damn well where she was," Lowden snarled. "She'd already killed herself. It was a total mess. We'd made the decision to give the baby up —"

"Who is 'we'?" Kaye interrupted.

"My wife, Monica, myself and Rachel."

"So it was a family decision?"

Lowden nodded.

"Why did Rachel take her own life?" Kaye asked.

"Her guilt over giving up the baby overwhelmed her, at least that's what her therapist told us afterwards."

"Why was she guilty?" Kaye asked.

Lowden stared at him before answering. "Rachel didn't want to give Crystal up. We had to convince her it was in her, and Crystal's, long term best interest."

"So the 'family decision' wasn't really a family decision," Kaye said. "It was a parental decision."

"Okay, yes," Lowden said. "But it was the right decision. Because Rachel died before the adoption went through, it became a nightmare."

"Where was Crystal born?"

"At our house."

"Who was Rachel's prenatal care provider?"

"Uh," Lowden stammered, "she didn't have one."

"Was that another family decision?" Kaye asked pointedly.

"I fail to see the point of all these questions," Lowden protested. "How are they relevant?"

"A young woman was murdered, Mr. Lowden. Your granddaughter, as it turns out. So I'll ask you again, when was the last time you saw Crystal?"

"I already answered that."

"You're saying you've had no recent contact with Crystal, is that correct?"

"That is correct."

"Have you ever heard of a website that reunites long-lost family members?" Kaye gave him the name of the site.

"I have not," Lowden replied.

"Your internet service provider seems to think you have," Kaye said, staring back. "According to information I have, the IP address of the hardware installed at your home was a frequent visitor to that site for quite some time until just a few months ago."

"Bullshit," Lowden spat.

"I think Lil Lost Redhead would disagree, Mr. Lowden. She agreed to meet you at the inverted fountain plaza on the UCLA campus. Does that ring a bell?"

"I'm assuming you're referring to Crystal."

"I am," Kaye confirmed.

"Let me ask you a question, then, smart guy," Lowden said quietly. "When was Crystal, or Valerie, or whoever she might have been, murdered?"

Time for the rubber to meet the road, Kaye thought. *If I tell him and he claims an alibi, I can either get past him or use it to hang him.*

Kaye gave him the date range of the weekend Valerie's body was discovered.

Lowden glanced at his desk calendar, then looked at Kaye. "I was in Sacramento that entire weekend. And I can prove it."

"Why were you there?"

"Convention and trade show," Lowden replied, obviously pleased with himself. "I stayed at the host hotel and met with a lot of people. Check it out for yourself."

"I will," Kaye assured the smiling man.

"You do that," Lowden said. "Now get the hell out of my office. This conversation is over." He reached into the top drawer of his desk and pulled out a business card, which he flipped across the desk in Kaye's direction. "My lawyer. You want to talk to me, call him and make an appointment."

Kaye put his notebook away and stood up, leaving the card where it landed. "Thanks for your time, Mr. Lowden. I'll be in touch."

He turned to leave, then stopped and turned back. "One more question. Ever read the scripture Matthew, eighteen, fourteen about the loss of a child?"

Lowden's eyes flew open and his face turned bright red with rage. "Get out!" He shouted. "Get out now!"

"Have a nice day," Kaye said to the wide-eyed Noreen as he walked out.

He left Lowden's office with the gut feeling he'd found his killer, or at least that if it wasn't Leon Lowden, the man knew who it was.

But as someone had recently reminded him, gut feelings are inadmissible in court.

He needed more, and he knew it. He first needed to check Lowden's Sacramento alibi, and he had to establish a tangible link between Leon

Lowden and Valerie Weber during, or close to, the time Valerie went missing and her body was discovered.

He decided to return to the station and document the interview while it was fresh in his mind.

Kaye was wrapping up before heading home when a pop-up notified him of a new email. The sender was Lt. Waller from RHD and the subject line was 'We screwed up'. Curious, he opened it. The first thing he noticed were multiple attached video files. He read the message.

'Don't know if you've heard, but Tom Gannett decided to retire instead of coming back to work. The IT people finally got around to closing his computer accounts and found these sitting in his Inbox. I skimmed through them, and based on the dates and locations I think they're connected to the Weber case. Sorry we didn't get these to you sooner, but we didn't even know about them. I hope they help.

Lt. Waller'

Kaye leaned back in his chair and almost laughed out loud.

You've got to be kidding me. Now? NOW?

There were eight video files from traffic cameras in the Silver Triangle area near Staples, and more from cameras at intersections on the approach to the Hollywood Reservoir.

Just as he was about to open the first Silver Triangle file, he was interrupted.

"Detective Kaye?"

He turned to see one of the PAs – he couldn't recall the name – from downstairs, a thick manila envelope in his hand.

"These came for you today. I tried to find you earlier…" The PAs voice was apologetic as he held out the envelope.

"Can't find me if I'm not here." Kaye said and smiled as he took the envelope. "Thanks for bringing it up."

"You're welcome."

Kaye flipped the envelope over and his pulse quickened when he saw the return address. 'Lt. Adamson' was handwritten above the printed Orange County Sheriff's Department label.

He tore the envelope open and extracted what had to be a half-ream of paper, tightly bound with rubber bands. It was exactly what he thought it was.

Greg Sebaly's original reports on the Glithero and Calhoun cases.

He started removing rubber bands, stopped after the first two, put the stack down on his desk and stared at it.

What's the point? He wondered. Glithero was dead, and he knew the man hadn't killed Valerie Weber. Gene Calhoun had been the father of Valerie's baby, which to Kaye meant he had likely been the one to savagely beat her, but was probably not who had killed her. He'd address that when Calhoun was arrested on the rape charge.

The only thing the reports might settle was whether Kathleen Shaeffer and Amelia Shaeffer, his Amy Shaeffer, were one and the same person.

Leave it alone, he told himself. *Makes no difference. She's dead either way and you can't bring her back.*

He sat there, staring at the stack of new paper bearing almost twenty-year old words, for a full five minutes. Finally, he put it in the trash can, stood up, pulled on the Big Boar jacket and headed for the Harley.

The squad room door hadn't finished closing behind him when he stopped.

I've got to know, or it'll haunt me for the rest of my life.

He spun around and went back to his desk. Without taking off his jacket, he grabbed the reports from the trash and ripped off the remaining rubber bands. The top page was a memo from Adamson, confirming that the contents were true and correct copies of the full, official OCSD records concerning the investigations of Dylan Glithero and Eugene Calhoun.

The Glithero case face sheet was next, followed by Sebaly's case file and investigative notes.

It wasn't what he wanted.

He shuffled nervously through the stack until he found the Calhoun case face sheet. He pulled it out and set everything else aside.

Two thirds of the way down the sheet was the 'Victim Information' block. Kathleen J. Shaeffer. Her date of birth was listed. Next to the DOB, the checkbox for 'Juvenile' had been checked, and below that were the names of her parents. Charles and Sylvia Shaeffer.

Kaye stared at the page.

It was Amy's birthday, her middle name was Julia and her parents' names were Charles and Sylvia.

He could hardly breathe. It was his Amy. His hands trembled so hard that the paper fell from them. Rage, not directed at Calhoun, directed at Amy, overcame him.

Why didn't you tell me? Did you really think it would have mattered? I loved you! I I loved you! Non-stop through his mind, over and over.

He forced himself to focus and control his breathing, which helped settle his emotions. He remembered he'd felt the same rage and a desire for revenge after Roy Dobson had killed her.

The lesson of what had actually happened wasn't lost on him now.

He grabbed the stack of reports, put the Calhoun case face sheet on top and headed for Captain Thompson's office.

The lights were off and the door was closed and locked.

He'd have to wait until tomorrow. He locked the reports in his desk and again headed for the bike and home.

He'd cry when he got there.

***

He hadn't cried. He somehow managed to rationalize his way through all five stages of grief on the ride home, and was emotionally spent by the time he rolled the old Harley into the garage.

He sat on the bike for ten minutes, staring at the stairs that led up to the study. Amy's sanctuary.

Did she hide up there to escape me?

Finally he swung off the bike and headed for the house, knowing he'd probably never set foot in the study again. It was now a reminder of mistrust and betrayal.

CHAPTER 45

On the ride in, Kaye made a short-term plan. He'd gather his information and resources, then sit down with Captain Thompson. He'd brief his boss, then hand him everything he had. He wanted nothing to do with any further investigation into Amy's death.

Then he'd hunt down Valerie Weber's killer, if it was the last thing he ever did as a cop.

He spent an hour distilling his investigative notes on the Weber case to identify the people he'd talked to, those he thought should be talked to now and the linkages he'd found. He wanted to present solid information, not speculation, to the Captain.

When he finished, he gathered everything up, took a deep breath, and headed for Thompson's office.

The door was open and the Captain was at his desk. Kaye stopped at the threshold and knocked.

"Come on in," Thompson said, looking up.

Kaye took his usual chair and laid his notes on the desk. Thompson eyed them suspiciously.

"What's all this?" he asked.

"Something came up in the course of the Weber investigation," Kaye replied. "I just got confirmation and I need to separate myself from that part of the case. These are the pertinent notes."

"You want off the Weber case now? Care to explain why?"

"Not the Weber case. This will need to be a separate case, and I can't work it."

"Again," Thompson said, "care to explain why?"

"Amy," was all Kaye said.

"Amy?" Thompson stared at Kaye. "Your wife? What could she possibly have to do with this?"

"I don't think her death was an accident. I think she was murdered. Somebody needs to look into it, and it can't be me."

"Okay," Thompson said slowly, "can you give me some sense of how you reached that conclusion now?"

"It's in the notes."

"If you don't mind, I'd like to hear it from you, Detective."

Kaye took a deep breath and began with how what he'd expected to be a simple case of a high school girl getting beat up had totally blown up on him. How he'd identified Dylan Glithero. How that had led him to Eugene Calhoun. The old trial transcripts. The unidentified juvenile victims, one in particular. How Calhoun had done hard time, then hooked up with Glithero again after getting out.

"And that connects him to the Weber girl?" Thompson asked.

"Yes, sir," Kaye replied. "I also have DNA proving Calhoun was the father of the baby Valerie Weber was carrying when she died."

"Holy crap," Thompson muttered. "Sounds like motive for murder to me."

"I can't prove it, but my guess is that Valerie told him she was pregnant and he beat her. But I don't think Calhoun killed her."

"Why not?"

"Think about it," Kaye said. "Valerie was killed only a few days after she was beaten. If Calhoun had wanted to kill her, he would have done it the first time around."

"Do you know for sure who did kill her?"

"I'm focused on her biological grandfather and gathering evidence."

"So, how does this connect to your wife?" Thompson asked.

"She was one of Calhoun's rape victims when she was in high school. That's what I finally confirmed yesterday."

Thompson's jaw dropped and his face went blank.

Kaye continued, explaining how he'd checked parole records and what he'd found. His visit to Lancaster and the discovery that for years Calhoun's cellmate had been one Roy Dobson.

"Wait a minute," Thompson interrupted. "Roy Dobson. Isn't that the name of the guy who…?"

"It is," Kaye nodded and saw comprehension dawn in Thompson's eyes. "Royal Duane Dobson killed my wife and he was a cellmate of Eugene Calhoun, who hated her for keeping him from being paroled."

"Oh, my God," Thompson whispered, collapsing back into his chair. "Oh… my… God."

"There are visitor records that show Dobson's daughter, Sharon, visited Calhoun multiple times before and after Amy's death."

Thompson was silent for a full minute, digesting and connecting what Kaye had told him.

"A payoff," the Captain said finally. "Calhoun paid to have Amy killed for keeping him in prison. Roy Dobson had nothing to lose, he was dying anyway, so Calhoun paid his daughter."

"That's what I think, too. Obviously, I can't investigate it. I got in enough trouble when I thought it was an accident."

Thompson nodded. "Agreed. You want this to go to RHD?"

"No. Jurisdictionally, this is a Laguna Beach case. I'd like you to give it to J.J. and Burke and let them dig into Sharon Dobson before we say anything to Laguna Beach PD. Then they can help work it as an outside agency assist if Laguna wants them to."

"Good idea," Thompson said, nodding. Then he got serious. "Ben, I can't tell you how sorry I am. Losing Amy in an accident was bad enough, but this...? Well, this..." He shook his head. "I can't imagine. You want to take a few days?"

"No, sir," Kaye said instantly. "I made a promise to a mother. I've got a murderer to catch."

Thompson tried, not altogether successfully, to suppress a smile. "That voice is back, is it?"

Kaye just nodded, stood up and left the office.

Kaye returned to his desk and gathered his emotions. The conversation with his Captain had been painful, threatening to drag him back into anger. He sat for a moment, then went to the break room and brewed himself a cup of tea. When he returned he could see J.J. and Burke meeting with Thompson behind closed doors.

It's not your case, he told himself. *Leave it alone.*

He spun his chair and reached for his keyboard. He opened the email from RHD with the traffic cam videos attached and downloaded and saved them to his local drive. Then he sorted by date and time to get a sense of what he had.

Tom Gannett had done his homework before calling the traffic guys and asking for footage. Because Kaye had known what time Valerie Weber had been picked up behind Staples, Gannett had used an expanding radius search pattern, and as the distance increased, so did the time window.

Gannett had also known that Valleyheart dead-ended going west, and reached the same conclusion Kaye had: Whoever had picked up Valerie had either cut through a parking lot or reversed course to get back to Ventura Boulevard. The Staples video time window wasn't long enough to make the determination.

Kaye started with the assumption that his suspect had cut through a parking lot, and watched the footage from Ventura Boulevard and Coldwater Canyon first, looking for arrivals and departures. He saw several white SUVs, but was able to disqualify them all.

Then he watched the files from Ventura and Whitsett.

Still nothing.

What if he came from the North and turned around to leave that way?

He selected the file from Whitsett and Moorpark.

The first southbound, white SUV passed through the intersection only seconds after Kaye hit the 'Play' button. He paused it and studied the image, noting that the time stamp was a full twenty minutes before Valerie had been picked up. There was still enough ambient light to see that the driver was a woman.

He clicked the 'Play' button again. There was more traffic than he'd expected, given the location and time. On most of the signal cycles, southbound traffic stacked up at the red light. Waiting vehicles were close enough together that all but the first vehicle's front license plate were obscured by the car in front of them. When the cycle changed to green and cars proceeded, the differences in driver reaction time and acceleration rates meant that not every front plate could be seen.

He stopped the video several more times to check out possible matches, with no luck. He watched the time stamp click closer and closer to the time Valerie had been picked up. About to give up and try another camera, he decided to check two more signal cycles.

The Whitsett light cycled to red as a light-colored SUV approached from the north and was the first car to stop. It had gotten dark enough that color resolution was fading, replaced by gray tones. He couldn't tell the exact color of the SUV, but he could see the VW emblem on the grill.

The intersection had two streetlamps, diagonally opposed, both of which had come on. As luck would have it, one was on the southeast corner. That maximized the distance from the now stopped VW, but improved the angle of light enough to better illuminate the SUV's interior. The driver was lit up from mid-chest to just above the nose. The passenger seat was empty.

Kaye paused the video and scrolled down until the front license plate was centered in the image. It took two enlargement clicks before he could read it.

It was the plate number he'd written down from the 'vehicles registered to' record of Leon and Monica Lowden.

He scrolled back up and focused on the driver. It wasn't a great portrait shot, but Kaye saw enough to convince him that if it wasn't Leon Lowden driving, it was his body double.

"Got'cha," he muttered aloud.

He continued watching the video. Minutes after the pick-up behind Staples, the VW again passed through the intersection, northbound this time. Kaye noted the time, closed the file, opened the opposing camera file and fast forwarded to the same time.

He passenger seat was occupied, and to Kaye it looked like Valerie Weber.

He pursed his lips and nodded his head.

Okay, I know who, now I just have to be able to prove it in court.

He took a break before diving into the Hollywood Reservoir approach videos. Because the area was larger and the time window much less defined, there were more of them and they were longer. That was somewhat obviated by the fact that because of the hour there was much less traffic and Kaye could fast forward more often. Still, it took him all afternoon to grind through them.

He didn't find Leon Lowden and his VW Tiguan.

Though it was late, he tried Kayla Okafor's number.

"You called just in time, Detective," she said when she picked up. "Ten seconds later and you've have gone to voice mail limbo. What do you need?"

"Who's the on-call warrant judge this weekend?"

"Hang on." She went quiet for a brief moment, then came back. "Okay, Schlemburg has it until six tomorrow morning, then Stiffler until Sunday morning and Franklin until Monday. Why?"

"I think I've identified Valerie Weber's killer," Kaye replied. "I need search warrants for his car and DNA."

"Good news," Okafor said. "I'd love to hear more, but I've got to run. Look, send me the affidavit. I'll check my email periodically and submit it for you electronically, if you'd like."

"That's okay," Kaye said. "Take your weekend. Judge Franklin is up on this. I'll talk to him Sunday. It'll give me time to write it up."

"Call me Monday?"

"Will do. Thanks, Counselor."

Kaye bent to outlining the search warrant affidavit requesting access to Leon Lowden's VW Tiguan and a sample of the man's DNA. It was nearly midnight when he was satisfied enough to send the document to the printer, retrieve it from the tray, grab the Big Boar jacket and head out.

When he reached the turn off from PCH onto the road that climbed the canyon toward home, he slowed, then rolled back on the throttle and kept going. Fifteen minutes later he stood alone in the darkness at the end of the Paradise Cove pier, leaning on the railing and staring out to sea.

His thoughts were a jumble as he tried to come to grips with all that had happened to Amy. What else hadn't she told him? Was she afraid he would leave her? Was she simply too ashamed about what Gene Calhoun had taken from her to talk about it? He wished he could seek advice and counsel from Roshi.

He stood there for an hour, raising far more questions than he found answers for. In the end, he decided there was only one thing to do.

Go to the source.

CHAPTER 46

It was almost noon when Kaye rolled the Road King out of the garage and headed for Orange County. He took PCH through the tunnel onto I-10, then took the 405 south.

As he rode, he contemplated how best to approach Charles and Sylvia Shaeffer. Amy's parents had never warmed to him, making it clear that they considered the hulking, ex-Marine biker not good enough for their daughter. As much as he hated to admit it, their animus toward him had become his motivation for earning a degree and entering law school. The nature of his relationship with them was best demonstrated by the fact that he hadn't spoken to them since Amy's funeral, when Charles Shaeffer's parting words to him had been, "I hope you're happy. You and your damn motorcycles killed my girl."

Though he loved riding PCH, Kaye by-passed both the 55 to Newport Beach and the 133 to Laguna Beach.

This wasn't a pleasure ride.

He took the Crown Valley Parkway exit and headed for the coast. A little over six miles later he crossed PCH and rolled to a stop at the Monarch Bay gate guard shack.

"This is a private community," the guard told him bluntly.

"I'm aware of that," Kaye responded politely. "I've been here before. I'm here to see the Shaeffers, Charles and Sylvia."

"Really, now," the guard said sarcastically, raising an eyebrow. "Why don't I just call and see if they're expecting you?"

"I'd rather you didn't," Kaye said. "Look, I used to be married to their daughter before she died. I'm passing by and just want to stop in and say hello, and see how they're doing. Is that okay with you? If you need some proof I'm not a bad guy, try this." He reached into his jacket and showed the guy his badge and ID.

The guard studied the badge. "Okay, that'll fly with the boss," he said as he opened the gate.

The Shaeffer house occupied a prime promontory above the beach, its expansive glass offering broad vistas of the coastline and open ocean. Seeing the house brought back a flood of bad memories. He and Amy had planned on being married there, but Sylvia had refused to allow it. After the marriage, visits were sporadic because of the strained nature of his relationship with Charles and Sylvia, and they had actually been on the way home from one of the rare visits when Amy had been killed.

He parked on the street, not even able to bring himself to use the driveway, walked around the frolicking dolphins fountain to the front door and pushed the doorbell.

Sylvia Shaeffer, past sixty but still working hard at being glamorous, opened the door.

"Why, hello Ben," she said in a Texas drawl Kaye knew was affected, "What are you doing here?"

"I need to talk to you. Is Charles home?"

"He's playing golf. What is it you want to talk about?"

"Amy."

"Ben, I don't think –"

"That's your problem, Sylvia," Kaye interrupted angrily. "You don't think about anybody but yourself."

She stared at him for several seconds, then started to close the door. Kaye put his hand on the door and stopped her.

"Invite me in," he said evenly. "Trust me, you'll want to hear this."

Sylvia stared at him again, then swung the door open, stepped aside, and gestured for Kaye to come in.

"I'd offer you a seat and some refreshments, but you won't be here that long," she said frostily as she closed the door behind him. "Now, what's this about?"

Kaye turned to face her and said, "Eugene Arthur Calhoun."

Sylvia's expression didn't change, but Kaye caught the flash of panic that flitted across her eyes.

"Doesn't ring a bell," she said casually.

"Really? You don't remember the name of the man who raped your daughter when she was in high school?" He paused, then added, "Your daughter Kathleen?"

Sylvia Shaeffer wilted. "How did you...?" She barely whispered.

"Let's sit down."

When they were seated, Kaye began. He told her about Valerie Weber and how the investigation had led him to old Orange County court records. He told her about the trial transcripts and how he'd tracked down Greg Sebaly.

"In the process I came across Eugene Calhoun, and it turned out he was linked to my case."

"Linked?" Sylvia asked. "I don't understand."

"After Calhoun got out of prison," Kaye told her, "he picked up right where he left off, preying on young girls."

"He killed the girl?"

"No," Kaye replied. "But he got her pregnant, just like he did Amy. Or should I say Kathleen?"

"You don't understand," she said softly. "You couldn't understand."

"Try me."

Sylvia sighed. "Yes, when she was born we gave her the first name Kathleen. But after what happened, the trial, the publicity and the angry mobs, she just couldn't go anywhere. Even going to school was a nightmare, so we moved and put her in a private school, thinking it would help. It did, but only for a while. Eventually, she just threw in the towel and changed her name. Her life went back to almost normal." She took a deep breath. "Except for one thing."

"What?"

"She became obsessed with keeping that monster in prison."

"You knew she went to the parole hearings?" Kaye asked.

"We did. We tried to convince her to just let it go. To move on, live her life. But..." Her voice trailed off.

"I have to ask one question." Kaye said.

"Go ahead."

"Why didn't she tell me any of this?"

"She was afraid she'd lose you. I know that you know Charles and I were against her marrying you. But she loved you, Ben. I mean truly loved you. She was petrified that you'd walk away, especially if she told you she could never have children."

"I wouldn't have."

"You can say that now, but what if she'd told you before you got married?" Sylvia said. "There's really no way to know, now."

"I loved her, too."

"We knew that," Sylvia said.

"Then why were so you against us getting married?"

Sylvia took a another deep breath. "Ben, you've proven yourself to be a very capable individual. I'm not trying to insult you, but at the time Charles and I just didn't think you'd be able to provide Amy with the kind of life we'd hoped for her."

"What gave you the right to decide what kind of life Amy wanted?"

"All parents have dreams for their children."

"That's almost funny," Kaye said, "given that she ended up providing me with the kind of life I never dreamed of having."

"We weren't surprised by her success. We just thought you might hold her back. You didn't, but, obviously, one of your lifestyle choices ended up killing her."

Kaye looked at her and knew the debate was pointless.

"Do you remember the name Roy Dobson?"

"Of course I do," Sylvia said, her voice hard.

"I came across something very interesting during my investigation."

"What was that?"

"Dobson was an ex-con, and –"

"We knew that," Sylvia interrupted.

"We did," Kaye agreed. "What we didn't know, and probably never would have known if I hadn't randomly been assigned the Valerie Weber case, is that Dobson's last cell mate in prison was none other than Eugene Calhoun."

"What?" Sylvia said, eyes wide.

"Prison records show that Dobson's daughter visited regularly before Dobson was released," Kaye said. "They also show she kept going back to visit Calhoun after that."

"Why would she…?"

"Good question," Kaye replied slowly. "It's beginning to look like Gene Calhoun paid Roy Dobson to kill Amy as revenge for her keeping him in prison all those years. An investigation is on-going."

Sylvia's face froze in an expression of horror and she started trembling uncontrollably as she stared at Kaye.

"Amy didn't die because of my lifestyle choices, Sylvia," he said. "She was murdered. That's what I came here to tell you. I'm sorry for your loss. Our loss. But it wasn't my fault."

Sylvia wrapped her arms across her chest and began to rock back and forth, keening softly.

"Would you like me to call Charles and stay until he gets home?" Kaye asked.

Sylvia looked at him with blank eyes and shook her head.

"Fine," Kaye said, standing up. "I'll show myself out."

CHAPTER 47

It was an unwritten rule that detectives only bothered the on-call judge for warrant submissions if the circumstances required it. But it wasn't a court policy, and Kaye didn't feel like waiting even twenty-four hours. Nor did he want to miss his window of opportunity to present his affidavits to Judge Franklin, who was already up on the case.

Weekend on-call schedules for judges were notoriously flexible, with trades coming fast and furious on Fridays because of prior commitments and other factors, so when Kaye called the on-call number, he kept his fingers crossed.

"Judge Franklin," the man answered. Kaye relaxed a little.

"Your Honor, this is Detective Kaye, LAPD West Bureau. How are you today?"

"I'm fine, Detective. You?"

"Working on a Sunday, sir."

"Join the club," Franklin said. "What can I do for you?"

"I'm calling regarding a search warrant request on the Valerie Weber case."

"The young woman whose adoption file we opened," Franklin said immediately. "She was murdered, correct?"

"Yes, sir, that's her," Kaye said, his confidence buoyed by the Judge's recollection. "Honestly, Your Honor, if we hadn't already talked about the case, I probably wouldn't have called you on a Sunday."

"You're fine, Detective. I'm actually at the courthouse writing a ruling. What are you looking for?"

"I'd like to search a specific vehicle and house for physical and forensic evidence that would place the victim there immediately prior to her death, and I'd like to obtain a DNA sample from the vehicle owner."

"Is the owner of the vehicle also the owner of the property?"

"Yes, sir," Kaye replied. "Both are actually owned jointly, husband and wife. I'm interested in the husband."

"Who is it?" Franklin asked.

"His name is Leon Lowden. He's Valerie –"

"I remember who he is, Detective," Franklin interrupted. "I read the adoption file. Is your probable cause solid?"

"As a rock, Your Honor," Kaye replied. "It's all laid out in the affidavit."

"Let's do this, Detective," Franklin said after a brief pause. "Since I'm already in the office, email me the affidavit." He gave Kaye an address. "I'll review it immediately and email you my decision. Where are you?"

"I'm at the station, sir. I'll be here waiting for your decision."

"Three things," Franklin said.

"Sir?"

"One, if you share the email address I just gave you with anyone, I'll have your head. Two, do you swear that the contents of your affidavit are true and correct to the best of your knowledge?"

"I do."

"Good. Three, I want a printed copy of the affidavit, with an original signature, on my clerk's desk by nine o'clock tomorrow morning. And it had better match what you send me, word for word."

"It will be there, Your Honor."

"Okay, send it and I'll look at it right away. I need a break from what I've been doing."

Kaye promptly sent the email with the affidavit attached.

It took a little over an hour to hear back. The Judge approved the application and sent along copies of the warrant and conditions. Ten-day expiration, no nighttime service, and the vehicle could be impounded if necessary. DNA collection by ducal swab only.

Kaye was satisfied. He checked the time. It wasn't too late to ride to Northridge, but it was Sunday. He picked up the phone and called Devonshire Station. Five minutes later, assured he would have the resources he needed, he headed for the Harley.

***

Forty minutes later, Kaye idled the Harley down Lowden's Street. The Expedition and white VW were both in the driveway. He pulled around the corner to the elementary school parking lot, called Devonshire again, gave them his location and asked for a patrol unit. One was dispatched and he was given an ETA of less than fifteen minutes for the crime scene unit.

The patrol unit showed up in minutes. Five minutes later the crime scene team showed up. Kaye briefed everyone and explained what he was looking for, then they all headed for the Lowden house.

"Doorbell cam," one of the patrol officers pointed out when they got to the porch. "Think they'll answer the door?"

"We shall see," Kaye said as he pushed the button. "If they don't, I break down the door."

It was only a few seconds before the door swung inward. Leon Lowden glared at Kaye. "What the hell do you want? I told you to talk to my lawyer."

Nice tattoo, Kaye thought as he glanced at Lowden's left forearm. *No doubt military.* "I have a warrant to search the VW Tiguan and your home, and collect a DNA sample from you, Mr. Lowden," Kaye said. "You are not entitled to an attorney's presence while the warrant is executed. Feel free to consult with your attorney later if you choose to contest the warrant or its findings." He handed Lowden a copy of the warrant. "A receipt for any property we seize will be provided."

"Leon, who is it?" Kaye heard Monica Lowden's voice just before she rolled into view behind her husband. "Oh, it's you again."

"Says he has a search warrant," Leon said without taking his eyes off Kaye.

Monica craned her neck to see around Leon. "Why are you doing this to us? I told you about Rachel. Now you're harassing us?"

"I'm not harassing you, Mrs. Lowden," Kaye said patiently. "I'm conducting a murder investigation."

"Murder?" Monica said scornfully. "I told you, Rachel took her own life. It was fully investigated at the time."

"I've read the reports," Kaye said, then directed his attention to Leon and held out his hand. "Keys to the Volkswagen."

"And if I don't give them to you?" Leon blustered. "You break a window or something?"

"No, I just call a tow truck. Could be a week before you get it back."

"Damn cops," Leon muttered as he dug into his pocket, took out his keys and dropped them into Kaye's hand.

"Thank you," Kaye said politely. "Now, if you'll step outside, we'll let the DNA tech take the sample. Only takes a second." He turned and signaled to the tech, who came onto the porch, collection kit in hand.

Leon looked at Kaye with undisguised hatred as the tech explained the process to him and proceeded with the collection. Thirty seconds later, the swabs were sealed, labeled and back into the collection kit.

"Thank you, sir," the tech said and hustled off the porch.

"Mr. Lowden," Kaye said, "you can either go inside or stay out here. You're welcome to observe, but the evidence gathering team will not answer questions, and if you interfere with them you will be arrested. Do you understand?"

"I understand you're an asshole," Lowden snorted.

"Gosh, Leon," Kaye said. "I'm hurt. In all my years as a cop, nobody's ever called me that before."

The uniformed officer couldn't suppress his laugh, which drew a look from Lowden.

"I need a verbal acknowledgement to my question, Mr. Lowden," Kaye said. "Do you understand what I told you a moment ago?"

"I understand. Just do what you came to do and get the hell off my property."

"That's our plan," Kaye said, then turned around and walked over to where Karen Koenig, the crime scene team leader, waited. "Keys to the car," he said, handing them to her.

"You want us to start with the house or the car?" she asked.

"Use your resources as you see fit."

"Thank you." She turned and huddled with her people. Two headed for the Tiguan while the others headed for the house.

When it became apparent that the Lowden's weren't going to cause any real problems he released the uniformed officers.

The list of physical items on the warrant was limited primarily to digital devices. At one point Koenig came to Kaye and asked, "Do you want me to seize their cell phones?"

"No, just note the numbers and provider information," he replied. "I can get the records."

"Do you want to take the computers with you?" she asked, holding them up. One was a laptop, the other a tablet decorated with colorful flower stickers. "There's also a desktop they're disconnecting now."

"No," he said. "I want as strict and limited a chain of custody as we can get."

"Makes sense," Koenig said and went back to work.

It took just over an hour to complete the search. No tangible physical evidence was recovered from the Tiguan. The results of the swabbing and vacuuming would take a few days. Drain collection and surface processing protocols were also completed inside the house.

Leon Lowden shut the door in Kaye's face when Kaye handed him the receipts.

Kaye and Koenig's people met again at the school parking lot.

"Well?" Kaye asked.

"No obvious smoking gun, if that's what you're asking," Koenig said, then smiled. "But I did see a Glock nine mil in the master bedroom nightstand, just so you know. I think our best chances are the computers and finding DNA in the trace and surface samples from the car, but…"

"Yeah," Kaye said. "He's had quite a bit of time to clean up."

"You really think this guy is your killer?" Koenig asked. "His own granddaughter?"

"If he didn't kill her, he knows who did."

"I'll get this stuff processed as soon as possible," Koenig told him.

"Thanks, everyone," Kaye said. "Appreciate it."

CHAPTER 48

Kaye was waiting in the hallway outside Judge Franklin's clerk's office when she showed up. He gave her the quick-and-dirty and handed over the signed affidavit, the returns he'd received via email, and two copies of the receipt he'd given to Leon Lowden. The clerk assured him they'd be on the Judge's desk when he arrived.

His first call from the station was to Kayla Okafor.

"Good morning, Counselor."

"How'd it go?" Okafor asked without preamble.

"Too soon to tell. No results yet, but we didn't find pictures of Leon Lowden posing with Valerie's corpse, if that's what you were hoping for."

"It's never that easy, right?"

"Right," Kaye replied. "I did get computers. I can check for communications between Valerie and the Lowdens, and cell phone information if we need the records."

"But the bottom line is you didn't recover anything that specifically connects Leon Lowden to Valerie's murder."

"Not yet," Kaye replied. "The crime scene team lead thinks our best chance is any trace they got from Leon's car, but he had lots of time to clean up. We'll just have to wait and see what the lab comes up with."

"What will you do in the meantime?"

"Not much I can do, except wait."

***

The first hopeful news came when Karen Koenig called about an hour later.

"I thought I'd let you know," she told Kaye, "that we did recover epithelial cells from surfaces in the front seat area of Lowden's Volkswagen that we can test for DNA. The lab said they'd try and have it done by tomorrow."

"That's a start," Kaye said.

357

"The jackpot was the front passenger seat belt. Based on the fact that we found nothing anywhere else in the vehicle, I think Lowden spent considerable time cleaning it up. But he missed something big."

"How so?"

"We ended up with a hair; a medium-length red hair complete with follicle; in the vacuum trace bag used in the front seat area. I'm giving a hundred to one it belongs to your vic."

"I'm not taking that bet," Kaye said. "Good work. But nothing in the cargo area?"

"Nothing," Koenig confirmed. "Given that's probably where the body would have been had it been transported in that vehicle, either Lowden really cleaned it up, or the body was wrapped."

"Or it was never there," Kaye added. "What about the house?"

"Same as the car. We got some testable material, we'll just have to wait."

"Thanks, Karen. I appreciate the good work."

He'd barely hung up when his phone rang again.

"Detective Kaye, this is Scott from the digital forensics unit. How are you today?"

"I'm good. What's up?"

"I was just assigned the computers and tablet from the search warrants you executed yesterday." Scott read off the warrant and case numbers. "I need to know what you're looking for, specifically."

Kaye gave Scott a brief summary, including the URL of the adoptive family seekers website and the usernames he had. "I'm looking for anything that can confirm communications between the usernames Matt eighteen fourteen and Lil Lost Redhead. If you can recover any actual messages, that'd be great."

"This the same case I enhanced the video for?"

"It is."

"Did that help you find this Lowden guy?"

"It did," Kaye said. "If you can get into those devices and find the right stuff, it would greatly help me solve the case."

"Oh, I can get in," Scott said confidently. "I'll let you know what I find."

Next, Kaye set about checking Leon's claim he was in Sacramento at the time of Valerie Weber's death. It didn't take much digging into the Sacramento Bee's website archive to find the article covering the event Lowden said he'd attended. It had taken place at the Convention Center, starting the Thursday afternoon Valerie had gone missing, through noon on the Sunday her body had been found.

He read and re-read the article, but could find no reference to the specific host hotel where Lowden claimed to have stayed. It wasn't hard to discover that two major chains had hotels directly across the street from the convention venue.

He picked one and called.

"Sheraton Sacramento. This is Holly. How can I help you?"

Kaye introduced himself and told her, "I'm trying to find out if a particular guest stayed at your hotel on specific dates. Can you do that for me? If not, I need to speak with someone who can."

"When was it?" she asked.

He gave her the dates. "There was some sort of developers and builders trade show at the Convention Center."

"Oh, I remember that. Yes, that's recent enough. What was the guest's name?"

"Leon Lowden." He spelled it for her.

"One second, please." She put him on hold, but wasn't gone long. "Detective, I don't find that name in our guest records for those days. Was it possibly booked under a company name?"

"Mr. Lowden owns the company. It has his name in it."

"Then it would've come up. Sorry. Have you tried the Hyatt?"

"It's next on my list. Thank you, Holly."

Kaye hung up, then dialed the Hyatt next door to the Sheraton. He got a young man named Marcus. After going through the same introduction and reason for the call, Marcus asked for the guest's name.

"Leon Lowden," Kaye told him.

"Hang on, Detective." Kaye was again put on hold, but again didn't wait long. "Detective?"

"Still here."

"Yes, a Leon Lowden was a guest here that weekend. His reservation was for three nights, Thursday through Saturday."

Well, crap, Kaye thought, then asked, "Was there anything unusual about his stay?"

"Unusual, how?"

"Maybe a late check-in or early check-out, odd housekeeping or room service requests. I mean, I'm sure most of your guests come and go without a whimper, and a few are on your radar the entire time, right?"

"You got that right," Marcus agreed knowingly. "Hang on again. I need to go to a different computer."

This time the wait was longer, but there was hold music.

"You still there?" Marcus asked when he came back on.

"I'm here."

"The only thing I found was that Mr. Lowden called Thursday afternoon and asked for a late check-in. The note in the computer said 'flight delay'."

"Did you find his actual check-in time?"

"I did. One fifteen in the morning."

"Check out?"

"Just before noon on Sunday."

"Does the registration list a vehicle?"

"Uh," Marcus said slowly as he searched. "Yes, it lists a white Volkswagen Tiguan."

"Thanks, Marcus. Appreciate your help."

He leaned back in his chair and sighed deeply. It's almost six hours by car from L.A. to Sacramento. Leaving from Northridge would shave some time off that. He had video of Lowden picking up Valerie from behind Staples. Lowden had made a point, though, of telling Kaye he'd met with quite a few people in Sacramento, so Kaye knew there wasn't any doubt about whether it was actually Lowden who attended the conference.

He listed his car, not a rental on the registration, so he obviously didn't fly. He must've driven like a bat out of hell, Kaye thought. *Either way, even if he picked her up, I just established that my prime suspect was four hundred miles away when Valerie died. Nice work, Sherlock.*

The old advice bubbled up again. 'Don't find evidence to fit the suspect. Find the suspect that fits the evidence.'

CHAPTER 49

Kaye rode the '61 to work, hoping today would be the day the pieces of the Weber case puzzle would finally come together.

The email was in his inbox when he logged in. The sender was Dr. Mehrabi and the subject was Evidence and DNA Analysis Results, Valerie Weber homicide. The email itself was short and sweet.

'Detective Kaye; The report is attached. Call me after you look it over. Mehrabi.'

He downloaded the file attachment to the case folder, then opened it. The first page was a standard form, the boxes filled with case information and legal foundations for the analysis, information on the techniques used and the names of the technicians that had completed the testing. Kaye was surprised to see that Dr. Mehrabi had personally done the testing.

The second page was a generic orthographic projection drawing of a sport utility vehicle. Places where trace samples had been recovered were numbered and a list below the drawing matched the numbers to specific sample information. Testable material had been recovered from the front passenger seatbelt buckle anchor and the inner surface of the front passenger door release handle. Both samples matched the known comparator sample obtained from Valerie Weber during autopsy.

The hair Koenig had mentioned, recovered from the front passenger seat area, also matched Valerie Weber's DNA.

Other samples collected either lacked adequate material for analysis, or had not matched Valerie Weber. As expected, the majority of the touch DNA recovered matched the DNA sample collected from Leon Lowden pursuant to the warrant. Some were unmatched.

None of the trace collected inside the house matched Valerie Weber's profile.

Combined with the video, Kaye now had definitive evidence that proved Leon Lowden had picked Valerie up behind Staples.

Got'cha, Kaye thought. *Almost, at least.*

Progress. Probably enough to get an arrest warrant.

He suddenly remembered Mehrabi's instruction to call her after he'd read the report, grabbed the phone and dialed.

"Mehrabi."

"Doc, hey, it's Ben Kaye. I read the DNA report of the Weber case. Thanks for expediting it."

"You're welcome. I wanted to talk to you about something that's not in the report."

"Oh?"

"I didn't include it because it wasn't a comparison listed on the search warrant, and I want to rerun all the tests to confirm the results. But I thought you should know."

"Okay, Doc," Kaye said slowly, "now you've got me worried. What's going on?"

"According to the paperwork that came with the Leon Lowden DNA sample, you wanted it compared to Valerie Weber, hoping to establish a familial connection."

"Correct," Kaye said. "Everything I've found tells me Leon Lowden was Weber's grandfather. I wanted confirmation."

Mehrabi hesitated for a second, then said, "I almost hate to tell you this. Leon Lowden is Valerie Weber's grandfather, but that's not all."

"Excuse me?" Kaye said slowly.

"He's also her father."

A stunned Kaye was speechless.

"Detective, are you there?"

"I'm here. I just can't... That means..."

"Leon Lowden impregnated Valerie Weber's mother."

"Rachel," Kaye said softly.

"Who?"

"Rachel Lowden, Valerie's biological mother, was the daughter of Leon and Monica Lowden," Kaye said. "Doc, are you absolutely positive?"

"Like I said, I'm rerunning the comparisons," Mehrabi replied. "But based on the results I've got," she hesitated again, "yes, I'm sure."

Kaye went quiet again, trying to digest what Mehrabi was telling him. The doctor understood and waited.

Kaye gathered his wits. "Okay, thanks, Doc. You'll let me know if things change?"

"Of course."

"If they don't, I'll need the results in an official report."

"You'll have it."

He ended the call, leaned back again and tried to wrap his head around what Mehrabi had told him, and its implications. He finally gave up, his frame of reference unable to come to terms with it.

But as a cop, he got it. He now had motive to go with opportunity.

***

Kaye had been working on an arrest warrant affidavit for nearly an hour when his phone rang.

"Detective, this is Maldonado at the front desk. There are two gentlemen here to see you. A Leon Lowden and his attorney, Mr. Behrend."

"I'll be right down."

Leon Lowden was casually dressed in a long-sleeved t-shirt with a road grader printed on the front of it, jeans and tennis shoes. He wore an expression devoid of emotion. The other man was dressed in the *de rigueur* attorney's uniform: White shirt and striped tie under a blue blazer, gray slacks and a leather briefcase.

When Kaye entered the lobby, he locked eyes with Lowden, who turned to his attorney and said softly, "That's him."

"What can I do for you?" Kaye asked, noting that Lowden now avoided eye contact.

"Ted Behrend," the lawyer introduced himself. "My client and I are here to discuss a matter of mutual interest. I would appreciate it if you could make time to see us. In private."

"Sure," Kaye said, looking back and forth at the two men. "Let's go upstairs."

He led them to the same room where he and Patty had first interviewed Valerie Weber.

"So," Kaye said when they were all seated, "I'm assuming this has something to do with Valerie Weber. Are you here to contest the search warrant? Because if you are —"

"The court would be the place to do that," Behrend interrupted. "That's not why we're here."

"Cut to the chase, Counselor," Kaye said bluntly.

"My client," Behrend glanced sideways at Lowden, who nodded, then looked back at Kaye, "is here to confess to the killing of Valerie Weber, known to him as Crystal Lowden."

Kaye stared at Behrend for a full five seconds, then looked at Lowden. "Leon, you sure about this?"

Leon looked up at Kaye and nodded. "Yeah, I killed her. I didn't mean to, but…" He shrugged and looked back down at his hands in his lap.

"Are you willing to provide a statement?" Kaye asked, intending the question for both men.

"Yeah," Lowden mumbled without looking up.

"We are," Behrend added.

"Counselor, I'll need to advise your client of his rights."

Behrend immediately reached into his briefcase and removed some papers, which he laid on the table. "I've already conferred at length with Mr. Lowden on this matter," Behrend said. "Leon agrees to waive his Miranda rights, and I've taken the liberty of drawing up advisement forms and waivers. We've already signed them. If you'd like to look them over and they're acceptable, all you need to do is sign them."

Kaye looked them over. "These'll do." He signed them.

Kaye took out his cell phone, activated the voice recording function, put it on the table and looked at Lowden. "Tell me what happened, Leon." He settled back to listen, wondering how the man would spin it.

"First," Lowden began, "I want you to know it was an accident. I didn't mean for her to die. I was only trying to scare her, teach her a lesson."

"Okay, go on," Kaye said. "Tell me what happened after you picked her up outside Staples."

"You know about that?" A surprised Lowden asked, glancing at Behrend.

"I do," Kaye acknowledged. "I know a lot more, too, Leon, so don't bullshit me."

Lowden's expression hardened before he continued. "Crystal called me that day. Said some guy at school beat her up and her stepmom called the police about it. She was scared. She asked me to come pick her up so she could stay at my house until things settled down. I told her I'd pick her up and we could talk, but I didn't think it was a good idea for her to come to my house. I thought we'd drive around a little, I'd calm her down and reassure her, then take her back to her car so she could go home."

"What happened?" Kaye asked.

"When I picked her up, I was shocked," Lowden replied. "I mean, she was beat up bad."

"I know," Kaye said. "I took the report."

"She must've sensed I was upset," Lowden went on. "She was frantic, and just wouldn't calm down, so I decided to take her to the house. We were almost there when, out of the blue, she tells me she's pregnant, and the guy who got her pregnant is the guy who beat her up."

"And what did you do?"

"I got mad," Lowden replied softly. "It was like the nightmare with my Rachel all over again. You know about that, right?"

"I do," Kaye said, choosing not to tell Lowden just how much he knew. "Then what happened?"

"She became hysterical, crying and screaming," Lowden said. "I couldn't take her to the house, not with Monica there, and she just wouldn't calm down. I lost my temper. I yelled at her, she yelled back. I grabbed her. She fought back." He stopped and took a deep breath. "Next thing I know, she's...dead."

"How'd you grab her, Leon?" Kaye asked.

"By her neck, and her face. I just wanted her to stop screaming and listen. I didn't mean to. I swear before God, I didn't mean to hurt her."

"What did you do then?"

"I panicked," Lowden half-shouted. "I didn't know what to do." He took another deep breath. "I drove up into the hills and dumped her in some reservoir."

"Where was that?" Kaye prodded.

"I don't know, not far from the freeway," Lowden said. "It was dark. I just drove around until I found a good spot."

"Could you find it again?"

"I don't think so."

"Leon, tell Detective Kaye why you're here." Behrend spoke for the first time.

Lowden took another deep breath and looked Kaye in the eye. "I had to get this off my chest. When you came to my office, as soon as you asked me about the Matthew eighteen fourteen scripture I knew you'd figure it out. I can't live like this. I had to tell somebody, and figured the best course of action is to tell you. I'll take whatever I've got coming."

"So you were – are -- Matt eighteen fourteen?" Kaye asked.

"Yeah," Lowden nodded. "It was my username on that website where I found Crystal. Well, where we found each other."

"When was that, Leon?"

"Months and months ago," Lowden replied. "I don't remember exactly."

"I think we're done here," Behrend said, reaching up and grabbing his client's shoulder in a show of support.

"Agreed," Kaye said, turning off the recording. He stood up. "Leon Lowden, I'm placing you under arrest for the murder of Valerie Weber, known to you as Crystal Lowden. Stand up and place your hands behind your back."

Lowden complied and Kaye cuffed him.

"Leon, I'll meet you at the jail," Behrend said. "I'll do my best to get us before a judge today and arrange bail." He turned to Kaye and held out a business card. "Detective, if you would have that recording transcribed and notarized, and send a copy to my office, I'd appreciate it."

"I can make that happen," Kaye said. "Now, if you'll excuse me, I'll arrange transport."

He locked the interview room door from the outside, just in case.

***

An hour later Kaye turned Lowden over to Central Booking and headed straight for the D.A.'s office. Kayla Okafor was in court, but he was told she'd be back shortly.

He waited a little over ten minutes before a harried-looking Okafor came through the door, saw Kaye, and stopped.

"What now?" she asked testily.

"Good afternoon, Counselor," Kaye said as he stood up. "I'd ask how your day's going, but I think I know."

"Yeah, it's been one of those." She brushed past him and headed for her office. About halfway there she turned around. "Well, don't just stand there. C'mon back."

Kaye followed obediently.

"Okay," Okafor said once she settled behind her desk, "to what do I owe the pleasure of your visit?"

"I just arrested and booked Leon Lowden for the murder of Valerie Weber."

"I'll be damned," Okafor whispered. "Her own grandfather."

"Father."

"What?"

"Leon Lowden is Valerie's father, at least according to the DNA. Technically, I guess he's also –

"Stop! Stop!" A horrified Okafor stared wide-eyed at Kaye while she waved her hands. "He knocked up his own daughter?"

Kaye nodded. "Looks like it. The lab is redoing the test to verify the results."

"How did you finally connect him to the murder?"

"He and his attorney, Ted Behrend, walked into the station earlier today and Leon confessed."

"What?" Okafor asked. "He confessed?"

Kaye nodded again. "Yeah, but there's a problem."

Okafor stared at him, lips pursed and head shaking. "What's the problem now?"

"I don't think I believe him."

"Why would you not believe him?" Back to lawyer mode.

"He got some of it right, but his account doesn't even come close to squaring with the coroner's report."

"Coroners have been wrong before," Okafor pointed out. "That's why they call it *practicing* medicine."

"Yep," Kaye said with a smile. "Just like *practicing* law."

"Very funny," she said, unable to suppress a smile. "Let's get to the point. What do you want from this office? From me?"

"Time."

"Excuse me?"

"I need a day or two with Leon Lowden safely tucked away in County while I check a few things and either verify, or discount, his confession."

"And how do I do that?"

"Behrend was at Central Booking before I was. He told Lowden he'd try to expedite arraignment and bail. I need Lowden held, at least for a couple days."

"Okay, I'll call Behrend and be straight with him. What's a couple days compared to life, or death row, for murder? And I'll tell him I'll approve Lowden's release on his own recognizance if he goes along and the confession pans out."

"Okay," Kaye said, standing up. "Hope it works. Thanks, Counselor."

"Two days, tops," Okafor said. "Unless you can bring me the real killer, I file on Leon."

"Got it."

CHAPTER 50

The next morning, Kaye's first order of business was a call to Dr. Martinek at the Medical Examiner's office.

"What can I do for you, Detective?" the Doctor asked.

"I need to ask you about Valerie Weber."

"Valerie Weber... Oh, yes, the pregnant seventeen-year-old found in the Hollywood Reservoir. What would you like to know?"

"I made an arrest," Kaye told her, "but it's based on a confession and I have doubts."

"About?"

"Two things," Kaye replied. "First, my suspect, who was on my radar before he confessed, claimed during the interview that he unintentionally strangled or smothered Weber while he was driving and she was in the front passenger seat. Given what you saw in the autopsy, is that possible?"

"I would say probably not. The contusions in her neck were not to the extent we normally see in strangulation victims and there was almost no bleeding in the throat. Nor was the petechiae consistent with strangulation."

"So my skepticism is warranted?"

"I think so," Martinek replied. "I wouldn't say it's completely impossible, especially if the victim was somehow incapacitated, but there was no indication of that in the toxicology results."

"The second thing is the estimated time of death," Kaye said.

"What about it?" Kaye heard a hint of umbrage in Martinek's voice as she asked.

"The suspect claims he killed Weber in the car after he picked her up just before eight on Thursday evening. The body was discovered Sunday morning, obviously dumped."

"I remember, Detective."

"I've been able to reliably establish that the suspect was in Sacramento from very early that Friday morning until after the body was discovered."

Martinek was silent for a moment, and Kaye knew she was connecting the dots.

"Detective," she said at last, "based on my postmortem exam and what you just told me, I would testify for the defense on this one. Sorry."

"Don't apologize, Doc. That's what I thought, too, and it's exactly why I called."

"If there are no more questions, I have to go. Good luck," Martinek said and hung up.

Kaye leaned back and sighed. Lowden's confession was simply yet another misdirection, if not outright deception.

He called Kayla Okafor and got her voicemail.

"Counselor, don't file on Leon Lowden. Martinek at the M.E.'s office says there's no way the autopsy supports his confession or known whereabouts. Call me if you need details."

He hung up, leaned back and sighed again.

What am I missing? The thought ran through his mind over and over.

He lurched forward, grabbed a legal pad and pen, and started making a flow chart. He began with the morning he'd first interviewed Valerie and JoAnn Weber, hoping it would help him see sequences and linkages he might have missed. It grew quickly, but wasn't yielding anything really new.

Finally, he dropped the pen. It was lunch time and he needed a break. He grabbed the pages of the chart and the pen, walked around the corner to the deli and ordered his usual, then parked at an outside table. After a minute or two, he regretted not wearing his jacket. The sun was shining, but it was brisk. He ate slowly, spending time between bites on trying to expand and make sense of the sequence of events and possible connections. It wasn't working.

What am I missing?

He headed back to the station and heard his desk phone ringing as he crossed the squad. He recognized Okafor's number.

"Kaye."

"I got your message," the ADA said. "Are you sure you don't want to file on Lowden? I mean, your conflicts sound to me like things a jury should decide based on the evidence and testimony. Oh, and I did talk to Behrend, and he said he'd give us until tomorrow."

"I don't believe Lowden did it, and if I don't, no jury will," Kaye said. "Martinek even said she'd testify for the defense on this one."

"Seriously? Yeah, that cuts the odds of a conviction to about zero."

"If Lowden's innocent, he shouldn't be sitting in jail."

"Agreed," Okafor said. "You want me to call Behrend back and tell him?"

"You can if you want," Kaye said. "Or just call the jail and tell them to release Lowden."

"Let me ask you this," Okafor said. "Do you think he confessed to protect someone else?"

"It's possible, sure. But I don't know who, or why."

"What about Mrs. Lowden?"

"Both times I've seen her she was in a wheelchair, and one of their cars has a handicapped plate." Kaye said. "Didn't I tell you that?"

"If you did, I forgot.," Okafor replied. "So, you don't think she's physically capable of the crime?"

Kaye thought about it. "I don't see how a wheelchair-bound woman of almost sixty holds down and smothers a healthy teen-ager that's bigger than she is."

"Drugs?"

"Martinek said the tox screen was clear."

"Could she have had help?"

"I've asked myself that a hundred times," Kaye said. "If she did I have no idea who that might have been. It's her and Leon, and it doesn't strike me as a fulfilling relationship for either of them. Monica is pretty much housebound and Leon travels a lot on business. The weekend of the murder he was in Sacramento."

"What a mess," Okafor said, sighing. "Okay, I'll call the jail and tell them to kick Lowden loose."

"Sounds like the right thing to do."

"Okay, that's decided," she said with finality. "The plus side is that we're releasing him without charging him. If you get new evidence, we get a new warrant."

"Thanks, Counselor. And sorry about the wild goose chase."

She laughed. "My mother used to tell us that many a Thanksgiving dinner started as a wild goose chase."

Kaye chuckled. "I'll remember that."

He went back to the flow chart, carefully combing through the case file and his notes again as he searched for something, anything, he might have missed. It frustrated him that Valerie Weber's killing had led him on a tortuous trail to other crimes, including the murder of his own wife, but he had yet to bring the original victim's killer to justice.

He finally gave it up for the day. He was slipping into the Big Boar jacket when his phone rang.

Oh, perfect, he thought. *Probably Ted Behrend calling to tell me he's suing for false arrest.*

"Kaye," he answered.

"Detective Kaye, this is Scott in digital forensics. How's it going?"

"I've had better days," Kaye said laconically.

"Well, maybe I can cheer you up. I mean, no guarantees, but I found something on the devices from the Lowden search warrant I thought I should call you about."

"Oh?"

"I didn't have any trouble getting into them, by the way. One of the computers, the laptop, had nothing relevant on it at all. I found the accounts and websites you pointed me at in cache on the tablet and the desktop. I also discovered that the Matt eighteen fourteen account on the adoption website had been deleted."

"Do you know when?"

"The last login in was day before yesterday," Scott told him. "But that's not why I called. I found something... Odd."

"Really?" Kaye asked. "Odd... How?"

"On the desktop computer I found another user account for the same website that kind of sounded like another Bible verse."

"What was it," Kaye asked, now interested.

"The word Gen." Scott spelled it out G-E-N, "followed by the numerals one, nine, three, one, three and six. No punctuation, just the string of numbers all together."

"Hmm..." Kaye murmured, remembering Patty's mention of the G-E-N account Valerie Weber had communicated with during her search process, but the numbers didn't match. "Could be biblical, maybe, but could be anything. Did you find the password?"

"I did." Scott gave it to him. "I did not try to log in. I thought you should be the one to try that."

"I'll give it a shot. Anything else?"

"Just that the account was created the day before you seized the computer."

"Thanks, Scott," Kaye said, then added, "Oh, you should know that Leon Lowden had an alibi that checked out. He admitted to being Matt eighteen fourteen and to picking up Valerie Weber behind Staples, but nobody can smother someone from four hundred miles away."

"Well, shit," Scott muttered.

"My sentiments exactly. I appreciate the call, though."

CHAPTER 51

On his way home Kaye decided it was time to do something he'd been putting off. It was nearly 11:00 p.m. in the Central time zone when he made the call.

"Hi, Mom."

"Hello, Ben. What a nice surprise. Everything okay?"

"All in all, yeah. I've got a case that's driving me crazy." He paused. "And there's something I need to tell you."

She hesitated, then asked, "Is this about Amy?"

"It is." He took a deep breath. "I confirmed that Amy's death wasn't an accident. She was targeted."

He heard his mother gasp before she asked shakily, "Oh, my Lord. Are you absolutely certain? Why would somebody…?"

He told her the whole story.

"Amy never told you any of that?" she asked, amazed, when he finished. "I don't understand that at all, especially that she couldn't have children."

"Sylvia told me Amy was afraid I'd leave her."

"That's ridiculous."

"That's pretty much what I told her."

"Ben, I'm so sorry you're having to deal with this all over again. If there is anything I can do, please let me know."

"Thanks, Mom," Kaye said. "I hope we can nail someone's hide to the barn for what happened."

"Your father used to say that."

"I remember," Kaye said with a chuckle. "Usually he was talking about my hide."

"And you usually deserved it," she said matter-of-factly.

"Hey," he said, changing the subject, "while I've got you, can I ask you a Bible question?"

"Of course."

He laid it out for her, starting with the Matthew 18:14 reference, then gave her the character and number sequence of the account Scott had discovered.

"Hmm…" she murmured softly. "If it's from the Bible, it's got to be a reference from Genesis. That's the only book that starts with those three letters. Hold on a sec." Kaye heard her put the phone down. It wasn't long before she came back. "Okay, I'm looking at Genesis. What were those numbers again?"

He repeated them.

She was silent for a moment, then said, "I don't think it's a reference to chapter one. Genesis is about creation and the story of the patriarchs."

"Mom, I did actually pay attention when you took me to church."

"I'm just thinking out loud, Benjamin." She went quiet again for a bit, then said, "I think I might have figured it out."

"What do you think it means?" Kaye asked anxiously.

"I think it is a reference to Genesis, but chapter nineteen, which tells the story of Lot and his family escaping Sodom before God destroys it."

"And his wife looks back and is turned into a pillar of salt, right?"

"Correct. Lot and his daughters escape and end up living in a cave near a place called Zoar."

"That's it?" Kaye asked, his disappointment palpable.

"Well, no," she said. "These specific verses tell how Lot's daughters conspire to preserve their father's lineage by sleeping with him and getting pregnant."

"What? Say that again."

"Verses thirty-one to thirty-six relate how Lot's two surviving daughters end up getting pregnant by their father."

"Two daughters?"

"That's what it says," she replied. "Verses thirty-one to thirty-four tell how the idea was hatched and the older daughter following through. Thirty-five and six are the younger daughter doing the same thing. They both ended up having sons."

Kaye's head was spinning. Two daughters? And why would this account just suddenly show up? Was Leon testing him? Maybe baiting him?

"Do you think that's what the numbers mean?" his mom asked.

"Pretty sure," he replied. "Good catch, Mom. Thanks."

"You're welcome. And, Benjamin?"

"Yes?"

"I'll say some extra prayers for Amy tonight. You take comfort in knowing that she loved you, son, and sleep well. I love you, too."

"I love you, Mom."

***

Kaye did not sleep well. In fact, he hardly slept at all. He lay awake, constantly dissecting and examining the Weber case, trying to figure out what he should have done that he hadn't, or what he did do that he shouldn't have, and what he'd done wrong while he tried to reconcile his progress, or lack of same, with his conversation with his mother.

Two daughters?

But it didn't fit. Monica Lowden had used the words 'only granddaughter' when referring to Crystal during their conversation. To him, that meant she hadn't borne another child that could give her grandchildren..

Was she hiding something?

He remembered seeing 3:12 a.m. on the nightstand clock before being startled awake by his cell phone at thirty-nine a.m.

"Kaye, and this had better be good."

"Detective," a woman said, "I'm so sorry to call you at home at this hour, but –"

"Who is this?" he interrupted.

There was a slight hesitation before the woman said, "I'm sorry. This is Karen Koenig from Devonshire Division. I assisted with your search warrant last Sunday."

"The Lowden's," Kaye said, now awake. "I remember. So, tell me what couldn't wait," he glanced at the clock, "four hours."

"I just cleared my team from a crime scene," Koenig said slowly. "It was at the same house we searched on Sunday. The Lowdens."

"What kind of call was it?"

"It came in just after midnight as a possible shots fired, and they're working it as a probable suicide."

Kaye's mind raced. "Male or female?"

"Male. Same big guy who was such a jerk when we were there."

"How?"

"Gunshot through the underside of the mouth into the cranial cavity. Took most of the top of his skull with it on the way out."

"What about Mrs. Lowden?"

"No sign of her."

"She wasn't there?" Kaye asked.

"Nope," Koenig confirmed. "I heard the detectives talking. The nine-one-one call came from a cell phone, the caller was female, but refused to give her name. Patrol had to kick the door to get in. Mr.

Lowden was spread all over the living room wall, Mrs. Lowden apparently in the wind."

"Was there a note?"

"There was not," Koenig replied.

"But they recovered the gun, right?"

"They did," Koenig confirmed. "It was on the couch next to Lowden, practically still in his hand. A Glock, probably the same one that was in the nightstand when we served the warrant."

"Whose case is it?"

"Gerash," Koenig replied. "Late show. It'll go to Division for a second look, probably tomorrow."

"Thanks, Karen," Kaye told her. "I appreciate the call."

"You're welcome. I was worried about waking you up."

"It was the right thing to do."

He ended the call and dropped the phone on the bed.

Back to square one. Oh, wait, square one just killed himself.

He tried to go back to sleep. After a moment he grabbed his phone again, speed dialed Captain Thompson's office and left his boss a voice mail.

"Captain, it's Kaye. Been a bad night at Black Rock on the Weber case. I'll be in as soon as I can get enough sleep to function. Thanks."

CHAPTER 52

It was just after 10:30 a.m. when Kaye pushed through the doors into the squad room. He was still tired, but five hours of tossing and turning was better than one. He went to check with the Captain, but the office was closed and dark.

He detoured to the break room and brewed himself a cup of tea. When he got to his desk he found a note resting on top of his keyboard.

'Ben,

Burke and I are meeting with Laguna PD at noon regarding the connection between Eugene Calhoun and your wife's death. We found financial connections between Calhoun and Sharon Dobson and will be handing the case over to them for further investigation. Sorry we had to leave before you got in, but thought you'd want to know.

J.J.'

Kaye grabbed the phone and called J.J.'s cell number.

Burke answered. "Hi, Ben. J.J.'s driving. You calling about Calhoun?"

"Yeah. What did you find?"

"We had no trouble at all finding Sharon Dobson. I mean, the woman is certainly not trying to stay off anyone's radar."

"Did you find a payment to her, maybe through her father, from Calhoun?"

"Nothing obvious or direct. Calhoun was very cagey about it," Burke replied. "She went from living in an apartment and working as the manager of the bakery department at a supermarket to living in a very expensive home in a gated community in Anaheim Hills almost overnight."

Kaye knew that had to be where Sonny Eliason had been stymied by the gate after following Dylan Glithero and Audra O'Bannon to Orange County.

"The thing is," Burke continued, "the house and several expensive cars were paid for and are legally owned by wholly-owned subsidiary companies of the Calhoun empire."

"He gave her a phony job," Kaye said. "He's paying her a lot of money to do nothing."

"That's what we think, too," Burke confirmed. "Between that, the prior history in Orange County and the connection at Lancaster, the Captain told us to hand it off to the Laguna PD."

"I get it," Kaye said.

"One problem," J.J. spoke up, and Kaye could tell Burke was holding the phone up toward him. "If Sharon Dobson shows up in company records as an employee or consultant and they can show she actually participates in business operations, it legitimizes the situation. Makes it all look like a coincidence. A monumental coincidence, but…"

"I get that, too," Kaye said. "All we can do is give the Laguna PD what we've got. Thanks, and great work on such short notice."

"See you, Ben," Burke said.

"Later," Kaye said and ended the call.

All he could hope for now was that the Laguna detectives would work the case hard and find enough to convince a prosecutor to take it to a jury. He started running scenarios of how he would approach the investigation when he suddenly realized he'd gotten so wrapped up in the Lowden suicide and his conversation with J.J. and Burke he'd forgotten all about the Gen193136 account.

He opened the browser on his computer and navigated to the website where Leon and Valerie had found each other. First he tried the Matt1814 account and got a 'no such user' pop-up notification. Then he entered Gen193136 and the password Scott had recovered, clicked 'Login' and waited.

It only took a few seconds for the account home page to fill the screen.

It wasn't quite what he'd been expecting. The other accounts he and Patty had looked at were replete with information and photos. Each user searching for someone they weren't sure existed. This page was essentially blank, as though none of the field entries had been saved before the user logged out.

Except for one. On the sidebar menu there was a (1) notation after the word 'Posts.'

Kaye clicked on it, then stared, stunned, at the screen.

'Luke 17:32.'

What the hell?

His gut told him Leon Lowden had created the account and posted the message for him to find. Why? A joke? A taunt? And why would someone about to take his own life do such a thing?

One way to find out.

He opened another browser window, went to a search engine and typed in Luke 17:32.

It took only a few thousandths of a second to return several hundred thousand returns.

He stared at the screen in disbelief.

Luke 17:32 was three words long.

'Remember Lot's wife.'

What is that supposed to mean?

His fatigue clouded his reasoning, but an image from serving the warrant at the Lowdens' house flashed through his memory and it all suddenly fell into place. His eyes stayed on the screen as he leaned back and muttered 'son of a bitch.'

He'd been searching the roots when what he wanted was in the branches.

CHAPTER 53

After six caffeine-fueled hours of staring at the computer monitor, he found it. He was inwardly glad Tom Gannett wasn't there to skewer and roast him for not finding it in the first place. In his tired mind, though, Kaye constructed unnecessary defenses, which he rationally knew were just excuses.

I wouldn't have found it because I didn't know what I was looking at, or *It wouldn't have meant anything to me at the time.*

Plus, when he did find it, it didn't turn out to be what he'd started looking for. But what he did find gave him a much clearer picture of what had started almost twenty years before. He wrapped us his search by printing multiple copies of several screen shots he knew a jury would love.

It was too late and he was too tired to close the Valerie Weber case tonight. Tomorrow would have to do.

CHAPTER 54

It was a coat-and-tie, drive-the-pickup-to-work day. Rested, refreshed and more than a little anxious about the day ahead, Kaye left the house early, hoping to avoid most of the traffic.

When he got to the station he found Captain Thompson, surrounded by empty cardboard boxes, standing in the middle of his office.

"What's going on?" Kaye asked, looking around.

"I'm moving," Thompson replied, grinning. "Today's my last day."

"Today? I thought…"

"So did I. But yesterday, when I told the Boss I was definitely leaving, he politely suggested that today was as good a day as any. As much as he's screwed me over on this whole thing, I am more than happy to oblige."

"What are you going to do?"

"Teach," Thompson said, his grin growing wider. "One of those other irons in the fire I mentioned burst into flame. I took a job at a Junior College. Less prestige, but I get to stand in front of classes and actually teach. I don't have to move. I don't have to log a hundred thousand miles a year in traffic. The pay is about the same and they're tickled pink to have a Ph.D. of color who's been a cop for most of his life."

"Good for you, Cap," Kaye said sincerely. "Sounds like a perfect fit."

"It's as close as I'll ever get. Oh, I guess I should ask, since I'm officially still on the payroll, was there something you needed? The coat and tie were clues, by the way."

Kaye quickly recapped what had happened on the Weber case in the last few days, then, as Thompson shook his head in wonder, related what he thought was going on.

"With luck," he said in closing, "case closed by arrests, plural, today."

"Great work, Detective, as usual. And not to pry, but have you…?"

"Not yet," Kaye replied with a shrug.

"You'll know when it's right, either way. And by the way, it's very liberating."

It was Kaye's turn to grin. "Gee, Professor, I never would have guessed."

Thompson extended his hand. "In case I don't see you again today."

They shook hands and promised to stay in touch.

Back at his desk, Kaye got organized. He'd already decided on an approach to his first interview and made sure the screen shot printouts were on top of the stack. He took an unmarked sedan with a shield behind the front seat, just in case. By nine he was on the 405, northbound toward the Valley.

This time he didn't have to search for the address and went straight to the front office parking lot of TRT Trucking. The tricked out truck was again parked in the Reserved spot.

The same people were doing the same thing they'd been doing on his first visit, and he stood, unacknowledged, at the counter for a good thirty seconds before one of the men hung up his phone and looked at him.

"Sorry, how can I --?" The man stopped mid-sentence, stared for a second, and said, "You're the cop right? You were here before, but in biker clothes."

"That would be me. Detective Kaye. I need to see Mr. Rowell again."

"Does he know you're coming?"

"I doubt it," Kaye replied, noting several of the office occupants exchange glances. "Shouldn't take long."

The man picked up the phone and punched in a number. "Hey, boss, that detective that was here before is back. Says he needs a couple minutes." He listened, then hung up and looked at Kaye. "He'll be right out."

Seconds later, Rowell opened the door leading to the back offices, leaned around, saw Kaye and said, "Come on in."

They were soon seated in Rowell's office. Rowell didn't move his computer monitor, so Kaye scooted the chair sideways until he could see around it.

"Sorry," Rowell said. "I'll move it." He started to reach for it.

"It's fine, "Kaye said. "But you might want to close the door."

Rowell looked hard at Kaye, then got up and took the suggestion.

"So, what can I do for you?" he asked when he sat back down.

"I just need to ask you a few more questions," Kaye said, reaching into the file folder he carried and pulling out several of the screen prints. "Is this your truck? The one parked outside?" he asked as he laid them on Rowell's desk.

Rowell leaned forward to look more closely and Kaye saw him glance up surreptitiously as the color started to drain from his cheeks.

"Could be, I guess," the man replied. "Looks kind of like it."

"I can't tell for sure if that's you behind the wheel because of the visor," Kaye said. "But there are two people in the front seat. Got any ideas?"

Rowell ignored the question, instead asking, "Where did you get these?"

"Mr. Rowell, before I can answer that I need to advise you of your rights and inform you that I'm going to record our conversation. Are you okay with that?" He took out his phone, turned on the voice memo function and laid it on the desk.

Rowell, now looking thoroughly dispirited, gulped and nodded slightly.

Kaye went through the Miranda warning and asked Rowell if he understood, and what he wanted to do.

"What do you think I should do?"

"I can't offer you legal advice. But I think there's a lot more going on here than meets the eye, and now's your chance to tell the story. I can't make any promises, but cooperation with the police goes a long way with the District Attorney's office."

Kaye waited while Rowell fidgeted, trying to make up his mind.

"You should know," Kaye said, upping the ante, "these images of your truck, and I know it's your truck because I also have clear pictures of the license plates, are from traffic cameras near the Hollywood Reservoir. You can see the date and time stamps, right?"

Rowell nodded.

"They were taken only hours before a man walking his dog discovered the body of Valerie Weber, also known as Crystal Lowden, Rachel's daughter, floating in the water."

"What?" Rowell said, looking up with an alarmed look on his face.

"Trevor, I need you to verbally acknowledge that you understood the rights I read to you and if you want to waive your right to remain silent and talk to me."

"What happens if I don't?" Rowell asked.

"Then I leave," Kaye said simply. "I go see a judge and come back with an arrest warrant. Then we start all over again, except you'll be handcuffed to a table at the jail."

Rowell was silent for a moment before mumbling, "Okay."

"Okay what?" Kaye pressed.

"I understand my rights and I'll talk to you."

"First thing, then," Kaye said, pointing to the screen print, "this is your truck, correct?"

"You already know that."

"Is that a yes?"

"Yeah."

"I can tell from the traffic cam photo there are two people in the truck," Kaye said, "but based on your size I don't think you're one of them."

"I wasn't there," Rowell replied.

Kaye poked one of the pictures with a finger and asked, "Who's driving?"

For a second, Kaye thought Rowell was going to clam up, but the man finally whispered, his voice breaking, "My wife."

"Your wife?" Kaye asked, confused.

"Maybe I should start at the beginning," Rowell said.

"Please do."

"Okay," Rowell began, "first off, everything I told you about me and Rachel when you were here the first time was the truth. It just wasn't... the whole story."

"I hope you plan on telling me the whole story now."

Rowell nodded. "Rachel asked me to that dance and I took her. She was a lot more interested in me than I was in her, so when her dad threatened me with damnation and fire and brimstone if I didn't stay away from her, it was kind of a relief. It wasn't until after I found out what was really going on that I got pissed."

"What was really going on?" Kaye asked.

"Their dad was molesting them."

"Them?" Kaye asked, covering his surprise.

"Yes," Rowell replied. "Leah, Rachel's older sister, was in my class. I had a crush on her, but she wasn't really interested in me. She missed a lot of school, then one day she was just gone. I went to the dance with Rachel mostly to see if I could find out what happened to Leah. Then Rachel was just gone, too. I thought maybe they moved."

Two daughters, just like Job Kaye thought.

"How do you know Leon was molesting them?"

"Leah told me."

"And you didn't tell anyone else?" Kaye asked. "A counselor, your parents? Anybody?"

"She didn't tell me when we were in high school."

"When did she tell you?"

"I don't remember exactly," Rowell replied, "but it was a pretty long time ago."

"You were still in touch with Leah Lowden?" Kaye asked. "You just told me that one day she was just gone. How does that match up?"

"She was gone," Rowell confirmed. "I didn't see or talk to her for at least, gosh, almost ten years? It wasn't until after I quit baseball. Then, one night, I'm at this place on Sunset and I bump into her out of the blue. I wasn't even sure it was her, but she recognized me and said she'd followed my baseball career, such as it was. We hung out, and she told me we should get together and catch up. One thing led to another. You know how it is."

"I don't know how it is, Trevor. I need you to tell me."

Rowell looked at Kaye and smiled. "She's Leah Rowell now. My wife."

Kaye remembered Rowell's social media profile with the photo of him, his dark-haired wife and two young daughters, and tried to hide his surprise with a question. "Was Leah in touch with her mother back then?"

"No," Rowell shook his head emphatically. "But it was about then that she told me about what Leon did to them. He started molesting Leah when she was pretty young, then started in on Rachel, too. Leah told me that's why she had so much trouble in school, and that she even ran away a bunch of times to try and escape.

The reports, Kaye thought. *It wasn't Rachel.*

"Then," Rowell continued, "the day she turned eighteen she packed a backpack, told her dad to go to hell and walked out. She was an adult. He couldn't call the cops anymore. But Rachel was still there."

"Her mother didn't do anything to stop it?" Kaye asked. "The abuse, I mean."

"Not that Leah ever told me," Rowell replied. "And she hated Monica for it. Cut her mother completely out of her life and didn't contact her for years. It wasn't until about a year or so ago that I convinced her to reach out, that her mom should know she had grandchildren."

Kaye sensed a '*but*', and asked.

"My wife is still terrified of her father," Rowell told him. "But I finally convinced her. Leah wouldn't give her mom our address, they only talked on the phone or met in public places. That was also about the time Monica told her she'd found Crystal."

"Monica said she found Crystal?" Kaye asked. The flower stickers on the tablet suddenly made sense.

"That's what Leah told me. Monica claimed she found Crystal on some website, then met with her on the UCLA campus to make sure it was really her." Rowell said, dispirited. "If I had just left things alone instead of pushing Leah to contact her mom, none of this would have happened."

"Let's go to when you say Leah had your truck," Kaye said. "I'm assuming Monica called you."

"She called Leah. Monica avoids me whenever possible. She didn't like me back then, and she still doesn't. When she found out I was Leah's husband she got really upset."

"When Monica called, what did she tell Leah?"

"Only that she had a problem and needed help."

"And what night was this?"

"Saturday. The night before the date on the photos."

"What made Leah decide to go?" Kaye asked.

"Her mom was asking for help," Rowell said. "I wasn't going to let her go until Monica told her that Leon was in Sacramento until the next day. Then I couldn't stop her."

"You didn't go with her?"

"And do what with our two girls?" Rowell asked, shrugging. "It was late."

"Does Leah have her own car?"

"Of course," Rowell replied. "A Porsche Cayenne."

"So, why do you think she took your truck?"

Rowell just stared at Kaye, his expression saying, 'I didn't know then, but I think I do now'.

"What did Leah find when she got to her mom's house?"

"She wouldn't tell me. Said it was better if I just stayed out of it."

"She still hasn't told you?" Kaye followed up.

"No," Rowell said softly. "It wasn't until the day you came to see me that I started to wonder and ask questions. We had a huge fight and she threatened to leave me. She said it would be for my own good. I just…"

"How long was she gone?"

"Several hours," Rowell replied. "I tried to call her, but…" His voice trailed off.

"But what?" Kaye asked.

"Detective, you have to understand. Leon Lowden is a horrible human being, a monster. The last thing I wanted was for him to find out Leah was in contact with Monica."

"Okay, I think I have a sense of what happened," Kaye said. "But I want to make sure I have the timeline right. I'll go through it as I understand it, you correct me if I'm wrong, and if I jog your memory, please tell me. Will you do that for me?"

"Okay." Rowell nodded.

The two went back over what Rowell had told Kaye, who constructed a clean timeline. He wasn't asking for clarification as much as he wanted to circle back and see if the man's story changed.

"One more question," Kaye said when they finished. "Where were you this past Wednesday night, about midnight?"

"Home with my family," Rowell replied. "Why?"

"Leon Lowden was found dead in their house," Kaye replied. "Preliminary conclusion is suicide. But there was no note and, interestingly enough, Monica wasn't there when the police arrived."

He watched Rowell closely and could tell the man was wrestling with a decision.

"She called Leah about ten that evening," Trevor said after a moment, "and asked if she could come stay with us."

Before the shots fired call crossed Kaye's mind. *Planning her escape?*

"You went and picked her up?" He asked.

"Leah went, but not until later."

"Really?" Kaye asked skeptically. "Why would she do that if she knew her father was there?"

"She went totally ballistic when her mom called. She thought her dad was beating Monica again. I've never seen her that mad. She kept saying that it was something she had to do, she'd put it off too long, and I should stay with the girls."

"And she confronted her dad?" Kaye asked.

"I don't know. She won't talk to me about it yet."

"She brought Monica back?"

"No, she did tell me she took Monica to a motel. She didn't get home until after one o'clock."

"Trevor, is there anything else you'd like to tell me?" Kaye asked.

"There is one thing." Rowell looked away. "It was a long time ago and I'd forgotten, but I remembered it while we were talking."

"And what's that?" Kaye asked.

"When Leah and I sat down and talked for the first time after we ran into each other." He hesitated, then said, "She told me she never believed Rachel killed herself."

"She thought her father killed her sister?"

Rowell stared hard at him and said, "No. She thought her mom did."

Kaye looked across the desk at Rowell, saddened that something that hadn't involved the man all those years ago had now crashed down on his life, then reached and turned off the recording app on his phone.

"Trevor, I'll need to talk to Leah."

"I know," Rowell said glumly, then looked at Kaye. "You said you'd talk to the prosecutor?"

"I did, but remember, no promises."

"I got it."

"How far away do you live?" Kaye asked.

"Not that far," Rowell replied.

Kaye considered his options, then said, "Let's do this, if you're willing. Call your wife and ask her to come here. You can sit in while I talk to her, but you've got to keep your mouth shut."

"You'd do that?"

"I would."

"Thank you," Rowell said as he reached for the phone.

"Put her on speaker," Kaye told him.

Rowell nodded and punched the button before dialing.

"Hi, love," Leah Rowell answered. "What a nice surprise. What's up?"

Rowell looked at Kaye, who nodded, then replied, "The police are here. A Detective Kaye." He paused. "He needs to talk to you."

Several seconds passed before she asked, "What about?"

"The night you took the truck to help your mom."

Kaye heard Leah Rowell's sharp intake of breath, then a slow exhale.

"Okay, put him on," she said.

"Leah, you need to come here and talk to him," Trevor said gently. "Bring the girls if you have to. I'll watch them while you two talk."

"Trev, I can't just ---" she started to say and Kaye heard the rising panic in her voice before Trevor interrupted her.

"Yes, you can," Trevor said. "Leah, your dad's dead. You need to come to the office."

"What?"

"He's dead," Trevor repeated. "Wednesday night. The police think it might have been suicide."

"That's the night…" Leah's voice faded.

"You picked up your mom and took her to the motel." Trevor finished the sentence.

"Again," Leah whispered. "Like Rachel."

"Leah, listen to me," Trevor said. "You know I love you. I'd stand in front of a train for you and the girls if I had to. But enough is enough. This needs to end. Put the girls in the car and come talk to Detective Kaye. He knows, Leah. About you and Rachel. About Crystal and about your mom and dad. Please come tell him your side. You need to, for our family's sake."

Another silence, longer this time.

"Okay," Leah said at last. "The girls are playing over at Lydia's. I'll call and make sure it's okay, then come."

CHAPTER 55

Twenty minutes later the door to Trevor Rowell's office opened and a tall, slim woman, dressed in cowboy boots, jeans and a blue plaid work shirt, the sleeves rolled up to her elbows, walked in. Her long brown hair was woven into a single braid threaded through the opening on the back of an LA Dodgers baseball cap.

Horses, Kaye thought instantly. *That explains the truck.*

Trevor stood up, walked around his desk and gave her a hug and a kiss.

"Hi," he said softly, then, one arm still around her waist, turned to Kaye. "This is my wife, Leah. Leah, Detective Kaye."

Kaye stood up. "Thank you for coming in, Mrs. Rowell. Sorry it has to be under these circumstances."

"Me, too," was all she said before turning to her husband. "Trev, I need to talk to him alone."

"Are you sure?" Trevor asked. "Detective Kaye said I could sit in."

"I'm sure," Lean said. "Go do your truck stuff." She patted him on the chest, then stretched up and gave him another kiss. "I love you. No matter what happens, I love you."

Kaye had a sudden flashback to the night of Amy's death.

Trevor left the office. Kaye pulled the chair behind the desk around next to his and told Leah to have a seat.

"Mrs. Rowell," he led off, "before we talk I need to inform you of your rights." He restarted the recording app and went through the warning.

"I understand," she said, "and I'll talk to you."

"Let's begin with you giving me your full name, date of birth and current address," Kaye instructed.

She complied.

"And you are the oldest daughter of Leon and Monica Lowden, older sister of Rachel Lowden, correct?"

"I am."

"Mrs. Rowell, I'm here conducting a homicide investigation," Kaye began. "The victim was a young lady named Valerie Weber. During the course of my investigation I learned that she was born Crystal Lowden, and that her mother was your younger sister, Rachel."

"Okay," Leah said tentatively.

"Did you know that Rachel had a baby when she was barely seventeen?"

"I did," Leah replied. "I left home as soon as I turned eighteen, but Rachel and I stayed in touch. She told me she was pregnant, oh, about January."

"Did she tell you who the father was?"

"No, but I'll give a hundred to one it was my father."

"You're one hundred percent certain it wasn't Trevor?"

"Absolutely."

"What makes you think it was your father?" Kaye asked.

"Because he started molesting me when I was little, then raping me when I was twelve. Then he started on Rachel and left me alone for a while." She saw the look on Kaye's face and added, "Rachel was prettier than me. Then, right before I turned sixteen he started on me again and I got pregnant. I never told my mom or dad, and I miscarried not long after I found out. That's why I left home as soon as I could, and didn't want Trevor here now. I've never told him."

"I saw the runaway reports," Kaye told her. "I think I have a sense of the background. What I'd like to talk about are the events of the last several weeks." He leaned forward and put the traffic cam photos of the Ford dually on the desk. "This is your husband's truck." Kaye explained the timing and circumstances of how he got them. "Would you care to explain to me why you were in that particular place at that particular time?"

Leah's shoulders sagged. "I was helping my mom."

"With what?"

Tears rolled down Leah's cheeks as she answered. "She called and said she had to get rid of something. That if it was still there when my dad got home, he'd probably kill her."

"Did she tell you what it was?"

"No." She shook her head. "I didn't know until I got there."

"And what was it?"

"A dead girl," Leah whispered, choking back a sob. "She was really beat up, but I don't think my mom did that."

"She didn't. Your dad picked Valerie up the Thursday evening before she was killed and took her to your parents' house. I believe she called him because she'd been beaten up," Kaye told her. "Do you have any idea how long Valerie might have been dead before you saw her?"

"I have no concept of how to know that. Although now that I think about it, she was already cold to the touch and kind of blue in places." She shivered visibly. "I'd never seen anything like that before."

"Do you know who the dead girl was?" Kaye asked.

"Not then." She wiped her cheeks with one hand. "Mom told me it was another girl my dad had gotten pregnant. She told me the girl knew my dad was in Sacramento, and she'd come to the house demanding money. She said the girl threatened her, they struggled and the girl ended up dead. Mom said it was an accident."

"Did you believe her?"

Leah hesitated before answering. "No."

"What did you do next?"

"We took her body to the Hollywood Reservoir," she replied. "We couldn't think of anything else to do."

"You should have called the police."

"I know," Leah said softly. "But I knew that if my dad found out what happened, he would probably kill my mother. He beat her horribly when we were kids, even though she was in a wheelchair a lot because of her MS."

"Did she ever do anything to try and stop your dad from sexually abusing you?"

"Try to stop him?" Leah said, again almost laughing. "Not hardly. She blamed us for it, always quoting bible verses and stuff. I've never understood why."

"Valerie was naked when she was found," Kaye said. "What did you do with the clothes she had on and the bag she was carrying when your dad picked her up?"

"My mom put everything in the bag," Leah replied. "She had me pull into a convenience store and she threw it into their dumpster."

Long gone by now, Kaye thought.

"Okay," Kaye said. "I also want to ask you about Rachel's death. I saw the original report and had some questions, so I got a new opinion from the Medical Examiner's office. The pathologist who looked at the report doesn't believe Rachel could have inflicted those injuries on herself. Trevor told me that you told him years ago that you thought your mom killed Rachel. Is that true?"

"Yeah, I told him that not long after we found each other again," she said. "I didn't find out Rachel was dead until well after it happened.

391

I just stopped hearing from her and finally called a friend to see if something was wrong. That's when I found out she had supposedly committed suicide."

"And why do you think it wasn't suicide?"

"Because I just don't think Rachel would have done that to herself," Leah replied. "I mean, I don't have any proof or anything, but I can tell you that I've never let my mom in my house or left her alone around my girls because I think there's something wrong with her. I wish I hadn't let Trevor talk me into contacting her. She was a good mom when I was little. Then she got sick and spent a lot of time in the hospital, and had to take a lot of drugs. It changed her." She hesitated before asking, "Is my dad really dead?"

"He is." Kaye confirmed. "He was found dead, apparently from a self-inflicted gunshot, in the living room of the house. Your mother was not there when the officers arrived."

"Did they find a gun?"

"They did, pretty much still in his hand."

"Mom," Leah whispered.

"You think your mother killed your father?" Kaye asked.

She nodded. "Yeah."

"Do you know where your mom is now?"

"Not for sure," Leah replied. "She called for help again late Wednesday. Said dad had beaten her up again, she'd finally had enough and wanted out. I met her at the school around the corner, followed her to a motel and checked her in under my name. I don't know if she's still there or not."

"What time was that?"

"Oh, probably close to one a.m."

"Why check her in under your name?"

"So my Dad couldn't find her."

"Which motel?"

"It was off Tampa north of Parthenia. I don't remember the name."

"Leah, will you testify to everything you've told me today?" Kaye asked. "And remember, you're being recorded."

"Yes," Leah answered. "And I'll take responsibility for my actions, too. It was wrong to do what I did."

"One more question," Kaye said.

"Okay," Leah said nervously.

"Your Dad came to me last Monday morning and confessed to killing Crystal. I –"

"I don't believe that," Leah interrupted harshly. "I mean, he might have confessed, but my Mom did it."

"I didn't believe him, either," Kaye said. "Why do you think he would do that?"

Leah shrugged. "Maybe he was guilty about how he treated us all? I don't know."

"Okay, I think we're done," Kaye told her. "Leah, I could arrest you now, but I want the District Attorney to determine the charges first. I can't give you legal advice, but I will tell you that if I was in your shoes, I'd retain an attorney and work on turning myself in when the warrant is issued. Do you understand?"

"Yes, and thank you. I know what I did was horrible and there's no excuse. All I can say is that I was trying to protect my family."

Kaye gathered up the photos, his phone and the few notes he'd taken, then stepped to the office door and opened it. He could hear Trevor Rowell's voice coming from deeper in the building and followed the sound to the staff break room.

"Trevor," he said, "we're done. Leah will tell you what's going on, and the District Attorney's office will be in touch."

"You're not taking her to jail?" Rowell asked.

"No. I don't think that's necessary. I'll talk to the D.A. and we'll wait and see what happens, okay? Just don't leave town."

"We won't. Thank you, Detective."

CHAPTER 56

The motel was one of the lesser-known national chains, low enough on the hospitality industry pecking order that it was relegated to less desirable and visible real estate. It could've used some paint and the landscaping needed some attention.

Kaye first cruised the parking lot looking for Monica Lowden's Ford SUV. He found it backed into the end spot of the parking lot behind the motel. He parked outside the main entrance doors, went inside and found the registration desk. A young woman named Lupe greeted him.

"Checking in?" she asked cheerfully.

"No," Kaye replied and held up his badge. "I need to know if you have a guest named Leah Rowell?"

"Sure, hang on a sec," Lupe said, then stepped sideways to the computer terminal between the clerk stations. A moment later she looked up. "Yes, we do. Mrs. Rowell is in room two-twenty."

"Does it show when she checked in?"

Lupe looked at the computer again.

"One fifteen a.m. Thursday morning." She hesitated, then asked, "Did she call to complain because we charged her full price for Wednesday night?"

"No, nothing like that. Does the registration list a vehicle?"

Another glance down, then, "Yes, it lists a Porsche with a California plate."

"Thank you," Kaye said. 'How do I find two-twenty without taking the elevator?"

Lupe gave him directions and he set off.

Room two-twenty was directly across the hall from the fire exit stairwell when Kaye stepped out. The door had two peepholes, the lower one telling Kaye the room was configured for accommodating disabled guests. He knocked, stood a bit to one side and waited.

"Who is it?" came from behind the door and he recognized Monica Lowden's voice.

"Detective Kaye. You need to open the door, Mrs. Lowden. We need to talk."

"I have nothing to say to you. Go away."

"I'm afraid I can't do that. Open the door, or I'll get the Manager to do it."

He waited. Finally, he heard the deadbolt disengage and the door opened until it was stopped by the chain. Through the narrow opening he saw Monica Lowden peering out at him.

"What do you want now?" she asked.

"Open the door, Mrs. Lowden," he said sharply. "Last chance."

Monica hesitated, cursing under her breath, then closed the door far enough to disengage the chain before pulling it wide open. She leaned against the edge of the door, her left hand braced on the door knob. Her right hand held a cane, planted next to her right foot.

"There," she spat. "Happy now? Say your piece and get the hell away from me."

"Can't do that, either," Kaye said as he walked past her into the room. He immediately noticed there was no wheelchair.

"Mind if I sit down?" Monica asked as she made her way, supported by the cane, to the bed and lowered herself to its edge.

"Not at all," Kaye said, leaning against the cabinet for hanging clothes. "Where's your chair?"

"At home. Not that it's any of your business."

"Well, that's the thing, Monica," Kaye said. "You don't mind if I call you Monica?"

She glared at him but didn't answer.

"I think it is my business," Kaye went on. "I heard you left home in a hurry."

"And where, pray tell, did you hear that?"

"I had a very interesting conversation this morning with a gentleman named Trevor Rowell," Kaye replied. "Second time I've talked to him, actually. You remember Trevor?"

Monica didn't answer, so he continued. "I found it odd that you didn't remember Trevor's last name when I came to see you the first time."

"It was a long time ago," Monica said.

"It was," Kaye agreed. "But given that he's married to your oldest daughter, Leah, I should think you would have remembered. I also had a very interesting talk with Leah. About trucks and dumpsters and dead bodies and reservoirs."

Monica Lowden looked up at Kaye and he saw the fight disappear from her eyes as the color drained from her cheeks.

"I want a lawyer," she whispered.

"I think that's a capital idea," Kaye said. "Monica Lowden, you are under arrest for the murder of Valerie Weber, known to you as Crystal Lowden."

"What happens now?" Monica asked, barely whispering.

"Right now you need to gather your belongings," Kaye replied. "While you do that I'll call and have a female officer respond to help us out, and we'll start the process. You have a gun, or any drugs, with you?"

"Only what my doctors tell me to take."

While Kaye closely watched Monica gather and pack her things, he called in and asked for an Adam unit with a female officer to respond to the motel. The ETA was ten minutes.

"You know," he asked when Monica sat back down, her bag at her feet, "while we're waiting, I do have a question for you. It's not for the District Attorney or the jury. It's just for me."

"What?"

"Why?" he asked. "I mean, your own granddaughter? Why?"

She stared at him for a long moment.

"I'm not sorry for what I did," she said at last. "She deserved it."

"Why did she deserve it?"

"Crystal was just like her mom and just like Leah," Monica said bitterly. "Because I was sick so much they seduced my Leon and tried to steal him from me. I spent a long time looking for Crystal and finally found her. And what does she do? Tries to take Leon away from me by getting pregnant. Crystal got what she deserved. It was God's will. He will judge me, not a court."

"Monica," Kaye said, "Leon was not the father of Valerie's baby. It was —"

"Liar!" she shouted. "Don't try to defend her! She was a whore, just like Rachel and Leah."

Monica went quiet, clasping her hands in her lap and looking down.

"You should also know," Kaye went on, "that we'll be reopening the investigation into Rachel's death and Leon's death will be investigated as a homicide."

She looked up at Kaye with hate in her eyes. "The Lord will judge me, not you."

A knock at the door signaled the arrival of the uniformed officers. Logistics for transport were arranged. An hour later Monica Lowden had been booked on one count of first-degree murder.

CHAPTER 57

J.J. called Kaye at home on Friday night, apologizing for not getting with him at the squad. The meeting with Laguna Beach PD had been fruitful, with the Captain of Detectives assuring them there would be a thorough investigation. The Captain, though, had foreseen the same problems J.J. had, and not made any promises about getting an indictment.

For his part, Kaye thanked J.J. again and told him he'd accept the result was, whatever it was.

"Either way," he'd told Jefferies, "it won't bring her back."

***

Kaye rode the '61 to work. There was a light drizzle and the temperature signaled the change of seasons.

It was odd walking into the squad room and seeing the vacant Captain's office. He'd expected to find a new occupant and to be, along with everyone else, summoned into a meeting and told how things were going to change. For the better, of course, because that's how change is always sold to those it affects. But there was no sign of Captain Thompson's replacement.

At his desk, he started organizing the Weber case material so he could take it to the District Attorney's office. He hadn't been at it long when his phone rang.

"Kaye."

"Detective Kaye, this is Jim Whitman, Newport Beach. How's it going?"

"Making progress," Kaye replied. "But the day is young."

Whitman laughed. "I hear that, but I've got something that might brighten your day a little."

"Oh? What's that?"

"We booked Eugene Calhoun last night."

"Where'd you find him?" Kaye asked, elated.

"Getting off a boat at the guest dock of one of the local restaurants," Whitman told him. "Friday afternoon Laguna Beach tipped us they were looking at Calhoun on a possible homicide, so we put surveillance on the house. We saw him get on one of his boats, so we put Harbor Patrol on him. Wish you could've been here. That guy's a jerk."

"So I hear. Where is he now?"

"In our jail. We've contacted L.A. County and we'll process him out as soon as their transport people get here. Just be aware that Laguna P.D. might jump the line and want to talk to him first. I'm sure they'd let you sit in if you want to."

"Thanks, Detective Whitman, but that's not my case," Kaye said sincerely. "I appreciate your help, and the call."

"Hey, we've got to stick together. If there's ever anything else I can do for you, give me a shout."

"Same here. Thanks again."

He instantly called Kayla Okafor, hoping she wasn't in court. She wasn't.

"Good morning, Detective Kaye," she said cheerfully. "How was your weekend?"

"Great, actually. Yours?"

She chuckled. "I wouldn't give it a *great*, but it was good. To what do I owe the pleasure of your call?"

"Two things, both of which have to do with the Valerie Weber case, one of which you might already know about."

"Fill me in."

"Eugene Calhoun is in custody."

"No kidding? That's great," she said. "Who got him?"

"Newport P.D. hooked him up last night. Hopefully we'll have him by the end of the day."

"Local? I figured him for long gone."

"Me, too," Kaye said. "Just goes to show that money and brains don't always go hand-in-hand."

"You're telling me." Okafor laughed again.

"Watch for Calhoun in your workflow, please," Kaye said. "Laguna Beach is looking at him in connection to a probable homicide."

"How do you know that?"

"A link came up during the Weber investigation. We looked into it, confirmed the information, and turned it over to Laguna last week. No indictment yet, but the information is solid." He decided not to elaborate. "No bail for Calhoun here. He's got tons of cash and a private jet."

"I'll do what I can," Okafor said. "What's the second thing?"

"I'm closing the Valerie Weber homicide this morning."

"By arrest, I hope."

"Yes," Kaye said. "Over the weekend I arrested Monica Lowden for murder."

"Wait!" Okafor exclaimed. "Monica Lowden? Isn't she...?"

"Valerie's biological grandmother," he confirmed. "I'm also sending you the reports for review and determination of charges against one Leah Rowell. I think you've at least got abuse of a corpse. It was, and is, a real tangle. I'm organizing the case file now and you'll get it as soon as I'm done."

"Please do. I really want this case."

"I figured you would. One thing about Leah Rowell."

"Go ahead."

"She's as much a victim as participant in this whole mess. She wasn't present when Monica killed Valerie, but she got roped into helping dispose of the body."

"Detective, how does someone get roped into helping dispose of a body?" she asked, her skepticism obvious.

"It's a long story."

"I'm listening."

"Leah Rowell is the older sister of Rachel Lowden, Valerie's biological mother, and --"

"Wait, wait," Okafor interrupted again. "Rachel Lowden had an older sister?"

"Yes. Leah Rowell's maiden name was Lowden. Anyway, she knew how terrified of Leon Lowden the whole family was, so she agreed to help protect her mother, her husband and their two daughters."

"Sounds fishy to me," Okafor said.

"She gave me twenty years of history, which checks out in our records archives, and she pretty much handed me Monica Lowden's head on a platter for two more murders."

"Two *more* murders?"

"Yeah," Kaye said. "Leah's husband, Trevor, told me Leah always thought Monica killed Rachel, Valerie's biological mother. Doctor Archuleta at the M.E.'s office has reviewed the autopsy report and photos, and he doesn't think the manner of death is supportable as a suicide. I'll be asking for some lab work on the old case evidence. Leah also thinks Monica could be good for her husband Leon's death."

"Holy...CRAP!" Okafor said. "Can you imagine growing up under those circumstances?"

"Honestly, no," Kaye replied. "Makes me realize how lucky I was."

"Me, too," she said, then paused before adding, "Okay, look, I'll read the reports and background you send me and then talk to Leah Rowell's lawyer as soon as I know who it is. The abuse of a corpse charge gives me something to bargain with." She paused, then added, "You suggested that on purpose, didn't you? At any rate, I can't promise anything, but I'll see what I can do."

Kaye ignored the question about the abuse of a corpse charge. "Thanks, Counselor."

"No, Detective, thank you. Your investigative acumen frequently astounds me."

"Why, thank you," Kaye said, a little taken aback by the compliment. "But wouldn't it be nice if the world didn't need guys like me in the first place?"

"Never happen," Okafor said, sighing wistfully.

"We can always hope."

"That we can," Okafor agreed. "In the meantime, all we can do is put the bad guys away and mourn the innocents."

CHAPTER 58

Kaye rolled the '61 to a stop in front of the Weber house, shut down, leaned it on the stand and took a deep breath to gather himself. He'd debated calling JoAnn Weber to make sure she was home, but had decided against it, afraid she'd draw the wrong conclusion about why he was finally calling and start asking questions.

This was not the kind of news to deliver over the phone.

He rang the bell and waited. A moment later Miles Weber opened the door.

"Oh, hey, Detective Kaye," he said, surprised.

"Hi, Miles. Is your Mom home?"

"She is. Come on in, I'll get her," Miles said as he pulled the door out of the way, then turned and headed upstairs.

Kaye waited in the entryway. It wasn't long before JoAnn came slowly down the stairs.

"Hello, Detective," she said coolly. "I'd given up on you. Did you bring Valerie's computer back?"

"No, ma'am. I'm afraid I'm going to need to keep it for a while. Evidence."

"Evidence? Have you made some progress?"

"Is there somewhere we can sit down?" Kaye asked.

"Of course," JoAnn replied. "I'm sorry. How rude of me."

"That's okay," Kaye said as he followed her into the now-familiar living room.

"What news do you have for me?" JoAnn asked after they sat down.

"Three arrests have been made," Kaye told her. "One, a man named Eugene Calhoun, will be charged with multiple counts of rape and one count of aggravated assault and battery."

"Is he the one who beat her up?"

"He is."

"Was he the father of Valerie's baby?" she asked tentatively.

"Yes," Kaye replied. "I've also arrested a suspect in connection with Valerie's murder and charges are pending for a second suspect."

"Were they friends of that Calhoun man?"

"They were not," Kaye said. "The person charged with Valerie's murder is a woman named Monica Lowden. Also charged will be a woman named Leah Rowell, maiden name Lowden. The District Attorney will determine the charges against her."

"A woman killed Valerie?" JoAnn asked in disbelief. "Why would she...?"

Kaye patiently explained to her that Valerie being beaten, then murdered only a few days later, were separate and distinct chains of events. Those involved in one had no interaction with those involved in the other. Valerie was the only commonality.

"That was the big reason the case was so tough to break," Kaye said.

"Who was this Lowden woman?"

"Prepare yourself, okay," Kaye said slowly, then paused before continuing. "Monica Lowden is Valerie's biological maternal grandmother. Leah Rowell is Valerie's biological aunt."

JoAnn gasped as her hands flew to her mouth. "Her own grandmother killed her? That's... I don't understand that at all! How could she...? Oh, my God!" She broke into loud sobs.

Kaye took her hand and waited. Slowly, JoAnn calmed down and got control.

"JoAnn, it was a really bad situation all around, and it had been going on for years in the Lowden family. In fact, I believe the District Attorney will also end up charging Monica Lowden with the murder of Valerie's biological mother soon after Valerie was born." He saw the look in JoAnn's eyes and added, "It was ruled a suicide at the time, but there's new evidence."

"Thanks to you, right?"

"A lot of people are involved in this case."

She tried to half-smile through her tears, failed, and said, "After you picked up Valerie's computer, Miles told us that she'd already figured out she was adopted. I guess she really wanted to find her biological family."

"Let's say they found each other, thanks to the internet."

"And it cost Valerie her life."

All Kaye could do was remain silent.

"Where was her real grandfather in all this?" JoAnn asked. "How could he let this happen?"

Kaye looked at her and said, "JoAnn, I'm not sure –"

"Tell me," she cut him off. "Please. I need to know."

"All right. Monica Lowden's husband's name was Leon."

"Valerie's grandfather."

"Yes," Kaye confirmed. "He's the one who picked Valerie up behind the Staples where we found her car after she disappeared. JoAnn, he was a child molester. My information is that he abused both of his daughters from the time they were young."

Her face went ghostly white. She tried to say something, but no sound escaped her lips.

Kaye watched her closely and after the moment of shock passed, he saw knowledge dawn in her eyes.

"He was Valerie's father," she barely whispered. It wasn't a question.

"Yes," Kaye said. "DNA confirmed it."

Her eyes narrowed. "Why didn't you arrest him, too?"

"He's deceased."

"Had to be recently, right?" JoAnn asked. "I mean, if he was in contact with Valerie."

"He died last Wednesday night."

"I hope he burns in hell," she said bitterly, then her voice softened as she asked, "What happens now?"

"It could be a long, complicated process," Kaye replied. "There may eventually be a trial, but it could depend on a lot of factors, ranging from psychiatric evaluation to plea negotiations. It seems almost endless these days."

"What do I need to do?"

"If the District Attorney's office needs you, they'll call. An Assistant D.A. name Kayla Okafor will probably handle the case. She's worked with me throughout the investigation."

"There must be something else I can do," JoAnn pleaded.

"Honestly, JoAnn," Kaye said softly, again taking her hand, "all you need to do now is love Valerie and treasure the time you had with her. No matter what she may have said to you in anger, by any measure *you* were her mother. You, your husband and Miles were her family. Keep her in your hearts, because as long as she's there, she's not really gone."

JoAnn walked him to the door, where, tears in her eyes, she thanked and hugged him.

Kaye returned to the '61 and swung over. A minute later he headed for home.

CHAPTER 59

There was a chill in the late afternoon air when Kaye took his second cup of tea out to the patio and settled into his regular chaise.

Be time for full leathers soon, he thought as he sipped the tea and looked out over the Pacific. LAX traffic was the usual endless stream of departures, no doubt matched by the arriving flights whose landing lights could not yet been seen in the distant eastern sky. The breeze had changed to offshore, silencing the traffic noise from PCH and it would be an hour or two before the nocturnal residents of the canyons above began to stir.

His conversation with JoAnn Weber lingered in his mind. Even after the arrests of Eugene Calhoun and Monica Lowden, with charges against Leah Rowell pending, Kaye had yet to find the sense of satisfaction and closure he usually felt after solving a tough case.

Consciously, he thought it was because Valerie Weber, though seventeen, was, to him, still a child. There is no justice for loved ones when a child is taken. JoAnn still had her life to live, but the daughter she loved was gone, and she would likely carry the guilt of that loss to her grave.

Though he'd done his job, Kaye also wondered if there would be justice in the case. Monica Lowden had suffocated her own granddaughter, but he harbored doubts about how the case should proceed. While certainly no psychiatrist, things Monica had said during his brief contacts with her put him on the fence regarding her competence to stand trial rather than being institutionalized. Her illness and her life with Leon had most certainly adversely affected her mental health.

Plus, in Kaye's mind, Eugene Calhoun and Dylan Glithero were ultimately responsible for Valerie's death. But their weapon hadn't been a pillow. It had been a carefully calculated progression of ingratiation, coercion, exploitation, dominance and brutalization. He only hoped Calhoun would face justice in Amy's death at the hands of Roy Dobson.

Kenny Vaughan probably handed out the only real justice in this one, he thought, then mentally chastised himself. That wasn't how it was supposed to work.

Is how it's supposed to work even working? He knew he'd have to decide that for himself before he made a decision about his future.

He again recalled Roshi's lesson from the Sufi mystic Rumi.

Don't spend time searching the branches of the tree if what you seek is found in the roots.

While he considered his future his gaze fell on the house-facing window of Amy's study above the garage. His thoughts turned and he wondered if he could ever go up there again because of his feeling Amy had somehow betrayed him.

How can I forgive her? She lied to me. It was all a front.

It suddenly dawned on him why he was struggling with the resolution of the Weber case. He was normally an impartial, objective outsider trying to solve the puzzle. Not this time. The Weber case had revealed Amy's murder, making him a participant in the entire chain of events.

I'm in the same boat as JoAnn Weber.

While he tried to put things in order the darkness deepened and the chill began to penetrate. He grabbed the long-empty teacup, rose, glanced once more at Amy's refuge, then headed for the house.

Halfway to the back door he stopped and stood there for what seemed like a long time before turning and heading for the garage. It took him two nervous tries to punch in the proper security code, then he entered and crossed the dark garage to the bottom of the stairs. He stopped again and looked up. Finally he steeled himself and climbed to the top, where he again stopped.

There was still enough ambient light coming through the window overlooking the ocean that he left the lights off. His emotions churned like the sea beneath a hurricane as he slowly crossed the room and sat down in Amy's desk chair.

He sat motionless for a few moments before putting his hands, palms down and fingers splayed widely, on the desk and gently caressing the surface as memories flooded his mind.

Why? He asked himself over and over.

He brought his hands together, bent forward, rested his forehead atop them and tried to fight off the tears until exhaustion overcame turmoil and he fell asleep.

He dreamt he was sitting *zazen* with Roshi.

405

"Roshi-sama," he tentatively asked his mentor, "have you ever read the Bible?"

"I have," Roshi replied. "Both the Old and New Testaments and the Book of Mormon." The old monk smiled. "I have also studied the Qur'an, the Tanakh, the Mahabharata, with special attention to the Ramayana and Gita, the Upanishads and Vedas and, of course, the Sutras and Tripitaka."

"Why would you study other Scriptures when you've committed your life to The Path?"

"Benkei," Roshi said seriously, "you cannot understand how others see the world and make the decisions that guide their actions unless you visit where they stand and develop empathy for where they abide."

"So I should –" Kaye started to ask as he jolted awake.

He sat quietly for a few moments, then rose and headed for the house and bed.

As he drifted off to sleep, he muttered, "*Arigato, Roshi-sama. Mata aimashou.*"

Thank you, Roshi. We will meet again.

www.ingramcontent.com/pod-product-compliance
Lightning Source LLC
Chambersburg PA
CBHW072258020726
47501CB00002B/308